THE CHIMERA

SEBASTIANO VASSALLI

Translated from the Italian by
Patrick Creagh

SCRIBNER

New York   London   Toronto   Sydney   Tokyo   Singapore

SCRIBNER
Rockefeller Center
1230 Avenue of the Americas
New York, NY 10020

First Scribner edition, 1995
Published by arrangement with HarperCollins Publishers Ltd

SCRIBNER and design are
trademarks of Simon & Schuster Inc.

Manufactured in the United States of America

1 3 5 7 9 10 8 6 4 2

Library of Congress Cataloging-in-Publication Data
Vassalli, Sebastiano.
[Chimera. English]
The chimera / Sebastiano Vassalli ; translated from the Italian by Patrick Creagh.
p. cm.
1. Inquisition—Italy—Fiction. 2. Witches—Italy—Fiction.
I. Creagh, Patrick. II. Title.
PQ4882.A8C4813 1995
853'.914—dc20 94-40963
CIP

ISBN 0-684-80260-0

Contents

PRELUDE

Nothingness

FROM THE WINDOWS of this house you look out on nothingness. Especially in winter, when the mountains vanish, the sky and the plains merge into one great blur, the motorway no longer exists, nothing exists. On summer mornings, or on autumn evenings, this nothingness becomes a vaporous plain with a few trees dotted about and the motorway surfacing above the mist to straddle a couple of by-roads, twice. Over there on those flyovers tiny cars are in motion, and trucks no bigger than models in a toyshop window. It also happens from time to time – say twenty or thirty times a year – that this nothingness is transfigured into a crystalline landscape, into a glossy coloured picture postcard. Generally this happens in spring, when the sky is as blue as the water of the paddy-fields it is mirrored in, the motorway seems close enough to touch, and the snow-covered Alps abide there in such a way that it gladdens the heart just to look at them. At these times the horizon is a vast expanse: tens and even hundreds of kilometres, with towns and villages and the works of man clambering up the mountainsides, and rivers that begin where the snows leave off, and roads, and the momentary spark of imperceptible cars on those roads; a crisscross of lives, of histories, of destinies, of dreams; a stage as huge as a whole region, upon which the deeds and the doings of the living in this part of the world have been acted out since time immemorial. An illusion . . .

At these windows, this nothingness before me, I have often chanced to think about Zardino, once a village like the others you can see over there – slightly to the left and a little beyond the second flyover – against the background of Monte Rosa, the most massive and imposing mountain in this part of Europe. On picture-postcard days the landscape hereabouts is dominated and

I

forcibly marked by the presence of this mass of ice and granite towering above the surrounding peaks as far as they themselves turret above the plains: a "white boulder" – thus it was described at the beginning of the century by my mad adopted dad, the poet Dino Campana – around which "the peaks range/to right to left and to infinity/as in the pupils of a prisoner's eyes."

Campana arrived in Novara by train one September evening, without seeing a thing because dark had fallen; but the following morning, through prison bars, Monte Rosa is revealed to him, and "The sky is filled/with a running of white peaks": an image as elusive and remote as the love he was at that time pursuing, and which he was destined never to find, because it never existed . . . A chimera!

From those heights, from the summit of that chimera, by a tortuous route gouged more than once through the living rock, flows the river Sesia. In the local way of speech there is a gentle, feminine sound to the name: *la Sésia*, and of all the rivers that rise in the Alps it is the most eccentric and unpredictable, the most deceitful, the most perilous both for man and for matter verging on its course. Even to this day its capricious spates invade the plains with floods of muddy water metres high, and it is hard to think of the havoc it would cause if over the centuries the labour of men's hands had not hemmed it in between two endless dykes of earth and shingle and, in certain stretches, of cement, restraining and guiding it towards its confluence with the Po.

In centuries past, however, it happened that every few years the Sesia broke its banks and changed course, shifting a hundred yards in one direction or a mile in the other, leaving marshes and quagmires where once had been cultivated land, obliterating whole feudal domains and villages from the map, and even modifying the frontiers between States; which in this corner of Italy, at the turn of the sixteenth and seventeenth centuries, meant (to the west) the Duchy of Savoy (a southerly appendix of France), and the Duchy of Milan, at that time subject to the King of Spain. And maybe this was the way Zardino vanished. In the mid-seventeenth century, or a little earlier, according to historians, a village of some thirty "hearthstones" was swept away with all its inhabitants by the spate waters of the Sesia and never again rebuilt;

2

though the facts are far from certain. Other possible causes for the disappearance of the village (the name of which, in mediaeval documents, is often to be found in the more "gentrified" form of *Giardino*, "Garden") might be the great Plague of 1630, which decimated dozens of villages in the Po valley; or it might have been some battle, or a fire . . . or the Lord knows what else besides.

In this landscape I have attempted to describe, and which today, as so often, is swathed in mist, there lies a story buried: the grand story of a girl who lived from 1590 to 1610 and was called Antonia, and of the people who were living in the same years as she was and whom she met; and of that epoch and this part of the world. For quite some while now I have had a mind to bring this story back into the light of day, to pass it on, to pull it out of nothingness as the April sun brings to light the picture postcard of the plains and of Monte Rosa; and I also had a mind to tell you about these parts, and the world Antonia lived in . . . But then I was always discouraged by the distance which separates our world from theirs, and the oblivion that enshrouds it. Who in this twentieth century of ours, I asked myself, still remembers Bishop Bascapè, Il Caccetta the bandit, Bernardo Sasso the executioner, Canon Cavagna, the *risaroli* who laboured in the paddy-fields, the *camminanti* or "strollers" who walked the roads of the seventeenth century? And then, of Antonia herself nothing was known: neither that she existed, nor that she was the "witch of Zardino", nor that she was tried and sentenced in Novara in the Year of Our Lord 1610. An episode that caused a great stir at the time had slipped out of the ken of history, and would have been irretrievably lost if the muddle of the world and of things in general had not rescued it in the most banal conceivable way, causing certain documents to end up in the wrong place, whereas if they had remained in their right place they would now be inaccessible, or for ever vanished . . . Italy, as we all know, is a land of muddle, and something is forever out of place; some story which ought by rights to have been forgotten always manages to turn up . . . But I, though I had the luck to stumble across the story of Antonia, of Zardino and the plains of Novara at the dawn of the seventeenth century, was hesitant to relate it, as I said, because it seemed to me something too remote. I asked myself what on earth can help us to understand the things of the present unless they are *in* the present? Then it dawned on me.

Looking out over this landscape, the nothingness of it, it came to me that in the present there is no story worth telling. The present is hubbub. It is millions and billions of voices all together, in every language, trying to shout each other down by yelling the word "Me!" It's all "Me, Me, Me" . . . To find the key to the present, and to understand it, we have to withdraw from the hubbub, to descend into the depths of night, to the depths of nothingness – over there, perhaps, slightly to the left and a little beyond the straddle of the second flyover, beneath the "white boulder" that today is invisible . . . to the ghost-village of Zardino, to the story of Antonia . . .

And this have I done.

ONE

Antonia

ON THE NIGHT of the 16th–17th of January 1590, the feast-day of St Antony abbot, hands unknown deposited in the revolving wooden hatch at the entrance to the House of Charity of San Michele Without-the-Walls at Novara, a newborn baby of the female sex, dark-haired, dark-skinned, dark-eyed. In other words, according to the tastes of the time, little short of a monster.

That winter was bitter cold. The "monster" had been bundled up in a blanket without any other specific garments to protect her hands and feet, and she would certainly have died had not a wet-nurse temporarily employed at the House of Charity – a certain Giuditta Cominoli from Oleggio – realized from the barking of the dogs and other signs that someone had approached the turning-wheel; and had she not risen from her bed to investigate, regardless of the polar cold of that moonless night, and tugged at the bell-rope, compelling the orphanage servants to leave their beds, bringing down on her head every species of curseword, such as *Blast your eyes! A pox on you!* and other such courtesies.

The monster survived. She was baptized two days after her discovery, on a Sunday, in the mediaeval church of San Michele, attached to the House of Charity, and named Antonia Renata Giuditta Spagnolini. "Antonia Renata" to indicate her rebirth on the turning-wheel on the feast of St Antony, the 17th of January, whatever her actual birthday might have been, Giuditta in homage to the wet-nurse who saved her from freezing to death, and who thereafter took care of her; and finally Spagnolini, because the darkness of her eyes and skin suggested direct descent from one of the numerous Spanish officers and men who formed the garrison of Novara, and were quartered in the castle built into the ramparts on the south side of the city.

In those days, when you baptized a child you had a right to give it not only a Christian name but a surname as well, so that if there was no father, either attested or alleged to, a woman could think up any surname she fancied, with an eye to the signs of the Zodiac or to her own private guesses as to the paternity of the child, or whatever else came to mind.

In Antonia's case invention posed no problems, even if on due consideration the colour of her eyes and skin, and the precocious abundance of her hair, proved absolutely nothing, and Antonia's origins might have been quite different from those her surname hinted at. To the making of the foundlings exposed on the turning-wheel of the House of Charity at Novara, others contributed besides the soldiers of the Spanish garrison, to whose credit indeed be it said that sometimes, from pride of race, or religious scruples or who knows what else, they would acknowledge their illegitimate offspring at the baptismal font and at the altar. The Governor of Novara in person, Don Juan Alfonso Rodriguez de la Cueva, officer commanding the Fifth Regiment of Halberdiers of His Most Catholic Majesty the King of Spain, as dauntless a lecher as ever ripped off codpiece, and champion of all the fornicators who ever rutted before the face of God, brought to the cathedral in person, that they might be baptized according to the rites of Holy Mother Church, half a dozen of his bastards male and female, every one of whom he had christened by the sweet name of Emmanuel (or else Manuela), which in fact means "Sent by God". Novara certainly boasted other categories of fornicator, apart from the Spaniards, but these could scarcely have shown their faces in the light of day in so brave and so brazen a manner. However it was indubitably the latter who made the hatch of the turning-wheel creak round more often than the Spaniards.

At the time of Antonia's birth Novara must have been without exception the most calamitous city of all the utterly calamitous cities which constituted the calamitous kingdom of Philip II of Spain; whose dominions, like those of his father before him, were so vast and far-flung as to have it said that upon them "the sun never set."

The troubles of Novara (by which I mean the really big

troubles – not the little ones which the city had always suffered from, like any other place) began in 1550, when the then Commander-in-Chief of the troops of the Holy Roman Empire, Don Ferrante Gonzaga, while looking at a map, had had a flash of inspiration and decided that Novara, Novara and no other city, should be made the stronghold of the Empire against France and her allies in southern Central Europe. A city-fortress, encompassed by impregnable walls, a bastion proof against siege and artillery, barring all access to the Po valley from both the Duchy of Savoy and the Alpine passes.

From the headquarters of the troops of the Holy Roman Empire the incumbent Mayor of Novara, Giovan Pietro Cicogna, received orders as peremptory as they were insensate: to see at once to the demolition of the outlying parts of the city, where three-quarters of the civilian population lived, and to utilize the rubble to reinforce the city walls, adding new buttresses, new bastions, new defence works . . . At stake, apart from Cicogna's own personal career, was the outcome of the conflict, the future, the Empire, the whole world.

This Cicogna, a man of unbridled ambition, hurled himself headlong into the enterprise without caring a damn about anyone, layman or ecclesiastic alike. He devastated everything he was told to devastate, and thereafter began to shore up the ancient bulwarks as ordered. But at this point in the proceedings he became aware of three things.

The first was that the relative ease of demolition was by no means matched by the expedition of rebuilding, and that to put in hand the works of fortification demanded by Gonzaga would require money – a flood of money.

The second thing Cicogna realized was that while he was razing the outskirts of Novara to the ground, the real theatre of war had irreversibly turned to other parts of Europe and of the world in general. And from this realization emerged the third: that Novara and its fortifications, might they ever have been of the least use to anyone, were at this point totally superfluous. The building works were abandoned and today no trace of them remains. In any case, they were defences made of mere pebbles, rubble and mortar that would hardly have withstood a real siege, and at the first direct smack from a cannon-ball would have collapsed like cardboard stage props; so that even from the military point of view the project was somewhat ill-advised. Novara lay exhausted in a sea of rubble. Of the sixty or seventy thousand souls living there before its troubles began in earnest, the majority had moved out into the countryside or gone to live in other towns.

But the troubles were not yet over. It would have been an intolerable humiliation to the Spanish civil and military authorities to say to the Novarese, "Dreadfully sorry, we made a mistake. Rebuild your houses and God be with you. Work on the ramparts will cease." Quite to the contrary the Spaniards, in the harshest and most uncompromising manner possible, forbade the construction of anything in the area now cleared of houses – not so much as a dog-kennel or a tool-shed for a kitchen garden. They let a little time go by and then coolly came up with a new load of exceptional and extremely crippling taxes, "to complete the works of fortification already under way", "to bring to a successful conclusion, to the profit of the citizens and to their exclusive benefit and advantage, the defensive works already put in train". And more to that effect.

Novara became depopulated once and for all. Within the city ramparts, apart from the Spanish garrison, there remained perhaps six or seven thousand souls; and most of these were priests or nuns, exempted by ancient privilege from paying taxes, or else persons who had devised some means of cashing in as quickly as possible, legally or otherwise as the case might be, at the expense of the "religious" and the military, of course. Adventurers of every race and kind, vendors of every species of merchandise, hucksters, whores.

The latter were particularly numerous. Despite Cicogna and his passion for demolition, and despite the ordinances of the Council of Trent, the fact remains that at the end of the sixteenth century the city of Novara could boast the most happy-go-lucky and hedonistic clergy in the whole of Europe; of friars the most scheming, of nuns the most frivolous, the fattest of canons, the merriest of abbots, the richest of vicars. Certain hospices, well known to the Novaresi, with delicacy and discretion received the country curates who came into town for "a change of air", as they put it. Which meant, to escape from the miasma of the rice-fields, and to do their business with a wallet and a winsome lass.

There were also private "houses" which provided the friendliest of welcomes, making available every degree of human warmth at a price to suit all pockets. Males and females, the ripe and the juvenile, surrounded the client with every attention and solicitude. Then there was gambling, bets were laid and cash ventured at exorbitant interest. The penurious straits of the lay population, strange as it may seem, by no means bridled the dynamism of the clergy. On the contrary, it even pepped them up. There were priests turned lawyer, priests turned usurer, priests turned "madames" of whorehouses and managers of gambling dens, priests turned innkeeper . . . There were also, and very numerous they were, the so-called *quistori*, adventurers who dressed up in priestly garb and ranged the countryside sermonizing and flogging "bulls" of indulgence and phoney relics, working miracles and doing business of every kind, though always in the name of God. The nuns, and especially the superiors of the convents, the abbesses, led a life of queenly splendour, both within their convents and without.

So, to come back to San Michele, and to Antonia, and the Foundlings' Hospital of the House of Charity at Novara, in view of how things were going in town can it be wondered at if the wheel of mercy, the notorious wooden drum of the turning-wheel, continued to turn, and indeed turned more speedily than ever?

The monster grew, and became a little girl with the darkest of eyes and most raven of tresses. From the lodge which housed the turning-wheel and the wet-nurses she graduated to the Hospice itself, a building divided into two parts, one for the boys and one for the girls, at the time of which we speak both administered by the nuns of the congregation of St Ursula. There they sheared off her hair, according to regulations, and put her into a green canvas shift that reached to her feet, which was the specific uniform of the foundlings for all purposes and all seasons of the year.

At five years old she began to make sorties from the orphanage, along with the nuns and her fellow foundlings, to walk in procession on Good Friday, Corpus Christi, the Assumption of the Virgin, and all the saints' days and the feast-days in the Calendar on which the foundlings, both the boys and the girls, with shaven head and candle in hand, gave the world inconfutable proof of a thing most prodigious and marvellous . . . To wit, the loving-kindness of man, destined to triumph over pride, over wickedness and over all the other evil propensities which in that particular epoch appeared to be the true signs of the times.

But that is not all. The public appearance of the foundlings, maintained by the charity of the citizens of Novara, and in the care and under the supervision of the nuns, was not merely a spectacle both edifying and of uplifting moral value; it also served to remind the onlookers that, by making a contribution to the House of Charity, any sinner could in the life to come obtain a substantial reduction of his sentence, in terms of years and centuries of Purgatory; and that by bequeathing all its worldly goods to the waif-factory the benefactor's soul would waft direct into the bosom of the Almighty, without a single touchdown on the way. And the more ample the funds of the bequest, the more radiant with glory and beatitude would be the reward.

In this manner, between one procession and another, one religious function and the next, passed the earliest years in the life of Antonia Renata Giuditta Spagnolini in the House of Charity of San Michele at Novara; all of them more or less alike, with their winters when the foundlings started coughing, then grew hectic with fever, and died, and were buried behind the church, between the hen-run and the gatehouse with the turning-wheel; with their summers, when the foundlings swelled up and turned yellow and writhed on their death-beds for two or three days or even more – because of the contaminated water, so the doctors said. Had it not been for that swift interchange between living and dead the Foundling Hospital would never have been able to accommodate all the infants who entered by the turning-wheel or were brought there by relatives, by parish priests, or by someone who chanced to find them by the roadside. So that the death of a foundling was not a tragedy: on the contrary! The most fortunate of all – said the nuns – were those to whom the Lord, in his infinite goodness and mercy, granted the ineffable grace of leaving this world before they reached the age of sinning, to wing their way straight to

Paradise without having to undergo the temptations and tribulations that would otherwise have saddened their adult lives.

As they grew older, the main occupation of the foundlings consisted in funerals: both the cheerful, hastily performed funerals of companions for whom nothing more was needed than a drop or two of holy water sprinkled on the self-same sod where as a rule the hens used to peck about, behind the gatehouse where turned the turning-wheel, and the solemn funerals of Benefactors which contrariwise dragged on for hours, in San Gaudenzio or in the three naves of the Cathedral all a-glitter with candles. But this did not mean that the foundlings had no time at all for the games proper to their age, or were more unhappy than was implicit in their very situation. Far from it: there is nothing that stimulates life in the young – and not only in the young – as does familiarity with death.

Since the demolition of the suburbs nothing out of the way had happened in Novara; life went on as usual, without dramas, people got by either better or worse according to their luck or their money, and things would not be worth narrating had there not occurred at that very time, while Antonia was at San Michele, another event destined to have consequences, in this part of Italy and of the State of Milan, as profound and enduring as those caused by Don Ferrante Gonzaga, by Spanish domination, and by Cicogna. This event, more important than spectacular, was the long announced and long deferred arrival of the new bishop, Carlo Bascapè; concerning whom there were rumours to give the shudders both to priests and to nuns, and to disturb the slumbers of a great many people in the city itself and throughout the diocese of Novara.

This Bascapè, said those in the know, had been the favourite of Carlo Borromeo, the demented archbishop of Milan who tried to turn all his monks and nuns into saints by force. He had been counsellor to two Popes, and in the running for the papacy himself; but luckily at the last conclave the fanatical party had been defeated, and the new pope proceeded to rid himself of its members by packing them off to be bishops in the most distant and uncomfortable sees, dispersing them to the four corners of the Christian world. In Bascapè's case, however, sending him into exile in Novara had been no swift or easy matter, for at the time he fell into disgrace he was superior-general of one of the most powerful congregations of the new Church, the Barnabites; and he had kicked against the pricks with might and main. But in the end he was forced to give in, and made ready to leave his congregation, and Rome, and the lofty spheres wherein he had thitherto lived, to come and bury himself in a small town, in a frontier diocese, at only forty years old, or scarcely more! An eagle caught in a net set for thrushes, a comet trapped in the puddles and swamps of the plain of Novara; where he would be the cause of heaven knows what disasters – said the plump, placid canons of San Gaudenzio, and of the Cathedral – if, taking no account of the local situation, he there forcibly attempted to realize that pious, inhuman, transcendental Church which he and other madmen of his ilk had luckily failed to impose upon the world at large.

After a lot of gossip, numerous heraldings and much tittle-tattle, the new bishop at last arrived; and his arrival was followed after a brief interval by the disappearance from San Michele of the Mother Superior of the Ursulines, Sister Anna, who wherever she went left a long trail of perfume, and frequently received persons who came to visit her in carriages from Novara; even after nightfall, and men at that! A new Superior arrived, a certain Sister Leonarda, with wax-yellow face and very bushy eyebrows. There was an improvement in the diet and hygienic conditions of the foundlings, but the burden of the Masses for the dead and daily prayers for the Benefactors became unbearable. Not only that, but tremendous punishments began to be meted out to children who fooled around during funerals or dared to whisper to one another in church: entire afternoons spent kneeling on spiky millet seeds, public thrashings and days of fasting spent locked in closets constructed for the purpose; so that the older foundlings took to escaping by night, scaling the boundary wall bristling with broken glass.

Fresh to the orphanage came a lay sister, by the name of Clelia, with the specific duty of teaching the girls their catechism and devotional practices. All games were thenceforth forbidden, as being useless and harmful to their correct training as Christians and women, and were substituted by special "recreations" in which the foundlings were made to learn by heart and recite significant passages from the Lives of the Saints. The very walls, from hearing them so often, were compelled to learn the stories of St Adelaide, widow of King Lothair of Italy and of the Emperor Otto the Great, who among the splendours of royal and imperial palaces wove her own winding-sheet; of St Pelagia, who was the most dissolute woman in Antioch until she was converted on hearing a sermon by Nonnus, bishop of Edessa, and who lived thereafter, humble and happy, in a cave on the Mount of Olives; of St Rita of Cascia, who as an act of obedience watered a post of dead wood and saw it put forth buds, and leaves, and clusters of muscat grapes; and innumerable other facts concerning St Cyprian, St Anthony, St Perpetua martyr, St Teresa of Avila, St Procopius, St Cunegund, St Vincent . . .

But along with the Saints of the past there were the Saints of the present, the *modern* Saints – the missionaries of the Christian faith who in those very same years were venturing to the most remote and unexplored corners of the new-found worlds, to carry the word of God to the savage peoples who dwelt there, and to be rewarded with martyrdom. There were the acts of heroism, the miracles, the great exploits and the small episodes of everyday devotion and sacrifice that led to the inevitable agonizing death of these present-day successors to the Apostles.

Like all the young "religious" of the time, lay sister Clelia dreamed of going as a missionary to distant climes (China, India, Japan, were to her and her contemporaries what for us today are the planets of the solar system – or, let us say, what those planets would be if they were inhabited by other human beings). She always carried on her person a special little notebook in which she had diligently noted down everything she had heard narrated by the missionary Fathers. Sometimes for a joke, or else to distract her from some prank they were up to, the foundlings would beg her to tell them the story of "the little Cingalese", or that of "the Chinese who were converted by spittle", or the other one – justly famous – "of the little Japanese boy who broke all his teeth with a stone so as to be able to take First Communion".

"Sister Clelia," they begged her, "please, please can we have that one!"

13

Then she would say with shining eyes, "Yes my dears, yes. Come gather round me."

But when it dawned on her that her stories were of no interest to anyone, that the foundlings were poking fun at her, then she flew into a rage. "Little vipers! Cheats! Baggages!' she screamed, pulling them by the ears and doling out such hard pinches that sometimes they drew blood. "Bread and water for all of you for two days! No, three days! An afternoon on your knees on the millet! No supper for any of you for two days! You she-devils you! I'll rip the evil from your living flesh, I will!"

At night, sometimes, it happened that one of the older foundlings would slip into Antonia's bed in the dark and begin to fondle her, with many sighs, in certain parts of her body and in such a manner that she was overcome with surprise and shame. She tried to fend them off, speaking in a whisper so as not to be heard by the lay sister sleeping behind a curtain at the end of the dormitory, and who, had she woken, would have inflicted heaven knows what punishments: "Who are you? Leave off! Let me sleep!"

"Hush!" the wicked one murmured back, endeavouring to disguise her voice (Antonia always recognized them, though). "I am your Guardian Angel, I will take you to Paradise . . . Give me a kiss!"

"I am the Blessed Virgin come to visit you . . . Soon you'll find you like it! Have faith in me!"

TWO

The Egg

AS SHE GREW, Antonia became a real beauty, a child in whom one could already guess at the form and features of the woman to be; and this despite her meagre nine years of age and her head, for reasons of hygiene, completely shorn of hair, like all the foundlings. Even the coarse green hempen shift (on account of which, until a certain age, the boys were often mistaken for girls, and the infants and the skinniest of the growing girls looked like scarecrows, or – as the nuns put it – "dressed-up broomsticks") was on Antonia a becoming garment. In character she was tranquil and inclined to hold her tongue, given more to thoughtfulness than to rowdiness and raptures. Very often, between one funeral and another, between one sung Mass and the next, instead of playing with her companions, or joining in their spiteful, gossipy gabblings, or the petty intrigues of small girls already versed in many of the troubles of life, she would sit on her own thinking her own thoughts or go wandering around the orphanage buildings.

She poked her nose into everything. She went to look at the capons confined all their lives long in wooden coops as cramping as could be, scarcely higher than the birds were tall and stacked up against the outer wall of the building which housed the nuns, right under the refectory windows. Those capons had the peculiarity of being extraordinarily aggressive, because of their breed and of their living conditions. Only put a finger near their cage and at once they rushed to peck it, infuriated by their imprisonment and even more by the heat. This according to old Adelmo, who at San Michele was the only grown-up of the male sex, with the double function of gardener and sexton. The cages of the *pulon*, said Adelmo every time Antonia met him, ought not to be kept where they were kept, because the sun beat down on them from midday till sunset. They ought to be in the shade on the other side of the building. However, the other side of the building was the entrance side, and the nuns understandably would not even consider keeping the capons on their front doorstep. So there seemed to be no solution to the problem.

Another indispensable visit during Antonia's rambles was to the dog-basket occupied by Diana, a pointer bitch who once a year would "go on heat" and perform breath-taking exploits, breaking down fences, cutting herself badly on the glass by trying to jump the boundary wall, biting Sister Clelia . . . and all this, said the nuns, for one absurd reason – that she wanted to escape from the orphanage and go and "buy herself puppies"! (What would she have used for money? And who would she have bought them from? Who sells puppies to dogs? Why, Antonia wondered, do people say such stupid things and talk in such a baffling way?) Diana was usually the gentlest of animals, and even this business of "heat" was far from clear. What did it mean, "to go on heat"? Apart from all else, these moods came over her in the winter-time! Antonia had even tried winkling explanations on the subject out of Adelmo, but not even he was inclined to talk too freely. "It's just that at a certain time," he said, "she comes all over hot like . . ."

Occasionally in her wanderings Antonia would meet one of the nuns, Sister Livia, who would stop and talk to her as to a grown-up, complaining about the weather, about her ailments, about the Mother Superior, who ill-treated her, and about the foundlings, who played tricks on her – sometimes cruel ones, such as putting dead mice in the dirty linen or stretching invisible trip-wires where she was due to pass; and pass she did, and naturally came a cropper. All this was narrated part in words and part in gestures, because Sister Livia was a foreigner, from a country called Naples, and Antonia couldn't always grasp what she was saying. For "he" and "she", instead of saying *lui* and *lei* she said *isso* and *issa*, *vien'accà* for *vieni qua*, a girl she called *guagliona* instead of *ragazza*, and so on. At San Michele Sister Livia was the "elderly lay sister" responsible for all the charring jobs, just as Sister Clelia was the "young lay sister" responsible for the foundlings' education. The other nuns treated her as a servant. "For goodness' sake, Sister

Livia," they would cry, "can't you see there's a spider's web on the refectory window? Can't you see these benches are always smothered with dust? As for the floor, it's filthy! Get on and clean it! What are you waiting for?" And they scolded her with a "Get a move on! We always have to say everything twice!"

Along she would come with her bucket and mop, shuffle-shuffle in her slippers. "Spider's web, my foot! And couldn't they clean up their own dust with their own fair hands?" One day, when Sister Leonarda had given her a real dressing down in front of the entire orphanage, Sister Livia answered back with a growl, and not in so much of an undertone that Antonia and the other girls failed to hear her, "Sister Sewer has spoken! My respects to Sister Sewer! It shall be done according to the commands of Sister Fart!"

"She's a little touched," said the nuns, tapping their foreheads. "Poor thing, she means no harm. She really is a bit gone in the head."

On the announcement of a visit to San Michele from the new bishop of Novara, Monsignor Carlo Bascapè (the usual well-informed persons said he would be arriving on foot from the city, accompanied by the seminary students and certain canons from the chapters of San Gaudenzio and the Cathedral), after lengthy conventicles the Ursuline sisters selected Antonia, from among all the foundlings, to recite the ode of welcome to the bishop; maybe because she was prettier than the other girls, or because she was more level-headed . . . who knows! For weeks and weeks before the great day came they compelled her to repeat and repeat some ghastly verses penned for the occasion by the Mother Superior, Sister Leonarda:

> ("We poor children miserable
> As well as we are able
> Hail with one accord
> Our bishop, champion of the Lord," etc.)

until she was all in a daze. They gave her sweetmeats to encourage her and pinches for punishment. They pestered her with admonitions: "Don't forget now! Be careful, mind! Don't go making mistakes!"

17

When at last it came, the day long awaited and feared, they hauled her out of bed before daybreak, took her to the laundry-room, stripped off her clothes and plunged her into a tub of such scalding water that when they saw fit to pull her out again she was lobster pink. They scrubbed her with water mixed with ashes, and then flayed her alive by drying her off with coarse cloths of flax and hemp which *they* called towels: the pain of it made her shriek. They dressed her in white from top to toe, and decked her shoulders with two pasteboard wings to which Sister Clelia had glued hundreds of pigeon feathers to make them look more realistic; on her head they placed a blond wig woven of maize-leaves and attached a pasteboard halo. Since in the meantime dawn had broken they compelled her to drink a raw egg, to "keep up her strength". This, at any rate, was how Sister Leonarda put it. In point of fact Antonia found raw eggs more sickening than strengthening, but there was no way she could refuse the kind offer. She had to swallow the egg as the nuns bade her, shut her eyes and gulp it down.

With the egg in her tummy, and Sister Clelia clasping her by the hand, Antonia had next to hasten into the church to implore God and the Blessed Virgin for their assistance, by reciting the prayers of the Rosary and others appropriate to the occasion. Meanwhile all the foundlings, both boys and girls, were already outside the orphanage gates, lining the road which climbed to the city walls at Porta di Santa Croce, and whiling away the time until the bishop came by singing hymns of praise and thanksgiving until they were hoarse. From the Castle came a squad of harquebusiers, who stationed themselves along the route of the procession. No one from the Curia had requested their presence, but the military governor in person had taken the initiative of despatching them to guarantee the safety of that *cabron* (billy-goat), that *loco* (lunatic) – i.e. Bishop Bascapè . . . "If his enemies wish to kill him," said *su excellencia* the Spanish governor, rolling his eyes in a threatening manner and twisting the long, tapering moustachios that were his pride as a *caballero* and the preoccupation of his life, "they will have to do it a long way from Novara!" He then added in an undertone, but loud enough for those nearest him to overhear and inwardly digest his words: "He's enough of a thorn in my flesh alive, that *cabron*. Dead he'd be double!"

Luckily, however, the foes of the billy-goat put in no appearance that day. He himself stepped forth somewhat late in the morning, when the foundlings no longer had strength or breath to sing, and a few of them had been on the point of fainting from the hot sun beating on their shaven heads.

The first to come into view, emerging in crocodile from Porta di Santa Croce at the top of the incline known as the "Salita della Cittadella", were the Cathedral seminarists, clad all in black, with shaven cheeks and scalps and heavy wooden crucifixes hung round their necks. After them came the canons, recognizable from their round hats and the purple trimmings on their cassocks. Outstanding among them even from afar, for his bodily bulk and ruddiness of complexion, was that Giovan Battista Cavagna da Momo who a few years later was destined to become more famous than he himself could either foresee or have wished. As we shall learn in due course.

But on the day he came with the bishop to visit the House of Charity, Monsignor Cavagna was still little known, a priest like any other; but already in circulation regarding him was the pleasantry that the mediaeval poet Dante Alighieri had predicted his birth three centuries earlier, and had him in mind when he wrote the line (*Inf.* XVII, 63) mentioning "a goose whiter than butter".

In provincial Italy, in the seventeenth century, this is the sort of thing the priests used to laugh about, and in Cavagna's case they had some reason for it, because the poor fellow, hailing from a part of the Novara backwoods teeming with geese, really did look like a goose himself, and an exceedingly plump one too, in his gait and his gabble, and in the very shape of his person. He had, in fact, an enormous posterior, narrow shoulders, and perched atop a long neck the head of an infant that moved this way and that as he walked, as if searching about on this side and on that. Only the colour of his habit, being black, failed to match in with this image of a goose.

In the wake of the canons came the bishop, clad all in white and shaded by a gilded baldaquin borne aloft by four seminarians pacing in step with him, he himself half a head taller than they were. He was skin and bone, of waxen complexion, his beard grey and grey hair beneath his mitre. But although his face was cadaverous and prematurely aged, it was evident, given a closer look, that in his youth this Bishop Bascapè must have been a vigorous fellow endowed even physically with a certain charm; and that at forty-nine (his age at this time) he was not yet the "living corpse" he described shortly thereafter, while consecrating the church of San Marco Apostolo in Novara. It was on that occasion, according to his biographers, that he pointed to his own body and addressed the citizens of Novara as follows: "This corpse which you now see living before you, and speaking unto you, you will soon see lying dead in this same place, where I wish it to be buried."

But in point of fact he was already a mere survival from another man, of whom I think it may be said without doing anyone an injustice, that he had ceased to exist when Bascapè – that is, his body – came to Novara as bishop in obedience to his superiors. That body, in bishop's garb, thereafter continued to fight and to function like the knight we read of in Ariosto's *Orlando furioso*, who with his head chopped off still roamed the battlefield swinging his sword with hefty swipes, because he hadn't yet realized he was dead . . .

A considerable personage, our Bishop Bascapè! A personage emblematic of an epoch long distant from us in time and, in itself, long dead; but emblematic also of a way of interpreting life and human destiny that keeps cropping up, and is certain to endure well beyond this twentieth century of ours. For the first part of his existence the darling of fortune, showered with her every blessing; but in the second part she frowned on him, depriving him of all her gifts and more besides. An aristocrat by birth, a man of exquisite education and culture, well versed in Latin and Spanish, the two international languages of the time, a brilliant writer both in Latin and Italian, an expert in ecclesiastical and in civil law, and moreover with a natural gift for administration and "business management", Bascapè had all his papers in order to aspire to change the world – for the better, of course – and to think he would succeed. Philip II of Spain, whose guest he had been in the royal palace in Madrid, knew him well and appreciated his worth. One archbishop, the well-belovèd Carlo Borromeo, and no fewer than two Popes, Gregory XIV and Innocent IX, had sought his counsel and co-operation. At forty years of age, indeed at thirty-nine, he had been informed of his forthcoming elevation to the cardinalate. Whereupon, almost as if following the prepared script of his own ascent to the threshold of the papacy, and thence to his canonization, he had gone into retreat at Monza, in a monastery of his own congregation of the Barnabites, "Where," in the words of one of his biographers, "with the Novices, he devoted himself to the washing of dishes and pans, and other such chores; with like sentiments, I do believe, as those of St Bonaventura; that is, that if he were discovered in the employment of such offices by one bearing him the Hat (i.e. the symbol of the cardinalate) he could tell him to hang it up somewhere, until he had finished what he had in hand."

All in vain, in vain! However many soup-bowls Bascapè rinsed, however many plates he washed, the cardinal's Hat arrived not. What did arrive, on the other hand, was the news of the death of Gregory XIV, and from that moment on, in the affairs of our saintly dish-washer, everything went from bad to worse. Cardinal Facchinetti was elected Pope but survived only a few weeks, to be succeeded on the throne of St Peter by that Ippolito Aldobrandini who in the twinkling of an eye stripped Bascapè of everything he had, appointments, distinguished connections, important missions and grandiose prospects, and packed him off no longer to cleanse pots and pans, but souls; and this in an obscure provincial corner of the obscure Duchy of Milan. Novara, in short.

Though dead in heart, Bascapè still kept up the struggle. He made up his mind that nothing had happened, that his projects remained unaltered. Instead of changing the face of the planet from a base in Rome he would change it from a base in Novara, and he flung himself headlong, as we have said, into an undertaking I scarcely know how to describe (desperate? demented?), that of transforming an outlying diocese into the centre of the spiritual rebirth of the entire Christian world. The new Rome! The City of God! As the Russian revolutionaries in 1918 aimed to force people to be happy, and wrote as much in their manifestos ("We shall compel humanity to be happy by force") so three centuries earlier Bishop Carlo Bascapè wished to compel his contemporaries to be Saints; and even if the words are different the substance is more or less the same. His actions, moreover, were quite coherent with and adequate to the immensity of his undertaking – which explains why the Spanish military governor was concerned for the bishop's life. In the less than five years he had been in Novara, Bascapè had excommunicated one mayor, a certain Alessandro Lessona, and a fair percentage of the clergy, canons included; he had come to blows with the Senate of Milan, the Governor, with every one of the religious orders represented in the city and throughout the diocese, with Buelli the Inquisitor of the Holy Office, and with the parish priests. Many of these last he had sacked, others he had forced to change their way of life. Nearly all the beneficed clergy had been stripped of their benefices. He had put a ban on singing, dancing, laughing, gaiety, celebrations. Death and despondency was his decree. His faithful (his "flock", on whom he never ceased to urge pressing counsels, fiery exhortations, appeals, admonitions, benedictions and rebukes) had attempted to repay him in his own coin, but without success. For how do you set about killing a corpse? They had tried with poison (twice) and thereafter with a volley from a harquebus, and finally attempted to brain him with the balcony of a house he was visiting. All in vain! The mortal frame of the deceased emerged unharmed from all these trials, and was now descending the slope, exceedingly slowly, among his seminarians, his canons, the Spanish Governor's harquebusiers, and the foundlings themselves, now all but bereft of voice, who croaked out:

"Long live His Excellency our Bishop! Long live Bishop Bascapè!"

Emerging from the darkness of the church, Antonia was stunned by the sunlight, the crowd, the uproar. Almost without knowing it she found herself on a raised platform facing the bishop and the canons, who were smiling as if to say "Buck up and recite your poem and get it over with." Every eye was riveted on her. A wave of faintness passed over her at first, maybe because she had left her bed so early, or else it was the raw egg they had made her swallow against her will. Everything seemed to go fuzzy and spin around her – the platform, the bishop, the House of Charity, the very walls of Novara. Summoning all her strength she babbled,

"We poor children miserable . . ."
and there she stopped, mouth agape, hands clutching at nothing. Behind her she heard Sister Clelia prompting:

". . . As well as we are able! *As well as we are able!*"

But she lacked the strength to utter a word. Then blackness overwhelmed her and she passed out, pitching down onto the boards of the platform. Her wings came adrift and the pasteboard halo rolled to the feet of Monsignor Cavagna who, with some difficulty on account of his corpulence, bent down to recover it. Bascapè had a spasm of vexation and murmured, "What on earth have they done to her, those nanny-goats?" (The reference was, of course, to the nuns.) He turned to climb down from the platform, and entered the church with the throng at his heels, seminarians, canons, foundlings both boys and girls, and even a number of the faithful who had followed him out of the city through Porta Santa Croce. A cry arose from the huddle of nuns:

"Long life to His Lordship our bishop. Long life to Bishop Bascapè!"

After lunch, as a token of forgiveness, Antonia was admitted to the nuns' refectory to kiss the ring of his Lordship the Bishop, who – said Sister Clelia as she accompanied her thither – had seen fit to give them all this example of his charity and love of his neighbour by enquiring about the health of a foundling ("None other than yourself, you understand") and even sending for her to bestow his blessing upon her. All that was needed therefore, warned Sister Clelia, was not to cause any more trouble; for example by mistaking one of the Monsignors of his suite for the bishop himself, or turning her back on him when she was dismissed, or committing some other tomfoolery, such as touching his hand with hers when she kissed his ring.

Antonia entered. She saw the refectory tables had been drawn somewhat apart: on the one side sat the bishop and his suite, at the other Sister Leonarda and the nuns, all making her agitated signals meaning "What are you waiting for? Get on with it! Can't you see His Lordship is waiting? Kneel down, for goodness' sake!"

Down she knelt. Contrary to orders received, she took the bishop's hand in the two of hers and examined it before kissing the ring. And a white emaciated hand it was too, with long diaphanous fingernails exquisitely manicured. It could, indeed, have been the hand of a woman, but for those knobbly knuckles and all those hairs, glistening like black silk, covering the back of the hand and two-thirds of each finger. She kissed the ring.

Bishop Bascapè withdrew his hand and began to rub at it with an embroidered napkin and considerable energy and attention to detail, in all the places where the foundling's fingers had so much as brushed it. He then asked her, "What is your name?"

"Antonia Spagnolini, at your Lordship's pleasure."

"It was the Devil himself," declared Sister Leonarda in forceful tones, "who entered into the body of this creature this morning, and prevented her from addressing Your Lordship with the prayer and the welcome to Your Lordship on behalf of all the foundlings here in our House of Charity." Then she repeated, in tones of loathing and execration: "No doubt at all. It was the Devil."

"How do you fare here at San Michele?" asked the bishop. "Is all well with you?" Antonia, expecting no such question, turned her head towards the nuns for some clue or some comfort. What she got in its stead was a glare so withering that it left her breathless. "Yes . . . Yes, Your Lordship!" was all that she could babble.

Monsignor Cavagna, seated on the bishop's left, had tucked a corner of his napkin between the top and second button of his cassock, though splodges of sauce were as plain as could be on his collar and chin. His face creased with laughter and his eyes twinkled as he asked the foundling girl, "D'you get plenty to eat? Every day of the week? Dinner and supper?"

"Twice a day! Dinner and supper, Your Honour!"

Again a moment of silence while Bascapè finished cleaning the ring on which the foundling's lips had rested, and Sister Leonarda glanced at the other nuns with an expression of mingled gratification and relief, as if to say "So *that's* over and done with! It didn't go off too badly." The bishop then put down his table-napkin and raised his hand. "Antonia," he said, "I bless you in the name of the Father, the Son, and of the Holy Ghost." Thereupon he dismissed her with a "God be with you."

The foundling got to her feet, curtseyed as Sister Clelia had instructed her, and started backing away with all eyes fixed upon her: she couldn't wait to reach the door. Monsignor Cavagna gave her a wave of the hand, raised his chin, made a goose-movement with his neck – an habitual gesture, because his starched clerical collar was very trying to him – and then at once held out his glass to the nuns for another drop of wine: "Just a drop, you understand . . . Forgive me, sisters, won't you. It's for my stomach's sake. Otherwise," he explained, "I'll never digest this fine fowl."

THREE

Rosalina

SPRINGTIME ENDED, summer came. The turning-wheel at the House of Charity continued to turn, though less frequently than in the past; and this too was a sure sign that the presence of Bishop Bascapè was changing many things in Novara, among the clergy and not only among the clergy. Fewer nuns were to be seen around in the streets, fewer parish priests in from the country, fewer women framed in the windows or striking poses which revealed their profession beyond any reasonable margin of doubt. In fact women of that kind seemed to have entirely disappeared from the streets in the centre of town, and one only saw a few of them on the city walls near the Castle, and in the evening, when their presence became a strict necessity in order to prevent soldiers out on pass, randy and shameless as they were!, from devoting all their energies to molesting respectable women. The inns put up their shutters two hours after sunset, the "complaisant" hostelries were no more – or if they existed they no longer displayed the sign at the door . . . and they kept no registers. The city, formerly pleasure-loving, seemed to have shrunk into a mood of frigid ostensible morality, in which no one any longer trusted anyone else, although everyone, as best he might, went on doing what he had always done in the past; with many more precautions though, and amid greater difficulties due to the greater risks being run. Everyone, in fact, cursed the new bishop and the great He who had sent him *there* of all places. "With all the dioceses there are in Italy," they grumbled, "he had to be foisted on *us*, to be a bull in the china- shop here in Novara. Wish he'd break his bloody neck and leave us in peace!"

One day at San Michele Sister Livia, the elderly lay sister who did the charring in the House of Charity, was nowhere to be found, and the matter at first appeared inexplicable. Had she run away? With whom? And how had she managed it? She could certainly not have got far, said the foundlings, unless someone had helped her. To Antonia who knew her well, however, it seemed unthinkable that Sister Livia could have set off into the unknown, let alone with a man. At her age, and unable to speak the Novarese dialect that everyone else spoke! Unable to understand a word anyone said. Come to think of it, mused Antonia, Sister Livia had indeed run away once before during her lifetime, when she had come there to San Michele. Relatives she had none, nor any friends outside the convent. If she'd run away again, where was she going? Back to Naples?

For their part Sister Leonarda and the other nuns first thought that the "elderly" lay sister had been taken ill, and they instituted a search for her, in the cellars, in the church. They even sent Adelmo to check on the stream that flowed right under the convent walls, in case she might have tumbled in and drowned. But no sign of her, so they gave up the search.

They found her at dawn the next day, when the chaplain arrived from Novara to say Mass, as he did every morning, and Adelmo went to ring the bell and couldn't find the bell-rope. He looked up, and saw Sister Livia hanging above his head with a swollen, blotchy face, her eyes white blanks and her lips drawn back in such a ghastly grimace that the poor man almost had a stroke on the spot. He emerged wild-eyed, staggering, unable to utter a word, and it was only from his gestures and expression that it dawned on the nuns what he had seen . . . They made all haste to the bell-tower and the first thing they thought of (once over the first horror of the discovery) was how to avoid a scandal. A nun committing suicide, and in church what's more, would have been a news item, and what an item! They must cover it up. The story of the suicide, the chaplain told Sister Leonarda and the other nuns, who were still crossing themselves and taking furtive upward glances, must not cross the threshold of San Michele. The foundlings must never get wind of it, and no one in town must be informed of it except the bishop. As far as anyone else was concerned Sister Livia had run away. Disillusioned by her life in the convent, she had hearkened to the glib blandishments of the

27

world and cast off the religious habit she had never deserved to wear. In any case, the priest asked himself, addressing the question also to the nuns, was that not the simple truth? If we interpret the term "habit" as this sheath of flesh which God had given us as a burden to drag through the world, and which is the casket of the soul . . . The body of that iniquitous lay sister, which she herself had rejected, must be buried in great secret, by night, in unconsecrated ground, by the light of muffled lanterns. With her body they must also bury all remembrance of her.

The nuns obeyed; but things thereafter turned out not quite as intended, because there in the orphanage everyone knew the truth about Sister Livia and her death; and if the story of it never reached Novara it was solely because, outside San Michele, Sister Livia was unknown to anyone. For Antonia, accustomed as she had been from the age of five or six to every kind of funeral and funereal rite, that event was her first real encounter with death. Never before had she seriously stopped to think about it, and only after Sister Livia's death did it strike her as a real thing, quite distinct from the trade carried on in the House of Charity with those so-called "Benefactors".

No, this was the thing itself. Even the life-story of Sister Livia, which she had never learnt anything about, and which had come to such a sorry end, puzzled her. Sometimes, during her lonely walks, she speculated on the whereabouts of that Naples which Sister Livia had left to come so far, to slave away as sweated labour and kill herself. She asked herself why she had run away from there, why she had become a nun. What mystery was hidden in that death – and earlier, in that life, that was such anguish for the woman who bore it and so insignificant to everyone else? What meaning was there in man's life, beyond the rather simple-minded stories recited each day in the orphanage, over and over again every day, which she believed in as one believes in fairy-tales . . . which means she thought they *were* fairy-tales. You lived, you died: what for?

That summer of 1599 Antonia was not yet ten years old, but she knew everything about sex: how babies are formed in a woman's belly after the male has mounted her, as a cock mounts a hen, leaving in her that coloured speck you see in the yolk of a broken egg; and about the "moons" that are the bane of womankind, and are the tangible proof of their inferiority to the male, of their impurity; of the pleasure women feel when mounted by a man . . . one that to a lesser extent they can experience on their own by doing a certain thing, or even without doing anything at all, as had indeed happened to Antonia herself one Sunday morning in the orphanage, as she was on her way downstairs from the girls' dormitory. All of a sudden she felt she was going to die and that something awesome was happening to her . . .

Events were as follows. She was coming down the stairs along with another girl, by the name of Carla, and they were both holding their breath from the effort and watching very carefully where they put their feet, because between them they were carrying the lidded earthenware vessel that was the communal piss-pot of the girls' dormitory – they had to get it all the way to the ditch and empty it. Ever since Sister Livia had been unable to render that service all the girls had to take turns in emptying the piss-pot; and that day it was their turn. Antonia, like her companion, was puce in the face from the weight of it and all of a sudden, as she moved, she felt a tingling feeling rise from her feet and flood her loins; a thing so intense, so unexpected, so out of this world, that she completely lost her head. She opened her mouth to say "I feel ill" or "Help!", or something of the sort, but, as from time to time it happens in dreams, no sound emerged. Instead, before she knew it, her fingers had relaxed their hold and when Carla shrieked "What are you doing! Take care!" it was already too late. The piss-pot fell, tipped up, and caused a flood. Both vessel and lid bounded from stair to stair, shattered into a shower of potsherds and proceeded to deluge Sister Leonarda, who had the misfortune to be standing at the foot of the stairs and naturally flew into a fearsome rage, trembling from head to foot. "You slut!" she bawled. "You did it on purpose to drench me, I saw you! You dropped it on purpose!"

The other girl, this Carla, was scared out of her wits by what had happened and thought only of making excuses for herself: "It wasn't my fault! I tried to hang on to it! It was her what dropped it!"

That day the foundlings one and all had the satisfaction of seeing the Mother Superior soused from head to foot in their own pee and more full of wrath than ever before witnessed. As for Sister

Leonarda, after washing over and over again and disinfecting herself with lye, and changing her habit and undergarments and everything else she had on when the crime was committed, she decreed that the culprit of that outrage against her person should be locked up for three days in the cell known as the "fasting room". This was a sort of grotto, practically underground, damp and full of cockroaches and spiders, where the foundlings were given, once a day, nothing but a little bread and water. Nor, before they had served their full sentence, were they let out for any reason whatever, not even illness. For this was the Rule of the House.

It was there in the fasting room that Antonia met Rosalina, a grown-up foundling with whom they, the younger girls, should have had no contact whatever, for the nuns forbade it. Rosalina it was who explained to her, in the minutest detail, exactly how the male "mounts" the female, and all the rest of it – the "moons", pregnancy, the magic formulas to recite so as not to get with child. ("Which," the girl admitted, "usually don't work, so it's better to use a bit of sponge, even if it's uncomfortable and sometimes gets lost inside you. I wonder what ever happens to all the bits of sponge that go up and never come down again?").

Antonia listened open-mouthed. "Is it true what they say," she asked, "that you get a lot of pleasure with men?"

"Incredible pleasure," replied Rosalina, very serious. "The greatest pleasure to be had in this world!"

Then she had second thoughts and pulled a face. "To tell you the honest truth," she corrected herself, "I usually feel nothing, or almost nothing. But that must be because I was ruined when I was little. Everyone says it's an extraordinary thing, absolutely marvellous, that you can really go mad at such moments. Even us women, you understand, and not just the men. Of course," she added, "if you really want to enjoy it you have to do it only with men you like. If you have to do it for money and go with everyone, as I did before I was brought back here to listen to the twaddle the nuns talk, after a while you get fed up. Even disgusted."

Rosalina was tall, with a good figure, blue eyes and tow-coloured hair. She was seventeen years old, almost twice as old as Antonia, and her experience of life was as near as could be complete, since the convent had disposed of her before her tenth birthday to a baker in

Galliate who had solemnly pledged his word to marry her as soon as she had her "moons", and had set her up a dowry signed and sealed by a notary – so many sheets, so many pillow-cases, so many towels, so many aprons and kerchiefs and the rest of it.

Before Carlo Bascapè the Terrible came to be Bishop at Novara, Rosalina told her, the foundling girls of San Michele were given away to any man who asked for them and promised to marry them, young or old, rich or poor, resident or on the road; as in fact had happened to her and many of her companions. Even though everyone knew what the inevitable end of things would be, and what sort of contracts *those* were, with the foundlings always getting the worst of it. No sooner had Rosalina begun to have her "moons" and become pregnant than the baker threw her out into the street and bawled after her, "You strumpet you! Get yerself off and marry the ram that tupped you!" The ram that had tupped her was no other than himself – but the same thing happened to all the other girls and there was no help for it: they had to go. Without the sheets and pillow-cases and all the other knick-knacks mentioned in the contract, and without a place to lay their heads, trusting to luck.

In her pregnant state Rosalina reached Novara, where an old midwife rid her of the baker's foetus and thereafter kept her under her wing, along with two other girls who plied their trade in a house in Piazza dei Gorricci, on the first floor. Each girl had a room of her own, showed herself at the window to be viewed by passing men, and received her own clients in private, as society ladies receive their visitors. She too was a lady in her own right, for even if the old girl took most of what she earned she still had enough left over to buy herself a silk kerchief, a liver patty or a flacon of scent. Rosalina had spent four years in the house in Piazza dei Gorricci, and there she had been happy, despite the fear of getting pregnant again, and of being denounced to the authorities as a prostitute; and despite the church hens of the parish who crossed themselves at the mere sight of her, and the urchins who shouted rude words at her in the street. She shook her head violently: "Stuff and nonsense!" she said. In a year or two, when they'd grown up a bit, those very same lads would be back begging for her favours, and then they'd take a very different line.

She was not in the least ashamed of having gone with men for money. On the contrary, she thought it a better way of life than a washerwoman's or a scullery-maid's. "Either way it's the same old story, every man-jack of them wants to mount you, but they want it for free, and then expect you to be their slavey. Whereas a prostitute," she went on, "has a whole lot of men always round her, bringing her little presents, promising to 'redeem' her, vowing to love her for ever . . . Most of my clients were country priests who came to town a couple of times a month or more, for 'a change of air'. Every one of them without exception declared he was madly in love with me and wanted to rescue me from the life of shame I was living, and (can you believe it?) wept over my guilt at the very same time as he was enjoying me. They really seemed to mean it. I'm sure they meant it!"

To cut a long story short, Rosalina had lived four years there in the house in Piazza Gorricci, with her country parsons who brought her sheep's cheese and honey, vegetables and fruits in their due seasons, and with the midwife who relieved her of certain of the risks of the profession. Until Carlo Bascapè arrived as Bishop of Novara, and it was like a spring day when the sun is suddenly blotted out and a grey, cloudy sky rumbles with thunder. The priests and all other clients thinned out almost to vanishing point, and then one morning the girls found themselves alone and penniless and not a silk dress to their names. The midwife had done a moonlight flit, taking with her the few objects of value and also, in her haste, forgetting to pay the debts she had run up in the past few months with the landlord, with the tradesmen . . . The constables arrived, interrogated the girls and then packed them off back to wherever they had come from, without punishment of any sort but with a solemn warning: it would go hard with them if they were found in town again!

Rosalina had been escorted back to the House of Charity, the last place on earth she would have chosen to go. She'd wept and she'd shrieked, even thrown herself on the ground in the middle of the street, but all her tantrums did her not a whit of good. She had once again to don the foundlings' uniform, the coarse green shift and those horrible wooden clogs that covered her feet with blisters and with sores . . .

The Ursulines, who then took on the task of redeeming her, gave her a number of jobs to do. First of all, every morning, she had to go out to the ditch and empty the piss-pot from the boys' dormitory. This, said the nuns, would benefit her both as physical exercise and by provoking in her a salutary disgust for the muck of which man is made. Having performed this office she had to work in the kitchens as scullery-maid, and thereafter down at the ditch as washerwoman; she had to draw the water from the well, keep the courtyard swept, and finally, at the end of the day, repair to the church and stay there until nightfall, practising her devotions – orisons, acts of penitence, dialogues with God. Her diet was the simplest imaginable: a slab of plain *polenta* and a glass of water twice a day, to prevent her "humours" (in the words of Sister Leonarda) from becoming "all aflame again in a body already the victim of sinfulness", and to make sure these inflamed humours did not incite the passions, instigators of the most loathsome sins.

Rosalina pretended to resign herself to all this, with a view to escaping later. And escape she did – or at least she tried. Hence her presence in the "fasting room". Clambering over the boundary wall of the orphanage she had cut herself badly on the broken glass, and to make matters worse that wretched hound Diana had started barking and snapping at her from below. Out rushed the nuns with lanterns, and even the sentries on the walls of Novara came down to see what was going on and have a good laugh at her expense. Utter failure, and at what a cost! Rosalina had both hands wrapped in bandages now practically black with dirt. She moved to beneath the barred window, unwrapped them and showed Antonia her wounds, already festering. Addressing herself she said, "It was stupid of me. Next time I try and escape it won't be by climbing the wall at night, that's for sure! I'll walk out of here at the main gate by broad daylight, even if I have to kill someone on the way!"

And she turned to Antonia: "You think I'm not up to it, eh?"

"But what will you do?" asked Antonia. "Where will you go?"

Rosalina re-bandaged her injured hands. She pulled a wry face and shrugged; and Antonia, who until that moment had thought of her as a grown-up, realized from that gesture that she was choking down tears. It lasted but a moment.

33

"I'll go to another town," she said. "At least to start with and to get me out of here. Maybe Casale, or Pavia . . . I'll work as a prostitute. What else d'you think we can do in life, we foundlings?"

She shrugged again, screwing up her face in a rather forced smile that was meant to look intrepid. She took Antonia's chin between two fingers and forced her to look her in the eye. She burst out laughing.

The child was beginning to feel ill-at-ease with this disturbing talk, and also with her companion's strange manner, but Rosalina talked on without looking at her again, and noticed nothing.

"Even you girls who are still little," she said, "you'll be prostitutes when you grow up. Or else drudges. There's no way round it. However many times you've told over your beads with an *Ave Maria*, or however many Communions you've made. Once you get out of here, all those tales the nuns tell you are worth nothing at all. The Blessed Virgin, the Saints, virginity . . . It's all rubbish!"

She tossed her head and went on: "They're the first to disbelieve it in any case, but they'd rather be skinned alive than tell you that both as women and as foundlings the only thing that'll help you to face the world is that thingummy between your legs. There lies Providence, the real true Providence, the only one that helps us out when the whole world is against us. All the rest of it is twaddle . . . Don't you believe me?"

She threw back her head and laughed again. Then with her bandaged hand she tapped Antonia's shift approximately on the spot where Providence was supposed to reside. Then she fell serious.

"That's the only resource mother nature gave us when we were born foundlings," she declared, "and a huge part of our lives depends on the use we make of it. You'd better take the word of someone who's seen the world and the way it works. You go out and face the world like the nuns tell you to, and they'll make mincemeat of you out there! You'll be martyred before you have time to turn round. And anyway, has it never occurred to you to wonder why these old crows came to shut themselves up in this place? Brides of Christ? My arse! They're here because no one

34

fancied them, or because of dirty linen they had to hide under their dreary nunnish habits, or for any other reason I don't give a damn about. I'm not likely to forget how they were here at San Michele in the days of Sister Anna. There was a coming-and-going between Novara and the Ursuline sisters such as under this other Superior, hideous as she is, wouldn't be possible for a moment! Men of all races – Spaniards, Piedmontese, Milanese, and on one occasion even a Moor . . . Hey, what's up with you? Stop it, will you?"

For Antonia had suddenly hurled herself at Rosalina, pummelling her with her fists and pulling her hair: "It's not true! It's all lies! You're a bad lot!" she screamed, then started sobbing: "You want to send me to Hell, you do! I'm not listening to you!"

She crossed herself over and over again, glaring at her companion. If this was the Devil, it was supposed to vanish . . .

Rosalina's mouth expressed nothing but contempt. "You little fool," she said.

She stood up. Thereupon Antonia rushed to the door, hands over her ears so as not to hear another word the other said, then stuck out her tongue at her.

"Look out or I'll call Sister Clelia," she threatened. "I'll tell her everything!"

FOUR

The Flatlands

FROM TIME TO TIME to the House of Charity came strangers
whom the Mother Superior, Sister Leonarda, took personally to
view the foundlings. Many of these persons were impoverished or
(as they used to say in those days "lack-purse") noblemen in search
of a pageboy. Others were craftsmen or merchants who needed an
apprentice and said to themselves, "Let's take a peek down at San
Michele. Happen there'll be a young feller'll fit the bill."

Once among the foundlings they behaved as if at the horse-fair,
looking them over one by one, feeling their muscles and asking
Sister Leonarda, "He's not the rebellious type, is he? Doesn't have
nasty habits, eh? Isn't diseased, by any chance?" And in the end,
out of all those poor little devils putting on a show of boldness but
in reality terrified by the thought of being separated from their
companions, they chose the one who seemed most suited to their
needs, in household or workshop. Off they would go with the
victim at their heels, crying his eyes out, while his chums, grown
solemn, shook his hand or simply gave him a touch, in a last and
silent farewell.

It occasionally happened that one of these visitors interested
themselves in a girl. Could they cook? Sew? Take care of an
invalid? But usually nothing came of it. Requests from private
individuals to be entrusted with girl foundlings had become
extremely rare at the House of Charity since Bishop Bascapè had
strictly forbidden the practice of conceding girls "on approval" to
men who said they wished to marry them. As had happened in the
past to Rosalina and to many others. From time to time elderly
gentlewomen would come in search of girls with particular
qualities, to take care of some bedridden patient or paralytic; but
after the most probing investigation they gave it up as a bad job

because there had never existed, at San Michele or anywhere else, a foundling to serve their purpose: sweet-natured, strong-limbed, hard-working, virtuous and above all ugly. Sufficiently ugly to put men off at first glance and to spare that lady's male guests the embarrassment of a pregnancy, with all the complications this would later involve. In short, whereas with the boys at the House of Charity the better looking they were the more they were in demand, the girls only found a taker if they were hunchbacked, lame, or as hideous as sin. A foundling such as Antonia seemed doomed to grow up in the place, because no benefactress would ever have accepted her, even though they all gave her a looking over. But they didn't have to be fortune-tellers or prophets to realize that in a few years' time that girl with the night-dark eyes and the mole on her upper lip would create turmoil around her, wherever she went.

"What is your name?" enquired the old dames.

"Antonia Spagnolini," replied the girl. Then they would stroke her shaven head and sometimes give her a sweet or a sugared almond. But they finally chose someone else, with a squashed nose and buck-teeth, or else simply went off shaking their heads. What a pity! In the whole of the House of Charity of Novara there was not a single girl with a hunched back, or a goitre, or bandy legs. They were all as pretty as pictures, and no one wanted them.

Came the year 1600, Holy Year, the dawn of the new century. One market day in April San Michele had two visitors of a type unusual there. They were peasants; and peasants, moreover, from La Bassa, the flatland region of the province of Novara, rich in spring water and, to the south of the city, prevalently rice-growing. He, Bartolo Nidasio from Zardino, was a man of fiftyish, short and stocky and grey-bearded. He smiled rather gauchely, as peasants do when they come to town, and from one hand to another shuffled his conical hat, the proverbial "pointed hat" then worn by rustics. His wife Francesca, her hand in the crook of his arm, had a chubby face you couldn't tell the age of, and two blue eyes that made you happy just to look at. Her body, on the other hand, swathed in a shawl and linsey-woolsey gown reaching to her feet, seemed out of shape and even slightly deformed, with a gigantic bosom and such a large bottom that as

37

soon as they clapped eyes on her the murmur went round among the girls of the House of Charity: "*There*'s a mum with a bum!"

The visitors were taken to view the foundling girls by Sister Clelia – for Sister Leonarda scarcely felt like putting herself out for a couple of rustics – and the Mum with a Bum was carrying a bag of the biscuits now called "Novara biscuits", but in those days (they were baked flatter and harder then) were known as "Biscuits of San Gaudenzio" or "Nuns' tack". This on account of a folktale that attributed their invention to the times of Gaudentius, first Bishop of Novara, and gave all due credit for it to the enclosed nuns. When it struck the girls that their visitor had brought the biscuit-bag with the express purpose of opening it on the spot and distributing the contents, the ecstasy of the foundlings knew no bounds.

"Up for Mum with a Bum!" they cried. "She's brought us a bag of Nun's tack!"

The children formed a storming party: "One for me! One for me!"

"It is strictly forbidden to feed the children!" shrieked Sister Clelia, as the girls besieged the biscuit-bag. "It is prohibited by the Rules of the House! Give it here! They shall be distributed at dinner-time."

Not a whit of notice did the visitor take. "Come on, my dears, come on," she said. "If I'd known there were so many of you I'd have brought more! I'll come again. I promise I will."

In the twinkling of an eye the bag was empty, and the girls joined hands in a ring around the two visitors, making up a song on the spur of the moment, changing the words of a nursery-rhyme they knew:

> *Three cheers for Mum, for Mum has come*
> *With a bag of biscuits and a big bum.*

"The old crows are ugly." One voice struck a jarring note. "Old crows" was the somewhat disrespectful epithet with which the foundlings, girls and boys alike, referred to the nuns, and Sister Clelia craned her neck to identify the culprit, but there were so many children milling around, laughing at her and making gestures as if to say "Bye bye!" that she suddenly adopted a brisk manner.

"Let's get the matter settled," she snapped at the visitors. "Take one of these little vipers if you're really set on it, and God help you!"

"And as for you" – she wheeled upon the foundlings – "I'll settle with you later! I say no more!"

"If it were up to me I'd take the lot of them," Signora Francesca told her husband, "But that isn't possible. We've got to choose just one."

She pointed to Antonia: "Would it be all right if we took this one?"

Antonia, who until then had been laughing along with the others, and hadn't given much of a thought to those strange visitors, felt the world swimming before her eyes. "Are they out of their minds?" she wondered. "It must be a mistake." She, who had no physical shortcoming, not even buck-teeth like Caterina, or the slightly ricketty legs Iselda had. She felt her eyes fill with tears. Why did these two want to take her away from her friends, her companions, to pluck her from her surroundings? Where were they carrying her off to? Why had they picked on her?

Next thing she found herself on a cart, squatting among sacks of seed and looking out at the world through a distorting lens of tears – the little square in front of the orphanage gates, the well, the avenue of poplars leading up to Borgo Santa Croce and the walls of Novara. On her left lay the ploughed fields, the woods, the horizon, the cloudless sky. Where on earth was she going? She burst into a flood of desperate tears. It was all coming to an end, just like that! It was already over! She was facing the unknown. Farewell to San Michele, farewell to childhood, farewell to the world she knew . . . Her sobs were such as to melt a heart of stone, and Bartolo, who was far from having one, looked a question – What should I do? – at his wife beside him on the driving-seat. She made a gesture that told him to stop worrying and get the cart on the road. Whereupon he picked up the reins and gave them a flick. "Giddy up! Giddy up! *Ve' chi assà!*" he cried (turn to the right). "*I si drè!*" (go left).

Clippety-clop, skirting the city walls, horse and cart arrived at

Porta San Gaudenzio, which stood more or less where we now see the Barriera Albertina, a monumental gateway constructed in the first half of the nineteenth century in honour of Charles Albert of Savoy, King of Sardinia and Prince of Piedmont. As ever on market days there was a tremendous bustle of carts in and out, and Bartolo had to wait a few minutes before getting into the main street. To help ease the traffic problem someone had scrawled an arrow on the Customs House wall, and beneath it the legend: THIS WAY TO VERCELLI, TO THE PO, AND TO TORTONA.

Francesca in the meantime talked to the child, trying to cheer and reassure her with the mere sound of her voice. She asked her "Why are you crying, Antonia?" She bucked her up by saying things like, "You're not losing a thing by leaving that house where they abandon boys and girls on the turning-wheel. You'll be far better off in the country with us. There are lots of children of your age in the village. You'll be able to play with them." She gestured towards Bartolo and herself. "You see," she said, "the two of us have never had any children, and we're alone. So if you're a good girl and feel at home with us, we'll take care of you as our own daughter, and when it's time for you to get married you'll be married like a real lady, not like a foundling. You'll have a bottom drawer all of your own, and a dowry to take with you. Do you hear what I'm saying? Do at least tell me why you're crying . . ."

The fact was, however, that Antonia had already stopped crying. Children have this edge on grown-ups: that even at moments of desperation they manage to get distracted. There she was hunched up among the sacks, her back turned to Francesca, gazing wide-eyed at the landscape she had never seen before, with the snowy Alps in the blue of the sky and among them the mass of Monte Rosa. An unforgettable sight – and she, Antonia, had lived ten years at San Michele, on the other side of the walls of Novara, unaware of the existence of those mountains which gave their name to the whole region where she herself was born – *Piemónte!*

Very soon, however, not only the landscape but other things began to attract the attention of our foundling. Bartolo Nidasio was guiding his cart into a suburb that seemed to have just been built, so fresh was the paint and the stucco, and so new it was in every detail, from the wrought-iron railings to the roof-tiles. In the street was a tremendous crush of horse-carts and hand-carts, of pedlars and peasants – easily recognized, the latter, by their pointed hats and the bags of seed hanging from their belts – elbowing and searching out and running after each other with yells and gesticulations, puce in the face from God knows what hagglings outside the doorways of hostelries each with its own inventive name: The Moon, The Crown, The Flaming Cross, The Hawk, The Blackamoor, The Eagle . . .

This huddle of houses and sheds, of storehouses, of pens for livestock, was the suburb of San Gaudenzio which, following the demolitions ordered by Gonzaga, had sprung up again without authorization a few hundred yards from the gate of that name. According to law it should not have existed, but exist it did, and moreover was the place where all the roads converged: bearing to the left on leaving San Gaudenzio you were on the way to Vercelli and the Po, whereas the right-hand fork led off towards Biandrate and the villages of the Sesia valley. This was the halting-place for all the baggage trains coming to the city, and here was all the bargaining and here were the brokers for every sort of merchandise, be it corn, land, brides, flunkeys or slaveys . . . Here, on market days, were the notaries who drew up the acts for property transactions and mortgages for bankrupts; and here too were the usurers who lent money at exorbitant rates of interest. Here passed all the news coming from the city, and hence it would spread by word of mouth throughout the region; news about the political situation, the progress of the wars, the epidemics afflicting men and livestock, and in short everything that might interest the inhabitants of this last outpost of the Duchy of Milan and the realm of His Most Catholic Majesty of Spain, on whose dominions, as mentioned above, the sun never set . . . Just as troubles and tribulations never ceased to pester the residents, preventing boredom and keeping them on their toes.

"As soon as we're home we'll get that foundling's shift off you," Signora Francesca told Antonia as they splashed through a ford in the Agogna, which is a little river with freezing waters, today no longer limpid, but at the time of our story crystalline, with long green weeds swaying on the gravelly bottom, and the purplish shadows of fish that vanished on hearing a horse's hoofs striking on the stones of the ford. "We'll search around among the clothes I had as a girl. There must still be some kirtles and bodices that'll fit you. And then we'll buy some cloth and make you new clothes. I can't stand to see you wearing that trash any longer!"

Beyond the woods in the narrow valley of the Agogna ("shady with dense foliage" as a local Flatlands bard, by the name of Merula, penned in Latin), the countryside which today looks as flat as a billiard-table was gently undulating, ablaze with many colours, from the blinding yellow of the rape to the sky-blue of the flax-flower, passing through every possible variety of green: the emerald green of rye, the lustrous green of wheat, the bluish-green of barley, the soft green of young bean-plants and of the grass . . .

Further on, where the land had not yet come under the plough, it was flowering wild horehound that spattered colour on the pallette of spring, making great irregular violet-coloured patches which showed up bright in contrast to the sulphur-yellow of the dandelions or the golden carpets of buttercups; and already the early irises were reflected in the puddles and the frail catkins seemed to shiver on the willow branches overhanging the ditches, as soon as the lightest breeze arrived to touch them.

At every crossroads along the way was a little shrine dedicated to the Madonna, to St Anne, St Martin, St Rock, to the Sacred Heart of Jesus. Where the road forked at Gionzana a chapel with a miniature portico provided an emergency shelter for travellers surprised in those parts by nightfall or an unexpected cloud-burst. The vaulted ceiling of the portico, which must at one time have been frescoed, was by now totally black, and soot-blackened also were the large stones arranged to form an impro-vised fireplace. As Bartolo's cart passed the chapel they heard from the village deep buried in the woods a gladsome peal of bells sounding the midday Angelus. Signora Francesca crossed herself, while Bartolo, in vacant or in pensive mood, rapt in one of those deep meditations that the rocking of the cart and the monotony of the all-too familiar route always provoked in him, shook himself, straightened his back, called "Giddy up now!", and cracked the whip to urge the horse on faster.

They passed through a wood of birch and oak, and as soon as she emerged on the other side Antonia realized that the landscape had changed. No longer terrestial, as up till then, but acquatic. This was the country of the paddy-fields, a lagoon dazzling with reflected sunlight, subdivided into countless compartments, square, triangular, rhomboid, trapezoid . . . A mosaic of watery mirrors with, here and there, a few dun-coloured patches where the water had got blocked up and turned brackish and boggy. Like the suburb of San Gaudenzio, which our friends passed through on their way out of Novara, so these paddy-fields, as far as the law was concerned, did not exist; for the Governor of Milan, the Marquis d'Ayamonte, etc. (the *etc.* stands for the fifteen or twenty titles of nobility that followed and completed the surname) had issued orders *"to any person whatsoever and of whatever rank in society, even though privileged, that they should not venture to plant rice, or to cause it to be planted, for six miles outside the city limits of Milan and around the other cities for five, with the reservation that in the region of Novara His Excellency desires it that no rice whatever be planted in that province without his express permission, the penalty for those who contravene the aforesaid Articles being to each and every one, at the first offence, the confiscation of the crop and a fine of one scudo per rod, pole or perch, at the second offence, the confiscation of the fruits and a penalty of three scudi per rod, pole or perch, and at the third offence if the offender be a tenant farmer, or a steward, or a day-labourer, three years imprisonment; and if he be the owner of that rod, pole or perch a penalty of six scudi for every rod, pole or perch and exile from this State for the space of three years; the which pecuniary penalty and the income therefrom shall be attributed One Third to the Government, one third to the Accuser in the case (whose name shall be under lock and seal) and the other Third to the Office of Publick Health."*

And this last, explained the Proclamation, on account of the fact that *"the sowing of rice in certain parts of this State has for many years caused infection and corruption of the Air, and in consequence much mortality among the populace."*

This Proclamation bore the date September 24th 1575, the year which saw the start of that epidemic which was to strike the city and region of Milan with redoubled force the following year, 1576: but what other incentive or motive could the authorities in general, and the Spanish Authorities in particular, put forward for interfering with the cultivation of rice, other than that of epidemics, a recurrent feature of life? But thereafter the epidemics passed and the cultivation of rice continued to flourish, and indeed increased, it being far more profitable a crop than rye or forage, enabling the city and rural area of Novara to bear a heavier tax-load per head of population than other towns. In protest against the Proclamations of d'Ayamonte and his successor Charles of Aragon, there rose in revolt the "Professors Medical of the College of Novara", who affirmed under oath that the paddy-fields *"little harm could do to the Aire and to the General health of Men, as long as they are distant one mile from the Town, in keeping with Y Excellency's decree or little less, and in places most unsuited to produce other crops, at a distance from the frequented throughfares, and above all ensuring that the Rice-Waters move freely along, and in no wise cease to flow, and turn marshy."*

In 1593, as the memory of that plague began to fade, the Governor Ferdinando Velasco, High Constable of Castile (etc. etc.), permitted the distances to be reduced: for Milan and Novara four miles, and three for the other towns. Since his successor, Don Pedro Enriques de Azevado, Count of Fuentes (etc. etc.), chose to pursue the same line, the City of Novara charged its Official Orator, one Langhi by name, to make formal protests at every time and place that seemed suitable. And this was because, in the words of a writer of the time (Cognasso) *"the rice-fields of Novara are to the west of the city, outside Porta Vercelli and Porta Mortara, stretching as far as Borgo Vercelli; and if it is forbidden to grow rice within four miles of Novara and three miles of Borgo, then there is practically no room left for growing anything. It was also pointed out that the town suffered no damage whatever from malodorous air, and that having no other source of income it met all demands* (i.e. tax demands) *with its earnings from rice."*

This Langhi thereupon informed the Governor of the arguments put forward by the Novaresi. The Governor heard him out, and left the laws as they were. It was in any case deliberate governmental technique at the time of the Spanish domination, to leave its minions in the grip of laws which were inapplicable and in fact not applied, keeping people constantly a fraction on the

44

wrong side of the law, and thereby enabling the authorities to catch them out at any time – when they wanted to scrounge money on the side, or intimidate them, or find a justification for fresh and even graver acts of embezzlement. This is how modern Italy was born, in the seventeenth century. It may be of some comfort to us Italians to know that public malpractice came to us from abroad, and is more recent than commonly supposed.

Returning, then, to Bartolo and Francesca's cart and the story of Antonia, such was the aspect of the Novarese countryside that April morning of that Jubilee Year when the foundling, crouched between two sacks, watched it pass before her astonished eyes. Who can tell what thoughts she had, seeing for the first time the shattered reflection of the mountains in the mirrors of the paddy-fields, the long rows of pollarded willows, and all the rest? Maybe she was still thinking of San Michele, and of what her former companions were doing at that hour, of Sister Clelia, of Sister Leonarda, of the dog Diana . . . Maybe she was trying to imagine what was in store for her: who can say! Or maybe – and this is the most likely – she was thinking of nothing at all, letting herself be lulled by the rocking of the cart and distracted by the novelty and variety of the images mirrored willy-nilly in her eyes and printing themselves on her memory: a heron upright in the middle of a paddy-field, a flight of ducks, a grass-snake swimming across a rivulet, and even, glimpsed through a grille in a shrine, the martydom of a Saint (it was St Laurence) with the executioners and the Angels in heaven . . . It happens often enough even to grown-ups, to live through the great upheavals of their lives – even though long awaited, or foreseen, or feared – in a kind of oblivion, a kind of stupor, that leaves no room for the logical connection of thoughts; in a vacuity of the will, all but a dream.

FIVE

Don Michele

"LOOK! OVER THERE! That's our house!" exclaimed Signora Francesca to the girl as she stood beside the cart, after Bartolo had taken her under the arms, hoisted her out from among the sacks and set her down on the ground. She pointed to a pretty two-storeyed house with wooden balconies and a slate roof, shrouded and partly hidden by an ancient wisteria. But Antonia wasn't listening to her. Her attention was fixed on the Nidasio's yard, as she stood chin on chest, peeping from beneath her brows. At the far end of the yard, where the cart had come to a halt, grew a fig-tree. After that came the cowsheds, the barn, the hired-man's cottage, the shed for farm implements, the chicken-coops, the dung-heap. Beyond the dung-heap was the rest of Zardino, or what you could see of it from where she stood: other cowsheds, other yards, other houses with wooden balconies, with roofs of slate or hump-backed tiles or thatched with mud-caked straw; other wisterias, other fig-trees, other hen-runs, more and more barnyards, divided one from another other by low walls bristling with nails or broken glass to keep the thieves and the urchins out.

Down there, beside the dung-heap, a little party of women had gathered. These were the Village Gossips, bundled up in their black or grey shawls, eyeing the foundling and nattering ten to a dozen among themselves about this extraordinary event: Francesca having to go off to Novara, at the other end of the world, to look for a snotty-nosed girl to take on, as if the village wasn't already full of brats, some sick some not, legitimate or otherwise, of every shape and size, but with one single character-istic in common – they all ate their heads off. And honestly! muttered the Gossips, she could at least have got herself a boy – boys grow up and work in the fields. But to go to the city and bring back a *girl* was unimaginable, utterly unheard-of! It simply didn't add up! "How times do change!" they commented. "Just to think that our own mothers, and our grandmothers before them, used to drown their female brats in the mill-race at birth if they had too many of them, or didn't have enough milk to suckle them, or in lean years. Yes sir! They drowned them as you do kittens or puppies, and no one protested at all, not even the priest!" The Gossips put the blame for anything odd or wrong-minded that happened in the world on the new century and its mania for novelty. "People aren't what they used to be," they said. "At this rate where will we all end up?"

Some little way from the party of Gossips stood two minuscule, wrinkled and almost identical women who stood eyeing the foundling but kept mum, though they exchanged certain glances that could only mean "I can't believe my eyes! She's been and gone and done it!" Or words to that effect. These were the Borghesini twins, next-door neighbours of the Nidasios, with whom they had a feud. But, as we have said, the other Gossips chattered away, and not only chattered but gesticulated, or stood with arms akimbo, or adjusted their shawls or their aprons in a marked manner. Shaking their heads in a way that augured no good, over and over again they repeated: "This is all we needed! A foundling in Zardino! Mixing with our own children!"

"A daughter of the devil! A little witch!"

Indifferent to the presence of the Gossips, or at least unaware of their spitefulnesses – she was too far away to pick it up in any case – Signora Francesca took Antonia by the hand and leant down to whisper in her ear, "Are you hungry?"

The girl had now raised her head and was looking in the direction of the house: at the black dog (in fact called Blackie, though she was scarcely to know that at the time) barking like mad and rushing back and forth as far as his chain allowed and nearly throttling himself; at the hens and the geese flapping their wings and uttering their inarticulate sounds; at the boys and girls of Zardino standing round her wide-eyed and open-mouthed, as if she were a supernatural vision, something from another world.

She nodded.

Signora Francesca burst out laughing. "Now *there's* a good

sign!" she cried. "No, in fact there are two good signs: that you're hungry and that you've given me an answer at last."

Two young girls now sidled up to the foundling. They were the daughters of the Nidasios' farm-worker, who lived on the other side of the yard. The younger one stretched out a hand, touched Antonia's shift with a finger, and quickly withdrew it. The other girl, a little older than Antonia, asked her, "Why've they cut all your hair off? Were you naughty?"

At this point a boy came rushing into the yard and panted out: "Don Michele! Don Michele!" At which Bartolo removed his hat, the Gossips wheeled round, and they all saw the person thus heralded pacing towards them with vigorous step, by his side the altar-boy with the bucket of holy-water. And judging from how he was swinging it around he must have spilt practically all of it on the way.

Don Michele was a sprightly little fellow, chubby though by no means fat, of indefinable age, though he must have been over sixty. He was dressed like a peasant (something completely new to Antonia, who had never seen a priest going around without a black cassock down to his ankles), in a pair of fustian breeches held up with string, and a tunic also of fustian and all over patches. Only the green stole embroidered in gold which Don Michele wore over one shoulder had anything to do with normal priestly attire. This odd sort of priest, Antonia noted, was not even tonsured. His hair, completely white, was close-cropped, his cheeks were shaven, his complexion rosy and his eyes, so light in colour as to appear almost yellow, reminded the foundling of a cat that used to turn up from time to time at the orphanage, and which the nuns would chase away with besoms, ranting and raging as if it had been some kind of noxious beast. When he reached Antonia Don Michele halted, took the holy-water sprinkler held out to him by the altar-boy, and blessed those present "in the name of the Father, and of the Son, and of the Holy Ghost," aspersing the water even over the Nidasios' horse, which backed away sharply and would likely have reared up, but for being still harnessed between the shafts.

Don Michele then turned to the foundling and asked, "What is your name?" And when she had told him he said, "Welcome, Antonia! Dwell in peace with the people of Zardino, and may they also dwell in peace with you. Honour and respect your foster-parents as if they were your own, sent to you by the will of God! Love God and keep his commandments. Be happy!" Then: "Let us pray together," he said. The Gossips drew near, mumbling their paternosters.

And while they are at their devotions it may be an apt moment to explain to the twentieth-century reader that Michele Cerruti ("Don" Michele) was, no doubt about it, a rather singular species of priest; one fairly common before the Council of Trent and the Counter-Reformation, but already by the first years of the seventeenth century nearly extinct. An abnormal kind of priest, who did not scruple to use the church to rear silkworms in, and who therefore at this time of year kept the place shut tight at all costs, because he still had to heat it with charcoal braziers. Not that at other times of year he held many religious functions. A magician-priest, who by children's scalps could foretell not only their physical development but the events of their lives; one familiar with the powers of herbs and of minerals, who knew how to mend broken or dislocated bones by binding them between two birch-wood splints and intoning certain phrases of which he alone possessed the secret. A false priest, if we are to call a spade a spade; a man who could barely read and write, and who liked to say that his studies in philosophy and theology had been pursued at the university of life: this as he roved the mountains and valleys teaching the peasantry that Hell is horrible, and anyone wishing to take the shortest route to Paradise must buy the indulgences which he sold them himself. In the diocese of Novara false priests like Don Michele had for centuries been called *quistoni*, and the official Church had turned a blind eye to them; that is, in practical terms, had tolerated them. But then, almost overnight, the Ecclesiastical Courts had begun to take notice of them, and thereafter the *quistoni* had become increasingly rare, indeed practically extinct. So at the time of our story there were very few *quistoni* left, and these few no longer went around preaching sermons or working miracles but hid themselves away, like Don Michele, either in some Alpine valley or in one or other of the most out-of-the-way villages in the Flatlands. When telling about himself Don Michele loved to recount how when he was only twelve years old his father had put him into service with a *quistone* who dressed as a friar, and that that was how he embarked on his career, going around from village to village, from market-place to market-place, along with this false friar who made the rustics loosen their purse-strings by telling them tales of the hereafter – complete with the wailings of the dead and the crackle of hell-fire – such as to keep them awake for many a night, starting up in the dark at the merest rustle. These things occurred, said Don Michele, when the *quistoni* were still tolerated and even respected, and in some villages the parish priest himself would give them a night's lodging; in those far-off days when Novara had bishops with high-sounding names (Cardinal Ippolito d'Este, Cardinal Giulio della Rovere) whom no one had ever clapped eyes on, and who may not even have known the whereabouts of that diocese so distant from the courts they frequented, confining themselves to raking in the revenue.

At twenty years old Don Michele set up on his own. From the slopes of Monte Rosa to the banks of the Po he demonstrated how well he had imbibed the teachings of that bogus friar, preaching such sermons in the village squares that the rustics, if only to get rid of him, bought his indulgences and everything else he had for sale. He had had great loves, great battles, great adventures. He had done eight months' forced labour for fraud and larceny to the detriment of a widow in Pettenasco on the shores of Lake Orta. He had caught the *mal franzese*, but had pulled through. For a couple of seasons he had tried his hand at trading in Sacred Relics (fragments of Holy Crosses, the teeth and fingernails of martyrs, threads from Holy Vestments, and so on). Then, on the threshold of his fiftieth year, it dawned on him that the Church and the world at large had changed so much since the times of his youth that if he went on exercising the trade of *quistone*, as he had done thitherto, he would end up down a mine with shackles round his ankles for the rest of his born days. Or even on the scaffold.

He had to change his mode of life. He went to Novara, where he had a few acquaintances among the monsignors of the Curia, and such were his blandishments, bribes and traffickings that he succeeded in being made a Minor cleric. He was thereupon granted what were then called his "patents" as chaplain of Zardino, paying out a moderate fee to the episcopal administration: twenty ducats, to be precise. Money like that, outside the Church, wouldn't have bought two rooms to live in, so he had indubitably made a good bargain. Moreover, with regard to his ability to celebrate religious functions, or any claim he might make to being a priest, no one bothered to verify the facts, and the whole business – at least on paper – bore the stamp of legality. In those days parishes and bishoprics were bought and sold for cash, as in Italy today one purchases a pharmacy, a tobacconist's, a bookmaker's establishment. The price varied according to the size and importance of the parish, its certified or presumed revenue in tithes, charity, donations and other benefits. A priest's credentials were not always checked up on, and, supposing they were, not always rigorously.

Legally, Don Michele became a priest. Despite the fact that his specific rank in the clerical scale (that of "ostiary") permitted him only "to open and close the doors of the church, ring the bells and bless the faithful." He celebrated Mass, very much in his own way and only when he really couldn't avoid it, with long homilies on the immortality of the soul, Hell, Purgatory and the Remission of sins. He baptized infants, he heard confession, he joined the inhabitants of Zardino in holy matrimony and accompanied them to the grave. But above all he organized the personal side of his life, exploiting a number of skills acquired during the years he wandered the world over as a *quistone*: years that promised to guarantee him a peaceful, comfortable old age in that secluded Flatlands village where he had retired to live and to die, safe from the buffets of fortune. He therefore equipped himself with cauldrons and limbecs for distilling pressed grape-stalks into *grappa*, with beds for the hatching of silkworms, and with blue maiolica vessels in which to preserve certain dried herbs and powders which the rustics from all the villages around Zardino came to buy, even in the dead of night, should they have the toothache, or the stomach-ache, or womenfolk in pain with their *moons*. Every evening he crossed the square from the church to the Lantern Tavern, which stood directly opposite, to consort with his parishioners and play cards. Once a fortnight he would harness up the old cart and go to Novara for a "change of air", just as the real priests did. He would lodge in various family boarding houses, all too hospitable (if we are to believe certain rumours) and run by ladies of less than stainless character; such as one Paola, one Gradisca, one *Isabela de Valves, commonly known as The Flirt*, who lived in the rag-trade district and was so run off her feet in her day as to leave her mark in the cathedral Registry (the Illegitimate Births Department) and even in the records of the Broletto Prison.

His life and affairs arranged in this manner, Don Michele had reached the age of sixty, with no financial problems and in perfect health both mental and physical. Until one day, like a bolt from the blue, the world collapsed around him, shattering his peace of mind and throwing all he had built up in the course of his life, and indeed his life itself, back into the melting-pot. Summoned to Novara, interrogated on behalf of the new Bishop Carlo Bascapè by the Dean of the Chapter of Milan Cathedral, Monsignor Antonio Seneca, poor Michele Cerruti was adjudged to be exactly what he was: an impostor and a usurper of sacred offices, worthy to be sent to the galleys or even to the scaffold. Only his advanced age, read the sentence of the ecclesiastical court, rendering him nigh to the judgement of a more solemn and tremendous Tribunal, could mitigate the censure of earthy judges and save his life. Handed over to the civil authorities then represented in the city by His Excellency Doctor *utriusque iuris* Don Vicenzo Zuccardo, the culprit Michele Cerruti ("a true *quistone* and false priest", as is stated in the proceedings of this second trial) found himself banished from Novara and its territory, and from all the lands of the State of Milan, under pain (if he dared to return) of being on the first offence flogged and then chained to an oar in the galleys or sent to work in the mines, and on the second of being hanged by the neck in the public square, in Novara or wherever he might be discovered, according to convenience and the decision of whoever might have discretionary powers in the circumstances.

Bewildered and terrified, Don Michele was escorted under guard to the banks of the Po. He spent a few days across the frontier, at Casale, then made his way as best he could stealthily back to Zardino, having come to the conclusion that however things fared with him he had no other place in the world to lay his head, and that he was too old to change his surroundings and his habits; and moreover that his troubles and those of all the other *quistori* turned priest would shortly be resolved by the decease of their common persecutor; that is, Bishop Bascapè. According to those who had had occasion to observe him at close quarters, this bishop was a sickly fellow afflicted with a vast number of ailments which plagued him every moment of the day, and which he compensated for by plaguing the next fellow. He was not likely to give up the ghost on the spot, alas, but, that notwithstanding, his state of health was such as to give reasonable hope that he would not long be able to administer a diocese such as Novara, let alone with methods such as his. It was common knowledge that in the diocese of Novara there were more than two hundred parishes without a priest, in the Flatlands, in the Alpine valleys, on the lake shores. What harm was done if some of those parishes were run and ministered unto by a *quistone*, or by a Minor cleric, or by any one of the priests at the very time being investigated in Novara for a multitude of sins, including simony, concubinage, usury, ignorance of Holy Writ, negligence in the performance of their duties . . . But, as Don Michele put it, such people did not just spring out of nowhere, just as they were! No, they too were children of Holy Mother Church, unlettered or illegitimate maybe, but her children none the less. How depraved a mother must be to cast aside her offspring because she objects to the way they're made or regards them as unworthy of her? Furthermore, who was there to take the place of these imperfect sons? There would never be enough priests to put Bishop Bascapè's plans into effect. And what was more, argued Don Michele, the world had taken another turn and no modern youngster, after studying and making sacrifices to become a priest, would think of coming and burying himself in a hole like Zardino. Praise be to God they had quite other ideas, did the youngsters of the time! If they were ambitious they thought of their careers, of becoming monsignors, of going to Rome; whereas if they were idealists or dreamers they planned to become missionaries in distant climes: in India, in Japan, in the Americas. The new Church, reborn from the Council of Trent, and the Pope in person, pressed them into service in those far-off lands.

Such were the reasonings that led Don Michele back to Zardino. But we must not forget that he was full of fears of being denounced, put in irons, sent off to slave away in some granite quarry or gravel pit. He therefore completely changed his mode of life: he moved around very little, he never went to Novara for any reason whatsoever, indeed he never left the village. He drank a lot more than in the past, at the tavern with friends but even on his own. He talked to himself out loud, asking questions and answering them himself. He did not say Mass, nor did he preach or administer any sacrament other than baptism. And in the Curia in Novara nothing more had happened with regard to him. Month after month, season after season, four years had passed since the sentence against him had been pronounced and there he still was; the guards had not come to arrest him, no genuine priest had turned up to take his place as chaplain, the bishop didn't die, nothing happened at all. It seemed as if time had halted in its tracks; and Don Michele was well content with this. If they left him in peace he could ask for nothing better.

So, when the praying ended Don Michele bent down, took Antonia's face between his hands and kissed her on the forehead. Then he ran his fingers over her scalp, behind her ears, down the nape of her neck. Gently he felt from her temples to the back of her head, and then the cheekbones; he took her by the left wrist and studied the lines on the palm of her hand.

"She will grow up healthy and beautiful too," he said to Signora Francesca, who had slipped into the house and returned at once carrying in both hands a huge tray of the deep-fried rice-cakes we call *frittelle*. "Judging by the shape of her head," he continued, "I foresee in her a generous, sweet nature, though perhaps a little capricious, so you should be in no hurry to find her a husband. The life-line in her hand is long and clear. There is only one break at about twenty years old, a possible danger of death, but she will survive it. The spouse willed to her by Providence seems not to be a young man from these parts but an outsider. From him Antonia will have one child and seven sorrows, as in her lifetime did the Blessed Virgin. She will be widowed when her son is already grown up, and will live to be old. She will not die a natural death but through some mischance, perhaps a fire . . ."

He let go of the foundling's hand, helped himself graciously to a *frittella* from the platter offered him by Signora Francesca, and took a nibble at it. "Excellent!" he declared. "My compliments to the cook!"

After which all those present pushed and shoved to claim their share of *frittelle*: the urchins, the altar-boy, the farm-hand's daughters, and even the Gossips, who until a few moments before had been so overcome with indignation about this foundling's arrival in Zardino, did not scruple to close in on Antonia and Signora Francesca to gobble up her *frittelle*. Only Antonia made no move, timorously watching the children milling around the platter. The host in person, Bartolo himself, had to intervene, take a couple of *frittelle* from the tray and pop them into Antonia's hand.

"Eat up, eat up!" he cried. "It was for you that my wife had Consolata make 'em – to celebrate your homecoming. They're yours!"

SIX

The "Christian Brethren"

AT EASTERTIDE the rains came down and the river broke its banks. It invaded the woods and the cultivated fields, it filled the ditches inside and outside the village with dark muddy water which in places spilt over into the streets, transforming the cobbled alleys into torrents, and the farmyards and kitchen gardens into swamps. For two or three days there was nothing to be seen but water, to north, to south, in every direction, right to the horizon. Then the waters gradually subsided, withdrew into their proper courses, and the landscape became itself again. The young scamps roamed around armed with nets and other gadgets to catch the fish trapped in the pools, and the grown-ups set to work to repair the damage wrought by the floods.

After Easter the *risaroli* arrived. These were the seasonal workers in the paddy-fields, pitiful-looking men clad in rags and tatters, with all their worldly goods in a bundle under one arm or slung over one shoulder. They often came tied together with stout cords or even chains, to prevent them from escaping, and were escorted by the self-same Overseers who had gone hunting and recruiting them as far as Val d'Ossola, or in the Monferrato beyond the Po, or around Biella; and who now shifted them from village to village, hawking the labour of their *risaroli*, plus their own services, to the husbandmen of the area.

The work in the paddy-fields was one of the most bestial ever known in the Italian countryside, on account of the working environment and working conditions – bent double in the water from dawn till dusk, often beaten like slaves and subjected to every sort of hardship. The scant testimony that has come down to us bears witness to the fact that this labour was considered worse than the fate of one condemned to the galleys, and that anyone who volunteered for it was either mentally deficient or at the end of his tether. In either case, they were practically always people with no other alternative but starvation. Many of these *risaroli* were men so disfigured by the smallpox or by leprosy as to be too repulsive to beg on church doorsteps; many others were crippled or of unsound mind from birth, packed off by their parents to earn their living this way, either simply to get rid of them or else, in their innocence, really believing in what they were told by the recruiters, that working "in the rice", as they said in those days, was child's play, some sort of pastime, a mere game; and that at the end of the season their sons, after having good fun splashing about in the water, would be handed a heap of money to see them through the winter. Quite a number of *risaroli* were old men who had lost their all and had ceased to care about their lives, but none the less would have been ashamed to beg; others again came from such impoverished villages, where they lived in such dire penury that hearing the blandishments of the recruiters they must have thought they were going to Cockaigne, to have a meal every day – and twice on Sundays – while raking in money for jam.

All such as we have mentioned, and others of whom it would take too long to tell, in order to obtain work as *risaroli* around Novara had either signed their name or made their mark at the foot of a printed document. In the case of mental deficients the signature was appended by a parent or next-of-kin. This document, which you can be sure they hadn't read, stated that they voluntarily waived their rights to be protected by the law, in so far as the laws of the seventeenth century offered protection to anyone not in a position to protect himself. In practice this document meant the acceptance of temporary but complete slavery, which before the expiry date laid down in the contract could only be terminated – as indeed it frequently was – by the death of the slave.

At Zardino, as in all the villages of the Flatlands, the *risaroli* arrived every year in mid-spring. If they had not been booked in advance by one of the husbandmen they were bargained for and bought in the market-place outside the church, where all the other marketing took place – livestock, farm implements – amid the cursing and swearing of the Overseers, the outpourings of the

57

peasants trying to beat them down on the price of every single *risarolo*, and the playful inquisitiveness of the young lads, which turned to utter delight if some recalcitrant *risarolo* was brought back to his senses with kicks, punches, and whip-lashes.

The *risaroli!* . . . This continent of Europe, since it started scribbling its history and the history of all the other parts of the world, has wept crocodile tears over the negroes slaving away in the cotton-fields of America, and every other sort of slave either ancient or modern, but it never uttered a syllable, not one!, about the fate of the *risaroli!* Even the Church itself, after the Counter-Reformation so prodigal of saints and missionaries who tended the lepers in far-off lands, and nursed the victims of the plague as far afield as Cathay, and attempted to convert the Japanese by addressing them in Latin, never became aware of these starvelings on her own doorstep. Nor were they few – there were thousands of them on both sides of the River Ticino, and many died like beasts every year, without medical care or the consolations of religion. So much is attested to in a memorandum written by the Magistrate (Minister) of Health and addressed to the Governor of the State of Milan in the Year of Grace 1589.

"Above all it comes to our notice," declared this diligent magistrate, *"that it behoves us to remedy the great cruelty the Overseers of the* risaroli *practise towards those poor creatures, who by various means, often fraudulent, are taken to harvest the rice-fields, and perform other labours connected with them, on account of which they suffer much from excessive toil, and from drinking those putrid waters, and from not being given a sufficiency to eat and being beaten like slaves, the which forces them to work even when they cannot, and when they are ill, so that they meet wretched deaths in farmsteads or the surrounding fields without Confession."*

The charge was a grave one, and the words left no room for doubt, but His Excellency the Duke of Terranova, to whom the memorandum was addressed, had, we must assume, other matters in hand. As apparently did his successors, since more than seventy years later, in November 1662, the situation of the *risaroli* appears unchanged or even worse, according to what we learn from a proclamation issued by the then governor of Milan, Don Luis de Guzman Ponza de Leon, etc., etc., (titles omitted).

"And because at the time of the rice-harvest," we read in the

proclamation, *"or of other works in the rice-fields, certain individuals known as Overseers of* Risaroli *manage in various ways to amass quantities of men and boys, whom they use with barbarous cruelty, inasmuch as conducting them to their destination by promises and flatteries they treat them harshly, not paying them, and not providing those unfortunate creatures with sufficient food, forcing them to work like slaves, with floggings and with severities worse than are practised upon those condemned to the galleys, in such a manner that many, even of good birth, die miserably in the farmsteads, or in the fields surrounding, without bodily, or even spiritual, assistance. His Excellency therefore demands that in future these men and youths should not be led to the slaughter, nor any person maltreated, or defrauded of his rightful remuneration, and that the name, traffic and fact of the aforesaid Overseers should be suppressed. He orders all concerned"* etc.

Useless to transcribe the punctilious list of ordinances, or the terrifying catalogue of penalties both *pecuniary* and *corporal*: these proclamations were made for history, for posterity, for us who are the true recipients, so that we as we read them might exclaim, or at least feel: "What a wise man, how compassionate to his kind and impatient in the face of injustice, how apt for noble and lofty sentiments was the *caballero* Don Ponze de Leon!" In everyday reality such proclamations served for nothing. In practice this trafficking in *risaroli* went on until the country was invaded and occupied by Napoleon and thereafter into the nineteenth century, when in Catholic countries the combined evolution of public morality and the profit motive permitted women to be utilized wherever possible to replace male labour in the most insufferable and worst paid jobs. Only then were the *risaroli* replaced by the *mondine*, the rice-weeding women who, had they existed in the seventeenth century, would have scandalized the world; not with their sufferings, needless to say, but with the display (inevitable, given the nature of that toil out in the summer sun, half naked in the water with the ignoble part of the body higher than the noble part, which is the brow) of their indecent femininity; which ought to have been scrupulously concealed and repressed, according to the dictates of Holy Church and the customs of the time.

★

59

"The *risaroli, the risaroli!*"

The cry spread from farmyard to barnyard until it reached the Nidasios'. Antonia, since her arrival in Zardino, had spent most of her time with Anna Chiara and Teresina, the youngest of the Barbero children, who lived across the yard and were the village girls who first approached the foundling on the day of her arrival. Anna Chiara had touched her with a fingertip, to test her reaction and see if she bit, and Teresina had asked her why her hair was all shorn. They helped each other to tend the animals, especially the geese, or else played around together, or with the neighbouring children. As indeed they were doing that day.

At the very first shout they all teemed into the piazza in front of the church and found the *risaroli* already there, guarded by two toughs armed with leather thongs, which were the characteristic weapon of the Overseers – a strip of leather as broad as your finger wound around their fists, which used as a whiplash printed such clear-cut stripes across the back that they might have been branded there with a white-hot iron. One of the two bullies had a black patch over one eye, a pistol in his belt and a horn slung around his neck. He grasped the horn, leering in the direction of the children in a way that made Antonia's flesh creep, and raised the instrument to his lips. He blew into it again and again, pausing every so often to take breath. Those long notes, evoking echo after echo, were intended to inform the peasants, wherever they might be within the radius of a mile, in the village or in the fields, that the *risaroli* had reached Zardino, and were mustered in the piazza. Come gather round and look 'em over! As he blew, this ruffian's cheeks swelled like a balloon and his mug, in any case no model of beauty, became a monstrosity. The children laughed fit to burst. One of them shouted out, "You look just like a pig, you do!"

"They don't do much business here at Zardino," said Teresina Barbero, who was nearly thirteen and had a natural bent for level-headedness, always speaking as her mother Consolata would have done. She explained, "Those two Overseers, the one with the eye-patch and his mate. Who knows who they are or where they come from? To me they look like a couple of bandits!" And she asked herself, or maybe her companion, "What does a farmer think he's doing, taking men like that under his roof!"

But Antonia was not listening. She stood there wide-eyed and open-mouthed, gazing at the *risaroli* huddled together in the corner of the piazza where there was some sunshine, pushing and shoving to get a place in it, wrapped in army blankets that to judge from their state of dilapidation must have dated from the times of Charles V, if not earlier. The teeth of some of them were chattering, and all were obviously chilled to the marrow after a night spent God knows where, but certainly out in the open. There were old men with white hair, the skin of their hands and faces a bluish purple; there were two pathetic morons, recognizable as such by the odd slant of their eyes and the shaking of their heads and hands; there was one man with a goitre so huge that he had perforce to keep it outside his jacket; and that monstrosity pulsed slowly beneath the skin and seemed to have a life of its own. It was a parasite hanging from the man's neck, a bloodsucker of freakish shape, of enormous size. There was one black-haired young man with a face devastated by a kind of leprosy that was eating away his lips, his nostrils, his ears . . . He raised his eyes to Antonia's, bright with fever, and the girl turned quickly away; she tried to say something to her friend, but was so upset she couldn't talk straight and merely babbled.

Teresina took her by the arm and asked, "What's up? Don't you feel well?"

"Those poor things," Antonia managed to get out at last. "Where do they come from? Who on earth are they?"

Her new friend gave a shrug. "They're the men who come to work in the paddy-fields, what d'you expect? They come every year." She paused, and added: "Even Farmer Bartolo takes them on. His'll be here any day now. Hasn't Signora Francesca told you?"

Antonia clenched her fists. "I'll help them escape!"

Her eyes shone. She whispered, "I'll stay awake at night, believe me I will. Then, when everyone's asleep . . ."

"Are you mad?" Teresina gave her a serious look, and warned her, "Don't you even dream of it! In the first place,' she explained, "our own *risaroli* don't escape because Farmer Bartolo and Signora Francesca treat them well. In the second place, if they did escape the Christian Brethren would recapture them and maybe even kill them . . . It's happened before now!" She glanced around her, as if someone were eavesdropping, then whispered to Antonia: "You know who the Christian Brethren are? Have you ever seen them?"

Antonia shook her head.

"Come with me," said Teresina, taking the girl by the hand. "Let's go. There's nothing to look at here except those poor devils . . . Come along into the church, if Don Michele has left it unlocked as he usually does. I want to show you the Christian Brethren."

She tugged, but Antonia didn't budge. Teresina laughed. "Come on! There's nothing to be afraid of! They're only pictures!"

On entering the church there was an enormous silence, an enormous darkness. The two girls groped their way forward grasping each other's hands and almost stifled by the heat from the braziers and the smell of the silkworms. But the dark, at first so dense, was in reality a half-dark to which their eyes swiftly grew accustomed, until they could see not only the red glow of the braziers but also the silkworm beds and even the paintings on the walls . . . A few of these Teresina pointed out to her friend: "That's St Agatha having her breasts cut off! That's St Julius, who crossed the lake on his cloak to rid an island of snakes. The knight on his knees is St Hubert, and look, in front of him is the stag with the cross between its antlers."

Directly to the right of the altar was a fresco on which the window in the apse shed more light than on the others. Thither Teresina led Antonia, and "That's them! Look! That's the Christian Brethren!"

The fresco depicted a saint, recognizable by his halo, blessing a group of men on their knees before him, all dressed in white tunics bound about at the waist and holding a torch in one hand and a leather thong in the other. Their heads were concealed by hoods bearing a red cross above the eye-holes. The whole scene, though frozen in the form of a devotional picture, gave the onlooker a sense of disquietude: where would those hooded men be going to, after the saint's blessing, and what would they be doing, equipped as they were?

"Those men in the hoods," said Teresina in a whisper, as if they, up there on the wall, might overhear her, "are the Christian Brethren of Zardino, and the one standing up without a hood is their protector, St Rock. Then she breathed in her friend's ear: "They ride at night with their torches, and as long as they wear the hood with the cross on it they have to defend each other, and stick together, united unto death! That's why they are called Brethren . . . They bring us back the *risaroli* when they run away, they protect us from the horse-thieves, from the ghosts of unburied men and even from the Devil . . . At least, that's what my mother says, and that's what everyone in the village believes."

Antonia, in silence, drank in the picture. She had already seen these Christian Brethren, though she had not known they went by that name. At Novara, during the Good Friday processions. Men there were with black hoods and scapulars (which are short, elbow-length cloaks) who advanced emitting the most ear-splitting din by whirling wooden rattles high above their heads. These were the *tenebrofori*, literally, "bringers of shadow", and behind them, in small groups, came the hooded figures from the villages of the Flatlands, with their red crosses, their black crosses, their two- and their four-armed crosses, processing with doused torches in the faint, faint light of the oil-lamps on the window-sills of the houses. So slowly they processed that it seemed they would never pass. And behind the hooded confraternities came others, hoodless, and then came the nuns, the seminarists, and the pious women all dressed in black and weeping tears, carrying the statue of Our Lady of Sorrows and an empty coffin known as "The Dead Christ". Behind the coffin, chanting the *Miserere*, came the religious orders, the secular priests, the canons of both the chapters, that of San Gaudenzio and that of the cathedral, and the Bishop's vicars, and the Bishop himself, and the civic authorities, and the officers, and the soldiers, and the torch-bearing mob . . .

She shook herself out of it. Teresina took her hand and led her towards the back door of the church, still speaking in an undertone of supernatural things. "My mother says that at night all round Zardino there are devils. They come down from the knolls or else from over near the mill. Hasn't Signora Francesca told you? There's one everyone calls The Biròn, and he's a goat with eyes as red as embers who carries off girls if he finds them out of the house after dark. He's carried off lots and lots! Even my big sisters, Liduina and Giulia, went out at night and The Biròn got them."

Behind the church there was nobody about – the village ended there, and the two friends seated themselves on the edge of a grey stone sarcophagus which, having been for goodness knows how many centuries the coffin of a certain Cornelius Cornelianus, a Novarese *decemvir* – according to what was still legible, carved on the stone – now served as a washtub and drinking trough for the livestock. It was a fine spring morning, bright and sunny, but Teresina had already launched into supernatural matters in Zardino, and for her the subject was irresistible, and thrilled her as did no other. Anyway, we all know that there are some subjects which must be talked about in the broad light of day, because when evening comes they are too scary! Antonia hearkened open-mouthed, without giving another thought to the poor *risaroli* still there in the piazza, and whose arrival had in a sense been the cause of that journey among the shadows and mysteries of the Flatlands. She hearkened with the instinctive eagerness that children of every time and place have for such tales.

North of Zardino – Teresina told her – at a place called Fonte di Badia there were *Le Madri*: fearful, wilful, cruel women, on whose altar and before whose images anyone who passed that way had to sacrifice something they were wearing or carrying with them, so as to placate their fury. Even the bed of the Crosa, a stream of spring-water that flowed in from the east and encircled the village, turning the mill-wheel in transit, was bewitched and full of dangers. There, on the stream-bed, lurked the *Melusia*, a woman with long green hair and legs like two fishtails. She would beguile boys or girls looking at their reflections in the water, and if she caught them she would hold them under until they drowned. How many children she had caught, the *Melusia*! And then, continued Teresina, there were the Knolls, those two little hills just outside the village, towards the Sesia. The left-hand of these knolls, behind which the sun set, was infested with vile talking snakes with red crests and human faces; the one on the right, where there was a gigantic chestnut-tree, was the meeting-place of witches. There at night could be heard the music of lutes and viols, and sounds and voices as of revelry, so that none of the village people any longer went to gather firewood from that tree, and the chestnuts, though abundant, in the autumn time were eaten by the pigs. Only one person in the village was brave enough to go up there every year to pick up a few chestnuts, climbing the Knoll without turning a hair, and that was Pietro Maffiolo, the field-guard of Zardino. A tall, stringy beanpole of a man, explained Teresina, who went about armed with a crooked stick and had such long legs that when he was astride his mule his feet nearly touched the ground . . .

"Isn't he scared of the Devils?" asked Antonia.

Teresina burst out laughing. "Not on your life! He's half devil himself! You'll come across him . . ."

SEVEN

Zardino

A MOTORIST HALTING today on the motorway from Milan to Turin in the vicinity of the viaduct over the river Sesia might, by looking southwards to his left, see arising from the middle of the woods the smoke from the hearthstones of Zardino – that is, if Zardino still existed, which it doesn't. In the spring of 1600, however, it was still there, and all unaware, what's more, of being fated to vanish within a few years: a small village like many another small village in the Flatlands, with its landscape of vineyards and woods towards the marshes and the river banks, its meadows and moorlands stretching towards Biandrate, its rice-paddies and fields of maize and wheat in the direction of Cameriano and of Novara. And with its two little hills, formed by deposits from the Sesia and known as the Knolls, which rose above the housetops to the north and shielded the village from the vehemence of the river when in spate.

The main street of Zardino was the road that entered from the direction of Novara and the "Mill of the Three Kings", and it ran the whole length of the village as far as the little piazza outside the church. Along this street lay the various farmyards and the houses, built part of brick and part of the very stones removed from the soil by the men who had cleared it for cultivation some centuries earlier, and were thereafter put to use either for building or for paving the streets. The balconies were made of wood, as were the roofs of the sheds for carts and implements. The cow-byres were not roofed with tiles, as the houses were, but with mud-caked straw. Everything that met the eye, as you stood among those houses, was grey, shabby, crude, and yet, in the summer months, bright with wisteria and climbing roses; ivy peeped over the walls, vine-shoots twined about the balconies and

66

the grapes hung so low that you needed no ladder to gather them: you had only to reach up.

Inside the houses you could touch the ceiling, the doors and windows were proportionate to the rooms (that is, extremely small), and even a handful of people living together immediately produced overcrowding and promiscuity. But small chance, at the dawn of the seventeenth century, that the people living in any one of these peasant dwellings should be few in number. Out-of-doors, in the lanes, in the vineyards, in the barnyards given an air of picturesqueness by the corncobs hung up to dry, the skins of rabbits and other small animals, the strings of garlic and onions, the sheets and various garments drying on the line, human life bubbled and seethed, no more absurd than anywhere else in the world: barefoot goose-girls kept an eye on the geese wandering at will along the ditches; old men bent by the years and deformed by arthitis laboured from dawn till dusk in little kitchen gardens rendered impregnable by hedges of spiky shrubs, banks of brambles, sharpened stakes and other contrivances worthy of illustration in a present-day manual of guerrilla warfare. And all to keep out the young scamps, the donkeys, the geese, the animals of every shape and size which grazed unattended in the village, doing whatever damage they could. In the walls small niches contained miniature altars and statuettes of the Black Madonna of Oropa and of other saints who by ancient custom were thought to protect the dwellings and their inhabitants from every sort of trouble: the evil eye, diseases of men and livestock, drought, hailstorms, feuds . . .

Every morning the women were off to the pool in the Crosa (the same pool where, according to Teresina, the *Melusia* lay in ambush to grab children) balancing their washing-baskets on their heads. From that side of the village you could hear the thump and slap of the sheets as they were beaten against the stones or on the water, and the talk and laughter of the washerwomen, the *lavandere*. You heard their singing too, and their shrieks and curses if some man molested them. This business of the *lavandere* being molested by passers-by occurred fairly often at Zardino, and time was when it had even given rise to rustic wars against neighbouring villages, with punitive expeditions and reprisals on either side. These might well go on for years, but there was no solution, for the communal washing-pool, the spot where the waters of the Crosa were clearest and deepest, lay right beside the road to Novara, between the village and the "Mill of the Three Kings". At every hour of the day, but especially in the mornings, there was a constant stream of the carts and hand-carts, mules, donkeys and horses of peasants taking their grain to the mill to have it ground: *melga* and *melghetto* (maize and buck wheat), wheat and rye, and even certain pulses, such as chick-peas, had to be milled to make food for humans and fodder for animals. But always in small quantities, for grain can be stored but flour cannot. These peasants also came from other villages in the Flatlands where there was no mill, or the miller charged more, or made a poor job of it; and not all these men resisted the temptation to take a closer look at the *lavandere*, with that great gift of God which they displayed when bent over the water; or else to bandy some rustic gallantry, some passionate offer of their own persons. If the men persisted, the women replied by inviting them to make the same offer to their wives, their sisters, or their mothers, and after a few more verbal exchanges the unrequited lovers went their way. But, as I have already had occasion to say, there had in the past been some serious quarrels, when a man laid not just eyes but hands upon the plumper parts of a woman. Then husbands and betrothed came teeming out from the village, and matters passed from words to deeds. There had been black eyes and even wounded, a few over-fiery spirits had been given a chance to cool off in the perennially icy waters of the Crosa, and on occasion came the flash of a knife . . .

But all in all this was the life of the Flatlands, with all their lights and shadows, and even if after one or other of those brawls there was a corpse left on the ground the relatives would bury it and everything finished there: the constables and magistrates from the city would certainly never have come to Zardino for such a trifling matter. In the seventeenth century everyone fended for himself and his own – to care for everyone there was none but God. The lawcourts of the time had far more vital matters on their hands!

As for the mill, since we have mentioned it, we need only say that it was called the Mill of the Three Kings because of the fresco, all but erased by time and the weather, of which only a few traces remained (indeed, three bearded and crowned heads) on the façade and above the entrance; and that it was one of the most famous and ancient mills on this bank of the Sesia from Borgo Vercelli right up to Biandrate.

The market in Zardino was held in the piazza in front of the church on the first and third Monday of each month. In came the hawkers and pedlars from Novara and from the towns in the Ticino valley (Trecate, Oleggio, Galliate) to display earthenware, agricultural implements, breeding beds and other equipment for the raising of silkworms, traps for wild animals and fishing-nets, footgear and fabrics. On those days the Lantern Tavern opposite the church burst into life as a real and proper market within the market for every sort of dealer, from the *bacialè* (marriage broker) to the tooth-puller, from the barber (who between one beard and the next busied himself with matters of health and of heart) to the vendor of marmot fat as a cure for arthritis; and the *pénat*, a hero in these villages of the Flatlands, the individual most hated and most fawned upon by the Gossips. Concerning whom there were unverifiable rumours which ascribed to him vices and wickedness such as to pale the memory of Herod, or Judas Iscariot, or the emperor Nero; but then, when the Gossips met him along the road all the frowns on their faces were smoothed out, and their eyes sparkled with joy. It was he, the *pénat*, who purchased the goose-down, paying them the lowest price they could possibly agree to, but paying in cash, and the love-hate felt for him by the Gossips can only really be understood if we remember that for the women of the Flatlands the sale of those feathers was their only means of earning money independently of their husbands; and that the little silver coins they acquired from the *pénat* the women, by ancient custom, shared with no one – it was their own money, the source of their economic independence, the very first step towards the emancipation of women in this part of the plains and of the world. Circulating among the Gossips, and passed down from mother to daughter, there were legends of certain *pénat* who had made vast fortunes by extorting high prices from the mattress-makers of Novara, of Vigevano, even of far-off Milan,

69

for the feathers that they, poor dears!, had been forced to sell for a song. Palaces, carriages, servants; quarterings or half-quarterings of nobility, with the consequent careers in the army or the clergy; and all set up by plucking geese – or fleecing Gossips . . .

Such things were usually talked about in the winter, when they met of an evening in the cowsheds to keep warm and have a chat. And here even – though in deepest secret – they whispered the name of a recently ennobled family in Novara who had risen in the world after the coming of the Spaniards and who, without the shadow of a doubt, were descended from a long, long line of usurers and feathermongers. These upstart noblemen – it was whispered in the cowsheds – now possessed titles and palaces, and over the great doors of the palaces were coats of arms carved in stone and representing a four-footed animal of no known species. But if they had wished to represent the true origin of their nobility, said the Gossips, those coats of arms should have depicted a goose. A fine Goose Rampant: *there* was the emblem for them!

To get a bird's-eye view of Zardino, above the roofs and chimney-pots, you had to climb either the bell-tower of the church (dedicated to St Rock) or else one of the two Knolls which the Sesia had formed over the centuries with its periodical spates, and which in the early seventeenth century were called respectively Red Stumps and the Tree Knoll. The two broad, low hills have vanished since time out of mind, as has the village. The stones they were formed of later served to construct the new river banks and the land has been flattened out, first using oxen and then bulldozers, to make room for the traditional crops of maize, wheat and forage, and the recent import from America, the Canadian poplar; so that it may truly be said that of the environment in which most of our story takes place there is nothing left, not even the memory. The plain, which in Antonia's day was undulating and in parts untilled, is now dead flat and every inch of it is cultivated; the long lines of poplars intersect at right angles along the edges of the paddy-fields, creating a landscape quite different from the primeval landscape of this region over the centuries, one of woodland and heath, marshland and meadow. Even the courses of the so-called *fontanili*, the spring-waters at one time meandering and unpredictable, here a torrent, there a streamlet, there again a pool, have now been redesigned with the set-square, and in many cases with cement. Everything is ordered and geometrical, everything is arranged to produce the maximum profit: an open-air factory for cereals, wood-pulp and fodder, practically bereft of a history.

But the two Knolls which loomed above Zardino were already very old by the beginning of the seventeenth century: centuries old, and maybe millennia. The Tree Knoll, which at one time must have had a vineyard on the village side, for the roots of the old plants still sprouted here and there, took its name from an ancient tree – a chestnut – so huge that two men alone could not encircle its trunk with their arms: it needed a third. On this trunk one could still make out an inscription carved with a knife, in capital letters with the Rs back to front; and all the inhabitants of Zardino read it, even if they couldn't read: ALBERA DEI RICORDI. Naturally, however attractive it might be to interpret this as "The Tree of Memories", it meant nothing of the sort. The real significance of the inscription was a claim to ownership of the tree and its produce by a family of share-croppers called Ricordi, immigrants from the country round Milan, or maybe even from the Veneto, who had left Zardino almost half a century earlier, having failed to put down roots there. Those who still recalled them spoke of them as arrogant, quarrelsome people, who had tried, without the least right, to establish proprietorship of a number of tracts of moorland and pasturage, the Tree Knoll included.

The other Knoll, known as the Red Stumps, was a vast bramble-patch, a mound of stones populated by large but absolutely harmless snakes to which, however, the folk imagination attributed the ability to emit sounds, to talk, to hypnotize people with their eyes and to achieve wonders if possible more extraordinary even than these. They went so far as to imagine them in the form of dragons, with wings and crests and fireworks darting forth from mouth and nostrils. The people of Zardino considered the "Red Stumps" accursed, on account of a thunderbolt that in the not-too-remote past had struck the two oak trees which graced its summit, at the same time destroying a votive image of Our Lady which, in its little wooden shrine, had been nailed to one of the trees. The stumps of the two trees, corroded by the damp and acted on by atmospheric agents, had with the passing of time become covered with a kind of lichen, a reddish mould which in the rays of the setting sun turned the colour of flame. This phenomenon, visible even from the other side of the Sesia, had caused the name of this Knoll to change rapidly in the course of only a few years, from Our Lady's Knoll, which it had always been, to the Red Stumps.

Less clear are the reasons why the inhabitants considered the Tree Knoll as ill-omened. The rumour which Teresina passed on to Antonia had already been doing the rounds for some time: that witches met there to hold their Sabbaths and worship the Devil; but how this rumour started no one had an inkling. There had been no witches in the past of Zardino, at least in the more recent past, and as for the Knoll, the village elders remembered a time before the Tree belonged to the Ricordis, and anyone who wished to climb it could do so – not right to the top but at any rate to quite some height, thirty feet or more. There used to be a number of rough-hewn ladders nailed to the trunk, and from there aloft (said the old men) when the sun was bright and the air was clear you could see the pinnacles of Milan Cathedral thirty-five miles away, as you could Moncalvo in the Monferrato, and the sanctuaries around Biella, and all the Alps from Mont Blanc to Lake Garda and the Holy Mount of Varallo. In short, you saw the world.

Then came the Ricordis with their claims to ownership. They had tried to turn the Knoll into a vineyard and quarrelled with anyone who attempted to approach the Tree. And thereafter the rumour of witches began to be whispered abroad – a thing previously unheard of in Zardino – and people no longer ventured up the Knolls.

Life was pretty humdrum in Zardino. Especially in the winter, when work in the fields was practically at a standstill. The livestock huddled in their straw waiting for spring and spring sunshine to come, while every species of social activity shifted from the farmyards to the cowsheds. There the youngsters continued their games, the ancients nodded off or else, on request, told tales of times gone by to anyone wanting to hear them, and the Gossips sat in a circle sewing and spinning, as they put it, but in reality gossiping their heads off until deep into the night. It was there that the rumours started – tittle-tattle, intrigues, slanders and assorted absurdities – which still today, on the threshold of the year 2000, are an essential and indispensable element of village life in the Flatlands; only that now, thanks to progress, they can intertwine with news from the papers and the television, and may spread in ways quite different from those of yore. For example by telephone, or even – thanks to the power of literacy – by means of anonymous letters . . .

But at the dawn of the seventeenth century rumours were entirely and without exception started by the obsessions and the rancours of whoever it was set them in motion, and there was only one method of communicating them: a whisper in the ear. But the final result had no reason to envy the media of today, for the rumours circulated with extraordinary speed from stable to cowshed, entwining themselves with other voices in other sheds, other villages, other winters . . . They wove an inextricable web of lies and half-truths, a delirium of words with everyone against his neighbour, that always ended by gaining the upper hand over the truth, conditioning it, concealing it, giving it unpredictable offshoots, until it replaced the truth, became the truth itself.

When the fine weather arrived the rumours continued to do their rounds and their damage, but people began to turn their attention to other things, to "barnyard feuds" and "water feuds", two factors which for century after century stirred up the otherwise sluggish temperaments of the Flatlanders, and guaranteed the city of Novara a dense colony of pettifoggers, shysters, conveyors, scriveners, land-surveyors and others concerned with judiciary matters – a colony second only in number to that of the priests and the "religious" in general.

And may I be allowed at this point in the narrative to lay down my pen, to pause a while to draw breath and reassemble my resources? For here the matter of my discourse rises to greater heights, and the writer's task becomes an onerous one. It would require a supreme poet, a Homer, a Shakespeare, to do justice to the barnyard feuds of the Flatlands, which almost invariably sprang from a mere nothing – a sheet hung out to dry, a dead hen, a child bitten by a dog – but which could go on and on for centuries with such an accumulation of hatred between the parties concerned that, even if this did not reach the point of slit throats and corpse-laden finales, it would none the less have sufficed to confer logical form and meaning on the most atrocious massacres in history. Yes, it is here, in the barnyard feuds, that human hatred became refined and exalted, attaining the uttermost peaks of achievement, becoming an Absolute. It is hatred at its purest – abstract, bodiless, entirely impartial – that which set the universe in motion, and that survives all things. Human love, so often sung by the poets, compared to this hatred scarcely counts for a fig: a speck of gold in the broad river of life, a pearl in the sea of nothingness and no more. The water feuds also, though born of reasons of self-interest and without the least trace of idealism about them, were capable of attaining, and indeed often did attain, some species of obscure and negative grandeur. What is more, they had social implications – class warfare and so on – of the kind which have made history; the reason being that all agriculture here, especially the cultivation of rice, is strictly bound up with the presence, particularly conspicuous in this part of the plains, of either river-water or springs. It follows that the true owners of the Flatlands were not the owners of the land, then still split up into many small or even minute fragments, but the masters of the water. That is, of the vast and vastly ramified network of springs and canals, ditches and channels, sluice-gates, warping canals and so on, which was then and is to this day, and for this region, what the circulation of the blood is for the human body.

The true masters were few but mighty: the Curia of the diocese of Novara, the great landed proprietors of Novara and of Lombardy in general, the Cathedral Vestry Board, the Dominicans, the Jesuits, the Hospital (including the "House of Charity") . . . Down there in the Flatlands they fought against these overlords in two ways and in two stages. In the first place by day, when the farmers met together in their respective communities and appealed to the High Court in Novara in order to obtain the water needed for their crops, and at the proper price; after

74

which, by night, they found their own means of unhinging the sluice-gates or piercing the dams, in the process often leaving their neighbours' paddy-fields bone dry; and achieving other feats which would be too lengthy a task to detail here.

Thus it happened that from the original trunk of a water-feud, like branches from a pollarded willow-tree there sprouted dozens and dozens of further feuds: the proprietor of the water against the individual farmer, that farmer against his whole community, community against community, or against a single farmer. And thus the canals and sluices were often guarded (as banks and public offices are guarded today) by thugs armed to the teeth, paid by the proprietors to dissuade thieves by their very presence, or to teach them a lesson if the dissuasion failed to have the desired effect. And every so often, as in the circumstances was only inevitable, the outcome was a corpse.

EIGHT

People of the Paddy-Fields

CAME THE HEAT, spring burst forth. A second spring, when the poppies set the fields aflame as far as the eye could see, and the soft greenness of the rice veiled and dimmed the mirrors of the paddy-fields, turning the plain into one huge sun-scorched meadow. At night the croaking of the frogs was deafening – after it had sounded in your ears a while you became unconscious of it. Antonia, although by now she had had a chance to get to know Zardino and every soul who lived there, and to make herself known to them in turn, nevertheless still had mixed feelings of fear and fascination about the new environment in which she had fetched up. She was scared of the men. Instead of speaking to each other they bellowed, they brought out sounds from their gullets without ever articulating them with their tongues. They understood only each other, and with what effort!

Or the women now. When she passed them in the road they stood stock-still until she had gone by, making certain gestures, certain signs, that they alone knew the meaning of. Some of the Gossips were hideous, so skinny and black-clad they looked like Death bent double, as you see him in cemeteries with the scythe in his knucklebones; or else so fat and saggy they no longer had any shape to speak of, ruined by toil and childbearing like that Consolata Barbero who lived across the yard and had made the *frittelle* for the foundling on the day of her arrival. Consolata was a great fleshy hulk of indeterminate age, with a face too titchy for the mass of her body and two little hands suspended in mid-air approximately where her hips ought to have been. Even Signora Francesca, who had never borne children or been obliged to toil too hard, had – according to her husband Bartolo – three things rather on the biggish side: the tits in the front of her, the bum at the

76

back, and the heart... This last, however, not in the sense of a muscular mass and bodily organ, but as the seat of the affections and of generosity.

There were types of humanity in Zardino quite unlike those Antonia had come across in the city. Work-horses. First and foremost the *risaroli*, who arrived in May, left in September, and slept on the other side of the yard, on a handful of straw up in the hay loft. Unlike the *risaroli* haggled over in the village squares, Bartolo Nidasio's had no Overseers. They were hill folk from the valleys above Varallo, and they came down to the plains each year of their own free will to "do the rice season", as they put it, and earn enough Milanese currency to keep them through the winter without suffering from hunger when buried deep in the snows of their mountains. At first the girl used to spy on them, awaiting her chance to talk to them and make friends. But the *risaroli* didn't exchange a word with anyone – they had nothing to say, either to her or to anyone else. They worked from dawn till dark, strung out in long lines, bent double as far as possible without losing their balance, up to their knees in water. They advanced at a snail's pace, transplanting the rice in the heat of a sun that scorched and stunned them, weeding as they went. They would sing, odd as it may seem, and in fact is. They sang not for joy but to alleviate the drudgery, to distract themselves with the sound of their own voices, to feel themselves alive.

As we already said, they were hill folk, and many of their songs, with minimal variations, were the same mountain songs which are still known here in Italy, and sung to this day. The words change from one century to another, but the tunes are as ancient, all but eternal, as the rhythmic and vocal foundation on which they are based – the gait of the uplander as he climbs to the mountain hut, his call echoing from valley to valley, the roar of the torrent, the ceaseless ringing of bells from the grazing cattle. Other songs, in which the mountains played no part, spoke of a swallow that flew off and never returned, of a moon that drowned in the bottom of a well, of a vow oft renewed and then forgotten, with rhymes like Cupid's dart – broken heart – lovers part. But even these songs were not all that different from their modern equivalents, and were almost all of them sad.

Antonia saw the *risaroli* once a day, when she took them their midday meal, along with her new friend Teresina and the other two Barbero girls. Signora Francesca and Consolata loaded the food into the laundry-barrow (so called because at other times of year it was used only to trundle the laundry to the washing-pool) and the four of them, at the stroke of the Angelus, set forth from the village. Bartolo, on seeing them coming, would sound a blast on his horn, at which the *risaroli* would straighten up, very slowly and not without trouble, for after so many hours of work their joints had a job to regain their rightful position. Staggering on their feet, stunned by toil, befuddled by the sun, they clambered up on to the bank, and once on dry land sat down and leant against a willow-tree, or simply threw themselves down wherever they found themselves and stared wide-eyed at the sky. If they spoke to each other – and this happened only as a last resource – they exchanged few words in a guttural dialect which the girls understood not at all. As a rule, however, they did not utter. They took the bread from Antonia's hands and sometimes did not so much as raise their eyes to see who was giving it them, or at others they would look at her in a way that struck the girl even more than their shaggy faces, their sparse yellowed teeth, their scars. They looked at her as one might look at nothingness, without seeing her. They fell on the food.

Another work-horse Antonia came across day after day was Giuseppe Barbero, Bartolo's hired man and the husband of Consolata. All the young girls in Zardino went in mortal dread of him, starting with his own daughters, as they had immediately told their new friend: "For heaven's sake don't get left alone with Giuseppe! As soon as you see him, start running, and if he calls after you, sprint! Perhaps he'd do you no harm, but you never can tell . . . Better not to put him to the test."

Giuseppe Barbero was a rather stumpy little man, practically bald, with arms too long for his body and not a tooth in his head as a result of an infection of the gums; on account of which he did not so much speak as mammer. But his lack of teeth did not prevent him from continuing to be what according to his fellow-villagers he had always been, that is: a lusty glutton for any grub that came his way as well as a drinkhard of unlimited capacity, as capacious indeed as anyone ever seen in the Flatlands; which is a region, we all know, as rich in water as it is thirsty for wine. To see him walking along the road, with the lower part of his face moving as if he were chewing on air, his eyes staring into space and his hands dangling down around his knees, he appeared to be a mindless entity, a great ape; but those who knew him best would tell you that Giuseppe Barbero was a crafty one, and not half! He was a *balòs*. Which means not only crafty but nasty with it.

How many children he had no one knew, because some of them were born of his wife and others again of his two eldest daughters Liduina and Giulia, who had long since gone to live God knows where and didn't keep in touch. A great worker, a great guzzler, a great toper as we said before, and also, of course, a great "stud" with the women, for more than thirty years Giuseppe Barbero had got drunk once a week, and on Saturday nights had attempted to mount all the mares in his stable, who at the time of our story comprised his wife Consolata and three daughters still of tender age, Teresina (thirteen), Luisa (ten), Chiara (eight). On the far side of the farmyard, one day in seven, a frantic din started up, and the girls would arrive in tears at the Nidasio's and ask to be put up for the night because "dad had gone all horrible." Signora Francesca put them in Antonia's room, where there were two beds and they slept two and two. Then, little by little, calm was restored.

Similar things happened in many other households in Zardino and the villages around. In any country district, in the early seventeenth century, Saturday night was a hellish night when things were done that the doers soon wished they had never done, but then unfailingly repeated a week later. Because there was no alternative: the work in the fields was hard, gruelling in fact, and entertainment was non-existent – television had still to be invented...

Of the Barbero sons only one, Inerio, six years old, still lived with his parents. Two elder boys, Pietro Paolo and Eusebio, worked as living-in servants at the Badia. Another son, by the name of Gasparo, was a groom in the service of a nobleman called Tornielli in Novara. And here we have to end our list, because Antonia knew only of these, and also because a complete catalogue of the sons and daughters of Giuseppe and Consolata

Barbero had never been made, and would have been lengthy indeed. Consolata herself, when she set herself to passing all her children in review, lost count. She brought her finger to her aid: "That one's alive and that one's dead," she'd say. "This one went off in '88 to work as a waggoner. That one was born to my Giulia in the year of the Eclipse – what year was that? Now *this* one lives in Ghemme and is a sexton. And *that* one left home the last time his father beat him up and we haven't had a word from him since. Maybe he's dead."

She would dry her eyes: her fingers soon ran out on her, so she'd sigh, with resignation, "That's how life is for a woman! Your children fly off, they go here there and everywhere, they either live or die, only God can tell where they are!" But she always backed up her husband, come what may. "That Giuseppe of mine is a decent fellow!" she maintained. "It's not true he's a dirty old man! He's a great worker! He slaves away from dawn till dusk and its only when he's drunk that he tries to molest even his own daughters. If he was really a dirty old man he'd be always on the prowl!" But she took it out on Zardino, and on the Flatlands... "In villages like ours," she would be heard muttering to herself, "the only bit of fun is to make children. There's nothing else!"

When evening came, if no one spotted her, Antonia would cross the yard, circle the dung-heap, and seek out Biagio, to teach him to talk. This Biagio (whose name, in the Court Records, always appears together with the adjective *stulidus: "stulidus Blasius"*, which is to say "Biagio the Village Idiot"), was a boy of twelve or thirteen, the nephew and drudge of the same Borghesini twins, Agostina and Vincenza, whom we first mentioned as neighbours of the Nidasios and on bad terms with them. These Borghesini twins were both spinsters, and owned a thriving vineyard and an excellent kitchen garden. They were also the owners of Biagio, who had been handed over to them when he was still tiny by a brother of theirs living in Pavia. This brother had tumbled to the fact that there was something not right with the child, and had made up his mind to take him to his sisters in the country, so that when he grew up he could be of service to them, as we find in the records of Antonia's trial: *"So that he dig the vegetable beds and perform the hard tasks which they as females are unable to perform themselves."*

It is not stated, but it is easy enough to surmise, that the boy was the son of that same brother, perhaps even legitimate. The word translated above as "perform" is, in the original records, *conzare*, which must have been a widely used term thereabouts and at that time, judging from the number of times it crops up in our documents. And not only in its specific sense of "arrange" or "adapt", but also in the more general meanings of "to do", "to make", or even "to go" *(si conzò a Pavia*, for example). Well anyway, whether due to the country air, or thanks to his own natural physical constitution, in the course of a few years poor Biagio grew into a burly lad; but his brain did not grow in keeping with his body. Indeed it appeared not to grow at all. However, he was very mild and docile. He did everything he was told to do and (according to a witness at the trial) he was often to be seen coming up from the vineyard dragging a cart, or carrying a beam on his shoulders, with one of the twin sisters behind him scolding him and beating him with a stick as if he were an animal, all without his showing a sign of rebellion. Big and strong as he was, he allowed himself to be beaten by the twins or anyone else. That was why everyone called him "the idiot."

Antonia was the only one who did not laugh at Biagio. In fact when the twins were not in sight she would go up to him, take his hand and teach him the names of things. "The house, the tree, the sky," she would say, pointing. (The tree was the fig-tree at the far end of the Nidasio yard). He would watch Antonia's finger: he seemed transfixed. He would repeat after her, "Te houze, te tree, te zky," for he had once fallen and broken a front tooth, so there were certain sounds he couldn't pronounce. Occasionally Antonia would take him by the hand and lead him into the cowshed or even into the house and give him something to eat which she had put aside specially for him; but this she had to do with great caution, because if the Borghesini twins had come to know of it they would have sued the Nidasios before the consuls (locally elected magistrates of Zardino) – as had happened before now – accusing them of "attempting to steal their nephew" and "giving their nephew appetising viands to inveigle him towards their house". Antonia would stroke his cheeks and say, "Poor Biagio, you must be patient. Sooner or later those two old hags will peg out!"

As at San Michele, Antonia every so often kept herself aloof, or went for a walk on her own. This is how she came to make friends with Maffiolo the field-guard, the one whom the village children used to call *il Fuente*. When he walked through the narrow alleys of Zardino, ramrod-straight as only old soldiers know how, and so tall that when he passed the tavern he had to stoop so as not to knock his head on the inn-sign, the urchins all cried out *"Viva il Fuente! Viva il Fuente!"* (Which being interpreted means: "Long live Count de Fuentes, Governor of the State of Milan, who, as a joke, they pretended to recognize in the figure of Maffiolo). If, on the other hand, he appeared astride his mule with his feet nearly touching the ground, they would shout *"Viva il Fuente e la mujé!"* (Long live the governor and his wife). Or they'd pull the animal's tail, or even hang on to it and have themselves dragged along.

But for Antonia the old warrior soon became "Grandpa Pietro", a friend who watched over her play and told her stories of how the world is. They would sometimes be seen walking side by side, the girl holding his hand, looking up and listening open-mouthed while he spoke of the wars he had fought, the far-off countries he had visited, the great men he had seen at close quarters, and even spoken to...

Of "Don" Pietro Maffiolo, field-guard of Zardino at the time of our story, apart from being the adoptive grandpa of Antonia little was known besides the fact that he had served as a soldier of the King of Spain, on various fronts, for over thirty years; and that when he retired to the Flatlands to work as field-guard he had brought his past life with him bound to his arm, as was then the custom with soldiers, in a metal box containing his three brevets: as picked soldier, sergeant, and standard-bearer; also an unspecified number of mentions in dispatches, testimonials, and the certificate of honourable discharge signed in person by His Excellency Don Pedro Alverez de Zuñiga, Captain General of the 27th *tercio* (regiment), stationed in Flanders. His hair was quite grey when he arrived, but that was not enough to restrain the amorous transports of the Gossips of Zardino and district; for the advent in town of a bachelor – and one so distinguished, so versed in worldly affairs – was not an everyday occurrence. Like many other regions of the Po valley at the beginning of the seventeenth century, the lower valley of the Sesia had a surplus of women, both widows and spinsters; and more than one of these, when Maffiolo came to the village, had got it into her head that he was their man of destiny, sent specifically to be her spouse. Among these was the widow Ligrina of the *Mulino della Morta* (a farmstead so called because of a stream that went underground at that spot), and Giovanna Cerruti, whose husband had been killed by brigands in October 1586 and who had never managed to catch another one. And also the Borghesini twins, who were stunted and ugly but owned a certain amount of land, as we mentioned above, and had spread the rumour that if anyone took the one of them it would be as if he had taken both. . .

When Maffiolo was first in Zardino all these women and many others would greet him loudly and pointedly, "Good morrow to you, Signor Pietro!" They would invite him into their kitchen gardens to sit down for a rest, or into the house for a glass of wine. They would ask him, "What kind of life is it, for a man all alone? Don't you ever feel the need for someone to look after you?' He would reply partly in Italian and partly in Spanish, give a deep bow, place his right hand on his breast, thank them for the wine and. . . off he would go! No need to describe the fury of the disappointed hopefuls. As often happens in such circumstances, their sincere and disinterested love was transformed into hatred. And the hatred of the Gossips, there in the Flatlands, begets rumours. In the case of field-guard Maffiolo these rumours were particularly persistent and virulent. They explained his aversion to women by attributing to him a relationship (how shall we put it?) a trifle special with his she-mule. For many winters it had been whispered in the stables of Zardino that he washed her hoofs each day with borage-water, that he fed her on beet and charlock-tops and other green things of the season, grown in kitchen gardens for human consumption. And that on bitter nights he covered her with a woolly quilt to protect her from the frost. That he kept her and treated her in every way like a wife, and there's no need to explain the meaning of the word "wife". . .

The field-guard was happy to keep company with Antonia, but at the same time he was a mite ashamed of such a weakness on his part. "Chattering away with a little girl!" he'd say to himself. "It's old age creeping on! I must be in my second childhood!" But then, when they met again, he would take her by the hand as he always did, ask her where she was going, and go along with her. He would tell her about the countries beyond the mountains, places he had become familiar with when he was a soldier – Germany, Flanders, even far-off Poland where in winter the nights are so very long, "much longer than here with us", and where you meet bears and wolves by the roadside. But most of all he talked to her about Spain . . .

"Spain," he told her (and the girl was all eyes and ears), "is the greatest country in the world! There you see the extremes in everything. There are cities so huge and so beautiful that words can't describe them, but there are also places where people still live in caves as in ancient times, when we men were only one of the many animals inhabiting the earth. From Spain come the greatest Saints, the greatest criminals, the richest of the rich, the poorest of the poor – the greatest in everything. There, miracles happen every day!" At Santiago de Compostela, declared the field-guard, before the Portico of Glory the blind are made to see, the halt to walk, the dumb to speak and crooked limbs are made straight; but in the streets of Toledo and Madrid there are people capable of having your knapsack off your back without so much as touching you with a finger. And even that, if you come to think of it, is a miracle! At every church door there are swarms of beggars, so stinking and diseased you can't go near them. And in their midst, abandoned by all, are decayed noblemen – counts, dukes and such – who pay thus on earth for their errors, be they gambling, the pox, licentiousness or crime.

"But among the Grandees of Spain," resumed the field-guard after a brief pause, "that is, among the great ones of the earth, there are those who come from the people, like us, who by their own efforts – you understand me, Antonia? – by amassing wealth in the Americas, or using their wits profitably here in Europe, have succeeded in turning destiny back to front and supplanting the ancient overlords. From having nothing to possessing all! A new aristocracy!"

He would halt, and sweep an arm through every point of the compass. "Thus is Spain!" he would exclaim; and no matter where he happened to be at the moment that gesture always contrasted strangely with the low stone walls, the hedges, the all-too-limited horizons of Zardino.

"*Thus* is Spain!" he would repeat in more subdued tones. "The grandest dream man ever dreamt! Hell and Heaven upon earth, mingled together for us that are living!"

NINE

The Tiger

IN THE SPRING of the year of Our Lord 1601 thousands of people from the lower Sesia valley, Antonia among them, made a pilgrimage to Biandrate to see the stuffed tiger and the other marvellous and monstrous animals with which their reverends the Missionary Fathers of the Company of Jesus were touring from village to village, from town to town, throughout the State of Milan and indeed the whole of Europe. This to stimulate the new "vocations" by showing Christian people the progress made by the True Faith in far-off, unexplored lands and to collect offerings of any sort: in money, of course, but also in sacks of rice, of wheat, of rye, or pigs and goats and live capons, whole cheeses or goose salami, which the peasants brought with them from the most out-of-the-way villages in the Flatlands.

Biandrate is a small town on the banks of the Sesia somewhat to the north of Zardino, and to reach it on foot our pilgrims had to leave the Nidasio farmyard before sunrise. There were seven of them: Signora Francesca with Antonia, Consolata Barbero with her daughters and little son Irnerio. The dog Blackie followed them for a short while out of the village, as was his wont. Then he turned back.

To support the Missions, but also to keep body and soul together on the way, the women each carried a pannier cram-full of all God's bounty: hard-boiled eggs, salami preserved in fat, *ciccioli* (crisped scraps of goose-fat) and plum jam. The children went hand in hand, Luigia with Irnerio, Antonia with Anna Chiara. Teresina, who was the eldest and thought of herself as already a grown-up woman, walked on her own and brought up the rear. They followed the white ribbon of road between the hedges of the kitchen gardens and the sown fields, and when they passed under the Knoll atop which, in the darkness, giant and black, the *albera dei ricordi* soughed in the wind, Antonia felt a chill run through her – she held her breath. She clutched Anna Chiara's hand so hard that the child whined "You're hurting me!"

Dawn began to break to their right, beyond Novara. Over a misty, moisty horizon rose the sun, a red disc, lightly veiled; but as it soared higher it acquired an ever-intenser light, it blazed in the water of the puddles and ditches and in the hems of the clouds, obliging the women, as soon as they left the shelter of the woods, to pull their kerchiefs down over their brows, and the children to shade their eyes with a hand. Antonia had never seen the sun rise, and she never forgot that dawn as long as she lived. She was to remember it later, in Novara, as a prisoner in the Guild Tower gazing out between the bars at first light and seeing the red of the roofs beneath her, and the mists down in the plain, and Monte Rosa rising above those mists, untouchable, unattainable, like her dream of deliverance . . . "Ah," she was to think in those last days of her life, "Could I but be up there!"

They reached Fonte di Badia when the sun was already clear of the mist, but the meadowgrass still sodden with the dew. Descending towards the stream they were surprised not to see *le Madri* mirrored in the surface of the pool, among the waterlilies and the overhanging willow branches dangling so low as to be interwoven with their own reflections.

"*Le Madri* aren't there any more!" exclaimed Teresina. They stared about them. The marble slab beneath the sundial that marked the passing hours of the Flatlands was still in place at the top of the grey stone steps of the well-head. On its stone-built base an inscription thus admonished:

TEMPORA METIMUR

SONITU UMBRA

PULVERE ET UNDA

NAM SONUS ET LACRIMA

PULVIS ET UMBRA SUMUS

("We mark the hours/ By sound and by shadow/ By dust and waterflow/ For we ourselves are dust and shadow/ Crashing water, crying eyes"). Just that and no more.

87

But the far side of the pool had been bereft of the two blocks of marble, shapeless and polished more by the elements than by the hand of man, in which the folk imagination for at least two thousand years had visualized the most ancient divinities of the region, the Celtic Matrons, who became in pagan times *Madri Matute*, and later, with the coming of Christianity, *le Madri*. They had been replaced by a crudely constructed altar, just a few bricks, a dab of mortar, and on top a blue and white ceramic Madonna raising her eyes to heaven in an attitude of prayer, in her hands a string of rosary beads.

"I wonder who it was got upset about *le Madri*," grumbled Signora Francesca. "They'd always been there, and as far as I know they'd never done anyone any harm!"

The two women sat themselves down on the steps of the wellhead, uncovered their paniers and handed round breakfast to the youngsters: a hard-boiled egg each and a chunk of flat bread. They felt uneasy. All around was an enormous silence: not a bird singing among the willow wands, not the flash of a fish on the surface of the pool. Perhaps – thought Signora Francesca – the place had always been as silent as this, but why had she never noticed it as she did now?

"Whoever took away *le Madri*, no good will come to him!" said Consolata, who in common with nearly all the women of the Flatlands was very attentive to every sort of omen and superstition. And she added, after a brief pause, "*Le Madri* will take their revenge!"

Teresina thought this over for a while, and said at last, "They weren't really all that frightening, however many tales were told about them. You only had to give them a little gift when you passed by – anything at all, a piece of fruit, a flower you'd picked along the way, and they were satisfied. Why have they taken them away? Who did it?"

They set off again when the sun was already high, and in almost no time they came within sight of the town. To Antonia, who had never been there before, Biandrate seemed like a small city. It even had colonnades (though very low), and a cobbled street which like the streets in Novara had stone-flagged runners to provide a smoother passage for the cartwheels. A mass of people, immense confusion, with carts and barrows everywhere and peasants in their Sunday best wearing their conical hats, women decked out, like Signora Francesca, in the costume of the Lower Valsesia, or else in black from head to foot, like Consolata Barbero. There were young men and "spouses", i.e. girls of marriageable age wearing the diadem of long hairpins known as the "silver", which was the emblem of their particular age and condition; there were little children, ragamuffins, toddlers firmly grasped by their mothers or else bound to them by a leather thong so they couldn't get lost.

The missionaries and their tiger had attracted a host of itinerants to the town: hawkers and pedlars, quack doctors, profiteers, speculators, jugglers, fiddlers, beggars and suchlike . . . Around these, as at a village fair, the usual rowdy, festive atmosphere had built up, and it sent our youngsters into transports of excitement and brought them to a halt at every step before one novelty after another: "Over there! The Strongest Man in the World!" "The Fire-Eater!" "The Man Who Walks on Broken Glass!"

"O please, please Mum, spare us a copper!"

"Yes, give us a copper to buy some sugar!"

They bought five canes and ate them as they watched the man walking barefoot over broken glass. But though later on they talked wonders about it, in reality they saw little except the backs of the people standing in front of them, and beyond the backs the face of the acrobat as he moved. A mate of his kept up a soft, unremitting drumroll while he, the acrobat in person, crept forward at a snail's pace, with eyes tight shut to aid his concentration. Every muscle in his face was tensed, and his hair was tied at the top of his head to form a sort of pigtail. When he reached his goal the drummer ceased his rolling, the man's eyes opened, the backs of the people shifted, there was a little lukewarm applause. A few hands fumbled in a few purses, a few coins tinkled on the cobbles. People drifted away, while the gypsy and his crony gathered up the coppers. Little Irnerio was beside himself with glee. He rushed on ahead, vanished in the crowds . . . Then all of a sudden he reappeared, shrieking about a new discovery. He hauled the women and girls in his wake. "This way, follow me! They're rolling dice! Hurry hurry!"

It was no easy matter to drag the boy away from a group of men – very questionable faces, long hair, daggers in their belts – who had clustered, part curious, part wary, around a character with a great red beard and a huge scar across his forehead, and around his miniature stall – a folding table inlaid with marquetry, on which the only wares on show were a wooden cup and a pair of dice. The game had not yet begun: everything was hanging fire. The red-bearded man was giving his possible adversaries the once-over, without a word. In his hand were a couple of silver coins, and he tossed them on his open palm. Consolata and Teresina were forced to lift Irnerio bodily up by the arms and carry him off, kicking and weeping hot tears.

Further along the way a vendor of earthenware and glass had laid out his wares on the ground and was tempting the little ones with small painted terracotta birds which you only had to fill with water and blow into to make them warble like real birds. They were somewhat dear – a whole *soldo* apiece – but it was at this price that Irnerio calmed down, and began to smile again, his cheeks still wet. To each of the girls Signora Francesca gave a terracotta money-box painted with flowers. Then on they trooped. The market thereafter broadened out, with vendors of herbal teas, ointments for every variety of sore, elixirs to make you live to a hundred, panaceas and universal remedies for all ills. "Theriaca, theriaca!" cried certain hucksters dressed in black from head to foot to resemble doctors. On their stalls were rows of bottles full of an oily preparation which, according to the dosage and the manner in which it was taken, cured all. "Theriaca of San Marco!" (This last, made in Venice, was considered the best). Further on they passed between two rows of painted ceramic statuettes and figurines, a feast of colour! There were the pale blues of the robes of the Madonnas, the flaming reds of the Sacred Hearts, the brownish tints of the St Antonies and St Francises, the yellows and golds of the haloes, the green of the pedestals, the ivory and rosy hues of the faces . . . All the country folk were spellbound, goggle-eyed. They gave tongue with "What lovely statues! Why, they look real!" (Meaning, I imagine, that they looked like living people). They purchased such huge Madonnas and Redeemers that to haul them back to their villages they had to strap them to their backs, wrapped up as best they could in a blanket.

But there was more to come. There were crucifixes of all sizes and fashioned in every sort of material: terracotta, wood, bronze, wood and bronze, wood and ivory, silver, pewter . . . There were reliquaries embossed, chiselled, studded with coloured stones and glass, and within them – very often – a microscopic scrap of a "Relic"; miniature caskets and crystal urns to contain devotional objects; sealed glass bells housing reproductions of episodes in the New Testament (the Annunciation, the Ascension, the Resurrection); images of the Way of the Cross, depicting the torments of Jesus as he heaved his cross to the place of martyrdom; perpetual lamps (so called); candles of every size and shape – coloured, embossed or swathed all about with enamelled iron fashioned into vine-shoots bearing bunches of grapes or inter-twined lilies and chrysanthemums. Also on sale were miracle-working waters, in ampoules that put on a fine show on the barrows or packed in straw. According to their labels those little bottles hailed from the holy places of the entire Christian world: from the abbey of Montecassino to Mount Athos, from Santiago de Compostela in Spain to the Sacred House at Loreto in the Italian Marches. And the genuineness of the waters contained in them was sworn to by letters patent, signed by reverend abbots and other high-ranking ecclesiastics, framed and hanging on the wall behind the vendors' heads. Nor, of course, were the waters of more local sanctuaries absent: those of the Holy Mount of Varallo, of the Madonna of Re, of the Black Madonna of Oropa, of the Madonna of the Milk at Gionzana. These last two were especially in demand by women who could not conceive.

Missals also were on sale, and devotional books, and Books of Hours, all variously tinted and illustrated, and prints "penny plain, tuppence coloured" of all the Saints in the Calendar, but especially those whose powers were well known in the Flatlands, and who were therefore the most frequent recipients of the prayers of the peasantry: St Theodulus, protector of the fields from hail, St Defendent, guardian of barns from fire, St John of Nepomuk, who restrained the Sesia from bursting its banks, St Christopher preventer of landslides, St Rock forfender of pestilences, St

Martin, patron saint of share-croppers, St Apollonia healer of the ailments of the mouth. Prints of all these Saints, and of many others, were hung up like washing on a clothes-line above the heads of the passers-by. The latter, if they stopped to look, first praised the expertise of the artist and then, speaking of the Saint, be it a he or a she, exclaimed, "Why, all they lack is a tongue! They might be alive!"

To Antonia, who had lived ten years with nuns and churches, devotions and processions, that market of religious knick-knacks brought little in the way of excitement. But the two women and the young girls, not to mention the boy Irnerio, passed from thrill to thrill, from surprise to surprise – at the prints of the Saints, the miracle-working waters, the Reliquies, the crucifixes . . . in short the lot of it. And between one gasp of wonder and the next, one purchase and another, at long last they reached the end of the market. Here the Missionary Fathers, the Jesuits, garnered and divided up the offerings: on this side the livestock, on that side all the rest. And our own friends also emptied out their panniers.

The crowd of sightseers was thereafter channelled into a single stream alongside the church, on the outer wall of which had been hung a long banner, brightly painted; beneath it other missionaries were struggling to tell the crowd of the glorious exploits of the venerable Francis Xavier, the founder (with Ignatius Loyola) of their Order, the first Christian missionary in Malaya, Japan and China, a champion and a martyr of the Christian Faith which, as we all know, is the True Faith and the only one that leads mankind to eternal salvation!

These Jesuit missionaries had shaven heads and enormous beards, and conspicuous on their habits they displayed a silver heart almost as big as a real one. They took turns in singing the praises of their founder – a great man, a true martyr to the Faith, they said over and over again, whom his Holiness Pope Clement VIII was to beatify the following year, 1602, – the fiftieth anniversary of his death – and for whom the case for canonization had already been advanced. The priests pointed to the pictures with long bamboo poles and explained to the populace: "In this illustration we observe Francis Xavier, by then a man of mature years, meeting Ignatius Loyola as a student at the College of

Beauvais . . . And here we are in Venice, as we can well see: on the right of the painting we observe the gondolas and the Grand Canal with its palaces, whereas on the left, kneeling, is Francis himself, about to be ordained priest . . . And here we are in India, in the city of Goa, where Francis is tending the lepers and victims of the plague with a smile on his lips, careless of the risk he is running . . . In this picture Francis is at Yamaguchi in Japan, where he is ministering to a man condemned to death. He succeeds in converting him before his execution . . ."

Little Irnerio at this point began to whimper that his tummy was empty and could they get a move on. It was well past midday, and the sun beat full on our pilgrims' heads, but, hemmed in and squeezed together as they were, there was no way of forcing a passage through the crowd. They must needs listen to the bitter end to tales about the Saint who, had he been given his head, would have converted the whole human race single-handed. But unfortunately things were made difficult for him by everybody, by the perfidious savages of Malacca and Japan, by his own lackadaisical, hypocritical clerical colleagues, not to mention a certain Captain Alvaro de Ataide, a rapscallion of the first water who had dished his mission in China. Our Saint was on his last legs, moribund, but he just *wouldn't die*. "I do wish he'd get on with it!" murmured Antonia.

At last the Saint *did* peg out and the crowd heaved a sigh of relief. There was but one thought in every mind: "So that's over. Let's take a took at the tiger and then get a bite to eat . . ."

They circled the apse of the church and entered a courtyard. There were the animals, in a large canvas dome that sheltered their stuffed corpses from the heat of the sun by day and the damp night vapours. But not a sign of a tiger.

Yet another priestly figure, also with a silver heart much in evidence upon his vestment, pointed out the wild beasts one by one with the tip of his bamboo cane. And not without taking advantage of the situation to impart a few extra moral precepts to the pilgrims. "This," he announced, "is the crocodile," – and the throng raised a general chorus of astonished exclamations and comments – "which first slaughters and devours its victims and then sheds tears, thinking of the wrong it has done. In the same way many Christians are lured into Sin (fools that they are!) deluding themselves that all they need to get to heaven is to say 'I repent' the moment before their last gasp. Unluckily for them, matters are on an entirely different footing. God gives no one Paradise for nothing. To reach Paradise is like climbing a mountain, and the steps are made of good deeds and acts of piety."

"This other animal on the right, with its long long snout, is the ant-eater, which thrusts its tongue into holes in the earth to find ants, of which it is inordinately fond. Just so we missionaries lick into every corner of the earth with the Word of God and search out souls to bend towards the eternal destination!"

"This monstrous serpent which you see before you, longer than twenty spans of a man's hand and thick as a roof-beam, is the beast named python. It first entwines its victims in its coils and squeezes the life out of them, then swallows them whole, however big they may be. And just so the devil does to mankind: he seizes their souls, he crushes them with vice, he casts them down into a dark place called Hell, where there is no appeal and no salvation, where resounds one word alone – the word *nevermore*."

Animal by animal they reached the big door of a barn, which must have been specially cleaned out for the purpose and was guarded by two persons. On the one side was a Missionary regulating the influx of visitors, allowing them in by eights and tens, no more. On the other side was a Moor clad in Moorish costume, in violet-coloured silk caboose reaching down to his toes and a turban on his head, holding out a collection bag to all those who entered. Nor did he remove it until he had heard the tinkle of a coin dropping in.

"There within," intoned the missionary, "is the tiger, the Satanas of Animals, the Cruellest of all Beasts. Gaze on it for the time it takes you to say an Our Father and then be off, and God go with you. Here there is nothing more for you to see."

While they were awaiting their turn Antonia explained to Irnerio what a tiger looks like. She knew this, or thought she did, thanks to a picture Sister Clelia had sketched in her notebook, where there were also sketches of the men who dwell in the Indian jungles, remote from civilization, together with their weapons and their huts, and a number of wild creatures whom the lay sister had more than once heard the Missionary Fathers speak of in the course of their homilies. "The tiger," said the girl to the little boy, who had begun to whimper again, "is a huge cat with whiskers *this* long! But a lot more ferocious and cunning than ordinary cats."

When their turn came to enter the barn Signora Francesca and Consolina dropped a little small change into the collection bag proffered by the Moor, but when they found themselves in the great torch-lit chamber itself words died on their lips, all but a long-drawn "Ahh!!" of mingled terror and wonder. The tiger was half-hidden in the shadows, way above the visitors' heads, forepaws raised as if springing from the darkness at that very instant. Its mouth, gaping wide and daubed with red lead, displayed fangs that put to shame the tusks of a wild boar, such as swashbucklers in those days made themselves necklaces of. The yellow glass eyes glittered in the light of the torches, the flickering of which diffused and magnified the living shadow cast on the walls and ceiling. Bigger than a calf it was, bigger than a horse, bigger even than an ox.

No one in the Flatlands had ever seen an animal like this, and no one imagined such a thing could really exist, except in dreams. The peasants doffed their hats, the women crossed themselves, the children mewled and clutched at their mothers' skirts, among them Irnerio: "I'm scared, I'm scared!" They moved around the stuffed monster without taking their eyes off it, holding their breath, as if they feared it might still come back to life and attack them.

On the tiger's right side, from the shoulder down, ran a scar – or to put it better a great gash – which the taxidermist had attempted to patch up this way and that, with stitches and with paint, but without success. Thence, thought Antonia, the tiger's soul had fled . . . And who could imagine what trap or weapon had got the better of such a beast! She shuddered.

Outside the barn again, along with the other visitors, and among the low walls and the kitchen gardens of that Flatland village, it seemed to her absurd that the tiger had once really existed and been alive, and that it had ended up there, in that barn with that crowd all round it, through the agency of those missionaries with their great long beards. She knew then that she loathed them. What right did they have, those priests, to tamper like that with the things of this world?

TEN

Don Teresio

BEFORE ME ON MY TABLE as I write is a colour photograph I myself took a long time ago, maybe in 1970, maybe a couple of years later. I never imagined I would find it again, so long had I sought it! The photograph of Antonia. On the back are a few words written in my own hand, "An adolescent Madonna with a mole on the left side of her upper lip, photographed at . . ." (somewhere between the Sesia valley and Biella). Many were the youthful Madonnas with moles on their lips painted over the years by the itinerant painter Bertolino d'Oltrepò, here in the Flatlands but above all in the Alpine valleys. And who knows if there are not a few surviving on the outer wall of some farmstead or rural oratory.

The one I photographed alas exists no longer, and indeed it is already evident from the picture that the porch over the fresco was giving way, and that the rain of twenty years before had begun to seep down into the wall where the painting was. At that time I knew nothing of Bertolino d'Oltrepò, nor had I had any occasion to stumble across the story of Antonia. I was totally innocent of all I am telling you now.

In that spoilt and faded fresco the thing that drew me was the Madonna's face, so alive it seemed quite foreign to the rest of the painting; and it held you spellbound there to gaze at it. Those eyes as dark as night yet clear as day, that mole on the upper lip, the plump, red lips themselves, and then that riotous ringlet escaping from her draperies onto her left cheek . . . It took me many years to discover that these adolescent Madonnas with the mole on the lip are the only recognizable sign, a kind of signature, of that *madonnaro* or painter of madonnas who went by the name of Bertolino d'Oltrepò; concerning whom it appears, from the

97

records of Antonia's trial, that in a votive shrine at Zardino he made a portrait of the witch at fifteen years of age, attired indeed as a Madonna . . . who knows how many small frescoes of fifteen-year-old Madonnas have existed in centuries past between Monte Rosa and the Flatlands! And who knows how many prayers have been prayed before those devotional portrayals of a witch? But such, by good fortune, is Italy; and such also is art.

As for Bertolino, it is my belief that he went on painting Antonia's face because he was in love with that image; or, to put it better, with something that image would preserve for him for ever, whereas in the original it was destined to perish: the bloom of youth. Artists, at times, do fall in love with such things. What Bertolino wished to depict in the portrait I have before me – and which in some way and to some extent, with his native talent and the means at the disposal of a rustic painter, he did in fact succeed in depicting – was not so much a time of life as a state of grace. A season of the soul to which all of us, and artists even more than others, would wish to return; a springtime in the form of a lady . . . or of Our Lady. Other painters before him had tried to give womanly forms to springtime, but Bertolino had to gratify the tastes of the unpolished persons who commissioned him, to give them Madonnas with haloes and cloaks spangled with stars, just as they wanted. He was no Botticelli, he was no Raphael. He, at the utmost, could express himself in the faces: and so he did. This Madonna's face is a May day in the Flatlands, full of light, and poppies, and clouds mirrored in water . . .

But at this point I must introduce you to a new character in our story. Don Teresio Rabozzi, the young priest who was to play so great a part in later events in Antonia's life, arrived in Zardino on foot from Novara one Saturday in October in the year of Our Lord 1601, at the hour of Vespers. No one was expecting him or knew who he was. He passed the Lantern Tavern, and the yokels seated there under the pergola turned as one man to take his measure, as they always did with strangers. Who was he? What was his business in Zardino? His garb, and the crucifix on his chest, and the haversack on his back, were the same as those of the Holy Year pilgrims – the *Romei*, as they still called them at that time. But the Holy Year of 1600 had come and gone a good ten months before, and the way then trodden by the pilgrims now petered out among the cane-brakes of the Sesia, outside the village.

Almost as if he had read their thoughts, the stranger wheeled round, crossed the square to the church and strode as if he owned the place into the house of Don Michele the village priest, who always left his door unlocked until he retired to bed.

So! The plot thickened! Husbandmen and hired men one and all thereupon shrugged their shoulders, picked up the glasses and the cards they had laid down when the stranger appeared, and fell once more to thumping their fists on the table or shouting their heads off about insignificant topics, just as they normally did, to pass the time. In fact, though, they were awaiting the next developments of what they had just witnessed, and wondering who that pilgrim could possibly be. A friend of Don Michele's? A *quistone?* A "wandering scholar"? And in any case, why had he come there, to their village, to seek their priest?

Ten minutes passed, just enough for darkness to fall and for mine host, one Absolom, to emerge with a flaming brand on a pole to light the wrought-iron lantern which gave the hostelry its illumination and its name. Strange sounds then started to emerge from the priest's house, the slamming of doors, voices raised in anger, breaking glass. Candlelight was seen moving swiftly from one window to another, from one floor to the next. They heard a voice shout out, "Thou fornicator! Slave of Satan!" On the far side of the house Don Michele's dog was barking and yelping as if they were skinning him alive, and all the dogs in Zardino hastened to join in. Still impossible to tell what was happening in there, but whatever it was it was happening in a hurry!

Until an upper window was flung open and from it, one after another, flew the great ceramic vases of the priest's pharmacy, with all they contained in terms of herbs and mineral salts and other medicaments. They crashed down on to the cobblestones so hard they seemed to burst asunder, while there aloft the stranger was howling at the top of his voice: "Usurper of sacred offices! Priest of the Devil! No priest at all!"

"Don Michele, Don Michele!" cried the men from the hostelry, prudently keeping their distance from the trajectories of the jars, the alembics and the mortars that for nigh on fifteen years had been the sole pharmaceutical equipment existing in that part of the Flatlands. "What's going on? Give us an answer!"

"Quick, quick! Fetch the consuls and the field-guard!" cried someone in the rear to someone else deep in the shadows. "Get the lads here! There's a bandit in the priest's house!"

Meanwhile, "Scandal-monger! Corruptor of souls! Devil incarnate!" shrieked the bandit within the house.

When the very last pot of herbs and the very last alembic had joined its predecessors, smashed to smithereens on the cobblestones, and the entire square was littered with potsherds and as fragrant with dried herbs and elixirs as a herbalist's shop, there fell a moment of silence. The door of the presbytery thereupon opened and the stranger emerged, in one hand bearing a candlestick and with the other thrusting Don Michele ahead of him. "Come on, speak up!" he commanded. "Tell these people who I am and what my business is here in Zardino. Tell them an honest truth at last, after so many lies!"

Don Michele opened his mouth to speak, but the words choked in his throat and he burst into tears. At that very moment loud voices were heard: "Make way, make way for the field-guard!"

The little crowd made way, and by the light of the torches in strode "Don" Pietro, enormously tall and bony, with his hooked stick shoulder-arms like a harquebus and his right hand raised in a gesture as if to say: "Stop all that now! The field-guard's here and we'll soon get things sorted out." He then turned to the stranger and asked, "*Usted*, who are you?"

All the answer he got was for the mysterious pilgrim to turn back on Don Michele and bawl in his face: "Tell them, tell them! Own up, you scoundrel! Tell them who I am and who sent me. And speak loudly so they all can hear!"

"He's . . . he's the new priest," sobbed Don Michele, his chin on his chest. "He's brought letters patent from His Lordship the Bishop of Novara. There's nothing to be done about it – he's a real priest!"

There were flabbergasted murmurs from the crowd now: "Well, whatever next!"

"Bishop or no bishop," spoke up someone a little bolder than the rest, "if we're going to chuck this fellow out, let's do it at once." But you could tell from his tone of voice that there was no real conviction there, and that when it came down to it no one would lift a finger to stick up for the old priest.

"What should we do, Don Michele? *You* tell us what we should do!"

"I've already said," was the reply. "There's nothing to be done. Just go home!"

Upon which their new parish priest, Don Teresio, shrieked after them, "I expect you all tomorrow for Holy Mass! At the first stroke of the bell, mind you, the whole lot of you in church!"

That evening, at the Lantern Tavern in Zardino, not a man picked up his cards again. They sat around talking and talking, and when the church clocks of the Flatlands chimed three for half past midnight they drifted off to bed.

Next day every soul in the village was there in church to take a closer look at this great novelty, the new priest fresh from Novara. And as for himself, Don Teresio, he must have spent the whole night scrubbing, for the church looked spick and span from floor to ceiling. The tiles had been washed, the frescos toned up with a sponge, and the polished brasses shone like gold. In the window embrasures and the ribbing of the vaults not a single spider's web remained of the thousands that had made a fine showing until the day before. The entire church was aglow with candles. Within living memory there had never been so many alight all at one time.

Viewed by daylight the new incumbent was really very young, twenty-five at most, and even more pallid and emaciated than he had looked those few hours earlier, by night and the light of lanterns and torches that deformed things and made them loom larger. Hollow-eyed, waxy complexioned, cheeks as smooth as a woman's, with a scrap of ill-shaven stubble only on his chin. Erect in the church doorway he divided his flock, women on this side, men on that, and at the front the children. The boys and girls of marriageable age were arranged respectively to the right and the left of the altar, in the choir-stalls.

Then – he vanished. And when the farmers were beginning to grumble, tapping their feet with impatience and muttering half out loud, "What're we waiting for? Why doesn't he get a move on? *We've* got work to do!" he reappeared clad in gold-embroidered paraments of purple silk. He moved to the altar. He knelt, bending so low that his head touched the floor; he bounced to his feet again, wheeled round, flung wide his arms, uttered some Latin phrase in a sham nasal delivery that was a new one on everybody, and whirled round again; he leapt, or rather, he flew, to the left, light as a sparrow, knelt down again, sprang up again with wondrous elasticity, returned to the centre of the altar, bounded to the right . . .

His public, especially the females, stared wide-eyed at this ballet as if in a hypnotic trance, while a few of the young lads laughed out loud, without bothering to put a hand over their mouths. At a certain point Don Teresio seized the chalice, he bowed, he crouched before the altar mumbling incomprehensible words, then all of a sudden surged upwards as if the chalice he held were bearing him on high, towards the God the Father painted on the ceiling of the apse. A murmur of astonishment arose from the women's pews, while one voice broke out: "He's taken wing! He's flying!"

Finally, after dashing many times from one end of the altar to the other, reading from the mass-book in his ceremonial falsetto and answering himself in his normal voice, Don Teresio wheeled round on the faithful, fixing them with dilated eyes, and bawled out that although all those present in church had received baptism and called themselves Christians, they had in fact sunk to living like infidels, and that it was therefore his duty to carry out a thorough cleansing of their souls, a scrubbing not far different from that of the floor and walls of the church over which he had laboured all night long. And this at once, without delay! The matter was of the utmost urgency, and let nobody dare slink out of it or look for excuses! He quoted from the Gospel of St Matthew: "What man shall there be among you, that shall have one sheep, and if it fall into a pit on the sabbath day, will not lay hold on it, and lift it out? How much then is a man better than a sheep?" etc., etc.. He commanded that all the men, all the ancients, all the women and all the children over the age of ten make confession and take Holy Communion within the next few days, and certainly before the coming Sunday! A week later the names of any reprobates excluded from the Grace of God and the Communion of Saints would be nailed to the church door with a curse on them. He shouted aloud that by the express will of the Pope and the bishops convened at the Council of Trent no indulgence would be possible and no mercy extended to such persons. Rejected by God, until Easter next year they would live like beasts, excluded not only from the Church but even from the solidarity of their fellow men. Only at Easter, he warned, could this anathema be cancelled by pardon, by means of confession and expiation. Thus the reprobates, even here on earth, would have made an advance payment on Purgatory. During that time, he explained – and as he spoke his eyes dilated and his voice shook with wrath – this excommunication would also be extended to anyone who helped these reprobates or gave them shelter. Their relatives and friends must turn them out, their servants must abandon them and even men of medicine might not succour them, even were they on the point of death, under pain of being debarred from the exercise of their profession, and outlawed from human society. And on the death of one thus excommunicated, he would not be buried in consecrated ground, beside his parents and his relatives who had lived in the grace and fear of God, and following His laws. Nay, he would be interred in any old place, as luck would have it, without funeral rites or a prayer said, for the worms to feed on his body and the Devil on his soul. Thus it had been laid down by Holy Church – concluded Don Teresio – to defend the Faith against the assaults of the Devil and bring new strength to the People of God. And thus commanded his lordship Bishop Bascapè of Novara, who, after giving him his blessing, had in person entrusted to him, Don Teresio Rabozzi, the care of souls in Zardino.

The yokels hearkened agape to all this. Why, O why, they wondered, does this new priest not confine himself to threatening us with hell-fire in the life to come, as all priests do, and leave us to get on as best we can in this one? The choice between hell and heaven is our business. But they didn't know, the poor beggars, that more and worse was to come.

"Help me!" cried Don Teresio out of the blue, stamping his foot two or three times as if dancing a jig. "Help me to crush the head of Satan, the everlasting tempter, he who is here among you and never ceases to entice you with his wiles." He went on to explain that that accursèd paganism, vanquished everywhere more than a thousand years ago, even in the Flatlands, had all the same never been totally eradicated. Indeed it survived in many customs which must be constantly and tirelessly combated, with the help of God and Bishop Bascapè. The bishop, continued Don Teresio, had seen to the removal throughout the diocese of the last remnants of non-Christian cults, in the form of inscriptions and stone images venerated as fetishes; he had declared harvest and fertility festivals to be unlawful; he had banned musical gatherings and barnyard dances, marriage feasts and funeral banquets; and above all with particular severity he had banished from his diocese that vile and pernicious custom that goes by the name of Carnival, which more than any other and in the highest degree begets corruption, the decay of morals, the perishing of souls and the triumph of the Devil. It was therefore needful to supplant social gatherings in the byres by recitals of the rosary, dances by novenas, fairs by religious processions, and pagan harvest festivals by Te Deums and thanksgiving ceremonies. But above and before all else it was vital to keep Sundays and religious feast-days, daylong and from dawn till dusk, according to the edicts of Holy Writ and the Tables of the Law. Sunday is the Lord's Day, and must by all Christians be entirely devoted to Him, in thought and in deed. No hunting or fishing, no card games or toping at the tavern, no idle talk between the women or – heaven forfend! – illicit love-making between the young. No work! From crack of dawn till nightfall, swore Don Teresio, every feast-day and every Sunday in Zardino would be organized in such a way that not a single minute was left over for the Devil and his wiles, what with religious instruction for young and old alike, with hymns, benedictions, Vespers, processions, recitals of the rosary, public prayers . . . He had been preaching already for over an hour when suddenly he dried up, goggled wide-eyed and craned forward like a pointer scenting a hare.

"Hey, you." he shouted. "Yes, I mean you! Where do you think you're going? Come back!"

The congregation all turned their heads, just in time to see the man who had tried to sneak away return to his seat, scarlet in the face and mumbling something about a cow that had calved during the night.

"Shame on you!" shrieked Don Teresio. "Welshing in the middle of Holy Mass! Turning your back on God without a scruple!"

He then resumed his normal voice. He promised that as a result of his arrival the lives of all the inhabitants of Zardino would be changed from black to white, even though – he said – he did not underestimate the difficulties he would meet in reorganizing around his church a Christian flock worthy of the name. For a start, he announced, he would eliminate all the activities of the man who for years had usurped the name and function of priest, raising silkworms, lending money for usury, selling drugs and bodily unguents and performing every kind of act unworthy of a true priest. He quoted the Gospel: "My house was the House of the Lord, and you have made of it a den of thieves!" A true priest – said Don Teresio, stabbing a finger at his own breast – must live, according to Holy Writ, on the alms and contributions of the faithful. He became enraptured, rising on tiptoe as at the outset of Mass, when for a moment the Gossips really had thought he was about to take wing. Then, putting himself in the shoes of God the Father, he cried: "I, God in three Persons, ask of you: what in all these years has become of the tithes that were due to me, to the payments in kind and the donations linked by tradition to all the feasts in the liturgical calendar and to the names of my Holy Martyrs? Who has robbed me of them? And the right to mill grain, and to draw water, and to have so many cartloads of wood every winter, all rights established by notarial deeds: what sacrilegious feet have trampled them down?" He stabbed a finger at the men before him. "You! And you! And you! And you! All of you, fornicators and thieves into the bargain because you have stolen from God that which was God's!" His voice was by this time quaking with wrath, as was his raised arm. He glared in silence at his new parishioners, more or less in the same pose as Michelangelo in the Sistine Chapel had depicted Christ in Judgement: woe unto you! But then he lowered his arm and joined his hands in an attitude of prayer.

"For what was God's due in past years," he said, "and was not rendered unto him, He Himself will present the account when you come to die. But for what you owe now, for the current year and the months to come, it will be me, His humble servant, to call you to account. By my own poor means if these, as I trust, suffice. If not, then by appealing to the laws of men and their Tribunals, if such action be necessary to the greater glory of God and of his Holy Church. Amen."

ELEVEN

Il Caccetta

THE LEAVES FELL and the sky turned grey: winter came, and the ploughing of the fields, and the first snowfalls. True to his promises, Don Teresio strove at every moment and in every way to sadden and afflict the inhabitants of Zardino with his unflagging presence in farmhouse and farmyard, with his non-stop series of religious functions, all of them compulsory ("of obligation"), all of them of paramount importance, indeed indispensable to their salvation; with his pestering demands for donations and tithes, and with the clamour of his bells, which rang out full peals six or seven times every day, or even more. What crowds they were intended to summon, said Pietro the field-guard, *"Dios lo sabe"* (God alone knows).

But though his activities were frenetic, and his imagination inexhaustible, that latter end of the year 1601 and the early months of 1602, in Zardino as in all the other villages of the Flatlands, was not afterwards remembered by the people as "the winter of Don Teresio" but as "the winter of Il Caccetta" – who was no parish priest but a wealthy landowner from Novara (his real name being Giovan Battista Caccia) forced, on account of proscriptions and convictions, to repair to the far bank of the Sesia, to Gattinara in the territories of the Duke of Savoy. Whence, taking advantage of the fact that the river was low, and also of the scant control the Spaniards exercised over this frontier, considered safe on account of their alliance with Charles Emanuel I of Savoy, Il Caccetta's men made almost daily forays to plunder the villages of the Flatlands; and in all the cow-byres of all the villages, including Zardino, no one talked of anything except their exploits. Kidnapping, arson, outrages of every kind – material here for all sorts of stories, and for years to come! A fellow known as Il Barbavara, it was said in the byres, and another known as Il Marchesino, both notoriously Il Caccetta's men, had crossed the Sesia with a few other armed bravos and on the road to Carpignano had seized a pair of thirteen year-old twins, Costanza and Vincenzina, daughters of a barber named Mossotto living in those parts, and carried them off across the river. And again: a farmstead barely a mile from the village of Recetto set ablaze – five horses stolen; the owner, Farmer Nicola De Domenicis, a fine man, beaten so savagely that he died a few days later without recovering consciousness or uttering a word to anyone. In compensation a certain Iselda, twenty-four years old and nicknamed La Magistrina, who had vanished without trace quite a while back, and whom her parents lamented as dead, had reappeared in her village, Vicolungo, on the point of giving birth to the Antichrist with whom Il Caccetta in person, or one of the bandits in his gang, had got her pregnant . . . These and other stories went the round of all the cowsheds in the Flatlands every evening, and all the young girls, including Antonia, had to listen to them and their train of exhortations, prohibitions and warnings addressed specifically to them: "Mind now," the old Gossips hectored them, "Don't go out alone for any reason whatever! Don't open the door to strangers! Don't do anything rash in any way!" It was don't do this and don't do that until sooner or later, with all this natter, many of the girls ended up dreaming about the bandits. They dreamt of being abducted and carried off beyond the Sesia, to a great castle, where seated on a throne awaited Il Caccetta in person! Nor was he hideous or wicked, as their mothers told them, but quite the opposite – the Prince Charming of the fairy tales. And, as happens in fairy tales, he married them!

Il Caccetta, yes . . . If the fame men enjoy were not so ephemeral, and their memory so insignificant amongst men as in fact it is, long years ago the life of the Novarese nobleman Giovan Battista Caccia would have been reconstructed in black and white in an appropriate number of chapters, and he reinstated in his legend. On the contrary, it still waits to be written. I shall try to make up for this as best I may by saying that in that winter of 1602 he was but thirty years old, having been born in his castle at Briona on the 22nd of July 1571, under the sign of Cancer, of which

throughout his life he bore practically all the negative characteristics, both physical and moral. He was, in fact, very short in
stature, a real runt of a man (which saddled him with the
disparaging-diminutive nickname of "Il Caccetta") with a notice-
able disproportion between the upper half of his body – normally
developed, and indeed robust – and his legs, which were stunted
and puny.

Heir to an illustrious name and a conspicuous fortune, he grew
up amid a covey of women in his palaces in Novara and Milan, and
in the castle of Briona. His teacher and preceptor was a priest
named Alciato – the very same Rev. Alciato whom we shall find
(by then a Monsignor) among the judges in Antonia's trial for
heresy – who confined himself to falling in with all his pupil's
wishes, pandering to his every whim, excusing his every impul-
sive act; inwardly convinced as he was, like a large percentáge of
the clergy at the time, that there are in the world two categories of
people: those who are permitted to do anything and those who are
permitted to do nothing; and that even if our naked souls are in the
next world equal before God, in *this* world the difference between
men is so great that for a feudal overlord to kill a peasant is no
graver a sin than to snare a rabbit or hook a trout. This notion of
the world, already inherent in the teacher, was subsequently
assimilated by his pupil, who as he grew up even improved on it
and supplemented it with a very lofty and certainly exaggerated
opinion of his intelligence and of his rank, which the youthful
Giovan Battista Caccia considered vastly superior to the intelligence and rank of practically every other human being.

Before he was twenty years of age our hero married one
Antonia Tornielli, lovelessly and without any interest on either
side except the mercenary aims of their respective families, both
among the most wealthy and illustrious in all this part of Italy. She
bore him a son, whom he called Gregorio. In Novara at an age we
cannot vouch for, but certainly before he was twenty-five, he met
and made the acquaintance of a very beautiful and frivolous
woman, recently widowed and courted by all; and he felt for her –
or thought he felt – an immediate and irresistible attraction. "That
woman", thought he, "must be mine, whatever the cost!"

The merry widow (who might well have been a sight less merry had she been able to read Il Caccetta's thoughts) hailed from Milan, was called Margherita Casati, and had a none-too-secret relationship with Agostino Canobio, who at the time of our story was the most sought-after young man in the whole of Novara, the one whom all the young ladies dreamt of marrying. The sole heir of a family of bankers, he also had the good luck to be a handsome young fellow, of more than medium height, well knit, bursting with health and of a peaches-and-cream complexion. The exact opposite of our noble lord, who was stubby, ugly and waxen-faced, but who hurled himself into the conquest of this woman thinking he had no rival and not imagining he could ever have one. Who on earth would dare to oppose one such as he?

Agostino Canobio laughed in his face. As for her, "la bella Margherita", she must have had some notion of how dangerous this new suitor was, for she made a show of taking him seriously, saying, "My lord, how could I possibly reciprocate this feeling which you say you nurture for me, although it flatters me most highly? You are a married man, I am a respectable woman. So you can see for yourself that a relationship between us could never be; or, if it were to be, it could come to no good."

Il Caccetta gave no immediate reply; but a few days later the gentlewoman Antonia Caccia, née Tornielli, died. Heart failure, said the doctors; poison, said the Novaresi. And as if to prove them right, before the week was out Il Caccetta's cook died too, by falling off a roof; and God alone knows what he'd gone up *there* for. Margherita Casati took the hint and fled to Milan; not, however, before Il Caccetta learnt that she had been the mistress of Canobio, and still was: information, it was later said by those who knew him, which caused him the longest and most violent outburst of rage in his whole life. Things had come to a pretty pass if a petty bourgeois, the nephew of usurers, had had the nerve, or the recklessness, to imagine he could take *him* on – and even have a chance of winning!

It is at this point in the story that matters precipitated and the corpses were too many to count, because Il Caccetta, in attempting to kill Canobio, created a void around him by killing his friends, acquaintances, relatives and body-guards, while Canobio, who had not expected such a tempest and barely managed to save his skin (he was to die in 1602 at the age of twenty-seven and in circumstances far from clear: perhaps Il Caccetta did finally manage to bump him off, or possibly it was Canobio's fate to die young, and his death was natural . . . Who knows?), attempted to counter-attack, partly by ordering his retainers to kill Il Caccetta's retainers, partly by appealing to the law and the men who represented it in Novara and Milan: the Captain of Justice, the Podestà, the judges of the criminal courts. Let them, whose job it was, defend him from the fury of a raving madman who went around killing people and burning down houses for no apparent reason.

But Il Caccetta's victory over Canobio, total and over-whelming, had at least two features which, were they not concerned with tragic events, would certainly be comic. In the first place it was a futile victory, because at this point in our story all trace of Margherita Casati is lost: no one knows anything more about her. Secondly, it was a very costly victory indeed, which Il Caccetta was to pay for as long as he lived, and indeed was never to finish paying for. All the rogues and ruffians who worked on the fringes of legality, and not for a single master but as mercenaries, whose favours in terms of murder and arson Il Caccetta had requested in the past, now turned to him for their requital. They sent him word to this effect: "We have to knock off Tom, Dick or Harry," or else "We have to burn ditto's house down, and it's in your part of the world. Kindly see to it." How was he to sidestep claims of this sort?

Thus it came about that Il Caccetta's men – at Romagnano, at Orta, in the main square at Angera – started slaughtering people who had nothing whatever to do with his quarrel with Canobio, committing atrocities without the least scruple or second thought. At this point, reasoned Il Caccetta, and his desperadoes along with him, our debt to the Law is already so huge that however we add to it the punishment can't be worse: "We might as well be hanged for a sheep as a lamb!" Married women, nubile maidens, and even girls of nine or ten years old were carried off by force from the villages near by the fortress of Briona (which by this time Il Caccetta had made his stronghold), and were held there "at the disposal" of the overlord and his desperadoes. In the courtyards and kitchens of the castle there grew up a whole herd of "nobody's children", or rather of "anyone's children", fed like the dogs. People were slain just for the fun of it: a viol-player who had baulked at getting up in the middle of the night to go and make music at the castle; or a man at Romagnano Sesia who was slow to step aside. They perpetrated pillages and thefts of every kind imaginable, but especially of money and horses. They burnt down houses, they terrorized whole villages, because once having embarked on this course, what use was there in stopping? "I am in blood steeped in so far/ Returning were as tedious as go o'er" . . .

It was in 1600 that Giovan Battista Caccia was first sentenced to death by a Court, for having Agostino Canobio's uncle, Ottavio Canobio, blasted to death with a harquebus in Milan: in his mansion it was that before vanishing for ever from the face of the earth the luckless Margherita Casati had found a last refuge. What was to be done? The judicial system of the time, inflexible towards the poor and needy who had chanced to land up in its nets, offered real out-and-out felons every possible loophole. One of these, oft repeated in the proclamations of His Excellency Don Ferdinando Velasquez, Constable of Castile etc., etc., was that anyone who delivered a fugitive from justice to the authorities would be pardoned for a crime equal to that of the fugitive. In practice this meant that to get off a death sentence, and regain a clean record, all you had to do was turn over to the judges some other condemned man or, if he were dead already, at least his severed head. Our hero, in his castle at Briona, had an *embarras de richesses*. Which of his bullies did he relish least? Who knew the most compromising facts about his own activities? Finally he selected one, had him beheaded and dispatched the head to Milan.

The following year – we are now in 1601 – the same thing happened again. The criminal courts in Milan pronounced against Giovan Battista Caccia, Novarese landed proprietor, as many as two capital sentences: one to the gallows, for rustling cattle and other robberies; the other to decapitation for several murders. Il Caccetta, who in the meantime in his castle at Briona had had a vast amount of false money coined by an expert forger whom he had then disposed of by butchering him and, for safety's sake, his wife too, evaded both these sentences by handing over another couple of his bravoes to justice and then removed himself to Gattinara, on the far side of the Sesia, under the protection of Count Mercurino Filiberto di Gattinara and his Highness the Duke of Savoy. Here, taking up residence in the fortified monastery of certain friars known as the "Camisotti" on account of the white habits they wore, he began to spread word that he'd had enough of the Spaniards and their government and began to muster a cavalry force, no longer as bravoes and desperadoes and retainers of his own, but as soldiers, equipping them with "banners, plumes and white gartered hose" in the French manner, and "opposing those who wore the colour red" (this being the colour of the other side). He trained them in target-shooting at "the figure of a man said to be that of the King of Spain". In addition he made wild harangues to the reckless madcaps who every so often crossed the Sesia to seek him out. One Giovan Battista Comolo from Omeglia, for example, or one Giulio Gemello from Orta, or one Giovanni Commazzolo from Vercelli, or Blasino Caccia from Novara. They were all of them "rogues of consequence" with many influential connections.

These accursèd Spaniards, Il Caccetta told them, would soon be forced to leave Milan. The common people loathed them and the nobility, robbed of its rights and despoiled of its possessions, was by this time against them to a man. The essential thing was to be ready, to arm as many men as possible, and to wait for a move from Ranuccio Duke of Parma and Charles Emanuel I, Duke of Savoy, both of them his (Caccetta's) friends and protectors. Let them take it for certain, and be on the alert: the present alliance of the House of Savoy with Spain was just a passing phase, a political manoeuvre, and very soon Milan would be in the possession of *il Roi* (meaning the king of France, at that time Henry IV). He himself, Il Caccetta, had pledged to *il Roi* that when the time was ripe he would seize the castle of Angera, once the property of the Borromeo family, and march with other valiants upon Milan, where under the new regime obtaining in the State he would have the prominent position which his rank, and his commitment to the cause of *il Roi*, would have merited.

This was the time when the blue-and-white horsemen terrorized the Flatlands with their incursions, the long "winter of Il Caccetta", when the young girls never left the house and anyone who owned horses stabled them as far away as possible, in farms on the outskirts of Novara or even as far afield as the Ticino valley. Later, with the coming of spring, the river waters rose, flooding the fords, the bandits ceased their forays and life in the villages little by little returned to normal. The women were once again to be seen along the byways, or on their knees beside the watercourses doing their laundering; the children resumed their games and adventures, even far from home, in the depths of the woods; once again, in the fields, the sad, rhythmic songs of the *risaroli* were to be heard, and the fears of the winter paled, and vanished like ghosts in summer sunshine.

It is in any case a characteristic of the Flatlands, that everything goes hurrying by and nothing, or almost nothing, leaves its mark. Memory here does not cut deep: contrary to the way of things in the Alpine valleys, where the memory or the legend of an occurrence may endure from one millennium to another. The great plain is a sea in which the waves of time follow hard on each other and erase each other, event after event, century after century. Migrations, invasions, epidemics, famines, wars . . . all these are remembered today only because they are recorded in books. But for the written word there would remain no trace of them.

One afternoon on a day in late July of the year of Our Lord 1602 Antonia and Anna Chiara Barbero were helping Signora Consolata to weed a bed of turnips among the kitchen gardens behind the Lantern Tavern. It was hot, they were pestered by flies, and certainly no one was thinking that on that very day, in that very place, anything of importance could happen, when there came a clatter of hoofs on the road leading from the Sesia, and then a hubbub of voices, the jingle of metal, the barking of dogs. Windows were banged and shuttered up, people vanished from the roadways, and a single message flew from one end of Zardino to the other, one name that alone was enough to strike terror: "Il Caccetta! Il Caccetta is here!"

Poor Consolata was seized with panic. What should she do, both for herself and the girls? Impossible to get back home, for to do that she would have had to cross the road, and the road beyond the hedge was already chock-a-block with mounted men. There was also a closed carriage, with curtains drawn across the windows, and when one curtain was for a brief moment drawn aside, there appeared the face of a woman. Having no other way out, Consolata grabbed both the girls, pushed them down to the ground and thrust them by main force into the blackthorn hedge surrounding the vegetable patch. She did her best to crawl in there herself, on all fours so as not to be spotted. The barbs of the blackthorn ripped their skin and the flimsy stuff of their garments, pierced their flesh and drew blood; but none of the three females let out an "Ouch!" or made a move to find a less excruciating posture. Anna Chiara later recounted that she had held her breath as long as she could and stayed stock still, eyes tight shut, until the brigands had gone away.

Not so Antonia, who watched and saw everything. Despite the fact that the horses were close enough to the hedge for her to smell them, and despite the scare she got when the brigands turned in her direction and her heart missed a beat – *"They've spotted me! They're looking right at me!"* – she was less overcome by fear than by curiosity. She saw Il Caccetta, a ram-rod on horseback in the middle of the piazza, giving orders to his men: "If they refuse to come, bring them by force. But make sure that even by mistake you don't injure anyone!"

The whole piazza was jammed with horsemen, and sometimes you could see Il Caccetta, sometimes not. Despite all his exploits he was skinny, runtish, and ugly into the bargain. His face was the colour of tallow, his forehead bulbous and protuberant, and bulbous and glistening also were his eyes, like those – thought Antonia – of people with consumption of the lungs.

Meanwhile some of the men-at-arms, harquebus in hand, were battering at the windows and strutting around the yards yelling "Where are the consuls?" Then: "Come out of there, you clodhoppers, no one's going to hurt you!" In a matter of minutes they succeeded in herding on to the church forecourt some thirty of the inhabitants of Zardino. There was Absolom, keeper of the Lantern Tavern, with his two sons; there were the "consuls" holding office for that year (Benvenuto and Giacomo Ligrina); there were also a number of farmhands and day-labourers. And every one of them appealed to the clemency of Il Caccetta. "Be merciful. We've done you no harm. We are just poor worms. What do you expect from us?"

When he reckoned there were enough of them Il Caccetta made a sign to his men, who backed away and stood aside. He then addressed the peasants as follows:

"Do you know who I am? Do you recognize me?"

"We do," said Giacomo Ligrina, hat in hand like all the others. "You are the noble lord Giovan Battista Caccia, proprietor of the Castle of Briona and our overlord. Command us and we will obey."

Il Caccetta raised his left fist, with the thumb raised. He asked, "Do you know the meaning of this gesture?"

Nobody knew and nobody answered.

"I am the renowned He whom everyone calls Il Caccetta," he declared, "and if half the tales they tell about me in Milan and Novara had a word of truth in them I would be a cruel brute beast, addicted to bloodshed and every kind of excess, committing murder and arson and carrying off virgin girls. But as you can see, and as the proverb has it, the Devil is not so black as he is painted."

He stood up in his stirrups in a way that made Antonia think, "He fancies himself!" But it was only a fleeting moment. "Now clench your left fists as I am doing," he resumed at once, addressing the rustics. "Stick your thumbs up. Come right here to me, touch your thumbs to mine and cry aloud, 'Long live *Franza! Long live il Roi!*' Because your lord and master is Henri, *il Roi!*"

The horsemen of Il Caccetta's suite raised their plumed hats and flourished them above their heads, chanting in chorus: "Down with Spain! Up with *Franza!* Long live *il Roi!*" A few of them even fired their harquebuses into the air, and the echoes resounding among the houses made all the dogs in the village snarl and howl.

"Up with *Franza!* Long live *il Roi!*" yelled the peasants, though without much conviction.

"I am on my way to the city of Parma," Il Caccetta informed the inhabitants of Zardino. And he could well have regaled them with anything on earth, so strange and almost ludicrous was the fact that a feudal overlord should stop in a village and tell the yokels where he was going and why. "His Grace the Duke has summoned me," he continued, "and this means that great changes are in store for us – take heed! In a few months, a year at the most, I shall pass this way again, and all things will have changed, for over the castles in the lands of Milan and Novara will be flying the standard bearing the lily – the standard of *il Roi!*"

"Long live *il Roi!*" repeated the villagers as loud as they could. And it seemed to them they were getting off almost too lightly, for Il Caccetta to leave like this, without seizing any women or horses or burning down a single house. They reckoned that he had probably gone mad, and that they, at any rate, had had a great stroke of luck. As for *Franza*, and *il Roi*, they didn't care about them very much. In fact, if the truth be told, they cared not a hoot.

TWELVE

The Holy Bodies

IT WAS COLD and it was raining, that March day in the year of Our Lord 1603 when all the bells in the Flatlands began ringing out wildly, echoing from village to village for half an hour at a time, such as usually happened only on Easter morning; and all to tell the world these glad tidings: the Holy Bodies had at last arrived from Rome! Monsignor Cavagna had fulfilled the promise he had made the previous year, that he would bring to Novara enough Bodies of Holy Martyrs of the Faith and enough new Relics to equip every church in the diocese down to the most out-of-the-way parish. In Zardino Don Teresio nearly jumped out of his skin for joy. After pealing his bells far and wide until his hands were a mass of blisters he armed himself with a pilgrim's haversack, a heavy mantle with a leather hood and a pair of stout leather boots such as peasants wear for working in ditches, and thus accoutred set off for Novara, wading through all the mud, through the torrents, through the flooded canals along the way. He came back three days later – it was already Saturday – when many people in Zardino had begun to hope that he had drowned fording the Agogna and that the village was rid of him.

Quite the reverse: he was not only hail and hearty but beside himself with exultation, so happy and ebullient he appeared to be drunk. He sang as he strode along, he blessed every creature he came across, whether man or beast, he cried to the welkin the praises of the Lord. He carried his mantle rolled up under his arm, for in the meantime the rain had stopped and the skies were clearing. The huge grey clouds which had weighed upon the Flatlands without a break the whole week long were thinning out, rising until they revealed the distant mountains, opening up in gashes of deep blue, almost navy, above a landscape sodden and steaming as it started to bask once more in the spring sunshine. He went straight home to change his clothing and then, swinging the handbell he used to signal his movements from one farmyard to the next, he set out to make the round of the houses and inform the people of Zardino of the grandiose and miraculous events which had occurred during those days in Novara, destined to transform their city into a mighty centre of the Faith and of piety, second in importance only to Rome herself! The Holy Bodies, reported Don Teresio, had arrived at San Martino del Basto, at the Milan end of the ferry across the river Ticino, the previous Monday. And they came directly from Rome, and from the Catacombs! They filled the whole of a six-wheeled wagon, piled high with Bodies and Relics which Monsignor Giovan Battista Cavagna of Momo had personally, and with his own hands, dug out from recently-discovered Catacombs, and brought to Novara and to the people of Novara. Including, need he add, the outlying districts. Including Zardino!

"Yea, dear brethren," whispered Don Teresio to the yokels gawping open-mouthed at him, "It is all but sure: even we shall receive a Holy Body! An entire Body! It is too wondrous for words!" The wagon, continued Don Teresio, had for two days halted at San Martino to enable Bishop Bascapè's vicar-general, Monsignor Orazio Besozzi, to arrive and take delivery of it on behalf of the bishop, and for the faithful in countryside and town to organize along the route the most grandiose celebrations ever seen in this part of the State of Milan.

And so it came to pass. On the Wednesday, another day of torrential rain, the wagon at last started rolling again and arrived at Novara flanked by cheering crowds. At various places along its route prodigious events had occurred: a woman so doubled up with arthritis that her nose was level with her knees had suddenly stood bolt-upright, a man born dumb had spoken, an infidel had been converted, prostrating himself in the mud before the reliquary wagon, and had been lifted up and consoled by Monsignor Cavagna in person, who had heard his first confession and then baptized him, utilizing a few drops of rain fallen direct from heaven into the hollow of his hand. "And if these are not miracles," cried Don Teresio, raising a forefinger, "then I don't know a miracle when I see one, and have studied to no purpose, and am not a priest!" Of course, they must needs wait for the Church's confirmation before calling these prodigies miracles, and that would take time. But he, as a witness, already felt himself justified in narrating them.

Darkness was falling when the wagon bearing the Holy Bodies came within sight of Novara, and the walls of the city were seen from afar to be all lit up, despite the rain, "like the walls of Sion". Monsignor Carlo Bascapè issued forth from the Cathedral to meet the cart, sheltered by a canopy borne by seminary students and preceded by an awe-inspiring procession of canons, clergy, noblemen and religious confraternities. Never within living memory had Novara witnessed such a dazzling celebration, or in fouler weather! Triumphal arches made of painted wood (which unfortunately the rain had reduced to rack and ruin in a few hours) had been erected at all the gates of the city, the most magnificent being outside Porta Sant'Agabio, through which the cart was expected to pass. Fruit and flowers, such as the season permitted, had been strewn on the ground along the entire route, right up to the door of the Cathedral. Not a balcony without some sort of banner, not a window without some kind of lamp! The wagon had then been hauled into the Cathedral itself, directly in front of the High Altar (not by horses, because it is illicit for animals to cross the threshold of the House of God, but by faithful parishioners). And there it was locked in, waiting to be dis-burdened of its priceless load. Many of the faithful, Don Teresio amongst them, elected not to return home but to pass that night, and also the following night, sleeping or keeping prayerful vigil on the bare stone of the Cathedral steps or even on the cobbles of the piazza, beneath the portico which since time immemorial had been known – and never was name more appropriate and well-founded! – as the Portico of Paradise. Without feeling the least chill (swore Don Teresio, hand upon heart and riveting his blue-eyed gaze upon his listeners), because the very stone radiated such warmth, and so great a sense of peace and beatitude, that he had never in his life felt so well and so warm. Not even in his own bed in Zardino, beneath the huge goose-feather eiderdown that sheltered him from the frost on wintry nights . . .

The yokels hearkened, astonished and incredulous. Someone even suggested to Don Teresio that he should sit himself down and drink something restorative. He must be a weary-bones after all that rain, those nights spent sleeping on the stones, and trudging all that way through the mud! Perhaps he hadn't eaten? "Would you partake of something?" they asked. "Or have you had a bite?"

"No. Many thanks, but no," replied Don Teresio. "I am here to perform the Sunday Offices. But I can scarcely wait to return to Novara to beseech the bishop himself and Monsignor Cavagna for our share of the Relics for Zardino – a Holy Body!"

He raised his arms to heaven and widened his eyes to underline the immensity of such a request. He fell silent for a moment; then he said: "I realize, of course, that all this will need money; but with the aid of Divine Providence, and of all of you, we shall succeed in finding it." At which point the yokels felt their blood run cold, and either said no more or strolled away thinking: we should have known from the start that he was out for money! You just couldn't go wrong with Don Teresio: the words might change but it was always the same old story – "money money money". Whatever the location of that Paradise he spoke of every Sunday and every other day of the week, the road to get there was cobbled with coinage, and the more you gave the more comfortable your ride would be, maybe even in a carriage . . . Money money money: part exacted as dues, part solicited as voluntary donations, and part given to expiate some sin and save your soul. Copper coins, silver coins, alloy coins, gold coins . . . Since this new priest had arrived in Zardino, thought the peasants, it was as if the Good Lord had opened a bank in the middle of the village to rake in money on everything: on births, on deaths, on rainfall, on sunshine, on wheat, on beans, on maize . . .

While in Zardino people were defending themselves as best they could against Don Teresio and his money-grubbing, the high society of Novara, following the arrival of the Relics, was busy applauding a new hero, the same Monsignor Giovan Battista Cavagna da Momo who first appeared in the story of Antonia when she was still at San Michele and the nuns bullied her into reciting the verses of welcome to the bishop. The "goose whiter than butter" . . . How much headway in the world, with the help of God and God's representatives on earth (i.e. his religious superiors) had Monsignor Cavagna made since then! Headway in the career sense of the word, and real headway at that, first in Milan, where Bishop Bascapè occasionally sent him with letters and confidential messages to Cardinal Federigo Borromeo, and later in Rome, where he now resided, officially as secretary to Cardinal Gerolamo Mattei, but in fact as the right-hand man of the Bishop of Novara in the capital city of Christianity – a pair of eyes, a pair of ears, stationed near the papal Court to record the most privy of whisperings, the most secret of trends. It was very important and confidential in the extreme, this task which Bascapè had entrusted to the goose whiter than butter. Moreover the fact that for such a task he had chosen Monsignor Cavagna and no other signified, above all, that he considered him a faithful servitor of God and of his bishop, and equipped, what is more, with both merits and defects which rendered him especially qualified to live and operate in the City of the Popes. Cavagna's defects, according to Bascapè, were poking his nose into other people's business, a weakness for gossip and society life, gluttony, and lack of imagination. On the other hand, his merits included a stolid temperament and the lack of any ambition.

But on this last score Bascapè was mistaken. Cavagna was ambitious, as everyone is; he was merely ambitious in his own way and not in that of the bishop. Moreover he had in his character an element of gullibility which the bishop under-estimated. Given his scant propensity towards great flights of thought, and his scant aptitude for being overawed, Rome neither intimidated nor excited him. His curiosity, on the other hand, was aroused by certain traffickings going on around the basilicas outside the walls and the burial-grounds annexed to them, which at the time we speak of stirred the same greed and the same self-seeking as in other parts of the planet were stirred by gold. Adventurers, intriguing women, corrupt ecclesiastics . . . In fact, on account of the thriving trade carried on therein, the Relics and so-called Holy Bodies were a precious mineral, the only one existing in the sub-soil of Rome. Certain notions therefore started to gyrate in the head of Monsignor Giovan Battista Cavagna, and space in that head was found for certain rumours going the rounds of the drawing-rooms and the sacristies, concerning certain "bargains": the Holy Body of a martyr by the horrendous name of Gerund, duly authenticated and crated up, was available for only a hundred *giulii*, the equivalent of scarcely more than fifty Milanese *lire*; another Body, that of one Simplicius of Edessa, could be had for a mere ten *scudi* . . . Stupendous deals, unique offers, available only to those resident at the papal Court, or in its immediate vicinity.

What was to be done? Our good Cavagna discussed the matter with his bishop, giving him names, references, guarantees, and asking the bishop to authorize him to negotiate and acquire Holy Bodies for the churches of Novara and diocese whenever a good bargain presented itself. If one was to rekindle the flame of the Faith from the embers of apathy and indifference, then the moment – he declared – was propitious: it was now or never! Those Catacombs lay open for the taking, mines rich in treasures which would travel the world over and, with the fortifying presence of the martyrs, enliven and revive that sacred fire which in certain parts of Europe threatened to die out altogether, or was already dead, stifled by the ashes of heresy. He, Cavagna, begged only this privilege: to be able to give his life and strength so that Novara, of all the holy dioceses that constituted the Christian world, might be a little better defended than others from the assaults of the Devil, a little closer to God than others, a little holier than others. The bishop, after some indecision, gave his consent. And lo!, the results . . .

For some days in that month of March in the year of Our Lord 1603 Monsignor Cavagna, the goose whiter than butter, was the personage on everybody's lips in Novara, the hero of high society and the withdrawing-rooms, fiercely contested for by the ladies of the local aristocracy, who stuffed him with *gratòn* (scraps of crisped goose fat), with *fideghin* (miniature pig's-liver salami), with "nun's biscuits", while they listened ecstatically to his tales of marvellous adventures in the Catacombs, into which he had descended ("At the risk of his life!", whispered the ladies, between bewilderment and incredulity) in order to assure Novara of that profusion of booty which he had in fact succeeded in delivering: a wagonload of Relics! The Holy Bodies, said the ladies, unlike the relics of the previous year, had not been bought on the open market, where you only had to have money to get all the Bodies you wanted. No sir! These were bodies that no one knew were there, or where they were. They had to be dug out from the earth as truffles are dug for, and Canon Cavagna, big and fat and no longer young as he was, had transformed himself into a kind of truffle-hound, making his way along underground passages so cramped that he had to go on all fours, or even stretched full length and edging himself forward with his elbows, in places where everything might cave in: one sneeze and the world would fall on his head! Impossible to breathe – the place was airless! He was upheld, was Cavagna, solely by Faith and the silent appeal of those Bodies calling to him in the darkness, "Cavagna! This way! Do you hear us? We are over here!" All at the risk of becoming a holy martyr of the Faith himself – a thing very far from impossible, down there at a depth of fifty arm's-lengths – but never feared by him; indeed, devoutly yearned for. The heroic monsignor, murmured the ladies, in the bottom of his heart sought precisely that death, which would have enabled him to remain down there for ever in the company of the Martyrs! He had said this himself in the drawing-room of one of their number, while pouring himself a glass of a pungent, sparkling wine from the hills of Fara, or perhaps of Sizzano. He had paused with the bottle in mid-air and wondered out loud: "What better end could a Christian hope for, than to die in the Catacombs?"

The ladies went into raptures: "Monsignor, don't stand on ceremony . . . Another piece of *gratòn*? . . . We know you like it!" Or, "Do taste this white wine from Barengo. It's made by my father-in-law!" They enquired, "Could you see anything down there under the earth? Was it completely dark?"

"As at the bottom of a well," Monsignor Cavagna assured them, while introducing, with finger and thumb, one *gratòn* after another into a little mouth that turned heart-shaped to receive them. "When one is down there," he explained, "one lights one's way with tiny lanterns similar in all respects to those to be found in the tombs of the Martyrs. And if the oil spills, you're done for! You're in the dark!"

"Would you care for a little of this nut paste?" said the ladies.

124

"We made it yesterday." And, "Do eat a couple more 'Nun's biscuits'! They give you strength. Or a piece of cake . . . Don't wait to be asked!"

They drank his health: "To your next exploit in the Catacombs! To your next exploration!" And they promised him, "We will pray to God for you! We will invoke His aid!"

So passed a week. One Tuesday – we are already in the month of April – through Porta Sant'Agabio at Novara (coming, that is, from the road to Milan) there entered a mysterious personage who was observed by no one. He was travelling in a litter bearing no insignia, probably hired at the previous staging-post, with curtains drawn and windows closed. He was escorted by two bearded gentlemen whom no one in Novara had ever had occasion to set eyes on before, and by six horsemen complete with helmet and cuirass, with uniforms of vertical blue and white stripes. Those who knew about men at arms and armies said that they were Swiss, the famous "soldiers of the Pope".

The arrival of this mysterious personage caused a great pother. The traffic at Porta Sant'Agabio came to a halt, while there was an agitated exchange of messages between the gate and the castle; whence, a few minutes later, arrived a Spanish officer who personally escorted the stranger – who according to rumours later circulating in the city must have been a deputy of the Fiscal Procurator, which is to say the Minister of Justice in the Papal States – into the bishop's palace, together with his escort. And there, as far as our story is concerned, all trace of the illustrious personage is lost. Public report, which recorded his arrival, thereafter neglected to register his departure, which took place some time during the next few days, without any stir and probably in the first light of dawn. It did, however, concern itself with the consequences of his visit to Novara, which were immediate and immense. The following day, without any explanation or apparent reason, all the decorations vanished from the streets and the churches, and the Holy Bodies from the Cathedral. Also vanished was Monsignor Cavagna, without anyone knowing what had become of him. Some mishap? Some sudden illness? Those who came to the Curia to pull strings and wangle Holy Bodies for their churches – as did Don Teresio from

Zardino, and other priests from even further away, from the Valsesia, or Val d'Ossola, or the valleys opening onto the shores of Lake Maggiore – received disarming replies, such as: "Bodies? To which Bodies are you referring?" Or else they were asked to come back some other day because, as was explained by the monsignor to whom they had applied, "I know nothing about this whole business, and the person who does know something about it isn't here just now."

The truth began to filter out and make headway over the next few days and weeks, in scraps of information and unconfirmed rumours that little by little received confirmation, grew in strength, became certainties . . . And it was a tale to take your breath away! It was all a swindle! Cavagna's Holy Bodies and Relics – nothing but dogs' bones! Or, at the very best, human bones from any one of the cemetries around Rome – certainly not the bones of Saints! The bishop, the authorities, the entire city, had been the victims of a swindle, and a swindle so great, so infamous, that even the quips and japes of the roisterers and the inevitable witticisms put into circulation by the usual unbelievers scarcely raised a laugh. On the contrary, people fell to thinking. An enormous fraud, yes; but the more the matter came to light the more impossible it seemed that the person who had contrived it and carried it through was that very Monsignor Cavagna who (as everyone knew by now) was in prison, incarcerated by the order of the Fiscal Procurator, i.e. of the Pope, for having fabricated and fobbed off false Relics, defrauding his superiors and all the various religious and civil authorities responsible for superintending such matters both in Novara and in Rome. As much as to say that half the world had been hoodwinked by Cavagna! Perhaps in Rome such a thing might seem credible, but in Novara, no! Here Cavagna, Bishop Bascapè's goose whiter than butter, was well-known for his gluttony, for his vanity, and also for the gullibility which rendered him incapable of hoodwinking anyone at all. It was therefore clear from the very start that the first victim of the intrigue was Cavagna himself. A predestined victim, a prodigious numskull. "Someone" had got him into the Catacombs, given him a wagonload of trash telling him that these were Relics, and packed him off back to his home town well knowing how he

126

would be fêted; "someone" had given the bishop, and all the faithful in the diocese, time to make much of him . . . then he had unmasked him.

To what end had all this been done? Not for profit, thought the people of Novara. In the whole business very little cash had changed hands, and in any case one thing was certain: that unlike the specimens of the previous year, which were few, and bizarre, and paid for so much each, Cavagna's Relics had been, so to speak, a job lot, and acquired at a very modest price. Having reached this point in the argument the Novaresi asked themselves who had wished to exploit Cavagna in order to humiliate Bishop Bascapè? To humiliate the city of Novara! And even if they cared little or nothing for Monsignor Cavagna, and even less for Bishop Bascapè, they were intolerably affronted by the other fact of the matter: that "someone" – too powerful even to name! – had exploited them without the least regard for them or their feelings, as you use a stick to beat a person with. They felt humiliated, and reacted in the only way they were allowed to. By shaking their heads. By muttering. Cavagna's Relics, they said, were certainly no less authentic and plausible than many others in circulation in many other towns: Fragments of the True Cross, Holy Winding-Sheets, Holy Nails, Bodies of Martyrs or Fragments of same, which if their authenticity were gone into might well have a few surprises in store, and give rise to some comic tales to make the whole world laugh. But those Relics were religiously preserved in the churches, were displayed to the faithful, and it had never occurred to anyone to question them. True or false as they might be, authentic was the cult devoted to them. Therefore, asked many Novaresi, why were they alone forbidden to venerate Cavagna's Relics, welcomed to their city with public jubilation, for the sole reason that they were not authentic? Why, in the sight of God, was their credulity worth less than the credulity of others? For what reason had they been duped?

THIRTEEN

Rome

WHEN CAVAGNA LEFT the bishop's chamber, bowed and tottering, flanked by guards, Monsignor Carlo Bascapè stood motionless for several minutes, staring into space, his lips moving without emitting a sound. Then he put his head in his hands and went and sat down. There it was then – at last he knew the whole story! Now he understood all! He shifted the silver crucifix he kept in the centre of the table and replaced it by the death-mask of his friend and master Carlo Borromeo, as he did whenever he felt stricken, or had an important decision to take. What would Carlo Borromeo have done in his place? He passed his fingers lightly over those features: the broad and lofty brow, the prominent nose which had been the most marked feature of that gaunt, aquiline face . . . It was a wax mask, taken immediately after the death of the Archbishop of Milan with a view to casting a bronze bust from it; but that would have meant melting the wax, whereas Bascapè had been eager to keep it thus, in remembrance of his friend. In metal, he said, all faces are alike: impassive, hard, inhuman. Only wax, with a softness and warmth so similar to the softness and warmth of flesh, could, by moulding its lineaments, restore for him something of the life and spirit expressed in that belovèd face. Besides, the bishop asked himself, what matter is man made of, if not wax in the hands of God?

After some reflection, he gave himself an answer. This was, that whatever Carlo Borromeo might have done in such circumstances he, Bascapè, was no longer in a position to do. Times had changed, people had changed, the very century had changed and was, if possible, worse than the one already so godless, so addicted to every kind of vice, against which the Blessed Carlo had taken up arms. The stakes continued to rise, and would rise still higher.

To how many further trials, and how ferocious, would God subject his children before He consummated the triumph of his cause? It was war, thought Bishop Bascapè, out-and-out war, waged now for more than twenty years, within the Church and for the Church's sake! And although it was a certainty that in the end the winner would be God, far less certain was victory for one fighting at that moment, in the front line, that the Church of Christ and of the Apostles might rise once more above the squalors of the world . . . On the contrary, it was possible to succumb! He, Bascapè, was even then succumbing. The enemy was everywhere, outside the Church and within it, in Novara, in Rome . . .

He rose to his feet again; he paced the room. Now he knew! Cavagna's narrative, though interrupted by groans, sobs and sudden floorward dives to kiss his bishop's feet, had been as clear as daylight; nor, come to that, were the facts very complicated. What emerged, when touched up and corrected, was a seventeenth-century version of a Boccaccio story, the one about the fat-headed Calandrino who allows himself to be duped by Bruno and Buffalmacco, his two more astute cronies. In Cavagna's case the cronies had been one Giovanangelo Santini, a Roman painter, and a Novarese priest resident in Rome by the name of Flaminio Casella. The story had thereafter evolved as follows. Casella introduced Santini to Cavagna, and this Santini (who by all accounts was less than mediocre as an artist but well-considered by Cardinal Bellarmino and with many contacts at the papal Court) dangled the most astonishing and hitherto unthought-of prospects before the eyes of the goose whiter than butter. Would he – enquired Santini of poor Cavagna – be willing to be lowered into the Catacombs known as those of "Santa Priscilla" and take possession of the Holy Bodies with his own hands? If so, the thing could be arranged. Since he, Cavagna, and his bishop, were so eager to have these Bodies, it was only right to provide them, in the simplest possible way and without charging overmuch.

At first Cavagna was in two minds about accepting the offer, largely (according to his own account) because he was frightened at the prospect of having to descend into the bowels of the earth himself, at his age and with his physique. But later he allowed himself to be talked over. With small trouble and little outlay, Santini assured him, he would accomplish a memorable feat, he would earn the gratitude of his bishop and all the faithful of Novara, and he would become a great benefactor of his diocese, loved and remembered in centuries to come. Why dally? What was he waiting for? He, Santini, was in possession of a special pass, signed by the Cardinal Prefect of the Catacombs in person, which enabled him to enter the diggings to make copies of frescoes and remain there as long as was required for the exercise of his art. He would take Cavagna along with him, and ask nothing for it, not a penny. He would do it as a personal favour to a friend; and, as we know, in matters of friendship money plays no part. Once down there, of course, it would be necessary to disburse a few *scudi* to buy the silence and collaboration of a guide and three or four *tombaroli* (grave robbers). That was essential, indeed indispensable, because in the Catacombs no one can find their way on their own, least of all in the unexplored parts, where the Bodies lie. However, the painter assured him that this would be a negligible sum, truly derisory compared with the market value of the Bodies and Relics which Cavagna would discover down there.

The goose whiter than butter swallowed the bait. Thus began those descents into the unknown for which poor Cavagna, in a sling such as they use for unloading donkeys from ships, was lowered by winches and pulleys into fathomless shafts, at the bottom of which he found what Santini, especially for his benefit and using other, far easier means of access, had placed there the day before: ampullae full of Precious Blood, the remains of Saints torn to pieces by wild beasts, with the names of each martyr carefully engraved in the rock, enough whole Bodies to load a wagon with and, near the Bodies, a mass of lesser Relics such as Pieces of the True Cross, Holy Rings, Holy Fragments of Clothing and so on – sufficient to the needs of a diocese and maybe some to spare.

But after the triumphant outcome of those first expeditions things underwent a certain change. This perfidious Santini, to forestall any possible doubts on the part of Cavagna, whose suspicions might be aroused if he found the task too easy (and also perhaps to have a laugh behind his back), began to prostrate his victim with a series of unsuccessful expeditions. The workmen trumped things up to seem as if the rope had snapped, so that the goose whiter than butter, after plummeting down for some yards, found himself for a couple of hours at the bottom of a shaft in the cold, in the dark, and without any communication with a living soul. When his torturers finally decided to haul him out poor Cavagna had to be taken home on a stretcher, being unable to hold himself upright, even seated in a litter. He was ill (pneumonia?) for over a month, during which time the two cronies, Santini and Casella, put the finishing touches to their ruse by bringing to his bedside a false notary who had inventoried and authenticated all the Relics, and then procured him a permit (also false) for the Relics to leave Rome. They hired a six-wheeled wagon good for every kind of road – the "Juggernaut" of the time – and while by now half Rome, or the whole of it, was laughing openly at the credulity of this country bumpkin of a monsignor, who had the brains and the gait of a goose, and imagined he could roam around in the Catacombs without attracting the attention of the custodians, and the Prefect, and the chief of police, orders arrived from the papal Court not to interfere . . .

Why? the bishop asked himself, twisting the crucifix on his breast between his fingers. Why had Cavagna not been arrested at the gates of Rome, seeing that his documents were false and even the identity of the forger was common knowledge? Why were Santini and Casella at liberty, and no one levelling an accusation at them? Why, finally – and his eyes at this point filled with tears – had God willed the election as his Vicar on earth of that icy-hearted, stony, callous man who had taken the name of Clement VIII? What was the meaning of it all: Why did such monstrous things happen? Like Christ on the cross he cried aloud to the Father, "My God, my God, why hast thou forsaken me?"

He went to the window, opened it, rested his hands on the stone sill. His eyes roamed the humble rooftops of Novara, its modest bell-towers, its castle, and beyond the massive bulk of the castle the meadows, the woods, the horizon veiled in mist . . . That landscape, its hazy flatness, always cast a shadow over the bishop's thoughts, but on that day in April in the year of Our Lord 1603

Bascapè paid no attention to what he saw from the window: he was thinking of the Pope. Yes! He had known him before he ascended the throne of St Peter, as Cardinal Ippolito Aldo-brandini. In Rome in 1590 he had had occasion to meet him and also, to his misfortune, to clash with that arrogant, over-bearing man of abrupt, brusque ways, who considered Pope Gregory XIV's Milanese counsellors no better than heretics, and refused to hear about the reform of the clergy, the renaissance of the faith and of the Church, the *Holy* Church . . . Blasphemies! – said Cardinal Aldobrandini – The Church was already holy in the form it had acquired over the centuries, and was above dispute. To speak of improving it and adapting it to the times meant placing oneself *de facto* on the side of the Protestants and heretics. Moreover, he added in peremptory tones, false influences and false interpretations of the Council of Trent had led to unhealthy zeal which had to be disciplined and castigated, lest they produce hysterical mysticism and vacuous and theatrical cravings for sanctity . . . Certain persons, such as the late archbishop of Milan, Carlo Borromeo, had done almost as much damage to the Church as Luther and Melanchthon . . . But one day, when arguments of this kind were being bandied in the presence of the then Pope, Bascapè had rebelled. "It is my hope," he said to Cardinal Aldobrandini, his face pale with rage and sometimes a tremble in his voice, "that your lordship will be able to make such progress in true sanctity as in his lifetime did the cardinal of Santa Prassede (i.e. Carlo Borromeo), whose name, quite erroneously, has been linked by your lordship with those of the princes of heresy and the enemies of the Church, whereas Carlo was the prince of pastors and preachers of the true Faith."

The cardinal made no reply at the time; but shortly afterwards, when Gregory XIV died and he himself, Ippolito Aldobrandini, was elected Pope, he took his revenge on Bascapè. He despatched him to Novara, to become entangled in the massive problems of a minuscule diocese – and all might have been well if it had stopped there! Bascapè could have contented himself with being left where he was, on the fringe of the world, to work as a humble labourer in the vineyard of the Lord (as the Gospels put it) forgotten by Rome. But no. Year after year, season after season since Bascapè had come to Novara, scarcely a day had passed without his receiving from the papal Court some tangible sign that in Rome they had *not* forgotten him. Some small act of spite, some discourtesy, some obstacle put in his way . . . But this affair of Cavagna and the Relics was more than spite: it was infamy! They were out to discredit him in the eyes of his own flock, to cover him with ridicule . . .

"Who knows what wagging tongues are saying about it at the moment," said Bishop Bascapè out loud, "in the Vatican and elsewhere, all over Rome in fact . . . And in Milan! Who knows what has been reported to Cardinal Federigo Borromeo! And here in Novara what are people saying? What are the clergy thinking? . . ."

He felt a chill and closed the window. Perhaps he was feverish . . . He touched his forehead. Returning to the table, he opened a drawer and took out a small metal phial containing smelling salts. He breathed in deeply, first through one nostril and then the other, repeating the operation twice again. He replaced the phial in the drawer; he sat down. "Novara!" he sighed; and in that one bare word, and in the way Bascapè uttered it, was all the torment of a lifetime, condemnation and deliverance, the immolation of himself to God. Had he been able to choose his own destiny, Bascapè would certainly not have come to Novara even to be buried, no, not even for a day; but, since God had sent him there, he now loved his diocese with absolute dedication of himself and all his strength. Only, at certain times he felt his strength unequal to that enormous undertaking.

His thoughts turned back to Rome. He uttered the word "Rome!", and the wrinkles on his brow smoothed out and his eyes grew wide with the memory, the dream. Once more in his mind's eye he beheld the bridges, the river, the Porta Castello outside Castel Sant'Angelo, the Banks near the Tiber, the Pantheon, the piazzas . . . Once more he beheld the clear light of Rome, the immensity of Rome, the ruins of Rome, the landscape of Rome, and once more felt that strange allurement – love at first sight, almost a physical attraction – that he had experienced the first time he set foot there; he as a Milanese full of age-old prejudices against the ancient capital of the Empire, the city where no one does a job of work and everyone plots, traffics and lives from hand to mouth. But Rome, against all odds, had swathed him in her rarefied air, in her infinite history, her immense spaces; she had instilled in him a pleasure in being and feeling alive, a sprightliness of thought and of action, which thitherto he had never experienced in any place. She had entered into his bloodstream and his way of thinking, and had whispered in his ear, "Stay with me! One day you will be Bishop of Rome!" He had tried to close his ears to that voice, had always behaved as if it did not exist. The voice, however, persisted in existing . . .

He raised a hand before his face and fluttered it as if to drive away an insect, though in fact he hoped to drive away that thought, deep in him like a death-watch beetle deep in timber . . . Even when asleep, or busy with other matters, he had that gnawing death-watch at the back of his mind; both day and night it ceased not. At times he had just dropped off when that beetle jerked him back awake, bolt upright in bed, breathless as if he had run for miles, and streaming sweat. Then, if it was winter, Bascapè would throw a blanket round his shoulders, or if it was summer wrap himself in a sheet, hasten to the chapel of the bishop's palace, throw himself to the ground. He would sob, he would beat his breast: "Lord, forgive me! Have mercy upon me, O my God! Take no heed of my thoughts, they are not mine! It is the Devil tempting me. Help me to drive him out!"

He gripped his head between his two hands. His temples were throbbing and he thought with terror that he might have a return of the migraine, the most atrocious of his "Novara" maladies, attributed by the doctors to the vapours rising from the paddy-fields, the unhealthy climate, and the reverberations of Monte Rosa and its glaciers, which they said were the largest in the world. Before coming to Novara Bascapè had never suffered from migraine . . . His thoughts slid back in time and returned to Rome. There, in the House of the Barnabite Fathers where he had lived, was a spacious terrace overlooking the roofs and the domes of Trastevere, and there one could sit even in winter, when it was sunny, reading, studying, discussing theological matters . . . Then, in the spring, out through the walls at Campo Santo or Castel Sant'Angelo, to wander to the Isola Tiberina or towards the

Colosseum, in a cloud of almond, peach or cherry blossoms, among the ruins of temples and the gardens of the dead city, and the shanties more like sheds for livestock than human dwellings. There, amid those shanties, you still met shepherds with leather-thonged sandals carrying a lamb slung about their shoulders as the Good Shepherd did in the earliest Christian portrayals of him; and everywhere reigned a sea-breeze that stimulated and aroused you and made you feel hale and hearty: the *ponentino!*

Should you walk further you ended up lunching at one of the old hostelries outside the city walls, where you sat at long long tables with a horde of people, all of them strangers to one another: monsignors and pottery pedlars, pilgrims and abbesses, bishops and wagoners, highwaymen and painters and minstrels all jostled together elbow to elbow without a trace of embarrassment or irritation. And even if a cardinal had turned up, or come to that the Pope in person, the pot-boy would still have rattled off, among the dishes of the day, *cazzetti d'Angelo* and *zinne di Sant'Orsola, conjoni der Papa Re* and *pagliata dell'Agnusdei,* just as he had done with the rest of the customers. Then, having eaten your fill, the house would offer you a glass of **vin santo or of *lagrima Christi* in which to drink a toast to ***la faccaccia* or to *li mortacci* of anyone who happened to have his knife into you . . . These things, thought Bascapè, happened in Rome and could not have happened in any other part of the world. Only in that place consecrated by the millennia can all that has been and will be live cheek by jowl with all that is: both the high and the low, the old and the new, religion and profanity, pomp and poverty, even God and the Devil seemed to have found a solid and enduring equilibrium in that city where everything has already happened – and not only once, either! A thousand times! And thus it was also in those hostelries tucked away in the Roman *campagna,* along the old brigand-infested Roman roads, where at every step you might have your throat cut for the small change in your pocket. And there you sat

---

* The menu included: "angels' cocks", "St Ursula's tits", "Pope's bollocks" and "Lamb-of-God's offal".
** lit. "holy wine", "tears of Christ".
*** lit. "ugly mug", "rotten dead".

under the pergola and the strolling minstrels came with their lutes to sing *stornelli* in praise of love, or the Virgin's eyes, springtime or the *ponentino*. And there it was Rome, just as it was Rome in the cloud of incense and the thunder of Gregorian chants that shook the columns of the new basilica of St Peter's, the centre of the world, God's antechamber . . .

Bishop Bascapè's thoughts once again took a gloomy turn. For centuries, for millennia – thought the bishop – the city of Rome had been blissful in her sunlight, in her history, in her aromas of roast lamb and rosemary, and it seemed that nothing in the world, or almost nothing, could scandalize her. But one fine day there arrived on the banks of the Tiber a country priest, as big and fat as a goose and uncouth even in name (*cavagna* in Novarese dialect means a wicker basket), and Rome and the Pope had discovered . . . they had discovered that there were such things as false Relics and, to crown the scandal, that the Bishop of Novara was making a corner in them!

He got to his feet. He resumed his pacing back and forth, twisting the crucifix in his fingers. It was unjust, he thought, for the goose whiter than butter to undergo imprisonment. Cavagna would be sufficiently punished for his guilt, and above all for his ingenuousness, by the shame he now suffered and the discredit he would never slough off as long as he lived. As for false Relics, it was certainly not he who had invented such things, any more than had the men who duped him: they were part of the Church of that epoch and of the Roman way of life. The city of the Popes, even during the years when Bascapè lived there, was a foul though flourishing market in Holy Bodies, Holy Limbs, Holy Splinters, Holy Fragments, Holy Nails from the Cross and other such swindles which fed, and indeed fattened, an alimentary chain leading from the grave-robbers to the monsignors who (for a consideration) authenticated them; from the middlemen who procured the clientele to the notary who drew up the bill of sale, and thence on up to the Cardinal Prefect of the Catacombs himself. Into that free market which no Roman pontiff – not even Pope Gregory or Pope Sixtus –had ever seriously thought of suppressing, since it put food into the mouths of half of Rome, the cynicism and shrewdness of the Roman plebs succeeded in introducing unique relics, mostly destined for foreigners and especially for the French, who at that time and for some reason never sufficiently elucidated were considered more stupid even than the Milanese and the Germans – out-and-out boobies, in fact! The whole of Rome had had a good laugh over one Santa Mentula and one San Cunno (Latin names for the genital organs, respectively male and female) said to have been embarked at Ostia en route for Brittany; and this while Bascapè was still at the Court of Pope Gregory. The *Bargello* (police chief) had even set up an inquiry, but it led to no discovery of illicit dealings. Perhaps, in that particular case, it really had been a matter of a joke in dubious taste that, passing from mouth to mouth, acquired such numerous and specific details as to appear to be the truth; but the mere fact that it was taken seriously, and made the object of an investigation, was extremely revealing.

Be that as it may, the business dealings of those years, and of Rome as it then was, were actual and substantial: the frauds, the murders, the concealment of corpses ancient and modern, everything that occurred at that time around the Catacombs and the earliest martyrs of the Christian faith – not to mention the love affairs, the adventures, the fortunes made over-night . . . Material which, had it been possible to record it with impunity might perhaps have produced a new literary genre, a whole new literature, with its great writers and its immortal works. Never, in fact, in the thousands of years of the history of Rome and the world at large, had the dead and buried been more alive than in those first years of the seventeenth century, and never had their affairs been more closely interwoven with those of the living . . .

On the table stood a small silver bell. Bascapè picked it up and shook it two or three times. A door opened and in came a redheaded stripling of a priest, hands clasped on his breast. He bowed.

"Give orders downstairs," said Bascapè, "for Monsignor Cavagna to be released and to return to his home-town, to Momo or wherever he lives, and not to stir from there. When this business of the Relics is over and done with I will see to it in person that he is recalled to Novara."

FOURTEEN

Biagio

ANTONIA DEVELOPED SWIFTLY and, from what we may
gather from the records of her trial, she developed well: too much
so indeed for her social status and the tastes of the time. In the
unanimous recognition of Antonia's beauty on the part of the
Inquisitor, the judges, her fellow villagers and all who spoke at the
trial we almost seem to detect some uneasiness, or some indignation as in the presence of a guilty act: as a girl "of the people", and a
foundling into the bargain (this is what all the above seemed in
substance to be asking themselves), what right had she to be so
beautiful? Did beauty so excessive and ill- bestowed not imply
some scandalous and diabolical component, to wit, the ever-
recurring flatteries of the Old Tempter of mankind manifested *"in
the small mole, or birth mark, situated at the left side of the upper lip"*, in
the *"flowing gait"*, in the harmony of form in her face and her
whole person? For this reason Inquisitor Manini, at the conclusion
of the trial, began his final speech for the prosecution with
quotations from the Book of Proverbs (*"Exaltatio oculorum est
lucerna impiorum peccatorum"*: all that is too pleasing to our eye
induces in us sins of impiety); and also from a Pagan author,
Juvenal, who in one of his celebrated *Satires* wrote *"rara est adeo
concordia formae atque pudicitae"*, i.e. beauty and virtue rarely agree
together. As he proceeded with his oration the Inquisitor further
developed the theme of the unnatural character of Antonia's
beauty; which, if it were not the work of the Devil, he said, would
never have been able to flourish in regions "where the waters of
the paddy-fields stagnate, and the pestiferous miasma of the same
poison the air, causing the men to fall sick and the women to
languish, and even the children; so that anyone having a mind to
travel about those regions on the banks of the river Sesia must

encounter, in the people who dwell there, unmistakable examples of human degradation – yellow faces, eyes bright with fever, prominent bellies, precocious aging!"

These words of the Inquisitor's are translated from Latin, because in the records of Antonia's trial only the interrogations of the accused and of the witnesses are written in the vulgar tongue. As to their import, it must be said that the picture which emerges, concerning the miseries of the Flatlands, is without doubt exaggerated. Conditions in the plains of Novara at the beginning of the seventeenth century were not so catastrophic as Manini makes out. Indeed they were not much different from those in other country districts of Lombardy and Italy in general. In the hills, round the lakes, up in the mountains, work in the fields was everywhere gruelling; and everywhere the peasants looked prematurely aged, and there were cases of tuberculosis due to the hardships of the environment and the milk of infected cattle, and also of other diseases such as pellagra and malaria. But ricegrowing had many enemies, especially in the cities, and there was a strong prejudice circulating – which, to judge by his words, Manini shared – imputing to the Flatlands all the infirmities and degeneracies brought on mankind by unwholesome customs and unhealthy surroundings, and depicting their inhabitants as monsters; whereas, on the contrary, the Alpine valleys – riddled with consumption, rickets, goitre and cretinism – were exalted for the salubrity of the air, the excellence of the water and the quality of life. (And praise should also have been bestowed on the beauty of the women, if the Inquisitor's reasoning had had any basis of truth to it. But it appears that the mountain women have never enjoyed a reputation for universal beauty; nor, on the other hand, have the women of the Flatlands become proverbial for their ugliness. Throughout northern Italy, and indeed Italy in general, women have always been what they are today: some beautiful, some ugly.)

Having in the opening words of his oration demonstrated the wicked and heretical nature of Antonia's beauty, Inquisitor Manini went on – that torrid afternoon when the witch was tried, the 20th of August 1610 – to allude to a number of circumstances in which that wickedness had had occasion to manifest itself and

139

do harm; first and foremost the affair of *"stulidus Blasius"*, in other words the idiot Biagio. During the inquiries preliminary to the trial the story of the idiot had been narrated down to the last detail by the injured party, Agostina Borghesina, testifying also on behalf of her twin sister Vincenza. The latter, according to the records, had been obliged to remain in Zardino partly to look after the livestock, but more especially to keep an eye on the idiot, lest he strangle himself with the well-rope or get lost in the cane-brakes of the Sesia. Ever since Antonia had undone him with her magic arts, claimed Agostina, Biagio was no longer himself. He did things he would never have done in the past and could no longer be left on his own. Before the trouble started he had been a very well-behaved lad almost normal in appearance apart from the size of his head – which would have been excessive for anyone (so just imagine how it was for him, who had nothing in it!) – and as fit as a fiddle. He had never suffered from any illness, or, if he had, he got over it on his own, without any need of doctoring or medicines, and almost without their realizing anything was the matter. He slept on straw and was as strong as an ox: when the grapes were harvested he pulled the cart from the vineyard all the way to the house without pausing for breath, and he did all the rest of the heavy labour in both vineyard and kitchen garden – always under their direction, needless to say! On his own he was incapable of doing a thing, but if you knew how to manage him there was nothing he couldn't do. Before the witch destroyed him, sobbed Agostina, all the women in the village envied them him, because he did a man's work without giving the trouble a man gives. When he had done his work he didn't go on the prowl, off to the tavern or molesting other people's wives. No sir! He didn't drink and he kept his hands to himself. He just sat in a corner and stared into space. He had been a blessing to them, whereas now . . . She shrieked once more at the Inquisitor: "It was Antonia! You must send her to the stake! It was all her doing, the witch!"

With Agostina Borghesini, as with the other witnesses, the Inquisitor at first showed patience. He let her talk, get it off her chest, and confined himself to nodding occasionally and making a gesture as if to say "go on, go on." Later, however, he started to press her too with increasingly probing questions concerning the witch, the witches' sabbaths (her nocturnal trysts with the Devil), persons who had witnessed them, the magic arts practised by the witch and the consequences those arts had had for the un-suspecting inhabitants of Zardino. "That's enough chatter," he said. "Now let us get down to brass tacks!" For otherwise Agostina would have gone rambling on about things which had nothing to do with the trial and were of concern only to herself. The story of Biagio the idiot was in itself very simple, but it was also the continuation of a long-standing barnyard feud between the Nidasios and the Borghesini twins which had started before either Biagio or Antonia were born; and it was to that feud that Agostina kept harking back. There had been a court case in Novara because the twins wanted Bartolo to move the dungheap to another part of the yard, and he replied that the dungheap had been where it was since his grandfather's day and that he didn't know where else to put it. If anything they ought to move their house, because when it was built the dungheap was already there! Then Biagio arrived on the scene and the feud became further entangled because Signora Francesca (but Antonia in particular) had the impudence to treat the idiot as if he belonged to them. They talked to him, and even gave him food! One evening the idiot was nowhere to be found, and after searching all over the place Vincenza Borghesini finally discovered him in the company of Antonia. They were sitting with their backs against a walnut tree in a field just outside the village, and she was teaching him the names of things. "Now pay attention, Biagio," she was saying. "This is grass; that is the moon; I am Antonia; you are Biagio. Try and say this after me. Water. Grass."

"War-ter," said the idiot. "Gra-ass. An-ton-yah."

The whole business came to a head in the spring of 1605 when, in the very words of Agostina, the witch tried to gain power over the idiot by getting the Devil to enter his body. To outward appearances, however, it was Biagio who fell in love with Antonia, in his own particular way, thereby losing even that spark of reason he had retained until then, and with his lover's torments making the Flatlands and the whole world laugh. The poor lad was perhaps seventeen years old and Antonia two years younger, but she was already the most beautiful girl ever seen this side of the Sesia, according to the unanimous opinion of all who set eyes on her.

It all started one day late in April, or maybe the first week in May. The spring waters were freezing, as ever, but the sun was already hot. The girls of Zardino, Antonia among them, were round the big pool in the Crosa doing the washing and singing *La bergera*, a washerwomen's song and an ancient one – the earliest known versions are about the Crusades and the crusaders. It is in the form of a dialogue, with a solo voice and chorus. It tells the story of a young bride whose husband has gone off to the wars; seven years pass, seven long years, and no news comes of him; a wicked step-mother forces the girl to mind the pigs (in Piedmontese dialect *bergera* means shepherdess) and she languishes and pines away, until at the end of the seven years the husband comes home . . . and it was at this exact moment in the song that Biagio arrived. The soloist, a mannish redhead by the name of Irene, had already straightened up over her scrubbing-board, arms akimbo and bosom thrust out to announce to the world the return of the hero, when suddenly the girls behind her began screaming with terror and scampering hither and thither, and Biagio, after attempting to embrace each in turn, babbling "Anton-yah", leapt into the waters of the Crosa, having spotted the real Antonia on the far side. But as soon as he touched the water he calmed down. (A lover's bashfulness? The icy water? Unluckily for us Inquisitor Manini did not consider it expedient to dwell on this aspect of the matter, which in my opinion should at least have aroused his curiosity. Many authors of his time, including the Cardinal Archbishop of Milan, Federigo Borromeo, dealt in their writings with the property that water, especially if cold, has to expel Devils from the human body; and they recommended its use, by both immersion and ablution, in exorcisms and to liberate those possessed.) At any rate, poor Biagio stood stock still in midstream, arms outflung and up to his waist in water, as if turned to stone; and very possibly, indeed most probably, he had forgotten how he came to be there. At which point Antonia helped him to clamber out, dripping wet as he was, put her hand in his and led him home, while all the girls trooped after them right into the Nidasio farmyard, laughing and pretending to be bridesmaids. Until one of the Borghesini twins darted out from their house with a besom and set them running . . .

A few days later, before the echoes of the idiot's first exploit had died away, he suddenly started raving again and making an exhibition of himself in public, much to the amusement of the population of Zardino, adult and otherwise. One Friday evening it was, at the hour of twilight, when all his fellow-villagers had already supped, or were supping, or at any rate were at home, that a yell arose from the Nidasio barnyard, an uncouth voice bawling "An-ton-yah! An-ton-yaaah!" Almost at once the chase began through the streets and yards of Zardino, an exhilarating spectacle which, in a Flatlands version, anticipated the so-called comedies of the silent screen by three centuries, and made the Zardino folks laugh as they hadn't laughed for years. As slapstick, with involuntary actors, its effect was irresistible. The two titchy twins, fuming with rage, both armed with sticks like great clubs, scampered after their nephew belabouring him with blows. He pounded on, stopping every so often to shout "An-ton-yah!", but he was always cut off in mid-cry because the old women caught up with him and thrashed him mercilessly, in the face, on the head, wherever they could. In the end the twins managed to get the better of him and his follies and to take him home, stunned and bleeding, shaking his oversized head and with no idea what had happened to him.

This was the moment of their triumph and the beginning of their "treatment" for the idiot, whom the twins – in this first phase of the therapy – attempted to rid of Antonia's Devil by means of fasting and exorcism. They shut him in the little ground-floor room where he slept (it was in fact less of a room than a cupboard under the stairs which he could only crawl into on all fours), and there they kept him, without a bite to eat, for three consecutive days and nights. In the course of one of those nights, to poke fun at the rejected lover, the youngsters of Zardino scattered ricechaff between the Nidasio and Borghesini sisters' dwellings. This was an age-old custom, known in the Flatlands as *fè la büla*, to "chaff" someone. In Biagio's case, however, the chaff was wasted, since he most certainly knew nothing about it.

On the morning of the fourth day Don Teresio put in an appearance, preceded by two altar-boys bearing the holy water and the book of the Scriptures with which he proposed to cast out the Devil from the idiot's body. He planted himself firmly in front of the kennel below stairs and mumbo-jumboed, jumped about, crossed himself a dozen times, sprinkled water in all directions, even on the ceiling, and – reading from the book – roared out a quantity of words ending in-*us* or in -*um*, and went off thoroughly pleased with himself, having assured the Borghesini sisters that they could now be easy in their minds: it was all over, the Devil had departed their house and would not come back in a hurry – not with the lesson *he* had taught him! He'd got such a fright that even half as much would have sufficed . . .

Biagio emerged to look once more upon the light of day, and for three or four weeks his conduct was exemplary; he was as docile and hard-working as ever. But on the evening of the feast of San Giovanni, when the old hags were beginning to think that with a bit of luck Antonia's Devil really had done a bunk, and everyone else in the village was disappointed that the business had ended so soon and the idiot no longer made people laugh with his extravagancies, he suddenly went off his head again. He rushed from the house, followed by the old dames, surrounded by the enthusiasm of the villagers who openly incited and applauded him and then gave a big hand to his pursuers. He climbed onto the roof of the church, and thence onto the bell-tower, shouting at the top of his voice, "An-ton-yah! An-ton-yah!" A few young men, urged on by Don Teresio, made an attempt to reach him, but the idiot, who until that moment had never defied anyone, started hurling tiles and bricks at them, forcing them to climb down again. He would have stayed up there all night, calling Antonia, had not Bartolo brought a very tall ladder and Antonia herself gone up to fetch him; and he followed her down as a chick follows a mother hen.

The matter, for the moment, ended there, with the old spinsters taking the idiot home and bolting the door of his cubby-hole and the whole populace of Zardino going happily off to bed because they had been vouchsafed the extra performance they had been looking forward to. But no one knew, or could possibly foresee, that more and better was to come. In the middle of the night the idiot escaped – it was later learnt that he had managed to break down the door of his cubby-hole – and made for Antonia's house. It was full moon. The croaking of the frogs had ceased but shortly before, and it may have been the fourth hour after sunset (that is, one o'clock) when the silence of the sleeping village was rent asunder by the howl of "An-ton-yaah! An-ton-yaaah!" The dogs woke up and pandemonium ensued. The hired men and day-labourers – the agricultural workhorses of the time – violently torn from their dreamless sleep and enraged in consequence, rushed half-naked out into the streets to silence the idiot, carrying lanterns, mattock shafts, and the ropes they used to secure the bull in the mounting season. When at last they succeeded in catching him they reduced him to such a state that for the rest of the night and the following day he would give no trouble to anyone, nor so much as stir. He was hard put to it to keep his feet, the state he was in. The vindicators of the public peace and quiet half shoved and half dragged him to the door of his owners' house and handed him over with the threat, "If he wakes us up again at night we'll give him the chop!"

On regaining possession of the idiot the Borghesini sisters, to be on the safe side, bound him hand and foot. Then, after a confabulation that lasted until dawn, they decided that to restore their nephew to his senses and to hard labour they must castrate him, as one does horses, pigs and other farm animals. After all, was he not a farm animal himself? A Christian (that is, a human being) he certainly was not, even if at birth they had baptised him because they thought he was; mistakenly, as proven by the fact that thereafter the priest had given him no other sacrament, did not allow him in church, and would not so much as look at him. To castrate him or to castrate a chicken was the same thing: this, at least, was the conclusion arrived at by the Borghesini twins. The only snag was that it was more difficult.

"If it was a chicken we'd do the job ourselves, as we've always done with the cocks we want to turn into capons; but how do we set about castrating a man? And if he bleeds to death what will become of us, poor women that we are?"

So they sent to Ponzana, another village in the Flatlands of

Novara, for a certain *"Emiglio Bagliotti, Expert Castrator"* to come and minister to the idiot's needs. Come he did, armed with the surgical instruments of his trade, but when he saw what it was all about he had a moment's pause: "This is a good 'un!" Upon which the twins explained to him that this nephew of theirs, by the name of Biagio, looked like a man but wasn't one, and that he had to be castrated or else he would rove about at night, under the moon, on the lookout for females, and the men of the village would do him in.

"Very well then," said Bagliotti. "It's never come my way to castrate a man before, but I can do it." He asked two lire for the operation and the assistance of a barber named Mercurino. He assured them that once castrated the idiot would become as strong as an ox and as patient as an ass. He did the job, pocketed the money and went his way.

Biagio lay for three days between life and death, then little by little recovered. But not in the way Bagliotti had promised. He was weak and feeble, recounted Agostina Borghesini, and suffered from strange fainting spells, especially at the changing of the seasons. He would fall to the ground and remain there corpse-like for half an hour at a time. He was subject to everything: the phases of the moon, changes in the weather, the heat and the cold. He was almost always unfit for work, for which reason they, the Borghesini sisters, once again sued their neighbour Bartolo Nidasio, the witch's guardian, and also this Emilio Bagliotti, who was the material author of the damage, insisting that the pair of them pay compensation for the loss of their nephew. But when the matter was brought before the "consuls of justice" in Novara by the illustrious Attorney-at-Law Francesco Rivano it all went up in smoke; or rather, in gales of laughter. On their own heads be it, was the reply of those learned judges, if they'd had their idiot nephew castrated. They should have let him go with the witch, and he'd have worked twice as hard as ever! And other silly nonsense which, declared Agostina Borghesini, showed what the justice of the civil Courts was worth . . . But now, now she stood before the holy, infallible Tribunal of the Church, in which she had unbounded faith.

Called upon by the Inquisitor to sum up and explain her charges in detail, Agostina Borghesini accused Antonia of having persuaded the Devil to enter her nephew's body by glances, gestures and verbal enchantments, and of being a witch. But although the word *stria* (witch) occurred on her lips with great frequency and much wrath, Inquisitor Manini well knew that to find Antonia guilty would require further charges – those of heresy, black magic and taking part in witches' sabbaths. And it was to these, as we have said, that his oration turned, after the initial references to the diabolical nature of the witch's beauty and the catastrophic effects, described above, which that beauty had had on *"stulidus Blasius"*.

FIFTEEN

The Painter of Shrines

EVEN BEFORE SHE EMBARKED on the sabbaths and trysts with
the devil by night (the summer of 1609), Antonia gave proof of
"heretical depravity", we are told in the transcripts of her trial, on
three occasions sworn to by several witnesses. These were: having
her portrait painted in the pose and vestments of the Madonna of
Divine Succour in a votive shrine erected at the entrance to the
village of Zardino; provoking public scandal during a pastoral
visit of his lordship the Right Reverend Monsignor Carlo
Bascapè, Bishop of Novara; and lastly, fraternizing with a platoon
of lansquenets, known as *lanzi* (that is, German-speaking
mercenaries of the Lutheran persuasion) who for some mysterious
reason of their own were traversing the flatlands. In the accounts
rendered by the witnesses each of these events has a tangibility and
immediacy of its own, enabling us to see it in all its details, as in a
"still" from a film-track. The dates are unfortunately unrecorded,
but the chronological order of the three episodes is almost
certainly as given above. When she met Bertolino the painter
Antonia was still very young, probably fifteen years old, though
this is not certain. The encounter took place just outside Zardino,
towards the Knolls and the heath, where the track divided in two,
one fork leading to the banks of the Sesia, the other to the villages
further north, to Badia di San Nazzaro and Biandrate. It must have
been summertime, for Antonia was driving the Nidasios' geese
out to pasture, along with two other girls, maybe the daughters of
Barbero the farm-hand, whom we already know, or else two
other friends, who knows! It was hot. The geese were forging
ahead of the girls in a noisy, straggling group, stretching out their
necks and beating their wings as geese will. Whenever they
spotted a ditch they rushed to splash about in it, fishing in the

depths with their long necks and spraying up the water with their wings until in the dazzle of the sunlight you could catch every colour of the rainbow. Or else they would try to thrust their way through the hedgerows, and Antonia would have to race and chivvy them out again, for on the other side of the hedges were fields of maize, and if the geese got in there they'd wreak havoc with the tender young cobs. Far off towards Novaro could be heard the worksongs of the *risaroli*, and the girls, out of breath and giggling, halted every few steps to pluck the blackberries peeping from the brambles on either side of the track. They were chatting about the things all girls of their age usually chat about, and were so absorbed in their discussions about clothes, about girl-friends and sweethearts, that they did not hear the approach of the painter's cart; or rather, they heard it only at the last moment, when the cart was already on top of them and the painter had hailed them with a "Pretty sweetings!"

Their first impulse was to run away. Every unforeseen encounter outside the village in those days might conceal some deadly snare for anyone at all, but especially for young girls like them. And well they knew it. By instinct they cast an eye all around them: was there anyone working in the fields, was there someone they knew who might rush to their aid? But in the meantime the man who had hailed them had jumped down from the cart and was advancing all smiles towards them, in his hand a straw hat of a kind the girls had never seen before – broad-brimmed with a red ribbon around a low crown. "Pretty sweetings, don't run away," said he. "Don't you see my cart? Take a look! It's the Painter's cart!" It had for some time been common knowledge in Zardino that a painter was to come and fresco the new votive shrine that had stood all bare for a whole year and more, towards the Knolls near where the track forked. All it lacked was a fresco.

This shrine had been built on his own land by a certain Diotallevi Barozzi, in gratitude for having survived the collapse of a barn under which he had sought shelter in a summer thunderstorm. A miracle and no mistake! On that occasion, declared Diotallevi, he had really thought "It's all over! I'm a dead man!" But on the contrary: someone Up There had stretched out a hand and he had emerged unscathed. But, as everyone knows, miracles have to be requited, and Diotallevi, who in the first instance vowed to make a pilgrimage to the Madonna of Loreto, had – on further consideration of the length of the journey – fallen back on the construction of a shrine dedicated to the Madonna of Divine Succour. A shrine, he said, is always a fine token of gratitude, and what's more it lasts: pilgrimages come and go but shrines are there to stay! The masonry itself presented no problem. In the seventeenth century every peasant in the Flatlands was a builder on his own account for at least two weeks in the year, when winter set in and the roof and walls had to be patched up to withstand the bad weather. A slab of masonry in the middle of a field is, however, meaningless, unless it is painted. And it was at this point that the business of the shrine began to get tricky and complicated for our farmer friend, because he had never met a painter in his life and had no very clear idea as to where to look for one. For a start, were there any in Novara? "Of course there are," he was assured in Borgo San Gaudenzio by the brokers he applied to for advice. But when one of the latter, after consulting one such master of the palette, informed him of the artist's fees, Diotallevi felt his blood run cold. Ten *scudi* for three spans of fresco! ("What does he take me for?" he said to himself. "A loony who doesn't know the value of money?"). "With ten *scudi*," said the man-saved-by-miracle, in recounting the episode, "a fellow with two marriageable daughters, such as I've got, could set one of them up with a hope chest!" And for the moment there the matter rested.

A few months passed, until one day, as luck would have it, it came to the ear of Farmer Barozzi that on the other side of the Sesia, at Albano Vercellese, a painter called Bertolino d'Oltrepò was frescoing a rustic oratory, and the world and his wife was off there to watch him at work, he was that good! He painted walls with such figures, such faces, declared the locals, that just give 'em a tongue and they'd talk. They were quite scary to look at!

Early next morning (there was the Sesia to cross, and he had to take advantage of the fact that it was almost dry) Diotallevi saddled the mule and set off to see for himself how the said painter could wield his brush, and have a word with him. If he seemed an honest fellow, thought Diotallevi, someone he could talk business to as man to man, and not a raving lunatic like the one in Novara, he might even drop a hint about his shrine and ask how much he would charge to do the job . . .

He found him. This Bertolino was a sturdy fellow of more than medium height, with hair more white than grey; and to look at him while he mixed his colours, or handled his cartoons, using a nail to trace outlines on the wall – outlines later to be coloured in, angels' wings and hands, the robes of Saints and so on – he seemed perfectly normal, a man such as one might come across anywhere in any trade. Moreover he spoke a dialect fairly akin to that of the Novarese Flatlands, and this helped to reassure Diotallevi, who would not have known how to tackle a negotiation in regular Italian. The finished parts of the paintings were really beautiful, or at any rate so they seemed to Diotallevi. As far as he could make out they depicted the beheading of a Saint, but although the subject was gruesome the colours were vivid and gladdening, the eyes of the figures looked into yours and the faces were really and truly alive.

Well, when this peasant entered the little chapel Bertolino was scolding a lad of fifteen or sixteen, an apprentice of his. The boy had prepared the plaster for the fresco and was attempting to spread it on the wall as the painter had taught him to, with a swift, smooth movement of the wrist. But this operation was far from easy, and the plaster kept falling back off. Bertolino made a show of anger: "Curse the day I hired you!" he yelled at the lad, and covered him with insults: "Booby! If I'd hired a baboon he'd have done better!" But at second glance you saw he was more amused than enraged. Finally he thrust the boy aside and in a matter of seconds covered the wall, smoothing out the plaster right into all the corners and grumbling, "You good-for-nothing greedy-guts! You scrounger you! You'll never make a painter! You'll never be anything but a two-legged belly!" Plus further abuse even more elaborate than the foregoing. He used the cartoons to trace the design, the outlines of the faces, the hands, the draperies, the haloes . . . Then he began to lay on the colours.

It was at this point that Diotallevi Barozzi stepped forward to broach the subject of the shrine, deciding that having travelled all that way he might as well come to the point at once. He coughed two or three times and said, "Master, may I have a word?"

"Who are you?" returned the painter.

"I'm a farmer from over the Sesia, in the State of Milan," replied Diotallevi. "My surname is Barozzi and I come from Zardino. I've sought you out because I'd like you to paint me a Madonna of Divine Succour – just a little thing – in a shrine I put up in the fields to fulfil a vow I made two years ago. The picture should be four spans high by three across, with a spot of decoration around it. A blue and white Madonna, you understand, a quick job, nothing showy. But I must know in advance how much it's liable to cost me, because I'm a peasant farmer, as I told you. I've got two daughters to marry off and last year's harvest didn't go too well and . . ."

"Save your breath." Bertolino cut him short. "I know the whole tune. *And* the words as well. How much are you thinking of paying? Make me an offer."

Diotallevi was caught off balance: "What, me? . . . Make you an offer? I don't know! Really it's you who ought to name a price . . ."

"Very well," said the painter. "Let's leave it at that. You don't fork out anything for now, does that suit you? When I've finished the work and if you like it, you'll give me what you fancy, according to your conscience and what you can afford at the time. If you don't have cash you can give me whatever you do have, a pig, two brace of capons, a couple of kegs of wine . . . But I warn you: slap-dash work such as you suggest, saving on time and pigments, Bertolino doesn't know how to do it and doesn't try. If he paints you a Madonna, in a hundred years' time it's still as fresh as it started. Ask around, if you want to know about Bertolino d'Oltrepò!"

And thus, on the spot and without further formalities, they drew up the contract for the shrine of the Madonna of Divine Succour at Zardino. As a matter of fact, for Bertolino that way of doing business was perfectly normal. His humble clientele – peasants, silkworm breeders, parish priests of mountain and meadowland – were all people terrified that the painter might cheat them, and if he wanted to close a deal he had to throw in those two or three phrases which by this time he had on the tip of his tongue: "Let's leave it at that, don't advance me anything!

you'll pay when you want and as best you can! If you're not satisfied don't pay me a thing." In fact – and Bertolino knew it – the small customers paid up quicker and more handsomely than anyone, but they distrusted artists as a matter of course, and needed to be reassured, to cover their bets, to feel they were being crafty . . . If things came to the worst, if something went wrong, all they need do was not pay up . . .

Antonia and her companions turned back to look over the painter's cart, as he had bidden them to. They were all left round-mouthed with an "Oh!" of wonderment, as he had known they would be. And who could blame them! However dusty and muddy it was – Bertolino had splashed through the Sesia at the Devesio ford but an hour earlier – the painter's cart was an object unique in all the world, both as a vehicle and as a work of art, and to find it there before your very own eyes in the midst of the maize and wheat fields was bound to make a certain impression! Wide-eyed, they circled round it. On the varnished wooden side-panels of the vehicle was painted the entire gamut of marbles and other minerals, granites and porphyries, jaspers and alabasters, which had formerly been Bertolino's particular speciality, for which he was acclaimed and still occasionally summoned to work at in hilltop chapels or in city churches, elbow to elbow with the figure painters, the Masters. Who totally ignored him. Before he became an itinerant painter, and acquired the cart, Bertolino had worked for many years on decorative motifs and marbling, in places where the Masters arrived only when all the rest of them had finished their work, and wanted no prying eyes around to watch them tracing the outlines or laying on the colours. They were vainer and more capricious than high-society dames, more malignant and venomous than sanctimonious village biddies, more wayward than spoilt children. He, however, had had the chance and good fortune to observe the working methods of two of the leading Masters of the period, Stella and Lanino. This had fired him with a desire to follow their profession; and he had made a go of it, even though he had never studied under a master and was nothing but a simple *pitúr* (a local word which, like "painter" in English, can mean both artist and decorator). He had set up on his own account, with the cart he both travelled and lived in, that served him as store-room, shop-window, portfolio and bait. There were people enough in the Alpine valleys and the Flatlands who knew of Bertolino d'Oltrepò, the *pitúr*, solely because on the road one fine day they had happened to encounter that travelling cathedral of his and been dumbfounded by it, as Antonia was now; or because they had heard tell of it from someone who had seen it. Moreover, Bertolino was wont to say, for a wayfarer like him his cart had another advantage: it discouraged brigands, who recognized it from afar and saved themselves the bother of assaulting it. Without so much as a peep inside they already knew what manner of things was there . . .

To return, then, to Antonia and her friends, what brought them to a halt and left them gaping at the painter's cart as at a supernatural apparition was not the painted marbles of the sideboards but the canopy over the upper part of the vehicle, every square inch of it divided into panels and painted in bright colours like the nave of a church. On it was the entire repertory of Bertolino d'Oltrepò, painter of shrines and votive images. There were black Madonnas, white Madonnas, with or without the Child in arms, with suckling breast or heart in hand, with halo and star-spangled mantle and barefoot crushing the serpent. And there were the Saints: saints of harvest-time, saints to defend and safeguard folks from this or that, saints to succour them at birth and at the hour of their death, and saints people pray to for the miracles of health and of wealth – what they called "the favours". There they saw the Creator, and God in Judgement with raised hand, as you see him in mediaeval churches, but as no painter in the early seventeenth century any longer wished to depict him – yet he was still in demand! There were ex-votos, which according to Bertolino sold well and could have earned him a living without his needing to do anything else, if only he could have got used to haunting the same places year after year and putting up with a kind of competition that had nothing to do with art: for around the great Sanctuaries, where the ex-voto market flourished, it could even come to daggers drawn . . . Better to let it go!

The pictures on the canopy constituted a scaled-down sample of the paintings Bertolino executed with his cartoons, the ready-made stencils he used to trace his outlines. Here was none of that "improvised" painting that the figure-painters went in for, and it may have been that no one imagined he was capable of such a thing. But from time to time, unasked, he would make his client a present of one, as if to show him, or indeed to show himself, that Bertolino d'Oltrepò the *madonnaro* was neither a worser nor a lesser artist than the Masters who spoke with an affected French "R" and dressed in velvet and pranced down the street in such a way as to make people wonder "Who on God's earth was *that?*" . . . It sometimes happened that a peasant would recognize his own portrait in the face of a Saint, or that an ex-voto would precisely reproduce the spot where the miracle had taken place and the person it had happened to. Or indeed that God sitting in judgement should so obviously resemble the artist himself as to provoke a protest from whoever was footing the bill. And then, oh then, Bertolino would truly rise in wrath! "If you don't like the painting," he would tell the customer, "I'll whitewash it over and won't take a penny. D'you think your money's worth more than my art? Everything I do is done as a gift, and don't you forget it!"

Only when they had finished their tour of the cart, admiring the pictures and pointing them out one after the other ("Look, look there! That's the Madonna of Oropa! And there's St Christopher!") did Antonia realize that seated on the box of the cart was a lad of their own age regarding them with some interest, whereas they until that moment had not even noticed him. Where had he sprung from? Who was he? It goes without saying that the lad was the painter's apprentice, but his presence was sufficient to remind our girls that even the apparition of that cart in the midst of the fields, however much it shared with the stuff that dreams are made on, did in fact belong, like themselves, to the world of realities.

"The geese!" shrieked Antonia, suddenly remembering where she was and that she was there to mind the geese. "My geese! Heavens alive! They've gone and got among the maize!"

With hush and with stealth, with the silent cunning that domestic animals occasionally use to remind us that they too have brains in their heads, inferior to ours as they may be, that they can put two and two together, the geese had exploited the girls' momentary distraction to steal into the field of maize, vanishing completely from the sight of their guardians, who could guess where they were only by the racket they were making, tearing down the sweet tender cobs from the cornstalks and wreaking havoc with the crop. They must get them back at once! And the girls rushed off without answering the painter's questions or even saying goodbye. They left him standing there beside his cart, with pad and stick of charcoal, sketching away and crying "Come back, come back, pretty sweetings! What's ailing you?"

Thus ended that encounter of only a minute or two. And it may be Antonia would have forgotten it, as you forget a dream, or perhaps she would have remembered only the cart, a phantasmagoria of colour amid the green of the countryside and the young maize, a fairy-tale travelling the roads of the world on four wheels and drawn by a pair of horses, had it not been that some time later, when Bertolino had already finished his work and may even have left Zardino, a rumour began to go the rounds that the Madonna of Divine Succour painted in Farmer Barozzi's shrine had the face of Antonia – and not just the face either! It *was* Antonia, dressed as a Madonna and seated on a low wall with a goose at her feet. Everyone who trooped off to see it came back saying, "It's her all right. No doubt about it. It's Antonia to the life!" Needless to say the amazement was mighty, and they gossipped about it for months. And they did more than gossip. Throughout that winter, when Il Caccetta was already in prison in Milan and tales about him were not enough to fill an evening, they discussed whether or not it was lawful to depict the Blessed Virgin, as Bertolino had done, with the features of a girl of the people, with whom they were all acquainted, and a foundling to boot. Whether a blasphemy had been put into paint in the shrine on the outskirts of the village, as was maintained by the pious church hens and seemed to be the belief of Don Teresio himself (in any case he refused to bless it), or whether a Madonna, come what may, is none the less a Madonna, and the oddness of the picture must be ascribed to the eccentricity of the painter. Everyone knows that artists are all mad!

And there were those who based their arguments on grounds that were, so to speak, historical. The Madonna depicted in holy images must, they maintained, be of a particular age, varying from her twenty years or slightly less at the time of the

Annunciation to the fifty years, or slightly more, at the Deposition of Christ from the cross. Had anyone, they demanded, ever seen a fifteen-year-old Madonna? And if no one gave an answer they would provide it themselves, spreading their arms in an ample gesture: no, no one ever had . . .

Signora Francesca was in ecstasies. Whenever someone told her about the criticisms levelled by her fellow-villagers and the Gossips she shrugged it off. "It's all just envy," she said. "If it was one of *their* daughters on that wall they'd have a different tale to tell." Every time she passed the shrine she stopped and went into raptures: her Antonia! Painted as a Madonna! Perhaps she would have been a little less overjoyed had she been able to imagine what was to become of that painting and that shrine, and if she had foreseen, in the records of the trial, statements such as these: "*She* (Antonia) *answered me that she was devoted only to herself, and that she prayed to Besozzo's Madonna* (i.e. to Diotallevi Besozzi's shrine)." This from Irene Formica. "*They would say 'Look, there goes Besozzo's Madonna! Look at Besozzo's Madonna walking down the road'. And she, as she marched along, puffed up with pride.*" This from Isabella Ligrina.

SIXTEEN

The Blessèd Panacea

BISHOP BASCAPÈ'S long awaited pastoral visit to Zardino and other small villages on the left bank of the Sesia took place one spring day of a year unrecorded; perhaps the sixteenth, or maybe the seventeenth, of Antonia's life (who knows!). It was while Cavagna's Relics were still under distraint in Novara by order of the Pope, and Bascapè was still busy transforming his body into that "living corpse" which was to acquire its definitive and perfect form in the summer of 1610. In those first years of the seventeenth century, his biographers tell us, his physical afflictions had all of them worsened and, so to speak, acquired chronicity. The attacks of catarrh, of migraine, the "fluxions" (neuralgias, rheumatisms and other painful ailments), that kept him shackled to the world of the living by physical pain, had however reduced him to the shadow of a man; a devout ghost, similar in all respects to the phantom- saints and spectre-saints who at that time were being crammed, or had already been crammed, on the walls of the Lombard churches by painters often known by the names of their birthplaces: il Morazzone, il Cerano, il Tanzio da Varallo, il Fiamminghino, il Moncalvo and so on. In their canvases these artists depicted the very same anguish of living, and of living at that epoch, which Bascapè displayed in all his doings, and even in his body. Their pictures regale us with the gloomy histories of saints impelled by an implacable frenzy of devotions, of processions, of preachments, of ardent and ludicrous works; or of men rapt in spectral pleasures, or others again straying hither and thither without rhyme or reason.

It was after this fashion then – as in a canvas by Cerano or Procaccini – that the still-imperfect cadaver of Bishop Bascapè arrived at Zardino one spring morning when all the bells in the flatlands were pealing incessantly, answering one another from village to village. It came preceded by great festivities and followed by an imposing retinue, hermetically sealed in a black litter with curtains drawn, almost in darkness, afflicted with migraine, with allergies, and with so many other painful and mysterious ills that it would take too long to list them.

We are told by the chronicles of the time that as a gift to that little community, and in lieu of the Relics Cavagna had promised Don Teresio – but which never reached their destination! – Bascapè carried a fragment of the garment of a local semi-saint, the Blessèd Panacea. The bishop himself, in the course of his sermon, would provide an account of how she lived, setting an example of faith to all who knew her; and how, heroically, she died.

Amid the ovations and hurrahs of the children who had run to meet their bishop as far as the Mill of the Three Kings, or even further, his litter-cum-sarcophagus advanced at a snail's pace through the woods, the arable fields, the vineyards, along a roadway festooned with garlands of flowers and strewn all about with rose-petals. One sole cry resounded throughout the Flatlands: "Hurrah for the Blessèd Panacea! Long live Bishop Bascapè!"

The bishop's litter, borne by two mules, was preceded by a carriage in which travelled five men: two ecclesiastics, in the persons of Canon Clemente Gera and Canon Antonio Mazzola, whose task it was to assist the bishop in the cure of souls; and three laymen, whose names are unfortunately not recorded, but who were the Fiscal Registrar of the diocesan curia and his two assistants, an attorney-at-law and a scrivener. These three, and especially the Registrar, represented an important and, as it were, autonomous part of the bishop's pastoral visits; for wherever he made a halt they set themselves up a species of office, either indoors or out; and not only did they collect the land taxes due to the Church on rural properties, they also saw to the settlement of wrangles with both private individuals and whole communities, and the restoration of certain Church rights fallen into disuse; which in the diocese of Novara were many and of considerable magnitude.

Behind the bishop's litter, armed with harquebuses and seated stiffly on account of the breastplates they were obliged to wear in spite of the heat (able to decide for themselves they'd certainly have done without, but such were regulations and such the orders from on high), were the four men-at-arms of the escort. After these (who were of course on horseback), shambling and plodding along on a wide variety of mounts – chiefly mules but also donkeys and extremely mangy pack-asses – came the curates and parish priests of a dozen Flatlands villages which Monsignor Carlo Bascapè had visited in the last few days or was about to visit. Bringing up the rear of the *cortège* rumbled a cart drawn by a pair of oxen. And on this cart, once the bishop had passed, the peasants placed offerings of capons, pulses, rice, skeins of hemp or flax, salami, lard, vegetables, flour, walnuts, and others of the products of their soil, which two young seminarists saw to dividing up (foodstuffs on one side, the rest on the other) and to stowing into a huge wicker basket if there was a risk of their spoiling in the sun. These provisions were for the most part destined for the sustenance of the Seminaries of the diocese, and were to be delivered to their destinations that same evening . . . And while the little procession moved ahead the bells rang out full peal, and all over the plain arose the cry, "Hurrah for the Blessèd Panacea! Long live Bishop Bascapè!"

It was a day of dazzling sun and crystalline air. Piedmont and the distant Alps and all the world were basking and revelling in the blue of the sky and the verdure of the plains, and right at hand rejoiced and exulted in the conflagration of poppies that every-where accompanied the rising wheat, in the flowering of iris and wild rose, in the sparkling of waterways, in the light breeze ruffling the puddles and, along the ditches, swaying the young fresh willow-wands. All nature was a burst of aromas, of pollens, of buzzings, of songs, of birdcalls, of colours. The animals went seeking each other out, launching their signals from the trees, from the sky, from the soil, from the grass . . . and the air was streaked with the myriad flights of a myriad species of bird. The waters overflowed, and with them the life of the Flatlands. The very air was saturate with humours, with fluids, with invisible and impalpable substances to propagate life.

Sealed up inside his litter, as we have said, in almost total darkness, runny-eyed, coughing, exuding rheums at every pore, Bishop Bascapè inveighed under his breath against the pollen that winkled its way through the window-frames and heavy, embossed velvet curtains, thick and tawny as a lion's pelt, and, via his nostrils, prompted what life he had in him to exit in repeated sneezes, forceful and sharp as harquebus shots. In his hands were two embroidered handkerchiefs impregnated with essences, many samples of which were arranged before him in little copper bottles and glass phials – gum benjamin, myrrh, sugar cane, cloves – and every so often he would raise these hankies to his nose, press them to his nostrils and imbibe their aromas. He groaned and he bewailed the migraine that now tortured him daily, at all seasons of the year but worst of all in spring; and at intervals he would recite the words of the Psalm, *"Domine, ne elongaveris auxilium tuum!"* – Do not for long delay thine aid, O Lord. He invoked the Blessèd Panacea (the Relic of whom, enclosed in a silver casket, he bore with him in his litter) and the Blessèd Carlo Borromeo, his friend and patron. He also invoked Paul the Apostle whose priest (as a Barnabite) he was. The deafening clangour of the bells of all the churches and farmsteads in the lowlands of the Sesia beat agonizingly in his head. He invoked Jesus Christ Our Lord, whose effigy he always wore on a small crucifix round his neck. "Lord, come to the aid of thy servant!" he prayed: *"Domine, adiuva servum tuum!"*

"Hurrah for the Blessèd Panacea! Long live Bishop Bascapè!" cried the children all rosy and flushed with health and with the run from the village to waylay the bishop on the road. They hustled and they bustled, they thronged around. "Long live the bishop! Hurrah, hurrah!"

He shifted the velvet curtain a fraction of an inch, barely enough to peep out, to see whether the village was still far off or if they were nearing their destination. He could scarcely wait to find himself inside a church, where the smoke of the incense and other liturgical aromas might perhaps counteract that accursèd pollen and allow him to breathe; but the church was nowhere to be seen, nor even was the village. All he could see were the children shouting and flinging their arms about in greeting, and beyond them the heath, the vineyards, the fields full of wheat . . . The scarlet of the poppies gave him a painful jolt. He dropped the curtain and returned to darkness.

"Long live the bishop! Hurrah for the Blessèd Panacea!"

But at last, somehow or other, paving-stones sounded beneath the hoofs of the mules, and the first houses hove in sight. Low, grey dwellings they were, with windows so small you couldn't imagine how any light got in, with a few napkins on the sills, a few embroidered fabrics hung from the balconies to honour the bishop. The bells were ringing madly and the faithful in church were heard intoning the Te Deum. And as if that din was not sufficient, three or four petards were let off in front of the canons' carriage, and the horses bucked and reared; but, luckily for Bishop Bascapè's already frayed nerves there were no volleys or drumrolls. The bishop's litter, as ever, came to a halt exactly at the entrance to the church. Canon Gera, fat and squat, hastened to open its door. The bishop issued forth, clad entirely in black with purple buttons, and so waxen-faced as to resemble a corpse rising from the dead. Only his eyes, set in their deep violet sockets, were really and truly alive, and there was also that mauve nose which constituted a blotch of colour quite out of keeping with a face in which even the lips were bloodless. Dazzled by sunlight the bishop swayed on his feet, and was forced to grasp hold of Gera with both hands to prevent himself from collapsing. But he recovered at once, straightened up, still holding a handkerchief soused in essences, raised two fingers to bless a knot of people who had remained outside to greet him (*"in nomine Patris, et Filii, et Spiritus Sancti"*), then turned and entered the church followed by Canon Gera, and also by Canon Mazzola who in the meantime had seen to fetching the casket containing the Relic of the Blessèd Panacea from the litter. On the threshold the bishop was obliged to halt – he would otherwise have tripped over Don Teresio prostrate on the ground. He bade him rise (*"Exsurge"*), and proffered him his ring to kiss. Before the altar the bishop knelt down in his habitual way, resting the palms of both hands on the steps and making obeisance until his forehead touched the marble. Then he rose, he turned. He looked down into the church crowded with faithful, the men on this side, the women on that, as

Don Teresio had instructed them. The front row, however, was entirely composed of the adolescent girls of the village – Antonia among them – all white-clad in devout homage to the virgin Panacea.

Bascapè opened with the words from *Exodus*, *"Qui est, misit me ad vos"* – *"I AM* (God, that is) *hath sent me to you."* ("Lord, what a headache! That cursèd pollen!")

He gave two, four, six crashing sneezes, burying his mauve nose in his embroidered handkerchief. Many of the girls in the front pew covered their faces to hide their giggles, but Antonia remained serious. The scandal which Don Teresio reported at her trial – that she had laughed obscenely (*"turpiter"*) in the presence of the bishop – if it really happened at all, happened later, at the end of the sermon, or even at the very end of Mass, when Bishop Bascapè consigned the Relic of the Blessèd Panacea to the faithful of Zardino. In any case both Don Teresio and Inquisitor Manini, for motives not hard to divine, exaggerated this incident of "offence to the bishop". Possibly there was no such incident at all . . .

Antonia, as we know, had already had occasion to meet Bishop Bascapè, and seeing him again before her eyes, there at Zardino, reminded her of that day in her childhood when she should have recited him Sister Leonardo's poem, and of all that had happened to her – the rising at dawn, the purifying bath, the raw egg . . . How many memories passed through Antonia's mind while Bishop Bascapè, between one sneeze and the next, celebrated Mass together with Don Teresio! Her thoughts returned to Sister Livia, Sister Clelia, the House of Charity . . . And then, maybe, she had a vision of the bishop's long, long white hand which the nuns had exhorted her not even to brush with hers, and which she instead had touched . . . In spite of his pallor and gauntness, at the time of his visit to the House of Charity Bishop Bascapè was not yet that spectre of a man he was to become. Some of the nuns – Antonia remembered it very clearly – thinking they were not overheard had exclaimed, "What a fine figure of a man!" And even to her he had seemed handsome then. Whereas now he had nothing left of beauty but his voice, a warm, deep voice with an attractive Lombard accent; and all the more agreeable for the contrast with Don Teresio's falsetto, that priestly, "Sunday" voice put on specifically for celebrating Mass. When the bishop began on the story of the Blessèd Panacea, Antonia allowed herself to be carried away almost unawares by the flowing melodiousness of that voice; and the same happened to most people in the church, understanding as they did but a few words and phrases of the bishop's homily, or even nothing at all, for the simple reason that the bishop was preaching in regular Italian while the peasants spoke dialect.

The story of the Blessèd Panacea, which at that time Bascapè was touring around narrating to the peasants of the Flatlands, is that of a luckless young shepherdess, born in 1368 in a village in the Novarese hill-country and dead at a tender age. The first misfortune in her life – a life beset with tragedies! – was very likely the name, Panacea, which her witless parents had imposed on her; but thereafter followed many others, each worse than the last. Orphaned on her mother's side – say her biographers, and so that day repeated Bishop Bascapè – she was slaughtered at fifteen years old by her stepmother, infuriated with her because she did nothing but pray. She had no sweetheart as did other girls of her age, she did not tend the flock, she did not spin the wool. She did nothing. She just prayed from morn till night and her stepmother beat her to death.

"Belovèd sons and daughters," (thus the bishop addressed himself to the populace of Zardino), "you should therefore know that the virgin Panacea was the daughter of a certain Lorenzo da Cellio of Val Sesia, born in the village known as Cadarafagno (Ca' de' Rafani) but later established at Quarona, where his wife Maria, a native of Ghemme, bore him this daughter, Panacea; but she (that is, the wife) dying in Ghemme, he took a second wife who, treating Panacea with exceeding harshness, charged her with grazing the flock, gathering the firewood and bearing it home, and also with a task of spinning beyond what was feasible, principally because, the girl being given to performing her devotions in the church of San Giovanni di Quarona, built upon the hillside where she led the flock to pasture, she there applied herself assiduously to reciting the rosary. The more the wicked stepmother raged and fumed the more her stepdaughter radiated patience and virtue, and the former went so far as to punish her even for good and pious deeds; and in order to dissuade her from her prayers – ungodly wretch! – she broke and cast away her rosary beads. But God in his benignity, not wishing to defer the reward for so great virtue, vouchsafed that at this point the iniquitious woman was roused to such a pitch of wrath that she slew the devout and innocent girl (who was then arrived at her fifteenth year) on the pretext of her assiduity in prayer."

Bascapè made a pause to blow his nose. From outside the church came the barking of dogs and the chirruping of birds: the usual sounds, thought Antonia of a village like the one Panacea had lived in too . . .

But the bishop resumed his tale: "Inasmuch as one evening when the hour had come for her to return, and she was already driving the sheep homewards, and preparing to shoulder the bundle of firewood, arriving at the stone upon which she habitually recited her orisons, she was unable to resist the desire to pause there and kneel again in prayer; and thus the sheep arrived at the sheepfold on their own. Observing this, the stepmother in her rage hastened to the grazing-place and, finding the girl at prayer, belaboured her cruelly with her rough mountain distaff, and driving certain spindles into her head, slew her. And therefore is the girl often-times depicted together with her stepmother cudgelling her. These tidings having been reported to the girl's father, Lorenzo, who had several times in vain rebuked his wife, he hastened thither and found the faggot of wood aflame, so it is told, and could in no wise either raise the small body or extinguish the burning bundle."

The bishop's voice assumed a graver note: "According to the account rendered by the priest Rocco (Rocco Bononi, incumbent at Quarona in the days of Panacea) and all the other writers, and the unswerving tradition of the two parishes of Quarona and of Ghemme, among the innumerable persons who, on hearing the town crier, flocked to this tragic and wondrous scene was the Magistrate General of Valsesia, His Excellence Ambrogio de' Pantaleoni of Milan; who, noting the continuance of this prodigy of being able neither to raise the body, nor extinguish the burning faggot, dispatched a swift messenger to Bishop Oldrado in Novara, and he made haste to come, along with the clergy, and seeing the portent still continuing after many days, by his command and his alone could that hallowed corse be raised.

"Borne to the foot of the hill, it was then laid upon a cart drawn by two young heifers, the which drew up at the property of a certain Lorenzo da Cellio (the very name of the father, be it noted!), who in no wise consented to the body being buried there. Whereupon the heifers of their own accord took another direction, making straight for the plains."

Bascapè paused again, and wiped the sweat from his brow. He then resumed more strongly: "Thus proceeded that strange procession, a bishop and his clergy, the civil authorities, and an immense host of folk, all of them in the train of two heifers proceeding at their own sweet will, and hauling a cart bearing a young girl's corse. The heifers paused for a quarter of an hour to graze at Romagnano, and the company paused also. Arriving at Ghemme they made another stay in a field known as the Campo de' Banchelli, and there drank at a spring where a holy chapel is still to be seen, with a painting of the event. And thence they proceeded until they stopped in the graveyard near the church, beside a briar above the spot where Panacea's true mother lay buried.

"What touching poetry there is in this daughter lately dead who miraculously seeks out her dead mother! Upon that site Bishop Oldrado, having for the nonce ordered that the body be lodged in the church, in the space of a few days caused a chapel to be built beside the church, and therein a grave dug, lined with stone and covered with marble slabs, where he in person laid the body to rest on the first Friday of May in the year 1383, which was the first day of the said month. On the anniversary of which the feast-day of the Blessèd Panacea is customarily celebrated with great piety in those and other parishes, and with a great concourse of people, either from spontaneous devoutness or the fulfilment of vows; and it is wondrous to see what multitudes flock to Ghemme even from the diocese of Vercelli to honour this virgin with prayers, with oblations and with holy offerings. On that day the entire populace of Quarona journeys there in procession for ten miles, together with its priest, and offers a ritual candle, to the cost of which every head of a family contributes; and likewise, it is said, the people of other parishes both do and must do according to their own statutes. In that church, moreover, not only was a chapel established, but also a benefice for the saying of Mass; and in many other churches throughout the diocese we may find altars and images of the Blessèd Panacea.

"Many declare," concluded Bascapè, raising both voice and hand in monitory gesture, "that they have regained their health and strength by invoking the blessèd Panacea, whose very name denotes 'universal medicine'. Nor have we in any wise thought fit to alter this ancient cult, approved on March 14th 1570 by His Holiness Pope Pius V, and instilled into our people by the divine Will, by virtue of this blessèd and most felicitous maiden! Whom from this day forth you too shall invoke, in the name of the Father, and of the Son, and of the Holy Ghost. Amen."

SEVENTEEN

The "Lanzi"

IN THE AUTUMN of the same year in which the bishop paid his visit to Zardino, another exceptional event took place: a detachment of lansquenets (*lanzi* for short) appeared in the village one morning and stayed all day, giving no reasons and without any one even knowing who had sent them. The *lanzi* simply installed themselves in the middle of the village, between the forecourt of the church and the Lantern Tavern, as if their presence were the most natural thing in the world; then, when night fell, they set off towards the river. A fine enigma, especially for the sort of man (or woman) who always wants to get to the bottom of things, to probe their causes. A real brain-teaser, enough to rob you of both sleep and reason! Word went about that the *lanzi* had been obliged to cross the frontier to carry out a mission on the far side of the Sesia, or that they were on their way to retrieve deserters, or that they had lost touch with their regiment, or that they were deserters themselves. There were theories of every sort, but in the absence of any confirmation or concrete evidence interest gradually waned and people began to busy themselves with other matters. Even the unit the *lanzi* belonged to remained a mystery. The only established certainty was that they were not attached to the garrison of Novara, where as far as was known there had never been any *lanzi* even in the past, and that they therefore came from further afield, possibly from Milan, or even from Piacenza. It was there, they said, in the Duchy of the Farnese, that such troops were on home ground!

The detachment was commanded by a veritable giant of a man with huge tow-coloured moustaches and side burns. He was so lofty that to enter the Lantern Tavern he had not merely to lower his head but to bend double, and once inside he had to keep stooping to avoid crashing his head against the beams. Not a man in Zardino, or in the whole Flatlands, was as tall as he. Not even Maffiolo the fieldguard who, so the old crones said, was "as long as hunger"! As soon as they set eyes on him the village children nicknamed him Attila; and we shall do likewise.

This Attila had outsize hands and cheeks of a bluish-purple which testified to his capacities as a great eater and drinker, along with a predisposition to die of heart attack. He spoke only German, as did his men, being able to utter but a few words or phrases in an Italian crippled by Spanish, or in Spanish itself, but even these were more or less incomprehensible. Finally, to judge from his manner of speaking and moving, he was in a permanent rage: with those who did not speak his language, with his men – who did – and with the world at large.

It was one October morn with the sun already high when he and his *lanzi* invaded the piazza of Zardino as Don Teresio had just finished celebrating Mass, that is at half-past nine or a quarter to ten; and he at once began to bawl for the consuls to be brought before him. That at least was what the villagers thought they understood. He yelled at the pious biddies leaving church, halting in their tracks to eye him, because they feared that if they made to escape it would be the worse for them: "Swine coughs and goat's blisters and shit-eaters all as you are! I will them consuls here! Beast's knell!"

(It goes without saying that Attila was not even aware that the headmen of the Flatland villages were called consuls; nor was the term "shit-eaters" or any of the other words in the above sentences to be found in his vocabulary. But by a fortunate concatenation of assonances and plays on words, by which the German words were "translated" merely by their sound into a rough equivalent, the gist was understood. Attila did in fact wish to negotiate with someone representing the whole village, and so it transpired).

After some minutes of yelling and turmoil, the consuls arrived. There were two of them, freshly elected each year as laid down in the statutes. Those summoned by the will of the people to guide the destinies of Zardino for that particular year were a certain Angelo Barozzi, of whom we know nothing but the name, and our old friend Bartolo Nidasio. Who on seeing himself surrounded by so many men armed to the teeth, with such faces as theirs, and hearing their hollerings, swore to himself that he'd never again be a consul as long as he lived. When at last they had their chosen interlocutors before them Attila and his men started talking ten to a dozen about "rooay", "spyzay", and "essen", about totally incomprehensible things in short, and going beserk when the consuls failed to understand them. They pointed at their mouths, even thrust four fingers in, shouting *"hombre, comida!"* (Food, man! Food!). Poor Barozzi, appalled by the prospect of having to feed more than thirty famished Germans, attempted to pacify them with talk, to gain time. He hoped – though how illusory that hope was we shall soon see – that from one moment to the next something unforeseen might occur, and that the *lanzi* would depart as they had come. He beat about the bush with bureaucratic cavils, saying "We were not advised in time" and "It is useless for you to insist, we are not responsible," and other statements of the sort, of which the Germans repeated single words, syllable by syllable: "ahd-weist", "riss-ponz-e-bäl", looking at each other to see if someone had spotted where the trick lay. Bartolo, on the other hand, thought mainly of what might happen if the *lanzi* finally lost patience, and made a sign to Barozzi: Give up trying! Let's give them what they want, just as long as they go away! Don't argue!

While in the piazza before the church negotiations for eating *(essen! comer!)* were dragging on, most of the *lanzi* had crowded into the tavern and continued from within to make their presence felt with incomprehensible shouts of "rote-vine" and "trinker" and inhuman cries such as "Many in cargo!" But some of the younger *lanzi* went a-roving round the lanes of Zardino, peering in at the windows or round the yards to see if there were any women about. They tapped fingertips on the shutters, said "psst, psst", or called out *"tosa, bèla tosa"* (*tosa* being Milanese dialect for "girl"); but as if by enchantment the women had all disappeared from the village. There was not a single woman to be seen in any of the courtyards, even an old one, even an ancient. And as for the men, if truth be told, there were very few even of them in circulation. Only the children were out on the streets, skipping along behind the strangers crying, "The *lanzi*, the *lanzi*, the *lanzi*!

hurrah for the *lanzi*!" with an enthusiasm somewhat at odds with the occasion and the persons in question. They scrimmaged amongst themselves to finger the belts, the regulation short-swords, the damascened archibuses; they coo-erred at their leathern doublets, their red-and-white-striped breeches, their daggers, their hunting-knives. "Look at 'im!" they cried. "And look at *'im!*" Some of the daringest among them made so bold as to enter the tavern, which according to unwritten but inflexible laws was out-of-bounds to young boys, even in exceptional circumstances. There they saw Maffiolo the field-guard engaged in conversation with the *lanzi* in their own language, and ran helter-skelter to impart the latest news. "Il Fuente's talking to the *lanzi* and they're answering him!"

To cut a long story short, Maffioli was summoned to the piazza, where negotiations between the village headmen and the commander of the *lanzi* seemed to have bogged down once and for all, and his mediation was crucial in explaining to Barozzi –Bartolo on his part had already grasped the fact – that talk was useless: the *lanzi* didn't understand it, and if they had done so they would have flown clean off the handle. For this reason Maffioli refused to translate it. What the German had to say was very simple: if you give us what we ask all will go smoothly, we shall feel ourselves among friends and peace will reign; if you choose not to give it, very well, we will take it ourselves, but to repay us for the effort we will take more, whatever else we can lay our hands on – money, women, whatever comes our way.

Having thus settled the preliminaries, Attila formulated the requests, which were as follows: hay and oats for two horses and five mules; for his men two pigs of not less than five hundred pound apiece, and everything required for the slaughtering, butchering and cooking of them in the German manner. Bread and wine on demand, but at any rate in vast quantities, because (explained the captain of the *lanzi*) his men had a mighty hunger on them and a thirst to match. There being nothing to be done but obey, the villagers produced the pigs and chopped them up. They set up two tables in the back yard of the Tavern, under the lean-to roof that usually sheltered the carts, because there was not room in the inn for the whole platoon of *lanzi*, but neither could they be

171

seated outside under the pergola, for the weather was damp, the skies were louring and rain was in the offing. Beneath that lean-to the *lanzi* ate and drank fit to burst, and thereafter began to sing some of their own songs, merry or melancholy, lewd or love-sick, but all having one thing in common: the words were German and therefore incomprehensible to the Zardinians.

Two of the *lanzi* were fine musicians, playing on instruments similar to the viol but much smaller, which they rested on their shoulders, providing an accompaniment for the solo parts and the saddest of the songs. For the others the *lanzi* furnished their own accompaniment, beating out the time with hands and feet and all sorts of improvised instruments, knives clinked on glasses, for instance, or metal platters rattled on table-tops. In between songs they yelled and guffawed and bellowed fit to make your blood run cold. And if they wished to void their bodies of some superfluous burden they left the tavern, crossed the piazza, and deposited it on the steps of the church or on those of the presbytery, amidst the handclaps and hurrahs of their mates, who through the bars of some railings separating the inn-yard from the piazza proper were able to watch them exhibiting themselves in their bodily functions without moving from their seats. The people in the adjacent houses naturally saw everything going on in the piazza, so that it may be said that the performance of the *lanzi* took place before a fairly large, varied and participant audience; but all the same, however odd it may seem to us of the twentieth century, the presence of a public did not in the least embarrass the actors. On the contrary, it seemed to goad them on! Almost all the *lanzi*, in the course of their stay in Zardino, were to be seen either upright or squatting, their breeches down below their knees, before the church door or that of the priest's house. Some, indeed, paid their respects to both. The appraisals and comments which the onlookers addressed to the performers, and the replies of the latter, were in German, or in some cases in Spanish, but with the aid of a little imagination the Italian-speaking audience succeeded in grasping, if not the individual words, at least the general drift of what was said. And they perfectly well understood what one of the *lanzi*, already hoary-headed, had to say after depositing a turd of notable proportions on the priest's doorstep. While hoisting up his breeches he shouted in Spanish at Don Teresio's windows, "Look, Mr Priest, here's your newborn brother!"

From outside the church-doors other *lanzi* called Don Teresio "Pope of Rome" *(Pabst von Rom)* and urged him to come to the window and bless their arses – which they displayed, naked and ready for that purpose. One of them who happened to have a piece of chalk in his pocket used it to foul up the doors and walls with a number of (luckily incomprehensible) inscriptions and numerous drawings which were, on the contrary, all too explicit. Meanwhile the Zardinians, bolted and barred into their houses, were wondering what Don Teresio was up to; whether he was hiding in the cellar, as was most likely, or peeping out through the shutters.

"O God, don't let him come out and confront those devils!" prayed the church hens. "Facing martyrdom he'd be, poor dear!"

"Don't worry your head," said the husbands one and all. "He's not even thinking of facing them! As a priest he's certainly a bit above himself, but when it comes to risking his hide even he cools off!"

Hours went by. Darkness began to creep beneath the lean-to in the yard and into the piazza. Attila – who after eating and drinking like an ogre, and singing at the top of his voice along with his men, seemed to have nodded off, dozing with chin drooped on chest – suddenly shook himself and was seized with his habitual wrath, as on his arrival, roaring out orders thick and fast and rampaging around like a madman. Whatever he wanted, thought the villagers, one thing was certain: he wanted it at the double! At the double the *lanzi* rose from the table, ran to fetch the animals from the inn stables, packed up their baggage, formed ranks in the piazza. At the double they set off to find Maffiolo the field-guard, who however arrived at his customary pace, perfectly unruffled, in spite of Attila's yells of *"Schnell, schnell!"*. At the double they made ready their torches for the darkling march; and as a last touch, with all the urgency the circumstances demanded, Attila probed the field-guard (*"Schnell, schnell!"*) about the neighbourhood of Zardino – where to find the ford to cross the Sesia, what lay on this side of it, were there any houses? . . .

When suddenly into the piazza came . . . a trio of girls! The exultation of the *lanzi* exploded in a "Three cheers" so thunderous, so unexpected, a *Lebe hoch!* roared in a moment of such overwhelming exhilaration that even Attila was disconcerted by it, forgetting all about the rush and hurry . . . Three live girls!

The most overwhelmed of all, not unnaturally, were the girls themselves. Overwhelmed but, even more, scared out of their wits. What on earth was going on there in the village? Who were these men all dressed alike, with red-and-white striped breeches and leather doublets? Antonia, Irene Cerruti and Teresina Barbero had gone out early that morning to gather mushrooms, and had filled a panier which now lay overturned in a corner of the piazza. Re-entering the village they were amazed not to meet a soul, to find all the doors bolted, the shutters barred and the domestic animals, even the dogs, shut up in the stables. But before it dawned on them that something was wrong, that they ought to turn back, there they were in the piazza surrounded by *lanzi*. Imagine the scare they got, especially Irene and Teresina. As for Antonia, the fact that the field-guard was there put a little heart into her, especially as he gave her a look and a signal which meant "Don't worry. You'll come to no harm. *I'm* here!"

The excitement of the *lanzi* was sky-high. They clapped their hands and shouted, *"Tosa! Tosa!"* Antonia peered at their faces. The old ones really did have horrifyingly ugly mugs, but there were also a few fair-haired, blue-eyed youngsters who didn't look particularly wicked or dangerous. One of these stepped smilingly forward, gave a bow, took her by the hand. The same instant the two musicians struck up with something very rhythmic and spirited, the rest started beating time with their hands, and Antonia, who had never danced in public and indeed never danced with a man at all, found herself dancing with a stranger there in the piazza by the light of the torches before she had realized what was happening and what she was doing. And as she danced she wondered "What am I doing? Have I gone mad?" But in fact and in truth she quite enjoyed it. It didn't last long – maybe a couple of minutes. Attila then came to his senses with a bestial cry: the music broke off, the dancers stopped, and at once came a salvo of orders as sharp and peremptory as harquebus shots. Off! Away! *"Schnell, bist schnell!"* (Beast's knell, Beast's knell . . .). Teresina Barbero, who had stood dazedly watching her friend dance, took advantage of the sudden confusion to dart forward and grasp Antonia by the arm.

"Come away!" Her voice was all of a tremble. "What have you done, what have you done Antonia!"

"An-tóina," mimicked the German who had danced with her, over and over repeating the name: "An-tóina, An-tóina . . ." Then he pointed to himself: "Me, Hans." From round his neck he took a little silver medallion hung on a leather thong and put it round Antonia's neck, saying *"Undenchen. Recuerdo."* Then he fell in with the rest of the troop. The *lanzi* were even then moving off towards their unknown destination and the two musicians, screened from view by their companions, struck up with a tune very different from that of a moment before, a melody that seemed to rise from the earth itself, as they disappeared into the darkness; that told of another land of plains, of mists, of forests . . . They were already clear of the village when came the last hail: *"Lebe vol, An-tóina! Lebe vol!"* . . . Farewell!

Don Teresio showed his face the following day, but only in the afternoon. And this despite the fact that the pious women had since the crack of dawn been cleansing his doorstep of all traces of *lanzi*, and despite the fact that by mid-day a small crowd had gathered in the piazza knocking at his door and calling, "Don Teresio! Don Teresio! Are you all right? Please come out!" But he at that time refused to answer, withdrawing into an offended and indignant silence which not a few people in the village mistook for funk. ("He still senses a whiff of *lanzi*, I tell you," said Bartolo Nidasio to his wife. "As long as he thinks they may come back he won't come out").

But a few hours later, unexpectedly and in typical manner, Don Teresio did reappear. Having seized the bell-ropes and hauled at them for at least a quarter of an hour, he started rushing around from house to house and barnyard to barnyard collecting as many old wives and as many peasants as were needed to form a solemn procession to the four corners of the village, because – he shrieked – the Antichrist had been in Zardino and everything had to be reconsecrated. From stable to stable, from yard to yard must they go, with the Relic of the Blessed Panacea and the life-sized crucifix they carried on Good Friday, to bless what had been profaned.

Before starting the procession, however, Don Teresio urged his flock in the direction of the church ("To church, to church!"), in order to give thanks to God – thus he bawled at them when they had there assembled – for having saved their crops and homes, but above all to ask God's pardon for having been such poltroons the day before, when faced with the Antichrist; for not having risen in arms in defence of the church, the presbytery and the true faith. Whereupon the rustics stared at him wide-eyed and muttered, "Rise in arms? What arms? And where had *he* been, anyway?" But Don Teresio was inexorable, implacable, impervious to any doubt or criticism.

"Cowards!" he shrieked in their faces. "That's what you are: a bunch of cowards! Without exception, old and young, men, women and children! Can there be a moment in life," he demanded, and his voice trembled with genuine scorn, his eyes flashed the fire of unsimulated wrath, "or any special condition on account of which any person can be exempted from bearing his own witness to God, albeit at the price of martyrdom?" He shot onto tiptoe, as when he flew while saying Mass. He stabbed a finger at his parishioners, shouted at them, and put himself, as was his wont, into the shoes of God the Father: "Where were you yesterday while the Antichrist fouled up My house and the house of My priest? Who amongst you rose to defend My name and to bear witness unto Me?"

He returned to earth, declaring (in his everyday voice) that after reconsecrating the village to God with the solemn procession from yard to yard and house to house, it would be necessary also to reconsecrate the populace with a thorough-going "triduum," i.e. a period of three days entirely devoted to prayer, religious functions and alms-giving in terms of both money and produce. ("Just imagine him letting slip a chance of raking in money!" thought the rustics). At the end of the triduum, concluded Don Teresio, God might perhaps forgive them, but he would assuredly not forgive them all. One person there was amongst them for whom he, a simple priest, could do no more, so heinous were her iniquities; and he therefore washed his hands of her. He stretched

176

out his arms to pronounce the anathema: "She who danced with the Antichrist in the public square may never again set foot in church, nor receive the Sacraments, nor be buried in consecrated ground, until the Bishop of Novara, or the Pope in person, has vouchsafed her that absolution which they alone – not I! – can grant."

EIGHTEEN

The Last Winter

THE WINTER OF 1609-10, the last winter of Antonia's life, was fiercely cold in the Flatlands, but also very liberal with crystal skies and sunshine and fine landscapes. This was largely thanks to the snow which had covered the whole plain at the very onset of December and thereafter, turning to ice, had remained intact until the beginning of March. In fine weather when the sun shone the peasants would go off into the woods to set traps for foxes and snares for rabbits, to lime twigs and lay nets to catch birds. Some would even venture among the spring-water swamps bordering the Sesia, to capture the huge pike reduced by hunger to grabbing at anything that moved in the water: a glitter of metal or broken glass was enough to lure them up from the abysses of the liquid, freezing Inferno where they lived. There were those who had sighted wolves, or thought they had, and others who claimed to have spotted the tracks of lynx or bear. But that had been the case with practically every snowfall since time out of mind, and when the snow melted the bears and lynxes melted away with it and were heard of no more.

For the children winter was the wonderfullest season of the year; more so than summer (sweltering and rendered intolerable by mosquitoes) and more wonderful even than spring and autumn, when the labours of sowing and harvesting, there in the Flatlands, did not spare even the young "hands" like themselves. "First as a boy and then as a boss," says an old local proverb, "it's always work, work, work."

For the women, on the other hand, winter was the season of work-bees, of long evenings in the cowsheds, spinning, weaving and listening to tales around the lantern, their breath condensing in clouds and, in the shadows, the heavy presence of the livestock – the season of rumours and of gossip.

And even from the point of view of the work-bees it was a grand winter, with really fine natters and exceptional (sometimes prodigious) happenings, tales to be re-woven and re-concocted until they became brand-new. The most-told tale that year in all the byres, in all the gossipy evenings throughout the Flatlands, was the story (part old, part new) of Giovan Battista Caccia, nicknamed "Il Caccetta", the Novarese feudal lord and bandit of whom we have already said that his exploits were as famous in their day as now are the exploits of certain heroes of the football field, certain television "personalities" . . . Especially in November and December the gossips spoke of no one but Il Caccetta, but every time they named his name they broke off to make the sign of the cross, for Il Caccetta had been dead for several weeks. He was executed on September 19th 1609 in the Corso di Porta Tosa, in Milan, after seven years' imprisonment and a trial lasting for six: beheaded according to the law and in the presence of such a public as is proper to grand occasions – the nobility, the clergy, the high officials of the State, the religious confraternities with their banners, and behind these the throng of burgesses and peasants who had flocked in from all over the district to savour the great pleasure of seeing an aristocrat (one of the many richly deserving of such an end) mount the steps of a scaffold decked out at his own expense, and away with him amid whistlings and raspberries, ridding the world of his presence and leaving it that little bit better. It took two companies of halberdiers, it was rumoured in the cowsheds of the Flatlands, to protect the scaffold from the riff-raff, eager as ever to turn the beheading of a nobleman into a festive occasion with a little modest trading on the side, and possibly even going on the spree and dancing for joy through the streets and squares of Milan.

The performance, according to the chronicles of the time, was well up to standard, in all respects worthy of the notable traditions which Milan – even under Spanish rule – had maintained in this sector of the administration of justice. The scaffold was completely swathed in top-quality black velvet with trimmings of silver thread, and round it burnt twenty smokeless Genoese torches, each of four pounds' weight. In one corner, displayed for all who wished to see, was the carved walnut coffin in which the two pieces of Il Caccetta would, subsequent to the beheading, be recomposed for the solemn obsequies to follow.

Giovan Battista Caccia arrived at his last rendez-vous in a stylish black carriage with curtains mid-way between blue and violet (periwinkle blue, in fact – much in vogue at the time). At the foot of the scaffold his shackles were knocked off, while the gentle-women made remarks upon his physique. Disappointed, and in some cases even scandalized, they asked each other if this could be all there was to the renowned Caccetta. They could scarcely credit it, said they, that such savage crimes, such fearsome rapes, and all the rest of the exploits for which the name of Il Caccetta had been a byword, had been committed by a runt of a man knee-high to a gnome, remarkable only for his bulgy, glassy toad-eyes and his two legs stunted and wonky enough to raise a chuckle from a ricketty chicken. Such confabulations were held – or rather, on account of the uproar, shrieked – within a few yards of the soon-to-be-headless one, well situated to hear them had he not had far different thoughts to occupy his mind . . . It goes without saying that Il Caccetta was listening to no one and hearing nothing. He wore a wide-brimmed black hat, for all his hair had been shaved off; he stared into space, his lip trembled. At the topmost step he stumbled, and the executioner, Master Bernardo Sasso, his hood already lowered to conceal his face and wearing the pectoral with the cross on it and the leather apron, stepped forward to support him as far as the block. There, according to custom, Master Bernardo asked Il Caccetta's forgiveness for what he was about to do; but getting no answer, nor so much as a hint that he had understood, he twirled him around like a puppet towards the priest who had earlier confessed him and who now held out the crucifix for him to kiss – or, to be more exact, pressed it to his lips then plucked it away. From the mob came whistles and catcalls of disapproval at the scanty part Il Caccetta was playing in his death. One voice rose above the others: "Buck up, Bernardo! Lop off his head and have done with it!" The executioner raised a hand, asked the condemned man, "Have you anything to say before justice is done?"

The latter nodded, and immediately in the crowd a great silence fell, a silence laden with expectation. What could he be going to say? At this point Il Caccetta tugged off his hat and burst out sobbing. With lowered head he burbled "I . . . d . . . d . . . d . . . "

"Speak up!" howled a hundred voices from the front rows. "Can't hear a word!" And the mob joined in with "Spit it out, mate!"

"I die," – Il Caccetta brought it out in jerks – "I die for the sins I have committed and likewise" . . . – with his eye on the Authorities – "for those I have not committed!" And who in the world could imagine what he thought he was on about? Plainly the wording had been carefully thought out, but it moved no one and fell completely flat. Il Caccetta turned round dispiritedly, and Master Bernardo, a man of sterling good sense and a first-rate executioner, realizing that his decapitee was about to come out with some rubbish thought up on the spur of the moment, or do something he ought not to do, gave a signal and the drums all round the scaffold started rolling. Up stepped the headsman's two assistants, a pair of hefties standing head and shoulders above Il Caccetta. They seized him in the very act of shouting the words (inaudible anyway) "Down with Spain! Up with *Franza* and *Il Roi!*", they bent him double and chained him down so speedily that he didn't even know what was upon him, still yelling as he was. Master Bernardo raised the axe and clove it down – the drum-rolls ceased, one of the assistants picked up the severed head by the ears and displayed it to the mob. Seen thus from afar it looked a fake, a plaster mask; and a little grotesque with its lolling mouth, its staring eyes, the tip of the protruding tongue.

"Justice is done," intoned the headsman, bowing towards the Authorities. From every part of the Corso and every balcony rose cheers of approval, a veritable ovation: "Long live Master Bernardo! Bravo!" "That's the stuff!" "We've got him out of our hair at last!" "He died like the pig he was!"

The sentence which condemned him states that Il Caccetta ended up on the scaffold for committing *"many murthers"*; in fact he was got rid of because strongly suspected of plotting against Spain and Spanish rule; and also because by now there were too many people he would have endeavoured to kill if returned to circulation. But in the cow-byres of Zardino, and throughout the Flatlands, the story of Il Caccetta and his misdeeds was at once supplanted by the Legend of Il Caccetta: the tale of a criminal for love's sake, strong-handed with the strong, magnanimous with the weak and a "parfit gentil knyght" with the ladies. Above all, talk turned once more to that lovely creature Margherita Casati, for whom the twenty-year-old Caccetta had lost his wits and his good name. She, it was said, was the cause of all his misfortunes and all his crimes. A love, moreover, so violent and so tragic could not have gone up in a puff of smoke as everyone supposed. On the contrary, it survived after death! For on that 19th of September, declared the gossips, Margherita was there, in Milan, in the front row, right beneath the scaffold. Like stone she stood, expiating her share of guilt, for we all know that in these matters the woman is always just a little guilty – for beauty is never without sin! Yes, even before, in prison, she had been to visit him. Many times had she entered his cell, and this was made possible by the intercession of a very great lord – in some of the byres they whispered of a Savoia, in others of a Farnese – who had dropped a word into the ear of the Count of Fuentes, Governor of the State of Milan, and succeeded in moving him to pity . . .

Not all the Gossips, however, agreed with this version of the story, focused entirely on Margherita Casati. There were other versions, for though Margherita had been the best known and perhaps the most beautiful of Il Caccetta's women she had been by no means the only one, let alone the last. After her they had come by the dozen, some even from the common people: peasant-women, innkeepers' wives, married damsels and mature women, all claiming their part in the legend and, in some cases, cash: and in many cow-byres in the Flatlands they had their supporters. A certain Marzia from Sizzano and a certain Francesca from Oleggio, though they had both been carried off by force and violated for months on end – and not just by Il Caccetta either! no, by his whole gang – now maintained that all that ravishment had given rise to profound passions with promises to match: promises of marriage, promises to recognize their issue as legitimate and name them sole heirs of the Counts Caccia . . . Unluckily for

Francesca, and also for Marzia, Il Caccetta subsequently died in the manner known to all, without being able to carry out his good intentions . . . But they had hired two attorneys-at-law (each, needless to say, unbeknownst to the other) to safeguard the interests of their respective offspring and see to it that they were not deprived of their due. Not by anyone! Useless to wonder what became of those lawsuits: most likely they never even began . . .

Also in circulation during those early months of 1610 was a print of Il Caccetta's portrait, the work of a Milanese engraver who had seen his subject only on the scaffold, and that for a split second, and had subsequently immortalized him. A number of gentlewomen of Milan and Novara, who if they had actually known Il Caccetta in the flesh, as they were eager to make out, would never for a moment have credited that etching which bore virtually no resemblance to its original, shed genuine tears over it. But that is part of the natural order of things human, and requires no comment. In the stalls and stables of the Flatlands, however, after the first spurt of excitement over Il Caccetta's death and his luckless and intemperate love-affairs, talk continued for months about his money – how much he had and who would inherit it. Two schools of thought came into being, two factions: those who maintained that Il Caccetta, and therefore his heirs, possessed at least a hundred thousand gold *scudi*, which in current terms would have made him a billionaire, and the opposite school, which held that Il Caccetta had been rich, very rich indeed, but at the time of his death had nothing left at all. If no sensational titbit came to light in the way of undiscovered wills or bastard children recognized as legitimate, Il Caccetta's sole and universal heir was bound to be young Gregorio, son of the deceased and the gentlewoman (also deceased) Antonia Tornielli. A splendid looking lad he was, said the gossips, a real Prince Charming, tall and dark with black eyes, and in character the clean contrary of his father. But one day news reached the byres of the Flatlands that Il Caccetta's estate had been confiscated at the very moment of his death on the scaffold, and that even the city of Novara was putting in a claim for it. The disappointment was colossal. "Well, I call that really unfair!" protested the Gossips. But at length, reluctantly, they turned to other matters . . .

Also under discussion in the stalls of Zardino that winter was the Nidasios' Antonia, as they called her, who had had the nerve to turn down, among many other claimants to her hand, such a personage as Pier Luigi Caroelli, nephew of Count Ottavio Caroelli who owned half Zardino and half the Flatlands to boot! Who did she think she was? What was she setting her sights for? The marriageable girls and their mothers, aunts, grandmothers and sisters-in-law, which is to say practically all the women in the village, were highly incensed. Antonia, they said, is a witch who ensnares men with her magic arts just to make fools of them, since she has no intention of marrying them. She had been seen about at night but she had no sweetheart. Who was she going out with? She was one who "wore out" other girls' sweethearts for them, made them weak at the knees, diverted their attentions, sent them all of a dither simply by her presence, drove them mad to no purpose. And they numbered on their fingers the swains the witch had "worn out" for others. The first in order of time was poor Biagio, the Borghesini sisters' idiot nephew, but he was of no interest to any girl and no one envied her him – let her keep him! But then the genuine suitors had come along, and within living memory, declared the gossips, no one in Zardino had seen a girl who "caused so much chaff" (i.e. sent so many suitors packing) as had Antonia. How dare she turn her nose up at their boys? Did she, a foundling, aspire to marry the heir to the throne of Spain? Among the "worn out" suitors were two of the village lads, Giovanni Ligrina and Cristofero Cerruti, worth their weight in gold and acceptable even with your eyes shut: hard-working, thrifty, not a vice to their names. What's more, one of the two, Ligrina, had fallen sick as a result of her refusal, pining away to the extent of not wanting to look at any other woman and declaring that he intended to remain "a boy" (that is, a bachelor) as long as he lived.

Other suitors came from elsewhere, lured by the witch's magic arts, and no wonder, decreed the Gossips, since in the words of the proverb, *"L'om, l'asan e 'l pulòn in i püsè cujòn"* (men, donkeys and capons are the stupidest beasts in the world). One Pietro Balzarini from Casalbeltrame and one Giovanni Beltrame from Vicolungo had time and again despatched lutenists to Bartolo Nidasio's house to serenade Antonia, but nothing had come of it. And there had been stories in the past which had ended badly. A certain Paolo Sozzani, for example, of whom the records tell us nothing except that he was not a local, unable to bear the notion of being repulsed, got drunk, lay in wait among the kitchen gardens and attempted to take the girl by force. She had struggled to her feet and made off home, but – it was whispered in the cowsheds – with "the seed on her apron": a mark of infamy!

"That girl is a witch," repeated the Gossips, and they censured Francesca Nidasio for not teaching her her place in the world, and indeed for treating her better than if she had been her own real daughter, allowing her to get above herself beyond all right and reason . . . The new age was also to blame, of course, so free and easy! "There was a time," grumbled the Gossips, retying the knot of their kerchiefs under their chins and then raising their hands to heaven, "when such things didn't happen. A nobleman turned down by a foundling, indeed! Where's it all going to end? What else will we live to see? Ah, misery me! . . . "

The Gossips, of course, knew the gentleman in question and were aware that his gesture of sending a marriage-broker to ask for the hand of such a girl as Antonia had been an eccentricity, not to be taken amiss but not to be taken seriously either. To be perfectly frank, would any girl in the Flatlands have married that nobleman, bald as a coot and no longer in his first youth? Pier Luigi Caroelli, the *perdapè* as he was called by his landowner uncle's peasants and share-croppers, possessed nothing of his own but an aristocratic surname and this untranslatable nickname which in our part of the world was, and still is, bestowed on idlers, dreamers, failures and the like; on such as do things haphazardly, for the sake of doing them, but never get anywhere. Pretending he was a good bargain was a lie, and if it had been a question of their own daughters, and not Antonia, the same Zardino hags who were singing his praises would soon have changed their tune.

Nor was the *perdapè*'s physical appearance of the best. Tall, bony, without a trace of colour in his cheeks, with a goatee and moustache trimmed according to the fashion of the time, Pier Luigi Caroelli was a *giuvin vecc*, a juvenile at thirty-five (give or

185

take a year) who rolled his R's to excess and dressed rather affectedly in stylish patched-up clothes made to measure for somebody shorter and more thickset than he, maybe his uncle the count, or one of his wealthy cousins. He lived in Novara, in Palazzo Caroelli, where he had a ground-floor room in which he slept, wrote, received rare visits from his friends and, when he felt disinclined to go to the kitchens to eat with the servants, could prepare himself a couple of eggs or a salad. In return for the room put at his disposal, and the cast-off clothes he handed down, Count Ottavio his uncle condescended to use him as his steward and right-hand man. Thus the *perdapè*, astride a mule, appeared now and then in Zardino, where the Caroellis had woodlands, pastures and farmlands, to keep an eye on the share-croppers – Cesare Ligrina, Andrea Falcotti and Antonio Scaccabozzi by name, this last of La Torre (a farmstead now vanished). The *perdapè* made sure that they did not fell trees or, if they were supposed to plant them, that they did so. He saw to it that they did not turn the watermeadows into paddy-fields to make more money. He also saw, or pretended to see, to the sharing-out of the produce, making meticulous notes of sacks and bushels, firkins and kilderkins, the number of faggots and of capons, of hogs and the quality of the same and so on, registering them in a parchment-bound account-book which he always carried under his arm and which the peasants (who knows why!) called his "bread-and-butter book". When it came to writing he adjusted athwart his nose the bottoms of two bottles held together by a spring. These he called "eye-glasses", and they sent the children into fits as they clapped their hands and cried, "The owl! The owl!"

But the fact that everyone in the Flatlands spoke ill of him was purely the result of human ingratitude. Within living memory none of the stewards of the Counts Caroelli had let himself be swindled so easily, and with such courtesy, as did the *perdapè*. And that was not all: he spoke to the peasants in polite, formal terms and didn't lay hands on their women, not even on the sly. He neither molested them nor attempted to mount them, as had the stewards who preceded him, and this fact eventually came to trouble the thoughts and dreams of the peasants, who were darned if they could find a reason for it. They racked their brains and wondered what was wrong with the *perdapè*, (or was it with their women?) that he didn't make a pass at them. He didn't even cast a glance in their direction! Until one day they solved the problem by deciding that he was a *cüpia*, that is, "one of those". (All the sexual aberrations catalogued by Krafft-Ebing were, in the Flatlands, summed up for centuries in one single human type, the *cüpia*, and in this single word for it). Wherever Pier Luigi Caroelli went, his account-book under his arm and his "eye-glasses" in the inside pocket of his doublet, on every side of him bloomed forth allusions, double meanings, winks, obscene gestures and words in local jargon. So that later, when it was known that he had sent a marriage-broker from Borgo San Gaudenzio to Bartolo Nidasio, to ask for Antonia's hand in marriage, they all woke up with a start. "Well I'll be jiggered!" commented the flabbergasted peasantry. "Who ever would have thought it? The *perdapè!*"

What the peasants of the Flatlands did not know, but of which posterity ought by rights to be informed, is that the nobleman Pier Luigi Caroelli dreamt of being, and set out to be, a poet. *"Let the plains rejoice and Pan summon to the gathering"* is the first, electrifying line of a volume of *Lyrics* printed in Milan, at the author's expense, in the year 1612. His sole production, for Caroelli never had the money to print another. An unreadable book, in our day and age, and probably even when it first saw the light, stuffed as it is from start to finish with Nymphs and Fauns and Satyrs, with the haunts and heights of classical mythology and clichés repeated *ad nauseam*: the "Prime Mover of the Skies" (God), the "brilliant suns" (women's eyes), the "most vile of plains" (the Flatlands), the "freezing Eagle" (north wind) that assails the "genial hovels" (houses) of the ploughmen . . . A pointless book, for me who, alas, was forced to leaf through it. Not a trace of Antonia or of other characters in our story, but only anonymous unknowns (*"to the most illustrious and excellent poet"*, *"to the sovereign poet"*, *"to the favourite nephew of the Muses, supreme in Parnassus"* etc.), Caroelli's fellow-artists to whom many of the pieces in the book are dedicated. Therefore, at least for the moment, while waiting for some piazza in Italy to be graced with a statue to the Unknown Poet (for which with every day that passes we realize the increasing urgency) I would maintain that this trifling mention of the poet Caroelli, and of his unreadable *oeuvre*, will suffice . . .

NINETEEN

The Indictment

IN THOSE FIRST MONTHS of the Year of Grace 1610, with Il Caccetta dead and his gang broken up, the Flatlands were deprived of brigands terrorizing the highways and the villages, and furnishing material for the wintry-nightly tales in the cattle-byres. Partly for this reason, perhaps, and partly because human beings have always had (and probably still have) a need for dangers to keep their spirits on the boil and vital functions ticking over, word went round once more concerning the Fearsome Beast, or – more simply – the Beast. This Beast, which according to place and time acquired dozens of names in dialect, and even altered in a number of characteristics while remaining essentially the same, was a monstrous and fabulous animal which for long ages incarnated the terrors of the inhabitants of this region, roving from the Alps to the Po and making its presence felt now and then over the years with the slaughter of peasants and shepherds and the massacre of livestock, but most of all on account of the scare it put into folk who had the mischance to bump into it; after which they, as long as they had breath in their bodies, never ceased to relate that encounter and relive that thrill. Especially on festival days, and most of all when under the influence. To get the latest on the Fearsome Beast, not only in the seventeenth century but also in those that followed, you had simply, on a Sunday, to cross the threshold of any tavern in any village in the plains or the hills, and strike up a conversation. Nor would I dismiss the possibility that, by searching around with pains and with patience, one might come across someone who had met it even today. We have descriptions and depictions of the Fearsome Beast illustrating its metamorphosis over the ages. We know, for example, that in the Middle Ages it was seen with enormous horns, huge crests and a scaly hide, whereas in modern and contemporary times – the very latest sightings date from the turn of the century – it took on shapes we are more familiar with, those of a young bull or a huge dog with the head of a boar; in short the "pigdog", an animal which for long aeons existed in the nightmares of mankind but now fast becoming extinct, surviving in Italian only as a coarse exclamation. Having now become intelligent (and how!) we may now sneer at this Beast, but at the time of our story, at the dawning of the seventeenth century, the Fearsome Beast still wreaked real havoc and claimed real victims. This happened mostly in the wintertime, and mostly in times of peace and prosperity, when there were no wars, no floods or other natural or historical calamities to vex the country folk; as was in fact the case in that month of February 1610, when if we are to credit the prattle of the Flatlands the Fearsome Beast awoke of a sudden after several decades of lethargy and began to rove ever wider and wider, from the Sesia to the foothills, making forays both by day and by night. There were corpses to show for it: first a carter on the road from Briona to Barengo – the very same haunts where Il Caccetta had ridden rough-shod for years – then a girl from Castellazzo, who left home at dawn to fetch water from the stream and never returned alive. Both corpses, it was said, bore the unmistakable tokens of the hoofs and fangs of the Beast, which was sighted in the following weeks by a dozen people, perhaps more, in various places including the vicinity of a spring bounding the territory of Zardino. These sightings usually took place in the early morning, just before sunrise, or soon after sunset. Those who saw the fearsome Beast were, as in the past, wagoners, wayfarers, peasants on the road to work in the fields or on their way home again, women going out at dawn to fetch water from the spring, or rising from their beds at dead of night to tend the livestock.

The Fearsome Beast, according to all who had seen it, gave far warning of its approach through the woods with the massive crashing of broken branches and a trampling of hoofs. Its voice was a blood-curdling compound of dog-bark and pig-grunt. It was huger than a heifer and very hairy, its head big and bristly as a boar's, and white fangs that glistened snowy in the gloaming. Its eyes – small and red – were eloquent of its diabolic nature. It vanished at a sign of the cross or if shown a medallion of the Madonna or other consecrated image, or if you recited a prayer. Everyone, therefore, having to reach the fields in the early morning and fearful of meeting the Beast, left home weighed down with medallions and sacred images, and thoroughly equipped to put it to flight . . . And there were even cases of those who, hearing the din of the Beast in the distance, and its threatening voice, had had time to grab a crucifix; whereat the Beast, though remaining fast by, had not appeared . . .

Towards the end of the same winter there began in Zardino a series of amazing, or out of the ordinary, or simply puzzling events, all of which, however, indubitably indicated the presence of a witch in the village. Or so the experts affirmed. Animals suddenly stricken with mysterious maladies and felled to the ground; women and girls who in the course of a single day were bereft of the power of speech; indecipherable signs in the snow in places where it was untrodden, no human footprint or animal track to be seen; letters of the alphabet written back-to-front to form unintelligible words, who knows with what intent! . . . These phenomena and more besides, mentioned in the course of the trial, were immediately linked by the gossips with all the talk that had gone on in the cowsheds that past winter, concerning the diabolic and witchlike artifices with which Antonia ensnared her sweethearts. Nor was it only the gossips who were worried about it, but also their menfolk. Many asked themselves, "How was it it didn't dawn on us before? A witch in our midst and we didn't even notice!"

All Antonia's words and deeds, and every move she made, were thereafter followed with the utmost attention and interpreted in the light of what ensued. For example, if Antonia entered a certain house to do something or other and during the next few days a child fell ill, or a dog died unexpectedly, or a calf was born deformed, that – they said – was the real reason for her visit. The concatenations of events, the coincidences, were legion: Antonia said hullo to a certain girl and the next day the girl fell out of the hay-loft; Antonia passed along a certain road and wood-chips were later found there, arranged on the ground in a way that was mysterious to say the least . . . Nor is that all. If she looked up it would later rain, or even snow; if she looked at the ground the well would run dry, or the cellar roof would fall in; if she pointed a finger towards the horizon you could be sure that over there, or at any rate in that general direction, sooner or later a fire would break out, or the Fearsome Beast would assault a peasant; and if she sighed it was troubles for all and sundry!

Everyone gave Antonia a wide berth. On the roads, in the farmyards, wherever she went people fled, dragging their livestock behind them if they had time to do so; if she called out to a girl-friend, or to an old crone who was indoors, they hastily barred the windows, the doors, sealed every crack, so that not only she but even her voice could not sneak in. Whosoever came across her in the street, if there was no escape or chance of turning back, crossed themselves and hurried by, averting their faces. And who knows how Antonia reacted, if react she did, to this sudden hysteria on the part of her fellow-villagers? Who knows what thoughts went through her head, when she saw herself treated this way by every single soul, even those she had considered her friends! No trial for witchcraft, as far as we know, ever concerned itself with the feelings of the witch. On the contrary, it was imagined she was overjoyed at any great wickedness done or about to be done: she was happiness personified! And the worse everyone treated her the happier she was, for that was the sure and unmistakable sign that her sorceries were flourishing. (But even if she suffered, all well and good! "The sooner she drops dead the better!" was the way people reasoned).

To defend themselves against the witch and rid themselves of her, the Zardinians turned to their priest. It was a handful of men who took the initiative, following a meeting of the Christian Brethren. They couldn't go on like this! Something had to be done. Anxiety was abroad in the village, and it wasn't just the usual old church hens either, but the farmers and the peasants too, run-of-the-mill people, the same who skimped on their tithes, went to church as seldom as they could manage, and had no love for Don Teresio. But black magic is a serious matter, and who is not afeard of it? "If the cattle get diseased, or the seed for planting rots on us, what are we to do?" Only yesterday, declared the men of the brotherhood, this cow belonging to that peasant gave no

192

milk; a quantity of fruit-trees died over the winter, and what could be the reason? Such-and-such's child has a raging fever . . . What on earth has come upon us? They appealed to the priest. It was up to him, who had the specific duty and authority, to draw the witch's fangs with exorcisms and other methods deemed to be effective. Or else to denounce her to the Holy Office in Novara because, they said, the matter was serious, very serious indeed, and they, the Christian Brethren, had proof of it. They could testify that the girl attended the sabbaths, and had been witnessed on her way there by every single member of the confraternity! Last summer, they averred, in the *risaroli* season, they encountered her after dark, not once but several times, in the vicinity of the Tree Knoll, but at the time they gave no thought to those trysts because they assumed she had a sweetheart . . . But Antonia had no sweetheart and it was only subsequently, during the winter, that it dawned on them why she was going to the Knoll. A place, let it be said, where witches had long been known to meet! But they had tumbled to this rather late in the day, when strange things had already begun to take place in the village: cows falling sick, entire households losing their voices, children tumbling out of haylofts etc. . . . "Help us, Don Teresio," they begged. "Give us some advice, at least! What is to be done?"

Don Teresio kept himself to himself for many days, without giving an opinion on one side or the other, in favour of Antonia or against her. "We must pray," he kept repeating. "We must pray abundantly. If there were more religion here in Zardino certain signs which denote the presence of the Devil amongst us would surely not occur!"

He touched on the subject at Mass one Sunday, while dealing with the topic of sin and retribution, the latter of which proceedeth always from God. He quoted the Bible, the *Book of Maccabees:* "Verily, verily I say unto you: you shall now by God's will have the just reward for your pride!" And he went on to speak of the Seven Plagues of Egypt which struck the People of Israel at the time of the Pharaohs; and he alluded to the two scourges of Zardino, which is to say Antonia and the Fearsome Beast, though he named neither of them. He simply confined himself to saying that the two scourges were just, predictable, and foreseen by him.

"Certain it is," cried he, stabbing his forefinger at the faithful, "that God would not permit such diabolic presences to rear their heads in these woods, and such events to happen in this village, if your barnyards and your byres had not (for years!) witnessed sacrilegious talk against Him, against His servant who is addressing you this moment and against his right to receive tithes and gifts in kind from his flock. With more devotion and more largesse of alms certain things would not occur!"

Another fortnight passed, during which a child scalded itself with boiling water, a hired-man injured himself badly by falling on his scythe, and a number of other untoward events took place in Zardino and neighbourhood without anyone daring to speak to the priest about the witch, and without his mentioning the subject to a living soul. After the sermon about the Plagues of Egypt the whole matter remained suspended in mid-air, and even in the village they talked about it less. Until one April day (it was a Monday) Don Teresio shouldered the haversack he used for important occasions and went to Novara to denounce Antonia to the Holy Office, indeed to Inquisitor Manini in person. As it is written in the records of the trial: "*Before the Most Reverend Brother Gregorio Manini of Gozzano, Inquisitor for purposes of heretical witchcraft throughout the diocese of Novara, appeared Don . . .* "

The entire proceedings of the ecclesiastical courts versus Antonia ("*contra quendem Antoniam de Giardino dicta la Stria*") took place between two dates: that of the legal charge (made April 12th 1610) and that of the sentence (August 20th of the same year), as we have stated above. What happened in the five months between April and August could perhaps be called an inquiry, which lasted practically the length of the whole proceedings. During that period, apart from the accused, a score or so of witnesses were heard, among them the accuser himself, Don Teresio, who in fact testified on two occasions: first on the day when he preferred the charge, and again on the following Monday. From the proceedings of those two sworn statements we learn that Don Teresio, in the course of his service in Zardino, had been promoted to the rank of Presbyter, or senior priest, and that indeed he was addressed by this title: "*Presbiter Teresius Rabozzi, rector ecclesiae Giardini.*"

194

On being encouraged to speak freely, Don Teresio seized the opportunity to unburden himself of what gnawed most keenly at his vitals, things which in the pulpit of Zardino he had no chance to say. He had had cure of souls for nigh on nine years, he began, and had still not managed to scrape together enough cash to "break the seals," as the phrase then was (i.e. to buy himself into the benefices of a real parish). Not that the village of Zardino – nothing more than a huddle of farmsteads, according to his description – was all that short of money; but the church had been abandoned for the best part of half a century, had fallen into the hands of *quistoni* who used it for breeding silkworms, spending all their time trafficking with the local peasantry and thinking of nothing else but lining their own pockets; so that he, arriving in that village from Novara on the evening of the very day he had been ordained priest, had thrown all his energies and enthusiasm into redressing a very gravely compromised situation, succeeding only in part . . .

He listed his achievements. He had been obliged, he said, to restore the crumbling bell-tower; to carry out repairs on the fabric both of the church and the presbytery; to repair the roof of a certain Oratory of Sant'Anna, previously unsafe; to acquire hangings and furnishings for the church, so lacking in liturgical accoutrements at the time of his arrival that for months he had had to make do with everyday pottery and glass, if not indeed with kitchenware. He had been forced to bear the expense of major lawsuits in Novara, and others were still in train: against Count Caroelli, against an aristocrat named Ferraro (for tithes never received), against one Fornaro (or Fornari) of Cameriano on account of a spring of water which the ancestors of this Fornaro had appropriated, even deviating the course of the stream, so that the suit at present seemed too difficult and costly to be concluded within the foreseeable future. Surveys and counter-surveys – a headache and no mistake! He had had, and still had, numerous disputes with parishioners who refused to submit to the intricate system of taxes, compulsory "gifts in kind", and offerings due in Passion Week, on Ember days, Rogation days and Saints' days, upon which depended the existence of the Zardino chaplaincy and that of the chaplain himself. Moreover, he had undermined his health in the struggle against dances, carnivals, Maydays, harvest homes and other occasions of sin; in uprooting magic and superstitious practices; in spreading the Word of God among those boors of the Flatlands who were – and in such terms Don Teresio described his flock – *"the stingiest and most hard-hearted individuals on the face of the earth"*. And had they in any way shown him gratitude? In no wise! On the contrary: they accused him of being fanatical and money-grabbing, they nicknamed him the Jabbering Jinx, the bloodsucker, the *zèccola* – their name for the sheep-tick. They had once deposited a dead crow – bird of ill-omen – on his doorstep; and some of them, passing him on the road, would cross their fingers beneath their cloaks to ward off the evil eye.

Then, in recent times, had come the business of this girl Antonia, who lived in the house of Bartolo Nidasio but in actual fact was a foundling, that is, born of the filthiest sin there is, the sin of the flesh; she who told the country boors that to make the wheat grow "a cartload of dung was worth more than all the priest's prayers", and that they shouldn't pay the Passion money or the tithes unless these were laid down in the "Notary's Instrument" (i.e. a notarized deed proving the ownership of land). And also that just as the sun rises and sets without the need of humans to help it, likewise man is born and dies without need of priests and other parasites. Because the priest does not work. Not a hand's turn. He is like the rat that gnaws the bread of others; and, if he finds no bread, "the rat dies."

All these things, Don Teresio told the Inquisitor, and many more besides which he was loath to report on account of the respect he owed to his auditor, had fallen from her lips in public and been heard by a host of witnesses, both in Zardino itself and in the neighbourhood, creating scandal and horror among all Godfearing persons. And this Antonia who incited the clod-hoppers to transgress against the law of the Almighty, and against His Commandments, and against His Tithes, was the very same who some years earlier had had the cheek to have her portrait done by some common dauber of Madonnas and Saints, and wearing the vestments and with the halo of the Madonna of Divine Succour; and this in a wayside shrine still extant and plain to see for anyone entering Zardino from the direction of the Knolls and La Badia – which had caused much pride in her, and sacrilegious arrogance. For on the occasion of the visit of Monsignor Carlo Bascapè, Bishop of Novara, she had had the temerity to laugh in his face. In church, what is more, and in the course of the sermon. And lastly, she had danced in the piazza with the *lanzi* when those Lutheran fiends had suddenly turned up in Zardino one morning and remained the whole day, befouling the church steps, plundering the peasant folk and committing their habitual infamies. In consequence of that episode, said Don Teresio, he had forbidden her to take the Sacraments or set foot in church until she had been to Novara and returned with the bishop's pardon, hoping (he declared) with the severity of that punishment to bring her to her senses. Instead, Antonia had thereupon started to talk freely and publicly in the manner alluded to above, maintaining – reprobate! – that priests were worse than useless and God along with them, and that it was better to enjoy your own money than hand it to the priest.

The matter of the sabbaths had arisen later, of its own accord and without any particular stir. But it was scarcely surprising, for with her precedents and inclinations what else could such a girl do, once she grew up, if not attend the sabbaths? And so indeed she did. Last summer, said Don Teresio, Antonia had been caught more than once in the open fields after nightfall by the Christian Brethren, who were out rounding up escaped *risaroli*, and recognized by them as a witch. With regard to this, Don Teresio explained that the trysts between the witch and the Devil usually took place (according to what they said in the village) on the knoll known as the Tree Knoll, under an ancient chestnut with a sinister reputation because of the satanic rites formerly enacted there. On the trunk of that tree was a mysterious inscription with certain letters the wrong way round, which the yokels insisted on reading as "Tree of Memories", whereas in point of fact, of course, it meant . . . Goodness knows what it meant, or in what language! The Devil, stated Don Teresio, called by Isidore of Seville *serpens lubricus*, and by St Bernard *indefessus hostes*, frequently expresses himself in dead languages unknown to most people; as is witnessed by Anselm of Aosta and other authors. (Banished as he was among the churls of Zardino our priestly figure would never have let slip that rare opportunity to flaunt his learning in the great city).

Concluding his testimony and indictment, Don Teresio appealed directly to the Tribunal of the Holy Office, and to the Inquisitor in person, that for the love of God he should investigate the witch, whether she had already consigned her soul to the Devil or could still be prevailed upon to abjure him; and, if this abjuration were no longer possible, he asked him, and indeed implored him, to remove that hotbed of heresy from his small flock of faithful, who had suffered not a little perturbation on account of it. Because, he said in summing up, *"verba movent, exempla trahunt"* (Words shift you, example *drags* you). Quoting from who knows which Father of the Church . . .

TWENTY

The Witnesses

ALTHOUGH THE HOLY OFFICE in Novara did summon Antonia, before hearing the accused herself they heard (April 20th) one *Agostinus Cuccus filius quondam Simonis*, Agostino Cucchi, son of the late Simone, and (April 25th) *Andreas Falcottus filius Ioannis*, Andrea Falcotti son of Giovanni, and also *Nicolaus Barberius filius quondam Agostini*, Nicolò Barbero son of the late Agostino (i.e. Teresina's father). All three were residents of the village of Zardino and all three peasants and managers of farms on behalf of the owners of the same – in other words, share-croppers. Interrogated separately they all stated that they were speaking for themselves personally and also, in the utmost confidence, by proxy in the name of the Christian Brethren; that is, for the other members of the Confraternity of St Rock who while patrolling after dark outside the village had come upon the witch on her way to her trysts with the Devil. As many as four times, they said, they had pursued and surrounded her with their torches, taking her for a *risarolo* disguised as a woman. On the first occasion they had escorted her home, that is to the house of Bartolo Nidasio, enjoining him to keep her locked in. Later on, discovering her in the neighbourhood of the Tree Knoll, they had asked her where she was going and whom she was going to meet. They had even struck her with their whips and she had spat at them and answered, "I am going to meet my lord and your enemy, who if he were to appear before you at this moment you'd tumble out of your saddles from sheer fright!" A phrase, they avowed, which at the time seemed of no importance at all, whereas it patently meant that the girl was on her way to meet the Devil.

They went on to list the venues of these encounters. All fell between the village and the Tree Knoll, where the road forks, one way to San Nazzaro di Biandrate and the other to the banks of the Sesia. On one sole occasion, they reported, they had spotted her on the road leading to the Mill of the Three Kings and thence to Novara. They could not, unfortunately, remember the dates, but Andrea Falcotti pointed out that unless·there were gypsies in the area, or reports of stolen livestock, the Brotherhood of San Rocco usually made sorties in the period embracing the weeding and the harvesting of the rice, which is to say from June to September, and that their encounters with the witch had therefore occurred during those months. Questioned as to whether they had themselves seen the Devil, and what he looked like, the horror-struck peasants answered no indeed!, and swiftly crossed themselves. They had a red cross painted on their cowls, they explained to the Inquisitor, for that specific purpose – to protect them from encounters with the Devil while they were abroad by night in the woods. Their duty was to defend the village from evil spirits and cattle-thieves. In addition to that, during the rice season they restored fugitive *risaroli* to their rightful owners. They took an oath they had told all they knew, and that it was the truth. If further facts came to light they would come back. Upon which they took themselves off.

The Christian Brethren and their zeal were followed, on April 28th, 29th and 30th, by the Gossips. In addition to Agostina Borghesini, of whom we have already said that she told the tale of the Idiot Biago, during that period Inquisitor Manini had occasion to interrogate Angela Ligrina, Maria, (also Ligrina) Francesca Mambaruti and Irene Formica; all of whom are described in the records of the trial as "*most pious women*", busy (or at least Maria and Irene were) with collecting church-alms from door to door or otherwise engaged in good works. Suitably questioned by the Inquisitor, these "most pious women" related, with a riot of detail, all the rumours concerning the witch's maleficent doings in the village – the dead chickens, the deaf children, the deformed calves and so on and so forth. In addition they brought proof that the Devil was there in Zardino, and of his trysts with Antonia. The sabbaths, they said, occurred regularly every Thursday night, on the knoll known as the Tree Knoll. Strange lights to be seen, weird music to be heard, while in the village there were also rumours that the devil in the form of a billy-goat had been seen prancing and dancing erect on his hind legs, displaying outsized privates. And that the previous year an old dame by the name of Flavia Maraschino, finding herself one Sunday all on her own in the vineyard, in latening summer at the time of the grape-harvest, was approached by a young man of winsome aspect who seemed to have sprung out of nowhere, dressed all in velvet like a great lord; and he asked her if there were any newborn baby boys in the village . . . But as soon as she made the sign of the cross he melted into thin air. "Pouf!" concluded Maria Ligrina, raising her hand and puffing across her palm.

Nor was that all. A girl of marriageable age, Caterina Formica daughter of the witness Angela Formica, having betaken herself last winter shortly before Christmas to gather a faggot of wood on the Tree Knoll, at her home-coming had witnessed a terrifying and supernatural occurrence: the logs and brushwood of the bundle were transformed into serpents, which crawled into the cracks of the floor and there vanished. They were Devils! Antonia, continued the Gossips, attended the sabbaths and coupled with the Devil, living without the Sacraments of Mass and Confession just like brute beasts or the savages of the New World. And she said heretical things, and was herself a heretic, without so much as bothering to hide the fact. For when one day Don Teresio chid her and threatened her with hell in the presence of Irene Formica, and of the declarant Francesca Mambaruti, she'd had the gall to reply that heaven and hell are here on earth, and that after death there is nothing: "a nothing as big as the skies and in that nothing the humbug of the priests." In the same way she scoffed at the innumerable "tributes", meaning payments in kind and donations based on custom and tradition, which Don Teresio was most assiduous in exacting, and in the prescribed quantities, sending Gossips round from barnyard to barnyard, or calling there in person . . .

The interesting thing emerging from the court records is not so much the tales of the bigots or the irreverencies of the witch as the wide-ranging and highly intricate system of tax-exactions which was the reverse side of the priest's – or at least the country priest's – profession in the early seventeenth century. A continual hurry and scurry, a full-scale commercial enterprise – keeping an eye on souls, yes, but also on the crops, whenever anything was gathered or a harvest meant a whack for himself. It wasn't simply a matter of raking in the tithes, those laid down in notarized deeds as due to the Church in perpetuity on the produce of the soil. No, there was more: there were tithes due on untithed produce, that is, on anything growing other than in the fields, either in kitchen gardens or in the wild; there were the cubic feet of water which the community and private individuals alike owed scot free to irrigate Church lands; and there was the forced labour that all farmers, be they land-owners, share-croppers, hired men or casual labourers, were obliged to contribute free of charge at particular times of year; there were additional payments at Christmas, Easter, Epiphany, Pentecost and the Feast-days of the local Patron Saint, laid down for each parishioner according to his means: so and so must contribute a pair of hen turkeys, someone else a goose, another a demijohn of *vino baragiolo*, the somewhat sharp wine they used to make around these parts; there were *donations* and *compulsory offerings* for processions and Saints' days; there was the offering for oil and the offering for the candlewax and who knows how many other odds and ends that in the proceedings against Antonia the Gossips didn't even bother to mention. But which existed and were collected, in the name of God and of custom.

On top of all this came the "measured sack" for Rogation days, to finance all those processions with which the priest made good weather or bad, inducing it to rain or shine, and the "Passiontide Half-Bushel", two crushing tariffs of olden times levied upon cereal crops or rice, depending on the area, which had little by little been falling into disuse in the Flatlands since the Spanish occupation. When that occurred the priests had had to renounce certain of their privileges to make way for the new overlords, but Don Teresio, after a lull of more than half a century, had achieved the feat of re-introducing these two taxes in Zardino with regular deeds under the seal of a certain Ragno, notary public in Novara. Don Teresio based his case on a tradition attested to by the archives of his church until the year 1556, after which it had fallen into disuse without, however, being abolished.

"Let the dominus (i.e. priest) of Giardino" – and we are here consulting a deed signed by the said Ragno in this year of 1610 –*"be obliged to recite the Passion at the High Altar every Sunday from the Feast of the Holy Cross on May the 3rd until the Feast-day of September 14th, and by ancient custom the people, idest every landowner or share-cropper, be obliged to remit to the dominus either a payment in kind in wheat, or in rye if they grow no wheat, or growing neither wheat nor rye obliged to remit a payment in chickpeas, lentils, beans, lupins or in any other vegetables, including the beans growing among the maize, with no exception whatsoever, the which tribute for Passiontide shall be paid from the gross product of the share-cropping, as we extract from the inventory of 1556."*

The prose may be idiosyncratic but the message is clear: whatever a peasant sows, whatever grows of its own accord, (writes this Ragno), he must stump up for it. Sacks and bushels, firkins and hogsheads . . . I must beg forgiveness for speaking in terms of old-fashioned weights and measures, and for deviating from the narrative of the "most pious women" from Zardino and the witness they bore in the proceedings against Antonia. But I felt it beholden on me to account in some way for a system of taxes and extortions that was obsessive and downright murderous for the economy of the Flatlands, when the man applying the system and claiming the dues was such a one as Don Teresio. A system now luckily lost in the mists of time. And with that I have had my say.

The following Monday, the 3rd of May, Inquisitor Manini questioned Teresina Barbero, the same who was Antonia's bosom friend, or at any rate had been – she declared so herself –until the day when Antonia met a certain Gasparo, overseer of *risaroli* to Farmer Serazzi (or maybe Seghezzi, for here the MS is in poor repair), in a village called Peltrengo, between Novara and Cameriano.

Teresina appeared in court together with her mother Consolata, whom she had already begun to resemble: in person and in mode of dress they were as like as two peas in a pod. Both women were dark of eye and black of hair, with full moon faces and bodies as shapeless as makes no difference. Both wore black linsey-woolsey garments down to their ankles, their heads were swathed in ample shawls. Teresina's testimony, had Manini taken it seriously, might have been enough to put an end to the whole indictment for heresy. She explained everything, without even a mention of the supernatural, and what is more she had the advantage that her testimony could be easily verified as to whom and exactly what she was talking about. Unfortunately for Antonia, however, no Inquisitor of the Holy Office, in any city whatsoever, would, in a trial for heresy, have dreamt of accepting as decisive anything so coarse and down-to-earth as to coincide with the evidence of the facts themselves. And least of all in Novara. Here, at the time of our story, the tribunal for the Defence of the Faith was presided over by this friar, Gregorio Manini da Gazzano, Doctor of Theology, of whom we will speak at length in subsequent pages; but we must state here and now that he on principle, and systematically, distrusted anything that appeared crystal-clear and self-evident. In all that was too simple for words he suspected the ruses of the Devil. Conversing with his assistants Manini loved to quote a line from Virgil: raising his eyebrows and a forefinger he would intone "*Perfacilis descensus Averni,*" the descent into hell is the easiest thing in the world! And he went on to comment: "And thus it is, dearly belovèd brethren, in this world which God had given us to dwell in, that the only truly easy thing is to lose our souls. All the rest is difficult, is obscure, is intricate . . . Remember this at all times." He exhorted them never to rest content with the surface of things. He made a distinction between reality and truth. "Not everything that is real is also true," he was wont to homilize. "Indeed, quite the contrary! The truth often appears in such guises that the foolish and unlettered laugh it to scorn, or else it is concealed beneath appearances and arrived at only by circuitous routes." He would quote the *Summa theologica* of St Thomas Aquinas ("Truth is in the mind of God primarily and intrinsically, while in the mind of man it resides intrinsically but only indirectly; in things, if it resides at all, it is indirect and always extrinsic") and St Paul in the *Epistles* ("For now we see through a glass, darkly; but then face to face . . . ").

But let us return to the testimony of Teresina Barbera, daughter of Bartolo's hired-man, now twenty-two years old. She declared that Antonia had fallen for a *camminante* (which in English we shall call a Stroller – and what sort of folk these Strollers were you shall shortly learn), and that she was so infatuated with him as not to be her old self at all, either with her, Teresina, or with the Nidasios. All day long she ached to see him, and at night she escaped through the window and down the wisteria to go and meet him outside the village, either at the Tree Knoll or even beyond the Mill of the Three Kings, in a field over Novara way, where he sometimes dossed down in a hut near the sluice-gates belonging to a nobleman named Cacciapiatti, who paid him something to keep guard over his water-supply. This affair with the Stroller, said Teresina, had begun the previous spring, perhaps in May, and continued until the end of October, when the *risaroli* went home, and Gasparo (nicknamed *Il Tosetto*) along with them, to seek out a fresh force of *risaroli* to work in the paddy-fields the coming year. But that was not the end of the story. Antonia continued to think about Gasparo, and at that very moment she was expecting his return, for Gasparo had given her his word and the rice season was due to start. But he had never made mention of marriage to those he should have approached, that is to Bartolo or Signora Francesca. Never had he made any serious commitment towards Antonia . . .

At this point Manini interrupted the witness to ask whether she personally had had occasion to get a glimpse of this Stroller of whom she spoke. "Twice," replied Teresina.

"And did you have speech with him? Did you touch him?"

"Why, no sir."

"That being the case," pursued the inquisitor, "how can you be so sure, as you evidently are, that this Gasparo or Tosetto or whatever name he goes under was not the Devil himself in the form of a man?"

Teresina was left perplexed. In all honesty no such possibility had so much as crossed her mind. But at once she pulled herself together and answered much to the point: "What do you expect me to say? I'm speaking of what I've seen and what I know. If things are really different from what they seem to be then it's up to you to find out, priest that you are, and not to me!" And then, in answer to the second part of the question, "All I know about this Gasparo is what I've already said, that he's Antonia's sweetheart.

And if I really had to add anything else, and make a clean breast of it, then it's this: I don't know what Antonia sees in him that's any better than the local boys she doesn't fancy. Maybe it's that he's a bit of a rascal, or that he's not from our parts. But as for him being the Devil, and not a man, well I can tell you that the couple of times I met him he certainly looked to me like a man!"

"And what have you to tell me of the sabbaths?"

Teresina shrugged. We have seen that of all the small girls in Zardino she was as a child the one with the best head on her shoulders, and her common sense seems to have grown up along with her, if we are to judge by the answers she gave the Inquisitor.

"In my opinion," she said, after due consideration, "this rumour that Antonia went to the witches' sabbaths only started because she chose a sweetheart who was a stranger in Zardino – an outsider, and what's worse a Stroller! If her sweetheart had been a boy from our parts the talk would have taken a different turn: whether he married her or not. Things like this have always happened and always will. But a young girl going to the witches' sabbaths, that's a new one! And the real reason is that people don't know her sweetheart."

On May 8th 1610 the Inquisitor questioned a man so small of stature that nothing showed above the table-top except his face. The face of a goblin, with a bulbous forehead, two glassy eyes, a few tufts of reddish hair round his bald pate and on his jaw, sparse teeth in a cavernous mouth. Periodically a nervous tic convulsed the right-hand side of his face, stamping it with something of a grimace. This goblin, who like all the witnesses so far interrogated had been summoned on the advice of Don Teresio, declared that his nickname was *Pirin Panchet* (literally, Stool Peter). He explained that his principal occupation was that of itinerant milker, and that it was his wont to move even in the hours of darkness from cowhouse to cowhouse with his stool (*panchet*) secured at the waist behind him. In that way he had only to bend his knees and (hey presto!) he found himself seated. As for a real proper surname, he had never had one. As his secondary occupation he was a sacristan: he pealed the bells, swept the church, took the collection during Mass . . . For him, he declared, Zardino held no secrets, and he was also well-informed about the neighbouring villages: let them ask what they liked and Pirin Panchet would tell them. Want to know about the witch, did they? No sooner said than done. He'd known these last two years that Antonia was a witch, and when he said witch (the Inquisitor had asked him what meaning he attached to the word) he meant a woman who attends the sabbaths and kills man-children, of course! He'd seen other witches in his time, in Zardino and round about, and had been present at their sabbaths – "out of mere curiosity, you understand, not taking part." Anyone acquainted with Pirin Panchet knew that he had one characteristic unique the world over: he never slept! Not in the whole of his life had he ever had a wink of sleep! Twenty-four hours a day he went the rounds with his stool bumping on his bum, and it so happened one night that just to pass the time he'd sauntered up onto the Tree Knoll and sat himself down behind a bush to watch the sabbath. Yessir! He'd sat himself down on his stool. As to when this happened he couldn't at the moment remember, but they could ask Luigia Cerruti, because that same night her newborn babby died in the cradle. Suffocated they called it. Suffocated forsooth! He, Pirin Panchet, could tell them who had smothered the brat!

This was the way of it. When he, Pirin, reached the top of the Tree Knoll he saw three women there, Antonia and two others much older than her who must have come from a long way off, because he had never clapped eyes on them. A great fire burnt under the Tree, and as they danced round it the women stripped off their clothes. At this point the Devil appeared and all three, starting with Antonia, knelt down to kiss his arse. Of how the Devil looked he, Pirin, could give a very precise description (the Inquisitor had in fact requested such a description) having already seen him on other occasions.

"The Devil," explained Pirin Panchet, "is in all respects similar to a man, tall and thin, with black hair and dark skin. He has no horns, or if he does they are so small as to be hidden in his hair; his thighs curve forwards and his legs and hoofs are like those of a billy-goat. There are those who say he has a tail, but I've never seen it. On the other hand I've seen the Devil's Privates (both words are spelt with capital letters in the manuscript). They are larger than normal and Purple in colour". Making use of these

Privates the Devil then coupled with all three women, according to the ritual of the sabbath, but before this happened the women, passing it nimbly from hand to hand, had offered him a newborn, wailing baby boy. He touched it on the brow and above the heart and the babe immediately stiffened and gave up the ghost. At these amazing and monstrous events the aforementioned Pirin, known as Panchet, declared he had been present the previous autumn, on a night he could not precisely date but was at all events in the month of October, "affirming under solemn oath that he had told the truth, the whole truth and nothing but the truth." The foot of this page, as every other page in the register, is sealed with the phrase "Praise be to God" ("*Laus Deo*"), or else, "Blessed be the name of the Lord" ("*Sit Nomen Domini benedictum*").

TWENTY-ONE

The Bride

ANTONIA APPEARED BEFORE the Inquisitor for the first time on May 14th, a Friday, considerably later than the date of the court order because Bartolo had for days been bluntly refusing to hitch up the cart and take her to Novara "just to do the priests' bidding." He'd stand there in the middle of the yard yelling "Who do they think they are? Do they want the world to jump to it at a flick of their fingers? Well I've got no time for them! I've my sowing to think of."

He yielded at last to the urgings of Signora Francesca. The seed market in Borgo San Gaudenzio was on, and he could make this a reason for driving the two women to Novara without renouncing his principles, since he never ceased repeating that nothing would persuade him to go to town just because of the beastly priests. Not on his life he wouldn't! If they wanted to question Antonia and judge her, let them come and fetch her away themselves! He had better things to think about! And he went on cursing under his breath as he led the horse from the stable and backed it in between the shafts. Over and again he said it: he wanted nothing to do with it, not at any price! He would take his wife and the girl as far as Borgo San Gaudenzio and leave them there. Let *them* deal with the priests. He, Bartolo, had known only too well since the day he was born what that lot wanted from peasants, whenever they took an interest in them. "Money, that's what they want! Just money money money! And a bit more for luck! Everything they scheme up is for cash and nothing else, and even this time they'll manage to squeeze blood from a stone, but don't let them think I'll lend them a hand. No sir, no! No, no and no again!"

The two women, busy dressing for town, took a long time to come downstairs and Bartolo, who as a rule never raised his voice, started bawling "Francesca! Antonia! Will you get a move on? If you're not down in one minute I'll be away on my own . . . " And off they rumbled beneath a sky as leaden as their thoughts. Antonia wore the local costume of the villages of the Lower Sesia: a black skirt down to her ankles, a brightly embroidered bodice, a white blouse trimmed with lace at the cuffs, and over her shoulders a black crochet shawl. On her feet were the heavy wooden peasant clogs known as *suclòn*. She was a sight to warm the cockles of your heart. Signora Francesca had insisted on putting her hair up, and had decked her out with the diadem of long hair-pins known as "the silver", which we mentioned earlier as the insignia of "brides", girls, that is, of marriageable age with their dowries pat and trousseaus packed and ready. Antonia would really have preferred to leave her hair loose or bind it in a kerchief, as she usually did; but Francesca was not to be budged.

"I know all about these things," she said. "I know the nasty bitching the Gossips have been up to, and the envy that's eating at them and their daughters. The sort of thing they've been telling Don Teresio to persuade him to accuse you. All the more reason, then, to show that you're a bride!" And she forced her from her bed before dawn, and tricked her out as neat as if she really was on her way to be married . . .

The journey to Novara was tedious, and it would also have been done in silence had not Signora Francesca, from beginning to end, never left off nattering to Antonia, as she dabbed at her eyes with a hand-stitched hanky, now with this hand, now with that. Much advice was forthcoming: "Be respectful towards whoever questions you," she said. "Keep your eyes lowered, like a godfearing girl, and never fail to agree with them: 'Yes, Your Honour,' or better still 'Yes, Your Excellency.' Then, when they come to accuse you of being a witch and doing what the gossips have told them you've done, you must deny it, but with good grace, almost apologizing: 'No, Your Honour, No, Your Excellency, I would never have done that for all the money in the world. I am sorry, but Your Worship has been misinformed . . . ' And if you really do have to own up to something, say you acted on impulse, without thinking, as young people will, and that the very next moment you were sorry."

210

Concerning those moonlight escapades, and the encounters with the Christian Brethren which as far as was known were the basis of the charge, well, in the first place, said Signora Francesca, Antonia ought to have spoken to her and confided in her: for if the man she was meeting was already married there was no point in coming up against the Holy Office, and being tried as a witch, simply to defend *his* name and reputation. Whereas if he was not married, then things could be arranged. Even if he was a Stroller as, according to the Barbero girls, he was – or even a gypsy – all that mattered was that he should know where his duty lay, was hale and hearty, and had a will to work! No one in the Nidasio family had ever suffered from hunger, thanks be to God! All he had to do was the proper thing – marry her. That yes! And right speedily! Or else he was a blackguard indeed, bereft of honour or the least vestige of dignity, a man unworthy to be alive or to call himself a man at all. But she, she, Francesca, refused to believe that a girl such as her Antonia could have fallen for an individual of *that* stamp . . .

While Signora Francesca rattled on Antonia spake not a word. She kept her eyes lowered, fixed on the roadway glistening with puddles and the trees reflected in them; on the paddy-fields swollen with clouds and grey as the sky. Bartolo, seated on the box, also seemed to take no notice of this chattering on, all taken up with his own thoughts and his dialogue with his horse, a dialogue (or, to be more precise, a monologue) bristling with sounds that can be neither transcribed nor translated. On and off he glanced up at the sky and grumbled, "The soil's bone-dry but *we're* always half drenched." He grumbled about the drought, about the weather in general, about the harvests leaner every year . . . The cart at their backs was piled with woven baskets ready for the rice seedlings Bartolo was going to buy in Novara, and this moment when transplanting and sowing coincided reminded him of another such journey on another spring day ten years earlier, when he and Francesca were seated together on the box and in among the sacks of seed on the cart was a small girl, all wide-eyed and shaven-headed . . . How many things had happened since then! Be it the goad of the foul weather, or of those memories, to Bartolo it seemed that a whole season of his life was drawing to an end, and that the drops trickling down his cheeks into the grizzle of his beard were tears. Huh! a likely story! A hulking great fellow like him couldn't burst out crying on the public road – so the rain did it for him.

Raining it was, in squally gusts, so that after a couple of miles Bartolo had to stretch a tarpaulin over the cart to shelter the women and the baskets, and over his own shoulders he even threw a waterproof cloak which as a young man he would have disdained to use. For in those days he loved to challenge the elements, thinking he was stronger than they! But now he kept the thing always to hand, folded up under the box of the cart, on account of certain aches and pains that troubled him, especially in winter, owing to the damp.

Thereafter the sky cleared. At the Agogna ford it was raining no longer and the clouds were thinning out, unveiling scattered patches of blue. At Borgo San Gaudenzio the highway was dry and everyone out and about – not a drop had fallen in those parts. Our travellers alighted at the Falcon Tavern and divided there and then into two parties. Bartolo went off to the seed-merchants' stalls and the two women made their way on towards Novara, walking briskly because the sun was already high and they had a fair way to go before they reached the lawcourts. They had to get a move on.

Porta San Gaudenzio on market day was a place of crowds and bustle and yelling and haggling, a great crush of peasants and pedlars, their mules and their donkeys and barrows laden with wares which, no sooner past the gate and despite the fact that tax had already been paid, the troopers of the garrison amused themselves by turning topsy-turvy, rummaging in them with both hands and shouting one to another, "Here, take a look at this!" (*Mira, mira!*), or "Take a sniff at what this rascal's got on him! New-baked loaves! Red wine! Fresh fish!" – and if the victim wasn't pretty nippy in slipping across a coin, or if the latter was adjudged to be insufficient, then the whole lot ended up on the ground, in the mud and the mule-dung. "What the hell's this?" (in Spanish, between the soldiers). They passed the coin from hand to hand, pretending to be scandalized at someone trying to corrupt them. "What the devil's this, then? You must be joking!" But every so often they seemed pleased, and demonstrated this in their own way – noisily, by clapping the unfortunate such a whopper on the back as to leave him more dead than alive, or pinching his cheek as if he were a small child. "Vaya con Dios!" they would bawl at him. "God be with you, and you can thank your lucky stars you bumped into *me*, and not some other bastard!"

Francesca and Antonia had neither bag nor baggage, and managed to get by without being molested. In addition, Antonia had swathed her face in her shawl, holding this raised in such a way that the soldiers paid no heed to her. Once through Porta San Gaudenzio began the paved way, the *Via Granda* – cobbled at the sides and flagstoned up the middle – and our ladies made their way along it towards the Piazza del Duomo. Between the rooftops above their heads the clouds had finally broken, and a sickly, watery sun was reflected in the window-panes, bringing to life the coloured stuccoes, the vivid red bricks, the terracotta friezes, the enamelling on the Madonnas and other devotional figures in their niches in the walls. The street was thronged and there was a great stirring abroad – artisans busily wielding their brooms on the thresholds of their workshops, or giving orders to their apprentices, or nailing up their shop-signs for the day, while fishmongers, greengrocers and all and sundry cried their wares.

Of Novara as it was in the first years of the seventeenth century three things in particular would strike a visitor of today, always supposing such a visit were within the realms of possibility: the overcrowding, the racket, and the excrement. Albeit the houses of the nobility were numerous, with their empty reception-rooms and uninhabited chambers, and numerous too were the churches, the congestion apart from in those places was that of an anthill: alleys narrow as burrows, miniature doors and windows with rooms equally small in proportion or smaller, outside stairways clambering up the walls, undersized balconies, garrets, and in every angle people poking out their heads, or snoring them off or yelling them off, patching linen or hanging it out, or plucking chickens, or suckling babies, or munching a meal, or swapping yarns from house to house . . . The noise produced by such a multitude is something out of our ken these days, in a world stunned by mechanical clangings, shudderings, detonations,

213

recorded din . . . It is almost impossible for anyone today to have the least notion of how such a town could curse and whistle and halloo and cough and bellow and sing and sigh and weep and whisper and bark and laugh and utter great oaths . . .

Not to speak of the excrement, which towns today conceal in the intestines of their sewers, but were at that time before the eyes and noses of all, in the streets and in every public place – mule-shit, horse-shit, donkey-shit, dog-shit . . . But above all the human ordure pelting down from the windows or deposited *instanter* and *in situ* by anyone taken short while passing down the street. With the torrential rains of spring and autumn, twice in the year, that is, the town was washed clean; a cleanliness albeit of short duration.

Returning then to Antonia and Francesca: having travelled a stretch of the *Via Granda* they reached Piazza del Duomo, "The Piazza" by antonomasia. They crossed it, and passed the Ministry for the Poor, better known to the common people as the "Minestrone for the Poor", since in times of calamity it provided a free soup kitchen. They continued on their way along the pinching, stenchy, lanes behind the Chapter House and arrived at length at the little piazza of San Quirico. This was their destination, the headquarters of the Inquisition in Novara. On one side of the square stood the church of St Peter the Martyr (then still in the course of construction) and the Dominican monastery, on the other the Tribunal of the Holy Office. Piazza San Quirico was clean and silent, far more clean and silent than any of the streets or squares Antonia and Signora Francesca had tramped on their way there, and absolutely deserted. Even a dog scratching around in one corner no sooner spotted the two women than he barked at them and took to his heels.

The Tribunal of the Holy Office was a two-storeyed building with a portico fronting onto the little square. Beneath the portico a white marble statue portrayed St Peter; beside the entrance a tablet wrought of the same marble reminded the wayfarer that everything that met his gaze (the Tribunal itself, the statue, the monastery, the new church) had been commissioned by Brother Domenico Buelli, O.P., Professor of Theology and Inquisitor in the city of Novara, who had also had the plaque affixed there in the Year of Our Lord 1585.

As they approached the great dark wooden doorway with its two bronze lions for knockers Antonia had a moment of panic and stopped in her tracks. Signora Francesca, gripping her elbow, encouraged her, urged her forward. "Come on now," she said, "keep your chin up. We're there now – we can hardly turn round and go back! The sooner we're in the sooner we're out. There's nothing to be afraid of."

They knocked, and were admitted by a burly, bearded, cross-eyed young man to whom Francesca attempted to explain – two or three times, since she had the impression that he understood not a word she said – who they were and what was their business there. He regarded her as squinters do, two ways at once, and then, having left her to gabble on for a while, motioned her to wait and turned his back on them. Then appeared a friar all skin and bone, with fifty years or so on his shaven pate. This was the "*dominus frater Michael Prinetti, cancellarius*", the Registrar, or Clerk of the Court, who would thereafter draw up the acts and records of the proceedings against Antonia, at the foot of each page inscribing a "Praise be to God!" He took Antonia by the elbow and said, "Ah, so you are this Antonia of Zardino . . . We've been expecting you since last month." This as he urged her towards a doorway surmounted by a crucifix. Signora Francesca started to follow them but the Dominican pointed to a bench: "You sit there!"

Antonia was scared out of her wits. "What now?" she wondered to herself. "What'll they do to me?" But in fact nothing happened at all. After a wait that seemed endless, alone in a little room with a prie-dieu in the middle and a large picture of the flagellation of Christ on the wall opposite, she was led to the upper storey by the same cross-eyed young man who had opened the door to her and Signora Francesca and now, with the excuse of guiding her, began to touch her here and there in a way at once impudent and clumsy. ("This is all it needed!" thought the girl, and as far as possible kept her distance). Up a staircase and across a landing and they entered a large chamber where church pews lined the walls, and in the centre a desk with two Dominicans seated at it: Chancellor Prinetti, of whom we spoke, and Inquisitor Manini. This was the Council Chamber, where the tribunal met to issue its judgements, and where Antonia herself would in due course be tried. It was not customarily used for questioning the suspects or the witnesses in a case, who were normally heard in a special chamber on the ground floor, equipped for the torture of heretics; but for some reason unknown to us Antonia's first interrogation was carried out in this room.

"Approach!" commanded the Inquisitor. And then, when he had her before him, he put his first question, which Antonia found no means of answering. Not because she was too frightened, or because the question was particularly embarrassing or complicated, but simply because she was not sure she had quite grasped what the friar had said. She studied Manini's face, she scrutinized his lips, and asked herself in agony, "Have I got it?"

Everyone had this problem to begin with. The fact is that Manini spoke in Italian, not in dialect, and spoke moreover as to this day do many actors, adopting Tuscan usage and following all the rules of proper Italian pronunciation – which never was the language of the Po valley, let alone of the Flatlands. He modulated this voice to add stress to his words, and accompanied them with appropriate gestures; he stretched wide his eyes and glared into the face of the person he was addressing, undulating his long, slender hands in such a way that the country folk were spellbound as they watched him. Even our own Antonia was at first bewitched by the Inquisitor as a rabbit by a snake: she stared at him and failed to utter a word. Then she began to be sure of certain words, and others were translated for her by Registrar Prinetti, who in this type of interrogation or exchange often also fulfilled the role of interpreter. She began to make answer. She strenuously denied being a witch, or ever having met with the Devil on these so-called sabbaths. She didn't even know what it was, this thing everyone was calling a sabbath! Of the three farmers who were accusing her she said that one, Agostino Cucchi, was an enemy of her adoptive father Bartolo Nidasio because of a water-feud which had been going on for ever between the two families, while Falcotto and Barbero were simply a pair of dirty old men who had several times molested her on the road or in the fields, promising to give her "good money" if she would "go" with them . . . And as for Barbero, it was common knowledge in Zardino and for miles around that he was a "man of foul lusts", a veritable pig; and that he'd set his cap at her, as at so many women before her. She admitted being caught outside the village after nightfall by the men of the Confraternity of St Rock and being unable to escape them in any manner, "since they were on horseback and I afoot." She also owned up to being then on her way after dark towards the Tree Knoll, and that she was going there, unbeknownst to anyone, to meet her sweetheart. She obstinately refused, though, to say who he was or where he sprang from, this sweetheart unknown in Zardino.

Questioned by the Inquisitor as to whether she believed in God, she replied "*Indeed I do, my lord*"; and on further inquiry as to exactly what God was this she believed in she replied that they had taught her to believe in "*God the Father, God the Son, and God the Holy Ghost, Amen.*" And she crossed herself in such a way that if Signora Francesca could have seen her, her heart would have leapt for joy and relief. The poor woman's worst fear, as she sat in the entrance, was that Antonia might be carried away by her temperament. That she might disclose to the Inquisitor, and in no uncertain terms, what she thought of Don Teresio and of priests in general. But throughout that first interrogation Antonia behaved level-headedly, and followed the advice she had been given. When Manini asked her whether she admitted to having caused a public scandal by laughing during the sermon pronounced by the Right Reverend Monsignor Carlo Bascapè, Bishop of Novara, she answered that she had absolutely no recollection of having laughed on that occasion. If she had laughed, she said, it was certainly not on account of the bishop, but at something that must have just happened, some trifle, maybe something a friend had said. Everyone knows that young people will laugh for no reason at all! With regard to her dancing with the *lanzi* she replied that she had found herself suddenly in their midst, without realizing what was going on or even knowing who the *lanzi* were; that the meeting had lasted "*the time to say a paternoster*" and no more; and that it had had no sequel. As for the statements reported by Don Teresio, to the effect that priests served no purpose, she said that all that was the spitefulness of gossips, who spent the winter inventing tittle-tattle in the cowsheds and then went and repeated

217

it to the priest. Lastly, she declared that she had always made confession and taken Communion every year at Easter, until this last year, having been banned from doing so by "*pré Teresio*". And that all she had said was the truth.

While Antonia was answering the Inquisitor's questions, down on the ground floor Signora Francesca had attempted to apply herself to a piece of needlework she had brought with her to while away the time. But a stranger had come and sat himself down beside her, so bald and squat and swarthy and sly in the face that she could not imagine what such a man was doing in a religious Tribunal. He told her his name was Taddeo and behaved as if he were the sole lord and master of the Inquisitional Tribunal. He inquired of her, without too many preliminaries: Who was she? Where did she come from? What was her business at the Holy Office in Novara?

Whereupon he began to talk in the most extraordinary way. For example he told her that he was the apple of the Inquisitor's eye, that the Inquisitor would listen to no advice but his, and when it came down to it did everything he, Taddeo, told him to. There in the Holy Office a word from him, at the right time and place, could completely reverse a person's fortunes "from that to this" (the last phrase accompanied by a swivel of the wrist – palm down, palm up). Francesca breathed not a word, straining to concentrate on her needlework, but that disconcerting bore showed no sign of leaving her in peace. On the contrary he became increasingly impudent, he manoeuvred ever closer. So close to her that she could smell his breath – and it certainly had not the odour of violets or rosewater – he asked whether at the Nidasio farm they raised capons, whether they were plump, if they made salami, and whether they produced wine. And then, what quality of wine? Sharp wine or mellow wine? Then he assumed the stance of a friend and protector, promising incredible things. "I will see," he said grandly, "what can be done for your daughter, to save her from this trouble she's got herself into!" And finally, just a minute before Antonia came down and the two women found themselves outside the courthouse, at liberty again among the little squares and narrow lanes of old Novara, he made the gross proposition which Signora Francesca had been expecting all along: "You take my fancy, signora," he said. "If you come back and see me in a few days' time, I'll give you news about how your daughter's interrogation went!" He laid a hand on her knee and she gave a start: "What d'you think you're doing? Are you out of your mind?"

TWENTY-TWO

The Stroller

CONCERNING ANTONIA'S SWEETHEART, this Gasparo, we have already told the reader that he was a Stroller, and of this there is no shadow of doubt. Despite the fact that Antonia to the last refused to give his name, and thus involve him in her ruin, the story is clear enough. They had met a year before the indictment in the spring of 1609, when she was only nineteen and Gasparo was a good deal older, thirty or thereabouts – who can tell! There never was a Register of Strollers . . .

Theirs was love at first sight; but before retailing their love, so brief and fleeting as we shall see, something must be said about these men who in the Flatlands were on everyone's tongue for centuries, and who are no longer mentioned for the simple reason that they no longer exist. To dismiss them with a word as "vagabonds" would not be fair. The Stroller was a presence specific to this part of the plain and of the world at large, an historical figure, so to speak, but one who always remained on the shadowy side of history, entirely enclosed in his here and now, in his selfhood, his sullen need for basic gratifications. And indeed he would have contrived to vanish from the memory of man had not a Novarese writer of the turn of the century, Massara, left us a last, heart-stirring witness of that "singular and enigmatic figure of our countryside, which the precise and picturesque speech of the peasants illumines with the name of Stroller." This Massara did by going back in time and delving into the collective memory, because the last of the Strollers, those alive in Massara's day, in a last-ditch attempt to defend themselves and their way of life against the encroachment of progress, electricity, tarmac roads and compulsory education, had become criminals and bandits. Such were *Biundin* ("Blondie") and *Moret* ("Darkie"), who long enlivened the chronicles of the Flatlands and received the tribute of mention in the National Press for their armed clashes with the police ("Old Jean") among the paddy-fields and the straw-ricks. (This was more or less during the years when the Wright brothers were making their first experiments in powered flight and Albert Einstein was working out the Theory of Relativity). But the Strollers, the real Strollers, were not bandits, and Massara recalls them in a few pages both heart-felt and inspired, which comprise at one time their epic and their epitaph.

"These anarchists of the countryside," he writes, "have, like wild beasts born in captivity, lost their bloodthirsty instincts while preserving something which seems to be still more indomitable and indestructible; to whit, hatred of any kind of servitude soever. And in the depths of those brute souls there is none the less to be glimpsed a reflection of some poetry of the wild, as the water of stinking ponds sometimes mirrors a patch of starry sky.

"Where do they come from and where are they bound? It is a mystery to all, even to themselves. Nevertheless, from time to time, even the coarser allurements of normal life entice them; and then they appear out of the blue at some village tavern, they guzzle and revel and sing merry songs, and dance maybe with the complaisant country wenches, and squander the money they disdain to own – they who lord it over those who do possess it . . . And since these Strollers dare to challenge the forces of law and order, which (perhaps in the manner of an aging, abandoned mistress) they call Old Jean; and because they rove the fields and impose conditions on landowners and tenants alike, out of rabid craving for a life of freedom and a spirit of fiery pride, it is only natural that the country folk, although they fear them, also admire them. And since they admire, they help them.

"They walk, they walk, rarely on the main roads, more often on pathways, but most of all, by some odd symbolism of things, off any route trodden by servile human sheep, following certain mysterious trails according as the whim takes them, the milestones of which are the banks of paddy-fields, the rows of poplars, the willow-lined ditches, the dykes of canals. They walk and they walk, in the dogday sun that matures the crops, or on the crunchy frozen snow that sheets the arable land, and after taking a nap here or there in mulberry shade on sweltering afternoons, or under the stars amongst the grating of the crickets on warm summer nights, and in the barns of lonely farms for most of the others, they request and receive the wherewithal to assuage their hunger with the fruits of that soil of which they feel themselves not servants but masters, and then they walk on, walk on . . . "

Gasparo Bosi, better known among the Strollers of the Flatlands as Tosetto, first met Antonia at that very Fonte di Badia where once *le Madri* used to be, and where carved into the stone was still to be found that recipe for mankind as a blend of "dust and shadow, crashing water, crying eyes." He was somewhat short in stature, blondish, with grey eyes glimpsed between slits of lids and a round, roguish, face without beard or whiskers. His clothes, as with all the rascals of those times, were flash and vulgar, with ballooning sleeves striped black and yellow, a yellow doublet, tight-fitting breeches to emphasize what we would now call his cock and balls but in those days were known as his yard and his cullions. At his belt he wore a short-sword and a hunting knife, and the ensemble was topped off by a plumed bonnet. Like all the Strollers of the period, as indeed before and after, he was a storybook character; or rather, a romance roving the world on two feet; a romance, moreover, that no one at that time would have dreamt of setting down. In the seventeenth century vastly different themes occupied the minds of Italian writers! Grand themes! Or, even if they deigned to deal with trifles, they bulked them out with mythological apparatus: Helicon and Parnassus were the slopes where they best loved to wander, before descending into the green pastures of Arcady; Apollo and the other Greek and Roman divinities were those with whom they habitually held discourse. But which god ancient or modern could have raised the Strollers into the empyrean of Art and Poesy? What Poet would have bothered to waste his time on them?

This Gasparo had been a Stroller from the day he was born, since long before he could walk, as stands to reason. For poets and Strollers are born, not made. His mother, a scullery-maid in a pot-house, had kept him with her until he was ten years old and then consigned him to his father (a vagabond by the name of Artemio who occasionally turned up to exercise upon her his rights of bed and board), for him to take around a bit and teach him life. Artemio, however, in the two or three months they stayed together, had confined himself to instructing the boy how to beg at church doors by pretending to be blind and lame, and to instilling in him a horror of work. He was particularly insistent on this latter point. "Work is the last resource of nincompoops!" he would bawl at his son as they trod the roads. "It's the last forlorn hope of failures, and don't you forget it! Keep your chin up and your shoulders straight and never do a day's work for any reason, not even hunger! They always start working because they're hungry, and then spend the rest of their lives bending their backs like workers do. Ever looked 'em straight in the eye, close up? I'll just show you!" And if they were in the country he would take him into a field to look into the eyes of a peasant wielding a mattock; or else, if they were in town, into workshops where artisans were plying their trades. He was nearly moved to tears: "Poor devils! Even they were born to be men, like us!" He stalked out into the street inspired: "I, your father," he harangued the child regarding him all in amaze, "have been more than forty years in this world yet I swear to you that I have never worked! Not for one minute, not even to discover what it feels like! Not even for a lark! Even to pretend would turn my stomach! Try and remember what I am telling you now, unless you wish to shame the race of Bosi!"

One fine day they were in the hills of the Monferrato, on the far side of the Po beyond Casale, and in a wayside tavern they had stuffed themselves with sausages and scrag-ends of boiled meat. Artemio was moaning, "Woe is me, I'm feeling poorly! If I don't do my business at once I'll do it in my pants!"

On the crown of the hill was a large cane-brake, where the man concealed himself. Ten minutes passed, then a quarter of an hour, and finally Gasparo started to call his father, to search for him in the cane-brake. No one there! All that could be seen from that hilltop were other hilltops, other cane-brakes, and the boy then knew that he was on his own from then on. No sense in crying: he had to walk. The world is a ravel of roads and if you follow them you find everything: life and death, delight and misery, tears and consolation, adventure, love . . . He got back down to the road. He started to walk . . .

At the age of eighteen Gasparo found himself for the first time in the port of Genoa. Here a man known to all as Crovogianco ("White Crow" in Genoese dialect) on account of his prematurely snowy hair and unpleasantly grating voice, succeeded with a flood of talk and wine in signing him up as a mercenary galleyman on a vessel bound for Sardinia. "Mercenary galleyman" was the term then used for oarsmen who were not convicts but volunteers; men in desperate straits who took ship for the pay and often, like our Gasparo, could hardly be called volunteers. "There's always a stiff breeze on that run, you'll never have to row!" Crovogianco had bawled at him over the pandemonium in the "Cross-Timbers Tavern", crammed with cut-purses and strumpets at every hour of the day and night. Taking care meanwhile, unnoticed, to keep both their glasses brim-full, and as soon as Gasparo had drunk his down to slide across his full one in exchange for the empty. "You won't be earning that money, you'll be stealing it!" he bellowed in his ear, referring to his enlistment pay. Which, however, Gasparo never caught a glimpse of because someone else had pocketed it even before the vessel put to sea. He only awoke from his hangover when land was already far in their wake, and row he must, contravening his father's instructions and his own principles. Bringing dishonour on the whole race of Bosi. He rowed, with the sweat running into his eyes and the smart of the lash on his back, from Genoa to Sardinia. And then to get back he rowed again, on two other vessels, from Cagliari to the Tiber delta and from the Tiber delta back again to Genoa.

This Crovogianco was a dyed-in-the-wool villain, a hardened rogue if ever there was one, and had taken precautions in case anyone had a mind to kill him. But our Gasparo came at him from behind as he was walking down the street. He stabbed him in the side before he had time to turn and then (his victim still struggling to make off, crying "Help! Help! I'm a goner! A priest, a priest! I must confess!") plunged his knife into his back and left him there wheezing on the cobblestones like a pig with a half-cut throat.

He lay low for several days, but the authorities of the Republic had better things to do than go searching for the murderer of Crovogianco, so Gasparo came back into circulation, free as the air he breathed. He explored Genoa, discovered the excitement of living in a big city bursting with life, with trade, with taverns, with women only too glad to go with you for money, or even without it. A city all built of stone, with houses as high as hills and labyrinths of alleyways where you could lose your way as in a forest. He would have liked to stay for ever in that city, but he was accused of stealing something he hadn't stolen and was sentenced by default to have his right hand cut off. A thoroughly unpleasing prospect which decided him to skip back over the Apennines into Piedmont.

Then it was that he began to recruit *risaroli* for the farmers of the Flatlands. He tapped a new area each winter, he walked the Alpine valleys, he reached the most out-of-the-way hamlets buried under yard upon yard of snow, where the men were as famished as the pike in the boggy flashes of the Sesia and the glint of a silver coin flaunted an irresistible mirage . . . To Val Vigezzo he went, to Valsesia, throughout the Biellese, to Val Strona above the Riviera d'Orta, to Val Formazzo. All this he did according to the letter of the law, on the basis of certain stamped documents you could buy in Novara from the Town Hall clerks. It mattered not at all, a lawyer had assured him, that neither he nor his victims could read what was written on them. All it took was for them to sign before two witnesses, or that two persons were prepared to say they had seen them sign.

In the winter of 1605 he had brought off an exceptional coup, enrolling all the able-bodied (and begoitred) men of an entire mountain village up above Varallo. Thirty-two begoitred labourers! Three squads of *risaroli*! Needless to say this did not happen again in following years, but Tosetto always managed to get one squad together each winter, and what is more to keep them at work until harvest time, which was perhaps the toughest part, because many *risaroli* tried to escape when they realized that they had been promised heaven and had fetched up in hell. Or else they were openly defiant. But Tosetto had not forgotten his adventure with Crovogianco, and he hand-picked his *risaroli* from among the desperate cases, the disabled, the chronically unhappy, those resigned to the worst that life could have in store for them. Of whom there has never been any shortage in this world, let alone in the seventeenth century. He had become an out-and-out rogue, as sharp as a ferret and utterly ruthless, as required by the age and environment it befell him to live in. Every spring he returned to the Flatlands, to villages where by this time he was recognized by all, such as Borgo Vercelli, Cameriano, Casalino, Orfengo. For a fair stretch of the Sesia valley – well to the east of Zardino – Tosetto was a Stroller worthy of respect, both as an overseer of *risaroli* and as a wage-earning water-guard to various landowners. Wages he earned by going from village to village, from tavern to tavern, letting it be known that this or that water-supply was "his", and in the event of theft the culprit would find himself with his entrails in his hands, contemplating them right there in the street.

Like all proper Strollers he was a creature of the wild. He had no regular place to sleep, no habits of any kind, not a friend to his name. When he visited a tavern he spent his time playing cards – bezique, ombre, quadrille – or betting on cock-fights or on *la rana* (a type of target-shooting), then the national sport of the Flatlands. On top of which he laid hands on and courted any woman who came within range, pretty or hideous, young or old, married or not. Experience had taught him that there was always something to be got out of them. "A hog or a woman, there's no waste in 'em," he used to say. He also had exclusive rights (or so she led him to believe) in the favours of a certain Widow Demaggi, a redhead in Novara endowed with conspicuous rotundities, who would open the door to him when he knocked in the dead of night, and never ask him a mortal question, neither where he was from nor how long he'd be stopping. She already knew he'd be off and away at the crack of dawn without a word. Without even giving her a nudge. They would drop off together and she would wake alone, like every other day . . .

This then was the man, or the romance of a man, who approached Antonia near Fonte di Badia in the spring of A.D. 1609, with his plumed bonnet, his hunting knife at his belt, and the swell of his privates much in evidence. And who can tell what Antonia saw him as, or saw in him? Who can guess what he said to her? She, as was only natural, fended him off; but something happened in those few minutes, something that was, not once but many times in the course of the day, to bring to mind the Stroller

226

she had met beside the spring. The attraction between human beings, as we all know, follows laws of its own that are highly illogical; but not always mistaken. That first fleeting encounter was followed by another, the next day and on the same road; and then another again, on which occasion Antonia and Tosetto betook themselves for the first time into the wood . . . Thereafter they began to meet by night, when summer was already under way in the Flatlands and the paddy-fields were mist-exhaling marshes breeding swarms of mosquitoes which dispersed into distant meadows, or else clustered together, rising above the treetops and forming clouds that were visible from afar. These night-time trysts, as has been said, almost always took place on the Tree Knoll, whence Gasparo set off for "his" sluice-gates, the villages on the far side of the Flatlands, and his usual traffickings. Some nights they stayed up there till dawn, under the chestnut in each other's arms until the sky in the east began to pale, when Antonia made a dash for home, just in time to avoid meeting the gangs of *risaroli* trudging miserably towards their daily grind. Up there under the great chestnut there were no mosquitoes, and Gasparo spoke to Antonia of many things: of the sea, the sea which she had never seen and attempted to picture in her mind's eye. "Just think of the sky," said Gasparo. "The sea is the sky turned upside down, an endless expanse of moving water with islands dotted about – the island of Monte Cristo, the isle of Capraia . . . All round the islands there's the sea, like the sky round the clouds. The sea never ends, not anywhere – it goes on for ever!"

Or else he told her about Sardinia, which in Gasparo's memory was a place of fabulous and terrifying landscapes, a world of windmills, bandits, talking rocks, grottoes and other marvels. But most of all he told her about Genoa the magnificent, the city distant as a mirage, intricate and indecipherable as a dream, where you meet people of every race on earth and there are buildings of stone, the Stroller assured her, as tall as the hills of Sizzano or Ghemme there in their own parts, and in the evening, at a certain hour, people gather on the esplanade to watch the fine ladies and gentlemen roll by in their carriages. A place where you can buy and sell anything in the world, and men can disappear from one day to the next, as a stone sinks in a pond; and no one gives them a second thought.

Antonia listened and she listened, head on his shoulder and eyes on the stars. From time to time she started at a flicker or a rustle among the leaves: "Someone's there! Down there in the bushes. I heard a noise!" He would shrug – "What of it?" – and tap his hip where he kept his hunting-knife, exclaiming loud and braggartly, "When you're with me you've no need to worry!" And then, proud as a peacock: "There's no one and nothing can put a scare into me! I'd go down to hell this moment if I had to! I'd dare the Devil himself! Don't you think I'm up to it?"

"Would you do it for *me*?" asked Antonia.

"Of course I would! Who else would I do it for?"

He made her colossal promises: to marry her, to take her down to live with him in Genoa, on the fringe of the sea . . . "Just give me a couple of winters," he said. "I want to try and save up a nice little bit of money, enough to buy somewhere to live. But even if I don't manage to do that, no matter, we'll go there all the same. I'll get a job as a bodyguard to some big mister down there, and wear his livery, and you'll find a place as a housemaid or laundry-maid . . . " He fell silent a moment, then added, "Speaking for myself I just can't wait to get back there! I'm fed up with being a Stroller, and roving around cheating poor bastards into coming here to croak in the paddy-fields."

Needless to say this was all humbug, since Gasparo had not the least intention of going back to Genoa to have his right hand cut off, and maybe even his head, and was as pleased as Punch with the life he was living; and for the torments of the *risaroli* he didn't give a tinker's cuss. This was simply the patter Tosetto used to chat up girls like Antonia. To widows, on the other hand, and pot-girls in public houses, he made other vows, of fine clothes and jewels . . . And as for entering the service of some great lord, that was such a gross lie that even he, hearing it from his own lips, was flabbergasted: what, him in livery! Livery on a Stroller? Until that moment not only had he never uttered anything like it – it had never even crossed his mind. A Stroller is not a mere rogue, a picaro, who can change his standing and situation without turning a hair: a beggar or a highwayman today, tomorrow, perhaps , some prince's pampered favourite. No, a Stroller is a Stroller and there's an end of it.

Antonia for her part said little. She remained there motionless in the dark, her eyes open, and who knows if she was paying attention to all that prattle, or whether she believed it . . . undoubtedly she was pleased to be there, and to be with her dreams; she liked to let her imagination run riot about things she had never encountered in her life so far. If she did speak at all it was to ask for details: what were they like inside, those ships voyaging from country to country across the sea? And had he ever been into one of the tall, tall stone-built houses? And the ladies who appeared at the evening promenade, how were they dressed? Were they beautiful? Who were their escorts?

It was early in August when Tosetto began to default on his meetings with Antonia. She would go to the Tree and wait for him there, and when he didn't come would start walking to meet him part way. Instead she met the Christian Brethren with their torches, who hustled her back home, red with embarrassment and shame and trembling with rage. The next day Gasparo would apologize: "Forgive me, I had to rush to the sluices on such and such a canal!" Or else, "Two of my *risaroli* escaped and I had to recapture them!" But you could tell from his expression that he was swinging the lead, and that as far as he was concerned Antonia was becoming a burden. What did she expect? She had had her share of promises, her summer adventure, the benefit of his tales . . . She couldn't be stupid enough to think seriously of marrying a Stroller!

They went a while without seeing each other. Then he began to seek her out again, and was as affectionate as in the early days, bringing her little gifts and telling her tall stories about fearful hazards he had had to face in the very last day or two, enemies he had been forced to rout . . . He renewed the vows already made and even bulked them out with further details. He was astonished and downcast when she was sulky with him: he, victim of the foulest plots of men or of destiny, and not even his sweetheart gave him understanding and support! At times he seemed really sorry for himself: "Ah Gasparo, you've got your deserts. Just what was coming to you!" They spent the night beneath the Tree and then everything started over again – the lies, the broken trysts, Antonia's encounters with the Christian Brethren – until one late October evening he announced that he was about to leave the district and would be back in the spring. He asked her to wait for him. Unlike his usual self he was down in the mouth and not at all disposed to talk big. He told Antonia he was sick of the roving life and begged her forgiveness for not having yet called on the Nidasios to ask her hand in marriage. He would do so – that was the last of his promises – the very next spring. He wiped away a tear; and who knows? Perhaps at that moment he even meant it . . .

TWENTY-THREE

The Two Inquisitors

THE NEWS THAT BISHOP BASCAPÈ had forgone the stately ceremonies for the sanctification of his master and motivator, due to take place in Rome early in November of A.D. 1610, and that he was already on his way back to Novara, was certainly not such as to gladden the heart of Inquisitor Manini, who learnt it from a Cathedral canon on the 31st of May, a Friday. Indeed his first reaction was one of vexation. There was, he thought, no way in which that . . . that man of God could stop plaguing those who had the ill-fortune to be around him, treading on their corns, putting spokes in their wheels and in any case and on every occasion behaving in such a manner as to make himself, and no other, the centre of attention. "If he comes back now this witchcraft trial goes up in smoke!" he sighed to himself.

Things stood thus. Bascapè had gone to Rome the previous autumn to plead the cause for the canonization of the Blessed Carlo Borromeo, which was being obstructed for non-formal reasons, i.e. for those concerned with questions of doctrine. He was ready to give battle in no uncertain manner for the marching, combative Church that had been the Church of Carlo Borromeo, and that now was his, against the stagnant, hypocritical Church of *that* Rome, of *those* Popes, and of those recent times. However, in the few months he was in Rome he had been told that the Blessed Carlo would be canonized very shortly, in almost no time at all, in fact at once; so his battle ended before it had even begun. From one day to the next a word came from Court, and Borromeo's canonization papers jumped ahead of other aspiring saints more popular than he and also longer dead, such as Ignatius Loyola, Francis Xavier and a host of others. But that lunatic of a Bascapè, instead of being overjoyed, had taken umbrage and was on his way back to Novara, where you could bet he would rush all over the diocese throwing spanners in everyone else's works, starting with the Holy Office and the trial of Antonia.

What, in the circumstances, was to be done? Manini talked it over with certain members of his staff, and also a number of the judges of his own Tribunal. The reply was unanimous: bishop or no bishop, said they all, the proceedings against the witch of Zardino, already well under way, must be brought to a conclusion with all due formality and solemnity. The time was ripe for the Tribunal of the Holy Office of Novara to begin once more to operate independently of the diocesan curia and any other peripheral structure of the Church. Moreover, the cause was true and just, the outcome a foregone conclusion. Why hesitate? They must act swiftly, arrest the accused, interrogate her, and if necessary put her to the torture and force her to admit her guilt. Once the witch's confession was down in writing and the Tribunal assembled in plenary session no one would ever be able to modify its sentence, not even the bishop. For that would have meant repeating the entire proceedings, and judging the same defendant twice for the same crime, which in normal circumstances was not licit either in canon or in civil law. If the Inquisitor was fully convinced of the excellence of his case, as were his aides, and if the Holy Ghost did not deny him its assistance, the trial could well be concluded within a reasonably short time. A month, say , or two at the most . . .

To gain a better insight into the Inquisitor's state of nerves, as well as the real significance which the proceedings against the "witch of Zardino" had in the mind of the person conducting them, we have to take a step back in our story and set down a few things not yet mentioned, concerning the Holy Office of Novara and the Dominicans, whose activities as inquisitors had, following the arrival of Bishop Bascapè, been obstructed for the best part of fifteen years, and transferred almost wholly to the bishop's own Tribunal. Above all we have to introduce a personage who in 1610 had been deceased for some years, but whose shadow still loomed over Novara, over Bishop Bascapè, over the trial of Antonia and the Lord knows how many other things. This unrevenged and unplacated shadow was that of

Inquisitor Domenico Buelli, Manini's predecessor, of whom we have already had occasion to say that he had had his name inscribed with pride on a memorial tablet in Piazza San Quirico to remind future passers-by that everything in sight was there thanks to him. As the Latin poet Horace was convinced, and expressed the conviction in writing, that he need not wholly die, having reared himself a monument in words, frail perhaps but destined to survive throughout the centuries and millennia to come, so in turn Inquisitor Buelli conceived the notion that he too had worked for posterity, and that this work of his would be long remembered, and with gratitude.

He was wrong. Seen in the flesh, while he lived, Fra' Domenico Buelli of Arona, professor of theology, inquisitor of the Holy Office and prior of the Dominicans of Novara, was a right plump friar, as broad as he was short, bald and bouncy; dogmatic, as befitted his office and a bit to spare; ambitious, as became a man whose friend and tutor had been one of the fathers of the Catholic Counter-Reformation, Cardinal Antonio Ghislieri, who, on being elected Pope with the title of Pius V, continued to support Buelli even in his defects. The first of which was megalomania, the somewhat impetuous craving for grandeur which had induced Buelli (for the sake of posterity) to equip Novara, far in excess of any real need, with one of the mightiest inquisitional machines in the whole of northern Italy; with a small palace for the tribunal and the Chancellery, a monastery-cum-barracks of Dominicans, a church all of its own – a veritable fortress of the Faith, with its centre (as we have seen) in a square called Piazza San Quirico.

Of Buelli's little kingdom, established with the help of a Pope in addition to the sweat and the fervour of the person who should have reigned over it, no trace remains in Novara today. Piazza San Quirico no longer exists, any more than does the palace of the Tribunal or the Dominican monastery. On their site is a piazza named after Antonio Gramsci, the Sardinian Communist, though to the present-day Novarese it is better known by its historic name of Piazza del Rosario. Even the church, part intact, part remodelled, has changed its name, from San Pietro Martire to the Madonna del Rosario, so that Buelli's work, and Buelli's name, have left not a rack behind – not even a memory. In that brief period which belongs to him, and was his, Buelli did indeed establish his kingdom, inscribe his name on a marble tablet, and (deservedly) make ready to reign there. But it happened to him, as it often does to men when they finally achieve the goal of their whole lives, that something crops up to prevent them from enjoying its fruits, and casts it all to the winds, and causes them to die in rage and despair.

This "something" was, for Buelli, the arrival in Novara of a bishop who in physical appearance was his exact opposite. In so much as Buelli was vigorous, ruddy, bouncing with life and energy even to excess, so the other was fleshless, diaphanous, lacerated by every species of infirmity of both body and soul. "He'll soon peg out," thought Buelli, as did everyone else. But he didn't know, poor wretch, that he would be the one to peg out first. Bascapè had come to Novara to build a Church of his own within the Church, and to use that springboard to change the world! Just imagine him putting up with anyone else changing it in his place, according to his own way of thinking and not the bishop's! Just imagine him leaving the struggle against heresy in the hands of others! Those infiltrations of Protestantism in the Alpine valleys, which Buelli had equipped himself to combat at long range, in the most formal and bureaucratic manner, Bascapè went out to fight hand-to-hand and house to house. In the words of one of his biographers, "by pathways precipitous, rocky and periculous, where the good bishop was forced to grasp for a handhold, and even to have himself borne upon a crude litter made for that purpose, and having sometimes to send persons ahead to dam the torrents so that he could ford them; and he also with great hardships traversed glaciers."

Nor was that all. He ordered the parish priests to report any suspicion of heresy directly to himself and to the Bishop's Tribunal. The bishop, he explained in a pastoral letter, was the inquisitor by ancient custom, and the Dominicans were mere coadjutors whom the bishop was free to use or not to use. Moreover (though this has little to do with the story of Antonia) he revindicated the ancient right of the bishops of Novara "to administer civil justice in their feud at Orta, and to settle all questions involving persons or possessions of the Church entirely themselves, without interference from the tribunals of the State" – thus laying the foundations of a lasting and irremediable conflict with the Mayor of Novara, with the Governor and Senate of Milan, with the Kings of Spain, and with the world at large. Poor Buelli was beside himself. He rushed off to Rome to appeal to the Holy Office and to his new protector Cardinal Bellarmine in person. He shouted, he wept, he stamped his feet and banged his fist on tables, and he yelled so much and got into such a lather that no sooner back in Novara than he died of heartbreak, i.e. a coronary, during the year 1603. Unexpectedly too, according to the chronicles. For one morning he had scarcely finished breakfast but he rose to his feet, his mouth gaping as if to yell something; but nothing did he yell. He turned purple, pitched to the ground, and after lashing out with a few last punches and kicks, gave up the ghost.

They gave him a very fine funeral, celebrated by the bishop in person and with all the civil and religious authorities in the diocese in the front row singing him the *De profundis*; but his death, as it turned out, was not in vain; for it was thanks to this death, and the good offices of Cardinal Bellarmine, that the adversities of the Holy Office in Novara finally reached the ear of the Pope. Now Clement VIII, as already mentioned, had little or no affection for Bascapè, whereas he was passionately devoted to the Dominicans. It was during his pontificate, and that of his successor Paul V, that the Inquisition in Rome lived its most glorious and terrible days – those of the burning of Giordano Bruno, and of the interdict of Venice. Scarcely a day passed but poor Bascapè was faced by another setback, and no mean ones at that! Just for a start, they covered him with ridicule with that business of Cavagna's Relics; in addition, denunciations by many citizens of Novara, who felt no inclination to become Saints against their will and even hired an "orator" (spokesman) to go to Milan and Rome and put their case for the removal of the lunatic bishop and the restoration to Novara of its time-honoured peace and quiet, found attentive ears in both of these cities, and also at the papal Court. Periodical inspections were ordered in the diocese of Novara. In the first instance the Bishop of Como, and later on Cardinal Piatti and Cardinal Gallo, were entrusted by Clement VIII to keep an eye on the doings of

Bishop Bascapè. The "living corpse" calmed down a little and Buelli's successor, Manini, thought that maybe the moment had come to bring off a spectacular trial in which the bishop had no part; to indemnify the memory of his predecessor, and to give tangible and public proof of the victory of a worldwide organ of Holy Church (i.e. the Inquisition) over the despotic ambitions of a provincial bishop. The citadel of the Faith raised by Buelli must be refortified, and the Devil in person brought there at last, there to Piazza San Quirico, to break his horns against his mightiest and most dreaded foe, rather than having an easy game against those meddling, bungling canons of the chapter, whom the bishop appointed Inquisitors as occasion demanded, without their having the least specific competency or ability in this field! Let the era of bungling canons end, and the Christian world hear once again of the Holy Office of Novara!

As luck would have it Don Teresio's charge against "the witch of Zardino" came along at this very point in our story, while Bascapè was in Rome to plead the canonization of the Blessed Carlo Borromeo. The action at law that resulted from the charge was a perfectly normal case of heresy, but there was an additional factor, both for Manini himself and for the Tribunal of the Inquisition of Novara, i.e. that it was exactly the right case at the right time, sent by divine Providence and not to be missed. A compensation for the past and a pledge for the future; a sure sign that in Novara and in the Church of Novara much had changed, or was in the process of changing . . .

Concerning Inquisitor Manini we have not yet mentioned that he was a man of tall, slim build, pale of face, pleasing in appearance, elegant in his gestures and even in his black-on-white monkish habit, which was cut close-fitting and rustled with his every movement. His hands, with their tapering fingers, were exquisitely cared for, while his mode of expression, stilted in pronunciation and recherché in its selection of vocables and figures of speech, was that of the great preachers of his era, when the churches were still theatres and people went there in part to weep, to laugh, to be amazed; to experience those powerful emotions, that stage-thrill, which the drama gives when it is applied to reality, or what is thought of as reality. As a matter of fact Manini himself had discovered his vocation in this very way. At the age of eighteen, hearing a Dominican friar preach the Lenten sermon there in Novara, he had felt an irresistible urge to be a preacher. He became a friar, went to Rome to study theology, and then took a specialized course in the arts of Rhetoric and of public speaking. His dream was of the great cathedrals, the soaring pulpits, and beneath the soaring pulpits the vast crowds, with the great ones of the earth seated in the front pews, in the half light, and himself on high, armed only with words, keeping them all spellbound; bringing them low, striking terror into them, annihilating them, and thereafter restoring them to hope, to repentance, to trust in God . . .

Destiny, however, did not second that dream of his. Or, to put it more precisely, it was his religious superiors who steered the course of his life into other channels, turning to account other qualities of his which would make him a fine Inquisitor: in the first place prudence, caution and the gift of diplomacy; the ability to deal with Church affairs, even on a high level, without committing indiscretions. At a mere forty years of age Manini had been appointed to the office of Inquisitor in a see such as Novara, rightly considered "difficult". And from then on the great cathedrals were banished for ever from his ambitions, giving place to the grand Benches and Sessions of the Tribunals of the great cities.

Two other things we know about Manini. The first is that he did not believe that reality was real. "Reality," our Inquisitor would declare, gesturing with tapering fingers and widening grey-blue eyes in the face of his interlocutor, "has no existence in itself, unless it be kindled by the breath of God's grace. It is merely an illusion, a faulty perception which will be erased by death." In the second place he was obsessed by the ideal and practice of chastity, to which he attributed virtually supernatural powers and devoted his only known (and unpublished) opus. The frontispiece of the MS bears the date 1618, and may still be found and consulted in an archive in Rome. For the twentieth-century reader it has at least one merit: it is short, being composed of two parts, each of six chapters, for a total of eighty handwritten pages. A pamphlet, if we compare it with the bulk of the unpublished treatises which the seventeenth century, most scribleomanic of centuries before our own, attempted to foist on future generations, and which woodworm and catastrophe together have not yet succeeded in ridding us of. But from a master of elegance such as Manini no other sort of work could have been expected. Elegant from the very title, *De Remedio et Purga haereticorum Libri XII*, and its informative sub-title in the vulgar tongue, which reads "Antidote and Purge of Heretics, in Twelve Books"; written by Fra Gregorio Manini da Gozzano, "*Sanctae Theologiae professor et Inquisitor Novariae*" (Professor of Sacred Theology and Inquisitor of Novara).

The basic assumption of this treatise, and its particular novelty with respect to all previous treatises on the subject, comes right at the beginning. In the very first lines of the first chapter Manini writes: "*Haeresis potest expurgari, vel etiam impediri*", "heresy can be suppressed, but it may also be forestalled." And he puts the question, "Why, apart from punishing heresy, and justly so, do those who are responsible for combatting it not attempt to obstruct and forestall it, by counter-attacking against the devil on his own ground? Any heresy whatever, argues the Inquisitor, proceeds directly from the Devil, who roams the world over in many forms, but is most wont to act in the guise of the "feminine of man", *idest mulier:* for the feminine section of humanity is that which most directly partakes of the nature of Satan, and of his very substance, while the male part, formed by God out of that universal element which is the soil itself, without any further changes or manipulations, was made by him in his own image, as according to Holy Writ, and is therefore, at least potentially, divine. From the foregoing it follows that the most efficacious weapon the Devil can wield for the temptation of man is seduction by women, and that men, and women too, can disarm him of that weapon, and triumph over him, by means of the practice of chastity. This said chastity, writes Manini, "*vere est summus Remedius, et maxima Purga haereticorum,*" (i.e. "is the greatest Remedy and supreme Purge of heretics"). He concludes with a memorable assertion: that wherever there is chastity there is no heresy, and cites the Epistles of St Paul the Apostle ("Without chastity there is no salvation") and the *Summa theo-*

logica of St Thomas Aquinas ("Chastity is the remedy for every vice").

Having thus cogently expounded his scheme for an offensive against heresy based on universal chastity, Manini proceeds to discourse on the unbridled lechery produced in countries north of the Alps by that monstrous heresy which he calls "Luttheran" (with double "t"), quoting excerpts from sermons, travellers' tales and various hearsay. At one point he owns up to having no first-hand experience of this phenomenon, but merely a vague notion of it in consequence of an episode during his early days as Inquisitor, when he travelled to the outermost confines of the diocese of Novara, and the Alpine passes which lead "*in partibus infedelium*" (that is, amongst infidels and heretics), and the Devils tried to obstruct his passage by swathing the entire region in dense fog. Unable, however, to force him to desist from his journey, they brought down upon his head, and those of his companions, a raging tempest in which at first were to be heard horrendous whistlings and the ululations of bears, lions, wolves and other savage animals. Then, seeing that the Inquisitor and the other clerics proceeded fearlessly on their way, giving no sign at all of retracing their steps, little by little the howls and cries of the beasts transformed into the music of viols and voices of women calling him by name, "Gregorio, Gregorio, where are you going? Stay your steps!" and entreating him to remain there with them, promising him joys and pleasures such as no one on earth had ever before savoured.

"At a certain point the mists rolled apart," – thus relates Inquisitor Manini in his book, and in his Latin – "and we saw before us the Old Enemy in most beautiful female form, most comely, and naked; who laughed obscenely, sticking out his tongue at us (*obscene ridens, linguam exerens ab irrius*) and beckoned to me in particular to approach him. A thing which I, naturally, did not do and he, after summoning me once more, made off."

One of the most interesting chapters in the manuscript is the one devoted to witches, concerning whom Manini openly states that, just as the Devil is the opposite of Christ (whose brides in this world are the nuns), so witches are the brides of the Devil – and not in a figurative sense either, but carnally and at the sabbaths.

Indeed on this point our Inquisitor dwells at some length, demolishing one by one all the arguments of those who maintain that of witches only the souls take part in the *congressus sabbathicus* (i.e. the sabbath), while their bodies remain inanimate, in bed or wheresoever. If it be thus, argues Manini, then the copulation of the witch with the Devil, and the Devil himself, are dreams; but the sins of one who sleeps and dreams are a mere echo, a pale reflection, of the age-old guilt of our first parents, that is, the sin of Adam and Eve, and are in no way fresh sins committed by the dreamers, since these are prevented from the exercise of their will and their persons, and indeed lie inert as the dead (*"immo vero jacentes sicut mortui"*). If, therefore, we hold that the guilt of witches is a fresh sin with respect to Original Sin, and therefore specific to their being witches, it follows that those wicked ones sin in body and soul and with every part of them, and knowingly.

Parenthetically to this latter question, that of sins and dreams, the Inquisitor dwells upon a detail that is far from irrelevant, and indeed surprising when we come to think that it anticipates Freud and the *Interpretation of Dreams* by three centuries. If, writes Manini, we accept the principle that in dreaming we commit fresh sins, then no saint would be a saint and no man, even the most continent and modest, would be chaste; for a dream is in fact an effusion and as it were a release of the soul (*"somnium est prorsus effusio et quasi eruptio cordis"*) and no one can be held guilty on account of his dreams, however lustful and licentious these may be. We must therefore distinguish between Original sin and personal sin. The sin of a dream is that of old Adam, that Original sin which echoes down the centuries (*"per aetates resonans tamquam imago pristinae culpae"*). It is not, nor ever could be, in any way the sin of the sleeper himself. *"Nulla enim culpa est in somnis."* A sleeper commits no sin.

TWENTY-FOUR

First Torture

THE SECOND TIME she came before the Inquisitor, dressed in the same rude clouts she was wearing at the moment of her arrest, Antonia was no longer the "bride" of a month earlier, the girl who had appeared in Court with the "silver" in her hair. But she was very beautiful all the same, despite having spent two nights in lamentations of despair, fending off the assaults of the prison rats in the dungeons of the Inquisitional Tribunal, and going a day and a half without a bite to eat because she refused to touch what the friars served up.

Now that they had brought her up, up into the light of day, she was seated on a stool no higher than two spans of a man's hand, crouched, bent double almost, her face in her hands. At first glance you might have thought she was weeping, but she was not. She sat, thinking of nothing, suspended in some kind of void, vacant to herself and to the world; and that vacancy – which was also weariness and physical prostration – would perhaps have been transmuted into sleep had not the sudden clamour of a bell, announcing the arrival of the Inquisitor, given her a start and brought her back to reality. Where am I? she wondered. What worse is in store for me?

Manini entered, just a mite out of breath, swirling the air with his habit as he passed. He stepped up to the centre of the rostrum, a position towering above that of the Registrar (who to beguile the time had meanwhile written the Latin formalities of the proceedings); he made the sign of the Cross; he loudly declaimed "Laus Deo" (Praise be to God). He then reached out for a small black canvas bag which some hand had deposited there with a view to his examining the contents; he picked it up with his left forefinger and thumb, handling it with great caution, as if some

241

venomous beast might issue forth from it; one after another he drew out three small wax-sealed earthenware pots and an engraved silver box which, shaking his head, he exhibited to Registrar Prinetti as if to say, "Just look what sort of thing we come across in a peasant house!" He asked the girl, "Do you recognize these objects?"

It is stated in the register of the proceedings that this second interrogation of Antonia took place on June the 14th, a Monday (the witch being already detained in the prison reserved for women), commencing at eleven in the morning on the ground floor of the Tribunal of the Inquisition of Novara in the chamber called, in fact, the "interrogation chamber", of which the late lamented Buelli had personally seen to the fittings, equipping it with the most modern and functional instruments of torture then available on the market. He, sad to say, had not been able to enjoy the use of them, due to the afore-mentioned clash with the bishop, but the machines had been maintained in good order, regularly oiled and tested so that they were ready for use.

In appearance the chamber was an ensemble of three things: viz., the court-room proper, the gymnasium – that is, a gymnasium more or less as we know it today – and the sacristy. Across the middle of the ceiling was a beam bearing a pair of stout pulleys. These in turn bore ropes which could be wound and unwound with great speed and ease by means of windlasses fixed to the floor. In one corner of the chamber was a thing both mysterious and sinister, a table as big as a full-sized modern billiard table and enveloped in a grey cloth, while occuping fully half of one wall was a vast cupboard with an enamelled iron plaque which read "*Supellex tormentorum*", indicating that it contained instruments of torture. And finally there were the rostrum of the Inquisitor himself and the judges who sat on either side of him during the interrogations, and on the wall behind it a Christ crucified fashioned in laquered wood, daubed all over with blood-coloured blotches, and wearing a crown of real thorns.

"Yes, my lord," answered Antonia. "They belong to me."

"Then explain what they are," said the friar, craning towards the girl with an interest perhaps excessive for the particular question, but spontaneous and by no means ludicrous. This was simply Manini's manner. Whatever he said, and to whomever he said it, his large grey-blue eyes sprang wide, or darkened in the pallor of his face, his lashes would blink time, while tiny expressive wrinkles formed and faded. He was by birth and temperament an actor, a great actor – vain and cruel as all great actors are – who had chanced to land up in the seventeenth century as an Inquisitor. It's an odd world . . .

Antonia reflected a moment and then spoke. Those three pots, she told him, contained certain herbs which grow on heaths and in kitchen gardens, and which you steep in spirits of wine to extract their rustic perfumes. And this, the girl admitted, in spite of the fact that Don Teresio had forbidden all women whatsoever, and the young in particular, to practise that type of distillation under pain of the wrath of God, Hell itself and a lot more besides! What's more he had – not once but many a time – expelled girls and women wearing perfume from church. But females, said Antonia, are not made after the same manner as men, and not everything they do is pure vanity. When they have their moons, for instance. Was it right for a girl to give offence to herself and those around her just to placate God, as Don Teresio said she must? What if the opposite were true, and God also was offended by the stink of women?

The Inquisitor raised his palms before him. "Silence, woman," he said. "Even before the Holy Tribunal do you dare to blaspheme the Lord your God? Confine yourself to answering the questions asked of you, and hold your chatter. The ointments contained in these pots, of what poisons are they concocted? What maleficent results do they procure? Whom have they done to death?"

"I have already told you," replied Antonia. "They contain herbs."

The Inquisitor raised the lid of the little silver box and peered inside. He rose to his feet. Not in haste, but slowly. Slowly he rose, still holding the box in his hand, while the expression on his face grew grimmer, as if something ghastly had met his gaze, the proof positive of some malfeasance. "This box contains human hair!" he cried. "Whose is it? Speak up, wanton!"

The hair in the box was Gasparo's, and at this point in our story we must tell you that Antonia and the Stroller had met one last time, at the very beginning of that month of June and just a few days before her arrest. Antonia had somehow learnt that he was back, and rushed to seek him out. Gasparo did his level best to avoid her, but since she didn't give up and came back day after day, he decided to face up to it and have it out with her. His right arm was bandaged and in a sling on account of a knife-wound and he had no desire whatever to pick up the threads of a romance that – to judge by the rumours about Antonia going the rounds – was not only tiresome but dangerous. So he deluged Antonia with talk about the miseries of the Stroller's way of life. He had been strolling, he assured her, for months and months, over the mountains and down the dales around Biella, defying every kind of adversity and hardship to put aside that little nest-egg that would enable him to marry her and go to live in Genoa, as he had promised her. But it hadn't come off! Yes, he had trudged the length of valleys and scaled the heights of mountains, dared the police in the State of Savoy and landslides and all the perils of a hostile environment without laying his hands on a single *risarolo*; because now, said he, people were growing prosperous. They had a meal almost every day, and desperate poverty was a thing of the past, even in the mountains! In fact, had a character by the name of Pollone, a carpenter by trade, not consigned him his three sons who had been driven insane by headaches which no doctor in the valley knew how to remedy, he would have returned empty-handed. What's more, he had gambled away his last year's earnings, had run up debts. And he was ill. Fearsome stomach-cramps would suddenly attack him, and every time he thought he was at death's door. What claims could be made on a poor Devil like himself? What could Antonia demand of him, that he had not already given? He was great-hearted, he had promised her the sun, moon and stars, and when things took a turn for the better he'd keep his promise, so he would! Tosetto's word was Gospel, and sooner or later it came to pass. But just now she should let things lie, and steer clear of him, because he was up to his neck in troubles, what with his creditors, with landowners out to sack him as water-guard, with the Law and with the whole damned world. Antonia ought really to be grateful to him for speaking the way he was, open-heartedly. Anyone else in his shoes would have come out with all sorts of humbug to go on taking advantage of her, but not he! No, he was removing himself frankly and of his own accord, without being told. He was sacrificing himself without a protest, solely for her sake . . .

Antonia spake not a word. The Inquisitor now definitely threatened her, looming down from his great height and the dais, goading her on to answer: "Answer me, wanton! Whence came this hair? From one of your victims? From the Devil himself?'"

"Maybe," stammered Antonia, "they're mine . . . "

"Slave of Satan!" roared the friar. "These are blond hairs, or tending to reddish! Your own hair is as black as your own soul . . . "

He replaced the little box on the table. He sat down.

"You have attended the sabbaths," he said, and his voice had in an instant become again placid, almost winning. "You've been seen! Under a tree that I shall order to be hacked to pieces and burnt, to prevent other witches from using it for their devilish rites. Denying the sabbaths will avail you nothing. There are too many witnesses. Therefore, you would do better to confess all. Tell us in what form the devil appeared to you, who were the other women who served him, what he ordered you all to do and if you all had carnal relations with him. Only an act of contrition can save you!"

"I know nothing about these things," said Antonia. "I have never set eyes on a Devil. I have nothing to say."

The Inquisitor rose. He clapped his hands: "Bernardo! Taddeo!"

At this point in the second interrogation of Antonia the manuscript laconically records in its rudimentary Latin that the witch "*Data est tormentis ad tempus quartae partis horae circiter,*" i.e. that she was tortured for a period of approximately a quarter of an hour. But things were not as simple as those few words would have us believe. Before submitting to being stripped stark naked and searched (you shall hear in due course what that involved), and put to the strappado, Antonia defended herself with all she had, fighting tooth and nail against the menials of the Tribunal-cum-prison, Messrs Taddeo and Barnardo, who managed to overpower her and tie her down only after a long struggle, and not without hurting her.

We have already had occasion to meet these two individuals, father and son, in the preceding pages: Taddeo, the man who sat down beside Signora Francesca during Antonia's first interrogation and evinced such fervent interest in her, not only in words; his son Bernardo, the cross-eyed, bearded young slob who opened the door to the two women and then escorted Antonia upstairs to the Inquisitor, clumsily fondling her the while. If anyone chanced to ask him how on earth he had acquired such assistants – not run of the mill, to say the least – Inquisitor Manini, raising his eyes to the heavens and fluttering his tapering fingers in the face of the questioner ("A miracle, a pure miracle! Men such as they! It was Divine Providence that sent them to us!") would reply that they were two laymen who had come to dwell with the friars to fulfil a vow to serve God and his Holy Tribunal. But the truth was somewhat other, and some people in Novara still remembered it. Taddeo and Bernardo had been a pair of Il Caccetta's cut-throats, and had sought sanctuary in church to escape the arm of the law, as the laws of the time allowed, and had stayed on with the friars, who had eventually taken a liking to them – or at least to the services they rendered, the which (they declared) they no longer knew how to do without. Inquisitor Manini in particular appeared to nourish towards those individuals feelings even he was not aware of: what amounted to a physical attraction. When Taddeo was speaking to Signora Francesca, in confiding to her that he was the Inquisitor's darling he spoke no less than the truth. It could be said that Manini, aesthete of aesthetes, was fascinated by those men, so utterly primitive and animal, who by instinct had adapted themselves to their new situation, their new mode of life, with an ease that was entirely unforeseeable and not far short of prodigious. Servile towards the friars to the point of nausea, assiduous in the church and at religious functions, attentive to all that happened around them and in the environs of Piazza San Quirico, these two rogues turned lay brothers had succeeded in putting down roots in the august and inexorable shade of the Tribunal of the Inquisition of Novara just as certain kinds of inedible fungus manage to grow in the most unlikely places, such as cellars or store-rooms. And not only had they put down their roots there, but there they flourished on every species of traffic and intrigue both inside and outside the monastery, where their enterprise disturbed no one; indeed, what was known of it was put down to their zealousness. "He is so thoughtful," Manini used to say of Taddeo, widening his great grey-blue eyes and waving his hands. "So solicitous and attentive to all our wishes, and also so pious!" (Indeed, whenever his dirty dealings forced him to be away for a few days from the Dominican monastery and the annexed Tribunal, Taddeo justified his absence by pleading devotional practices: vows to fulfil, pilgrimages or visits to sanctuaries, almsgiving and other works of piety).

Today, people's idea of what happened to witches is centred on torture: long, cruel torture. What is not known, or not said openly, or at least not always mentioned, is that these tortures were carried out on partly or totally naked women, and were always preceded by minute inspections of the witch's body to ascertain – this at least was the declared motive of the inquisitors – that they were not concealing about their persons any philtres or amulets or other devilries capable of nullifying the effect of the tortures. They peered under their tongues and between their buttocks; they wrenched their legs apart by brute force, and the gaoler, or even the friar himself, used his fingers to ensure that all was according to rules and regulations even in the most intimate parts of the body. (In Antonia's case the first inspection of her bodily orifices was carried out by Taddeo. He had earned this right and privilege by tossing for it with his son – and need we say he won? – while waiting for Manini to summon them in to the Interrogation Chamber).

The subsequent contortions to which she was subjected, strung up by the arms on the "strappado" or legs splayed wide on the rack, were all part of an unconscious ritual by which for centuries the Catholic Church (and the Protestant churches as well, come to that) vented its sexual tribulation and anguish on those poor women – its terror of womankind as "Devil" and its need for a Devil. When the era of those rituals came to an end, to the relief of one section of the clergy and the disappointment of another – the whole business of witches dwindled away and vanished, reduced by the light of retrospective reasoning to a plain misconception in which sex played no part; for in any case – and here the mistaken historical hindsight of the nineteenth century lends a hand – what manner of women were these witches? Horrible toothless hags with protuberant chins, and covered with warts and hairy verrucas, dropsical, obese old bags deformed by labour and flabby from childbearing. Who on earth, however sexually repressed, could desire such women, or even think of them naked, without a pang of irrepressible repugnance? But the physical ugliness of witches as a reflection of their moral ugliness is a mere fable based on a prejudice, a fable of Romanticism. In point of fact, if one were really to delve to the bottom of this business, it would very likely emerge that these so-called witches, in the vast majority of cases, were buxom, winsome dames between thirty and fifty years of age; and that among them some were in their first bloom of youth, like our Antonia, or of exceeding beauty, like that of Caterina Medici of Broni, whom Head-Physician Ludovico Settala, Archbishop Federigo Borromeo, and the Senate of the State of Milan condemned as a *"filthy female, a witch and a deadly sorceress"*, to be *"borne to the place of execution on a cart, tortured throughout the journey with red-hot tongs and thereafter burnt alive."*

I am here quoting a certain Signor Mauri, the nineteenth-century author of an *Historical Tale of the Seventeenth Century*, in which he reconstructs the story (which alas is true) of Caterina Medici, a young serving-wench burnt alive in the main square in Milan in February of the Year of Our Lord 1617. As regards old hags with protuberant chins, they certainly also existed, and some of them were also tortured as witches. Even so, is it not reasonable and human to suspect that the examination of their bodies was rather more cursory than in the case of the young ones, and that they were rather more often allowed to be put to the torture wearing some garment? I personally am convinced of it. I may be mistaken, but I think not . . .

Put thus for the first time to the physical and moral annihilation of torture, Antonia reacted with frenzy, forgetting all Signora Francesca's advice, all prudence, even fear itself, much like those animals which cannot bear to be caged, and hurl themselves against the bars until they batter themselves to death. She rolled her eyes, bit her lips, foamed at the mouth, shrieked, spat at her gaolers. In short, she behaved like a witch. In the end she said:

"untie me and I'll tell you everything you want to hear from me and maybe more."

At this point, Registrar Prinetti noted in the records, "*incipit confessio Strigae*" (begins the witch's confession). Questioned as to whether she had seen and met the Devil at the sabbaths the witch replied: "I do not know who it is you call the Devil; though if he is the opposite of yourselves, and of your God, then I declare myself his votary and his spouse."

Questioned as to whether during the sabbaths she had carnal union with the Devil, she answered that truly she did not know whether the person with whom she coupled was the devil or not, though she certainly coupled with someone. Questioned as to whether she had lured the females who had been her accusers – Angela Ligrina, Maria Ligrina, Francesca Mambaruti, and Irene Formica – to accompany her to the sabbaths, she replied with hauteur that she, at least, did not share her Devil with any other female. But that even had she consented to introduce him to the hags mentioned by the Inquisitor, he would certainly have been revolted by their loathliness and would not have coupled with them for a silver scudo apiece. (In this instance, perhaps, Antonia was underestimating her "devil's" devilry). But as the Inquisitor probed deeper into the testimony of Angela Ligrina, who had sworn to being several times urged by Antonia to accompany her to the witches' sabbath, the latter replied that she wouldn't have gone anywhere or for any money with that old bag, and that perhaps, and in fact for certain, Angela Ligrina was thinking of the wrong Devil and the wrong sabbath. Let them ask *her* who she'd gone with!

Asked if she had ever kidnapped little children to suck their blood, and to practise sorceries after she had killed them, she replied: "No, my lord. I do not know how to do such things, and have known of no one in the whole world, however wicked, who really does them. They are idiocies they talk on winter nights in the cowsheds, the result of the humbug told them by you priests."

When the Inquisitor asked her if she had ever stolen a consecrated host for her sabbaths, she replied that her Devil ate more substantial fare than that, and whether or not hosts were consecrated made no difference: they were still saltless flakes of bread scarcely bigger than a finger-nail – a meal for ants! A crusty roll, declared Antonia, with three or four hefty slices of cheese or salame was worth more than all the hosts on the face of the earth.

The Inquisitor listened without batting an eyelid.

"Am I compelled to transcribe these enormities?" asked Registrar Prinetti.

"Naturally," replied Manini. "That is what we are here for!" Then, turning to the witch, he addressed her one last question: "Is is true," he asked her, "that the Devil appeared to you in the guise and aspect of a Stroller, as vouched for in the presence of this Tribunal by the witness Teresina Barbero?"

"I met my devil," was Antonia's reply, "without knowing the first thing about him. Not even that he was a devil! But even if I had known that, it wouldn't have changed a thing. Stroller or Devil, I'd have gone with him anyway . . . "

"Very well," said Manini, "That will do for today." Then he ordered the two gaolers to escort the witch back to her cell by the shortest possible route without heeding a word that came out of her mouth and if possible without even looking at her.

"Even so much as a glance," he warned them, "can lead your soul to perdition. The Devil is wily!"

TWENTY-FIVE

The Pig

FRANCESCA AND BARTOLO NIDASIO appeared before the Inquisitor on June 28th, a Monday; and it is certainly to be numbered among the oddities of Antonia's trial that the evidence of the witch's adoptive parents was heard so late in the proceedings, after the other witnesses. As a rule, in accusations of witchcraft against young women and girls, the very first person to be interrogated was the witch's mother, as suspected of being a witch herself, and of having induced her daughter to attend the sabbaths, if not indeed of having taken her to them in person . . . Whatever the reasons for the delay, the couple was made to wait over an hour to be admitted into the presence of the Inquisitor who (as soon as Registrar Prinetti had taken down their particulars) grudgingly resigned himself to interrogating them. Why had two simple peasants like them applied to the *Pia Casa* in Novara to be entrusted with a foundling? And why, moreover, a girl? The rural areas, said the friar, were already pullulating with females that the peasants frequently considered a useless burden, and even today in some Alpine valleys would barbarously drown at birth without so much as baptism. What sense was there in coming to the city to acquire still more of them? And why had the foundling in question grown up in sloth and idleness, and never been employed, without making any bones about it, to attend to the livestock, fetch water from the well and do the laundering, as was proper to her state and as they themselves had declared to be their intention when signing the agreement for her adoption? Who did they think they were? Noblemen? Landowners? Gentlefolk?

As he spoke he held his head inclined slightly to one side, his hands before his face, fingertips together. On and on he went with his questions, modulating his tone of voice as ever, but it was clear that he expected no answer from the Nidasios. Quite the contrary: the pair of them there, standing before his throne, could not have committed a grosser blunder than to attempt to break into his monologue, to make him any answer. He hounded them. Did they realize, these Nidasio "aristocrats", that for more than a year this foundling of theirs had not set foot in church, and on the contrary spoke ill of holy religion, inciting the peasants against the priest and making heretical statements? Did they know that every Thursday night she attended the sabbaths to meet the Devil? That she bewitched young men, sucked the lifeblood out of infants, and committed every kind of atrocity? Had they anything to say on this score? If so, they'd better look sharp about it, because he, the Inquisitor, had other duties more important than listening to their vacuous chatter! From his pocket he drew forth a watch on which he had had engraved the image of a tree, and beneath this a quotation from the Book of Proverbs: "*Fructus iusti lignum vitae*" (The fruit of the righteous is a tree of life). He opened the watch, he set it before him. "Speak up then!" he snapped at the Nidasios. "What are you waiting for? Nightfall?"

Signora Francesca burst into tears, and then proceeded to sob, more softly, for as long as she was in the Tribunal. Bartolo, who had grasped more or less a third of the Inquisitor's discourse, but had felt the impulse, while the latter was talking, to turn on his heel and leave, replied perfectly calmly, saying that he was old enough to remember a time when the Church was less oppressive, and the priests did not compel people "to sing and to carry the Cross" at the same time, as they had been doing for some years now. And this – "singing and carrying the Cross" – is a saying in the Flatlands which merits an explanation. In the Holy Week processions the man who carries the enormously heavy wooden cross, with its life-size figure of Christ, the whole thing seated in a leather sling, is under such strain that he cannot be expected also to sing in time with the others. He simply walks and thinks only of bearing his cross; for the wisdom of the old peasants has taught him not to take on more than one exertion at a time.

"Therefore," said Bartolo, "I myself and other old men like me, not used to being plagued by the priest every moment of the day and for every half-bushel of beans, sometimes grumble out loud without curbing our tongues. And this alone is the origin of Antonia's arguments, which Your Honour describes as heretical." Concerning the witch's supposed magic arts, Bartolo had this to say: "This girl is beautiful, and men perhaps do wrong to run after her, specially those no longer of an age to do so, and those with bad intentions. But that is part of the natural way of the world." Sucking the blood of infants and practising sorceries were simply old wives' tales without any foundation. The only serious thing in the whole matter was that the previous summer Antonia had fallen head over heels for a good-for-nothing, a vagabond whom he and his wife hadn't even known the name of. Only in May of that year, when the proceedings of the Inquisitional Tribunal had already begun, had they got wind of this Stroller, known as Tosetto, who came every summer as water-guard to various landowners there in the Flatlands and to bring gangs of *risaroli* to their share-croppers. This fellow, and no other, was Antonia's Devil: a Devil of flesh and blood whom he, Bartolo, would much like to meet and have a few words with. And in fact he had searched for him, but without success. The only way of clearing up the whole matter, said the farmer, and to get to the bottom of it, was for the Inquisitional Tribunal (having the authority and the means to do so) to compel Tosetto to appear before it, and to confess the truth about those famous "sabbaths" which Antonia had been seen on her way to. "The girl is certainly guilty," he concluded, "but not of what she is being accused of. That is all I know."

Francesca dried her eyes and spoke up. She said that her husband Bartolo had made some enemies in Zardino when he was "consul", by refusing favours to a number of people and by holding out against transferring to the priest certain of the community's ancient rights, common lands which the priest was now claiming for himself; and that those enemies were more or less the same persons who were now trying to get Antonia condemned as a witch. She said that Agostino Cucchi was not a reliable witness, being in age-old conflict with the Nidasios on account of a spring which the Nidasio and Cucchi families had been squabbling over for centuries . . .

"Yes, yes, we know, we know," broke in the Inquisitor, who

when he spoke of himself to persons he considered his inferiors used the royal "we". "Enough of all this: we are in a hurry!" Then he barked out, "And what about you? Confess! Did *you* go to the sabbaths with the witch?"

"Lord save us!" exclaimed Francesca, crossing herself. "Is that a question to ask a body? Me . . . at the sabbaths!"

"Have you ever seen the foundling on her way to them?"

"She used to run off at night," said Bartolo, "after dark . . . When everyone else in the house was already asleep. At about one o'clock." (That is, at nine or half-past nine. In those days, in the small villages, the time was reckoned from sunset.) "She climbed out of the window and down the wisteria . . ."

Signora Francesca went on to explain: "She took advantage of the fact that in summer we peasants go to bed at sunset, because we have to get up very early – at half-past six or seven." (That is, half-past three or four in the morning.)

"She'd be back before dawn," put in Bartolo. The *risaroli* never met her on their way to work. Or if they did, I was never told of it."

The Inquisitor was bored. Even if he let them talk for another two hours, he thought, what on earth could these two blockheads tell him? He rose to his feet, picked up his watch. He stepped down from his dais and started to walk away. But at this point, it is recorded in the proceedings, the Devil "foolishly" tempted him with the offer of a pig, which he rejected. ("*Stulte Diabolus temptavit eum, praebens suem quem ille contempsit*"). In actual fact Bartolo's attempt at corruption was so utterly unexpected and unforeseeable as to paralyse the Inquisitor into a pillar of salt!

"Excuse me, Your Excellency, may I have a word?" whispered our farmer, tugging him by the sleeve. "I have a proposal to make to you." He glanced over his shoulder to see if the Registrar was listening. He wasn't. So he whispered, "Back there in the village I have a pig of six hundred pounds weight – a fine beast! If you agree to the bargain I'll bring him you tomorrow and take back Antonia."

He became aware that the Inquisitor's mouth had fallen open and that his eyes were widening. He tried to play it down, to put things right: "For the monastery, I mean! A donation!"

Manini's lips moved once, twice, but no sound came out. When at last his voice emerged it was a strangled cry: "Taddeo! Bernardo! Where are you?"

Then: "Throw this scum out! Never suffer them to appear before my face again!" He clenched his fists and offered at Bartolo threateningly, but the affront he had undergone was so grave that no gesture seemed adequate, and words even less so than gestures . . . He stamped his foot: "Get out! Get back to your equals, you boors! You beasts in human clothing! A pig . . . to *me!*"

Francesca, who had known nothing of her husband's intentions, did not even realize what had happened. It was only later, on the cart, when they had already crossed the ford over the Agogna and Novara was far behind, that he revealed how he had offered the Inquisitor a pig in exchange for the girl, and he also told her who had suggested this course. T'was Don Michele, the former chaplain, now living on the other side of the Sesia, in the Duchy of Savoy, doing what he had always done on this side of the river but without claiming to be a priest – patching up sprained limbs, treating people's ailments with herbal remedies, rearing bees and silkworms, distilling essences . . . He had even taken a wife, had Don Michele! A young woman who might well have been his niece.

When Bartolo went to see him he listened to this tale of Antonia and shook his head all the while: "Poor girl, poor little thing! I'd so much like to help, old friend," said he when the recital was ended, "but what can I do? You know as well as I do that I wasn't even able to help my own self! This Church of today, these priests . . . On the surface, all Saints! All of them Archangels brandishing swords against poor devils like us who deal in the things of this world . . . All the same, at second glance, they have a chink in their armour too. Take Don Teresio, for instance. He takes wing while saying Mass, he sends you straight to hell if you dare to go out after game on a Sunday, or work in the garden. But if once a month you take him round two fat capons . . . If you slip him a gold *scudo* at Christmas and Easter . . . Well, in that case you can do what you like, I tell you. The fact that you're a sinner doesn't matter any more! Your sins will be forgiven you (in fact, that's exactly what the Church is for!) and when your priest meets you in the village he'll sweep the street with his hatbrim . . . "

At this point Don Michele fell silent for a while, thinking things over. Then he said: "The Inquisition . . . It's a rotten business! I don't happen to know this present Inquisitor, thank heavens, but I met his predecessor, *magister* Domenico Buelli . . . A bloodhound if ever there was one! A man who never loosened his grip on anything, believe me: not a heretic, not a penny, not a privilege! When Bishop Bascapè came to Novara they went at each other like two bullocks in the rutting season, head to head without yielding an inch . . .

"Buelli wasn't afraid of anyone. If he hadn't died of a heart-attack, as in fact he did, not even the bishop would have managed to tame him. On top of that he had a genius for extorting money – he even wrung it out of stones, the devil take him! He it was who built everything: the Inquisition palace, the monastery, the church of San Pietro . . . In a word, you know better than I do: everything and everyone has a price, in this world. Try to get a word with this Inquisitor, make him an offer, I don't know what – a pig, a calf . . . It would be better to offer him money, of course – fifty lire, a hundred lire . . . For a hundred lire you buy the Pope himself! But you haven't got that sort of money to give the Inquisitor, so offer him a pig, the biggest in Zardino. In exchange for the girl. What d'you say to him? Say, 'Your Excellency, it's a donation! For the monastery!' Go on with you! Don't worry, you've nothing to lose! The worst that could happen is that he flies into a rage, and that'll mean the offer was too low, that the real price was higher, far higher, and that you, my poor Bartolo, could never reach it anyway . . . All the same, you have to try it, even if you don't like the idea, as I see you don't. But you must do *something* to help Antonia! So as not to suffer remorse as long as you live for having done nothing . . . Poor little thing! Weight for weight, she'd have been better off if the bandits had got her . . . "

On the morning of June the 4th, a Sunday, the mob of urchins ever on the watch in the main thoroughfare of Zardino, and the old wives returning from first Mass, were present at a notable event. Pietro Maffiolo the field-guard passed through the village as stiff as a ramrod astride the mule his "wife" ("*La mujé, la mujé!*", cried the children as they tugged at her tail), on his head the very helmet he had worn for thirty years, first as a common soldier and later as standard-bearer in the service of His Most Catholic Majesty Philip II of Spain, his sword by his side and the pouch containing his credentials bound to his left arm. He was going to Novara (though this only became known in the village over the next few days) to give Inquisitor Manini his own personal testimony regarding the case of the "witch of Zardino". He went of his own accord, without being summoned by the Tribunal and without consulting anyone, convinced as he was that it was his duty to say certain things of the greatest importance, things which would be decisive in the proceedings and lead to the immediate release of Antonia. The children, agog at the novelty of his uniform, ran before him clapping their hands and shouting "*Viva 'l Fuente, viva 'l Fuente!*" or even "*Viva 'l Fuente e la so mujé!*" (Up with Il Fuente and his wife!) He ignored them. He did no more than make an occasional gesture before his face, as if brushing away a mosquito. Under his breath he grumbled, "*Niños locos!*" (Silly children). He stroked the neck of his mule, he encouraged her: "*Vámos, ánimo!*"

The meeting between the Inquisitor and the ex-soldier, on the first floor of the tribunal in Piazza San Quirico in Novara, was a stormy one. Manini was just back from Milan, whither he had gone to inform his colleague there of the proceedings he had in hand, and to render him that homage which Buelli had never rendered him: that of recognizing him, de facto, as superior in authority to the inquisitors of the other dioceses of Lombardy, a recognition claimed by the Holy Office of Milan since time immemorial, but not always obtained. In exchange he expected to receive encouragement and a promise of support in all quarters, in Milan and in Rome, in the event of a conflict with the bishop. But he had received neither the encouragement nor the promise, and throughout the return journey he had been asking himself why. Why had the Inquisitor of Milan behaved towards him in this manner? Out of ill-will towards his predecessor? On account of something known in Milan but not in Novara? Yet Manini had attempted to inform him of the situation in Novara in the most telling and truthful way possible. He had told him about Bishop

Bascapè, the "witch of Zardino", the Inquisitional tribunal of the Dominicans which had been for so many years inactive on account of the bishop . . . He had spoken of present events. Bascapè (this Manini had told the Inquisitor of Milan, who remained silent, and smiling – who knows what at!) had returned from Rome in the greatest haste, many months in advance of the date laid down for the canonization of the blessed Carlo Borromeo, fuming (according to all report) at how the Pope had dealt towards him – or not dealt at all. On top of that he had broken a hand, which still hurt him, so that his assistants in the administration of the diocese said that he had alternate hours of black depression and sudden outbursts of rage, and that he was more of a corpse and more intractable than ever. What else could one expect from a man in such a sorry state, but that in a moment of wrath he should start interfering again with the proceedings of the Holy Office, and commit follies?

But the Inquisitor of Milan, when at last he deigned to let his voice be heard (in a patronizing discourse stuffed with quotations from the Scriptures and the Fathers of the Church, and with that perpetual smile on his lips – enough to make the Saints, from a distance, wallop him one) was very tepid, if not downright chilly, about the matter of the "witch of Zardino", going so far as to advise poor Manini to . . . drop the whole business! The fact was, he said, that in questions of witchcraft and sorcery the tendency prevailing in the Church at that time was to delegate these as much as possible to the lay authorities, that is, to the normal lawcourts of the State, and not to take action itself except in those cases – few indeed and drastic – which involved the very foundations of the Faith.

In vain had Manini raised heavenwards his long, tapering fingers and dilated his great grey-blue eyes in the face of the other, to convince him that the trial he had in hand was very much one of those cases! In vain had he called his attention to the special circumstances existing in Novara and the need – with a true and just cause and a just sentence – to reassert the independence of the Holy Office in a diocese in which that independence had been suppressed . . .

"No, no, what are you saying?" contradicted his colleague,

smiling still and regarding him as if he were a thoughtless youth babbling at random. "What do you imagine is so particular about the situation in Novara to set it apart from the general and world-wide problems of our ministry?" After which, accompanying Manini to the door of his study and bidding him farewell, he took one of the latter's hands in both of his and, smiling in that maddening way of his, twice repeated, "Be circumspect, be circumspect . . . "

Pacing up and down his room, Manini was still fretting over that encounter: "He deliberately humiliated me! Why did he do it, why did he do it?" He could find no answer.

When confronted by that unexpected visitor, whom Taddeo said had appeared clad in a helmet and armed with a broadsword like Orlando the Paladin, and that they had had to sweat blood to persusade him to part with his armoury, the Inquisitor opened by addressing him a few (naturally sarcastic) words of praise.

"Bravo!" said he. "You have done excellently well to present yourself before the Holy Tribunal, even though you have not been summoned, and what is more on a Sunday, careless of disturbing us in view of the importance of what you have to say!" He enjoined him to speak and to confess. He prompted him: "Could it be that you too attended the sabbaths along with the witch? Or maybe you were yourself her Devil! Speak up!"

"I will, sir," replied the field-guard, who had taken note not so much of what the Inquisitor said as of his particular manner of speaking, eyes, hands and entire body forever in motion. He, Maffioli, had once known a man who behaved in this fashion, and all of a sudden it came back to him ("*Madre de Dios!*"). Count Horacio Lope de Quirega, commander of the 22nd *tercio* (regiment) of the army in Flanders, the biggest *maricón* (faggot) who ever fought under the colours of Spain, and maybe also the most consummate madman – he insisted on perfect Castilian diction even from the German troops, and when he fell in love with a soldier he sent him a ring with his coat of arms set in rubies . . .

Maffiolo pulled himself together. "Last year," he said, "during the rice season I went every night to check on the sluice-gates of the Cavetto, a stream used for the irrigation of kitchen gardens, and therefore of public concern. One night of full moon, as I passed beneath the Tree Knoll, I happened to catch sight of Antonia, the girl whom you have imprisoned as a witch. She was in the company of a certain Tosetto, a Stroller and the overseer of *risaroli* in a village near Novara. A right scoundrel! I swear on my honour as a soldier that this is the truth, and that round and about them everything was normal. There were no Devils, no witches dancing the sabbath, no portents of any kind. That is all."

While the field-guard was speaking the Inquisitor regarded him with simulated interest, and even with astonishment, as if to say "By Jove! These indeed are vastly interesting disclosures!" Then his face hardened. He rose to his feet. To Maffiolo he said: "Shame on you!" And while the latter stared at him in bewilderment he raised an admonishing finger and repeated: "Shame on you for your blockheadedness and your arrogance! You, who are so blockheaded as to presume to know the truth, and so arrogant as to come here and tell it to *us* of all people, to God's Tribunal! And with the very same brazenness with which you would go and blather it to your drunken comrades in the taverns you are accustomed to haunt!"

He paused theatrically. Then he demanded: "Do you imagine for one moment that we were not already informed of this tale of the Stroller?" He pointed a finger straight in Maffiolo's face. "Who do you think you are, you presumptuous churl, to come and give lectures to the Holy Office? Who summoned you? Get out of here and never again dare to show your face before us!"

Of this grand invective of the Inquisitor's Maffiolo had understood only a few words here and there, but taken in the round he didn't like it. And when he saw that finger stabbing in his face, he paled, he took a step backwards reaching for his sword. Not finding it, his hand rose towards the pouch containing his credentials. He loosened the thongs, he brandished it like a weapon.

"I," said the field-guard, his voice trembling with wrath as his fingers opened the pouch and fumbled within for heaven knows what, "I have fought against Luther and against the Turk, against the Poles and against the English. Seven times have I been wounded in battle. I have been awarded two medals for valour and the honour of being standard-bearer for His Most Catholic

260

Majesty. If persons such as you are now in a position to insult an old man like me, it is thanks to my many brothers-in-arms (he crossed himself, he kissed his finger) who lost their lives on the battlefields, in Flanders or on the Danube or in still more distant lands."

He clicked his heels and turned to leave. "Farewell," he said, "go with God . . .

"*Quédese Usted con Dios!*"

TWENTY-SIX

Prison

THUS ENDED THE MONTH of June for Antonia – in prison. While outside the Tribunal of the Inquisition and in the Flatlands the daily round proceeded, and the sun rose every morning and set every evening in a sea of vapours and heat- haze, only she was locked up underground, receiving no visits but the routine ones of her gaolers and with no other company but the rats.

The prison of the Inquisition of Novara was in the cellarage of the Tribunal itself, the men's dungeons to the right of the stairs, those of the women to the left. Apart from the witch, at the time we speak of, there was also a "sodomitical cleric", of whom nothing is known but what is meant by these two words; but then this cleric had had to be transferred to the bishop's prison, leaving Antonia on her own.

The cells were minuscule: blind pits unpaved and windowless. The sole glimmer of light entered through a wicket in the door, at eye-level and scarcely bigger than a hand. Peering out through this hole Antonia saw a corridor which was lit by day from the courtyard through two iron gratings in the ceiling; at night by a lantern hung on a hook at some height on the wall facing her. Up and down that wall, almost unceasingly, at every hour of the day and night ran huge rats with shiny black fur on their backs and grey on their bellies. These were the black rats, destined later to die out in our part of the world, to give place to the brown (or grey) rat brought over from America; but they were still fully active in the summer of 1610, and not in the least concerned about the fate in store for their descendants. They entered Antonia's cell, approached her, "sampled" her by testing the edibility of her clogs and her clothing, and the moment she dropped off they had her awake again shrieking and kicking to drive them off. And this three or four times an hour or even more. Without the harassment of those rodents prison would have been almost tolerable and Antonia, into whom they struck terror and even horror, resolved to speak about it to her gaolers: first to the young one, Bernardo, with his squint and his sagging mouth, who listened and said nothing (could he be deaf?) and then to the old one, Taddeo, him of the shiny bald pate and the hollow eyesockets, who made a show of amazement and consternation. "Rats?" he said. "Here in *this* house? It'll be the worse for me if the Inquisitor gets to hear of it!" And he asked her a whole heap of questions, whether she was sure she had seen them, if there were many of them, if she had counted them. Finally, after a bit more fun at her expense, the old blackguard promised that he would see to it with great traps and poisoned baits, that he would wreak such slaughter among the rats in the prison of the Holy Office in Novara that even the memory of such beasts would be lost. However, the rats stayed on in the dungeons, every one of them from first to last: the poisoned ones to putrefy and stink, the live ones to go on scuttling. But with fewer of the latter Antonia's sufferings were somewhat alleviated, and she was able to snatch brief periods of sleep without being molested: a blessèd relief!

During her first days in prison Antonia underwent alternate outbursts of rage and inconsolable tears. She screamed to be let out, that she had done no wrong against the priests or anyone else, that she was innocent. She pummelled her fists against the wall and tore her hair. Later she quietened down. She just sat on the prison bunk staring at the tiny wicket in the door, and the wall opposite with the rats running up and down it, while the days and the nights above her head followed ever faster on each other's heels. She did not speak; she did not react even when Taddeo placed the bowl of boiled rice in her hands and ceremoniously announced, "Your dinner, milady. Milady is served!" Or when of a morning he inquired about the sabbath: had it gone off well? Were they all present the night before, her friends the Devils? Were they better than men, those famous Devils? Did they have bigger ones? And similar rot.

The medical examination, compulsory in trials of this kind, was carried out on the morning of July the 12th, before Antonia was interrogated by the Inquisitor for the third and last time, and it lasted almost an hour. The two experts, Ovidio De Pani of the College of Physicians of Novara and Giovan Battista Cigada of the College of Milan, dwelt at length and with great care upon two of Antonia's exterior features which apparently seemed to them suspicious. These were her black, frizzy hair and the profusion of moles on her skin. In particular they suspected the moles as possible *signa Diaboli* (seals of the Devil). They therefore subjected them to the test of transfixion, patiently piercing them one by one with a silver needle and finding some of them to be practically devoid of feeling, a grave indication of guilt, wrote the doctors, and almost certain proof (*"majus argumentum et satis ferma probatio"*) that possession by the Devil was already an accomplished fact. It is well known that bodies inhabited by the Devil frequently present numb zones, and indeed it is by these that we recognize them as such. Lesser importance, on the other hand, should be attributed to Antonia's other characteristic feature, the thick, frizzy black hair on her head and in the other parts of the body decreed to it by nature. Oftentimes, asserted the experts, one sees women who, though possessing the same physical attributes, are certainly not witches, but live every moment of the day under the dictates of wisdom and comport themselves most piously in devotional practices; so that it is expedient to make distinctions in such matters, and to proceed with great caution, without hastening to conclusions which might later prove to be erroneous. Lastly – maybe for humanitarian reasons, maybe out of scientific scrupulousness – the two doctors appealed to the Holy Tribunal, requesting that before judging her a last attempt be made to rid the girl of the Devil with pills of wormwood, bitter aloes, rue and such like; or with violent purgatives; or with emetics; because, they declared, such remedies had in the past proved effective, and the Devil had issued forth from the body of the woman *"in flatus, stercus, aut utcumque in corporis excrementa"* ("in wind, in excrement, or in other bodily matter"). But luckily for Antonia it does not appear that this expert advice was acted upon . . .

After a pause of a few hours in her cell, in the afternoon of the same day, July 12th 1610, Antonia was escorted up to the ground floor of the tribunal, to the room especially equipped for the interrogation and torture of heretics, there to be subjected to a further questioning which, according to the records, lasted until nightfall, and which gave a decisive turn to the proceedings. For it was in the course of this last interview that Antonia proved herself to be a dangerous heretic; not merely a "lamia", or witch deep versed in sorcery, but also the disseminator of heretical and schismatic doctrines amongst the inhabitants of the Flatlands: a Luther in skirts! A Devil in female form! The presence of the Devil, say the records of the trial, became manifest in this last interrogation from the witch's very first replies and without the need of any particular prompting on the part of Manini, who had, indeed, merely repeated numerous questions already put in the two previous interrogations.

"Is it true," he asked Antonia, among other things, "that as a number of witnesses have testified you went to the Tree Knoll to meet a man, a Stroller they call Tosetto, and not to meet the Devil? Speak up!"

"If my lover had been a man, as you say," replied Antonia, "he would have come to prove me innocent before the Tribunal. He hasn't come because he is a Devil."

"What does the Devil look like?" asked the Inquisitor.

"Exactly like a man. Like you."

"What did you do with the Devil?"

"Made love."

"And what else?"

"We talked."

"Did you have accomplices?"

"No, your worship."

"Did you kill children?"

"No, your worship."

To compel the witch to confess her crimes they thereupon submitted her to a first torture, using the "strappado". This particular torture involved tying the witch's hands behind her back, hauling her up by them two or three yards in the air, then letting her plummet down until checked abruptly by a taut rope before she reached the ground. This after a period of time established by the Inquisitor according to the circumstances, and measured by prayers. For example he would tell the torturer:

"Hold her up there for an 'Our Father'," or it might be a "Salve Regina" or a "Miserere Nobis". (All this business is, however, recorded in the minutes of the trial in two simple words, "Thrice shattered," which means that Antonia was hauled up and let fall three times in a row.)

The intimate inspection prior to the torturing had been carried out by the young man Bernardo, who on this occasion had refused to toss up for it with his father, but when the moment arrived stepped forward resolutely: "This job's mine!" Taddeo thereafter endeavoured to readjust the witch's dislocated bones, to enable the Inquisitor to continue his interrogation, which he did. In the course of this next grilling there were two further interruptions for the witch to be put to the torture twice more, first the "strappado" again, and the second time on the *lecta cruciatus* (i.e. the rack) which Buelli had had specially built for the Holy Office in Novara, introducing a number of innovations to the model then most widely used.

At this point in the proceedings Antonia was posed a whole series of questions which were, so to speak, ritual: whether or not at her sabbaths they trampled crucifixes underfoot, or vomited up the consecrated host, or abjured their baptism and other such matters entirely irrelevant to our story. Put to further tortures Antonia was driven out of her mind with pain. She wept, she shrieked, she implored her torturers to stop, she insulted In-quisitor Manini and Registrar Prinetti, she uttered horrific things and foamed at the mouth, she rolled her eyes, her tongue lolled out, she fainted away. In a word she conformed precisely to the normal behaviour of witches subjected to the "strappado" or stretched on the rack of the Inquisition. But in the answers she thereafter gave, and the Registrar transcribed, her anger and desperation are transformed into heroism, the will to overcome her persecutors in the only way possible, by proving herself stronger than they. It is in those replies that the character of Antonia, paled, alas, in the records of the trial as it is in the paintings of Bertolino the *madonnaro*, reveals to us its most genuine and vivid colours – her innocence, her pride, her determination. It becomes grand in its own right and in compar-ison with the judges, who can find in themselves no explanation for such courage, and fall back, as said, on giving all the credit to the Devil.

In his concluding address, pronounced on the 20th of August before the tribunal assembled in camera, Manini spoke of some supernatural and diabolic strength that had enabled the "witch of Zardino" to endure the most agonizing tortures many times over ("*peracerba et iterum repetita tormenta*"), without ever renouncing her malevolence ("*nunquam recedens a mala voluntate*"), but on the contrary reaffirming and reinforcing those uncouth heresies for which she had been cast into gaol, and which she had attempted to propagate among the peasants of the Sesia valley.

Of these heresies the Inquisitor provided the judges with a fairly effective and accurate summary. All the heretical statements made by the "witch of Zardino", said the Inquisitor in substance, were based on three arguments. The first of these was that priests served no purpose – mere parasites of the countryside and of the world at large; the second was the purely symbolic nature of Christ ("*There's been many a Jesus Christ since the world began, and many more of them women than men*"); the third concerned the origin of sin, what the Church calls Original sin, but which according to Antonia was religion itself ("*The first sin is the lying of the priests. They say they know what they don't know, and give a name to what has no name. That is the first sin. All the rest follows*").

It was at this point in the interrogation that Manini – according to Registrar Prinetti's report – rose to his feet, pulled his hood up over his head and exclaimed, "*Diabolus locutus!*" – the Devil has spoken!

It was hot, stifling hot, during this time. The Flatlands and the whole plain of Novara, that July of 1610, were an immense steaming marsh which gradually dried out and baked hard, waiting for the rain. To keep the paddy-fields flooded the peasants stole water from one another or from the landlords. The River Sesia, the common water-source, was almost bone dry – an expanse of stones as far as the eye could reach, and down the middle two or three trickles that all but went underground between one puddle and the next. Everyone waited, and prayed for storms, but the only clouds which rose at evening, above the cities as above the villages of the Flatlands, were clouds of mosquitoes. Matters standing thus, and while waiting for the Captain of Justice of Novara, who had been applied to, to put at his disposal for interrogation the Stroller known as Tosetto, that overseer of *risaroli* and water-guard whose name had cropped up several times in the course of the proceedings against Antonia, Manini went off on holiday. In any case he had very recently received assurances from Abbot Aimo and others of the bishop's assistants, that Bascapè would for once not butt in and lay down the law about the conduct of "his" trial. Bascapè had other things on his mind just then! Important as a general rule, affirmed the members of the Curia, that the Inquisitor should abstain from dealing with cases involving ecclesiastics, and that when faced with something such as the "sodomitical cleric" he should hand the accused over at once to *their* Tribunal, without so much as putting him a question. But with cases pending in respect of lay persons, no objections had been raised and no specific measures taken, so that one might assume that the bishop had tacitly consented to delegate them to the Holy Office: *Nulla negatio prorsus est assensus* (The absence of prohibition is in itself assent).

So as we said the Inquisitor set out for his birth-place, Gozzano on the shores of Lake Orta, and there he remained until the middle of August, now visiting the Sacred Mount of Orta, where at that time they were erecting almost a dozen holy chapels, now rowing on the lake or walking in the woods. In those earliest years of the seventeenth century, when the story of Antonia takes place, Lake Orta was a scene of enchantment, a fairy-tale place. Its waters had not yet been poisoned by industrial waste or furrowed by speedboats; the asphalt network hemming it in did not yet exist, any more than did the camping sites, the row on row of villas, the eight or ten storey blocks of flats, and in short all the work of twentieth century "development". Not even the Spaniards, the great despoilers in those days, both in Italy and elsewhere, had succeeded in getting their hands on that minuscule paradise, for the Riviera d'Orta (the lake itself and its banks) was by ancient privilege a feudal property of the Church conceded to the Bishops of Novara, and typically enough Bascapè had defended that anachronistic right of the Church to administer justice, enrol troops and mint its own coinage, with endless lawsuits which in that year of 1610 were still dragging on in a number of places – in Milan, in Rome, in Madrid. It goes without saying that all those suits were lost before they began, though certainly not for juridical reasons. They were (how shall we put it?) . . . they were ludicrous in relation to the times and the actual situation obtaining in those parts. In an Italy scoured in length and in breadth by armies of many tongues and nationalities no one – not even the Bishop of Novara! – could think of carving himself out a State of his own and reigning over it as if it were on the moon, instead of plumb in the middle of the Spanish dominions.

The Spaniards, in fact, ruled over the State of Milan, maintained a presence in Novara and threatened the Riviera d'Orta, where for the sole purpose of avoiding a clash with that madman of a Bishop Bascapè they had refrained from installing a military garrison, shelving the whole matter until the bishop was *muerto*: something that many hoped would happen *de prisa* (right soon).

In this enchanted lakeside setting Manini remained, as we said, for over a month, having heard from Novara that Bishop Bascapè had departed for the village of Re in the Val Vigezzo without leaving any instructions regarding the Holy Office or himself personally; so that at least for the moment, thought our good Inquisitor, there was no reason to return to the city to die of heat. The sultry weather, mitigated on the Lago d'Orta and in the Alps by frequent storms – little clouds formed by evaporation from the lake and the adjacent plains, and dissolving towards evening into rain – rendered the climate of the Flatlands quite unbearable. The city of Novara, according to wayfarers, stank to leeward like an enormous dungheap, and had in addition been invaded by myriads of bloodthirsty insects, flying, hopping, crawling into the pallets and the seams of garments, and even breeding on people, in the very clothes on their backs! The artisans shut up shop, all activity ceased, and even the Tribunal of the Holy Office, Manini assured himself, could allow itself a temporary pause: God and the Devil, both equally overheated, would wait for the air to cool off before contending anew for the human race as was their wont, with no holds barred and with all the vigour which so coveted a quarry demanded of them both! There were – already summoned – only two witnesses left to be questioned, two

269

witnesses called to give evidence concerning the Stroller known as Tosetto, because the latter, according to information communicated by Registrar Prinetti, was not to be found. But for two such witnesses the Inquisitor had certainly no need to put himself out: the Registrar was perfectly adequate. Let him deal with it . . .

The interrogation of one Spirito Fassola on Tuesday July 26th, and of a woman called Demaggi nicknamed Gippa on Saturday July 30th, took place in an atmosphere rendered leaden by the heat and the miasmas of the Novarese summer, and did little to sharpen the image of the witch's mysterious wooer, with regard to whom the records of the trial contain conflicting testimony, and whom Antonia herself had declared to be a Devil. Registrar Prinetti, almost naked beneath his heavy, woollen, black and white monk's habit, was so debilitated by the heat that not even the proximity of a woman such as Gippa could arouse his spirits – chaste but still extant! – and lead him into temptation.

This Gippa Demaggi, the Widow Pescio, once interrogated by Buelli in his time because suspected of being a witch herself, but later permitted by him to abjure, had a reputation for very lax morals and no great intelligence; in actual fact she was a simpleton easily taken in by the first comer, as long as he had a glib tongue and wasn't bad looking. In her youth attractively buxom, at the time of the trial Gippa was a full-blown matron with ginger hair and billowing rotundities which sent the garrison soldiers mad every time they laid eyes on her in the street, and still set the citizens of Novara wolf-whistling whenever she passed. She was half a span taller than the Registrar and a good deal more corpulent. When she spoke of Tosetto she constantly plucked out and replaced between her breasts a small embroidered handkerchief with which she dried the tears spurting from her eyes at the most significant moments of her discourse, though she did not actually weep. Tears of emphasis, so to speak. Tosetto, she said in substance, was a good lad who had once told her he would marry her and since then she had seen him every so often when he happened to pass through Novara but without doing anything wrong Lord save us! She swore as God could see her and judge her and as her deceased parents too if they were called to witness and were able to speak would attest to their daughter's correct behaviour in this as in other circumstances in spite of the tittle-tattle going on about her. Being a widow is a rotten beastly thing wherever you are and specially in a town like Novara, brimfull of malicious tongues even worse than other places. Tosetto, she said, had then had to take himself off to beyond the Sesia on account of all the talk and the hubbub caused in the Flatlands by the "witch of Zardino". Not because he was afraid of accounting for his actions before the law – being perfectly innocent – but because (wild creature that he was and as the Strollers are by nature) he would rather die or be on the run all his life than spend even a single day in prison. It was not right, concluded Gippa, spurting and asperging all her tears, that there are still these witches in the world doing every sort of harm to people and things alike and ruining decent young men.

Even more sparing with useful information had Fassola been some days earlier. He admitted only to having met the Stroller and having employed him as a water-guard in the summer of 1608 and again the following year. Apart from that he knew nothing about him and still less about his girl-friends. The Strollers, said Farmer Fassola, are a strange sort of folk: better to have nothing to do with them! And Inquisitor Manini must have thought so too when he came to draw up the indictment of the witch, where to all intents and purposes he says that Tosetto was nothing more nor less than a Devil. *The* Devil, in fact: the age-old Stroller who wanders the world endeavouring to ensnare men and women; who walks and walks, and is never weary of tempting them.

TWENTY-SEVEN

A Last Pilgrimage

BASCAPÈ DID NOT SLEEP. The heat, the sultriness, discomfort from the hand he had fractured in Rome by tumbling down the steps of San Paolo in Colonna and which no doctor had been able to reset, not even the Pope's personal surgeon, these things had for many a night robbed him of the balm of sleep, leaving him exhausted and lethargic throughout the following day. But there was no remedy, he knew that by now: for there were neither medicines nor prayers to quell the agitation of the present and of his thoughts, to restore calm to his mind, and the long yearned-for silence. He must get up, find something to read, or sit at his work-table and pass his fingertips over the wax mask of the Blessèd Carlo Borromeo, evoke him, speak to him as if he were still alive and present, tell him about what was happening in the world and also a little of what was happening to himself; and ask him to help him live, if he really refused to help him to die! Even by day Bascapè called upon his beatified friend to gather him to himself, and to make haste about it. "I would fain pass swiftly through what shadow is left to me," he would tell him, "and come into your light. I am weary!"

In the life of every man who in his youth has had a strong idealistic impulse there comes, there inevitably comes, a moment when once and for all, with no further hope, or illusion, or dream, he realizes the stagnation of things and of the world in general; when it comes home to him that faith does not move mountains, that the dark will always prevail over the light, that stagnation stifles motion, and so on and so forth. The seven months lately spent in Rome had served to make Bishop Bascapè look reality in the face, to strip him of his illusions. Now he *knew*. The Church which he and the Blessèd Carlo had dreamt of re-establishing upon faith, moral fervour and great works of devotion and piety had instead ground to a halt within the brief span of two decades; and thus it remained, like the Babylon of the ancient scriptures, a monument to wordly things and worldly politics. A den of traffickings and intrigues, capable even of shuffling off its own Saints, as indeed it did, and in the most cynical and shameless manner possible – by canonizing them! By putting them in the calendar, i.e. shoving them in the attic! For this reason he, Bascapè, had returned tumultuously to Novara, breaking off everything and without even taking his leave at the papal court; and for this same reason he had refused to take part in the festivities for the canonization of the Blessèd Carlo, which for the organizers had at that moment one sole purpose: that of ditching the dead and the living along with them – out with Carlo Borromeo but also with Carlo Bascapè! . . . As one of his biographers was subsequently to write: "*He wholly resolved to depart, affirming that he could not fully take pleasure in that canonization, in which at one and the same time someone was on this side being canonized, and on that being censured for his works.*" Strong words, even scandalous for those times! Words of open rebellion . . . though perhaps inadequate to express the dejection and anguish that moved Bishop Bascapè's footsteps, during those hot nights in July 1610, up and down the staircases and corridors of the episcopal palace in Novara, that impelled him to stand at the wir.dow, looking into the dark between the houses as into the depths of his soul . . .

How many thoughts, during those nights of sweltering and torment, passed through the head of Carlo Bascapè! His mind dwelt on the Pope, the new Pope, Paul V, on whom he had placed all his hopes following the death of Clement VIII, and from whom instead he had received an affront so searing, so painful, that he still smarted at the mere remembrance of it. In Rome, in the spring of that same year of 1610, Bascapè had spoken to the Pope about his feud with the Spaniards and the Governor of Milan concerning the Riviera d'Orta, and had entreated him to resolve the problem by writing in person to the King of Spain. "Make me out a draft of the letter," the Pope had said, and he, Carlo Bascapè, had lavished upon that letter treasures of juridical erudition, of literary artifice, of fervour. But when he returned to the Court to find out whether

His Holiness had read it, and if things were going ahead smoothly, he realized that the monsignors of the Pope's suite, though careful not to cross him openly ("The letter . . . Of course! Already submitted! The Pope? . . . No, His Holiness has not yet had time to read it") were sniggering at him behind his back, pointing their fingers at him and tapping their foreheads as if to say . . .

His thoughts dwelt on the Cardinal Archbishop of Milan, Federigo Borromeo, that first cousin of the Blessèd Carlo who had played on the latter and his fervour and spurred him on against those very enemies of the Church with whom he, the Cardinal, would later share a meal, engage in politics, and feel at ease. A great lord and a great man on the world stage, was His Eminence Federigo Borromeo! But first and foremost a great politician. A great child of the times. Whereas the other . . .

He thought of Rome. He had returned there after many years' absence, hoping to rediscover among its hills that breath of eternity which he saw as diminishing everywhere in the world, even in hallowed places and in the words and rites of the Church, and which he had first experienced there, with the utmost intensity, when he was still young; but his sojourn had been a disappointment. The spirit of God no longer dwelt there. Installed now in its place, was politics: the scarlet coloured beast of whom it is written in the Book of Revelation that it was full of names of blasphemy, that it had seven heads and ten horns and who knows what besides! And that political Rome, that new Rome, was the Babylon the Great of whom the ancient scriptures speak, she who gave herself to the kings of the earth and made drunk the inhabitants of the earth with the wine of her fornication, "having a golden cup in her hand full of abominations and filthiness of her fornication," we read in *Revelation*, "and upon her forehead was a name written, MYSTERY, BABYLON THE GREAT, THE MOTHER OF HARLOTS AND ABOMINATIONS OF THE EARTH."

The oppressive heat was driving him to frenzy. From the loftiest terrace of the episcopal palace he questioned the star-filled sky, the plain all dark to the remotest distance, and in anguish he asked himself: where should he go? Where should he flee? To die . . . Was he not dead already, there in that bogland that had witnessed the shipwreck of his dream? What was the whole world but an immense cemetery crawling with fanged worms that he, worm among worms, struggled to love but found himself loathing with might and main each and every time one of them happened before him? To love them in church, or in processions, or when they were gathered together – that was easier. They sang, they exhaled pleasant odours, they were "the flock" entrusted to him that he might pasture them and guide them in the pathways of the Lord; but when he met one alone, face to face in the rooms of that palace . . . When individuals came to pester him with their stupidity, pigheaded hypocrites inwardly convinced they had all the right arguments about everything, eager to persuade him to talk and think as they did, to act as they told him to act, then he no longer managed to restrain his rage, as once he could. He insulted them. Without raising his voice, without so much as looking them in the face. The words which came out of his mouth of their own accord were whiplashes that wrapped themselves around the victim, stripped him bare, skinned him alive, drew blood. Later he would repent. Even he would fain have been loved by his flock, and by the individuals who composed it . . . He knelt on the floor, he sobbed, "O God, forgive me! Help me, Blessèd Carlo!"

From the dark and desolate plain rose the din of the frogs, that tremendous croaking which would at times break off inexplicably, and a little later start up again just as before, without a reason in the world. During those moments of silence, on certain nights, a nightingale could be heard singing from the castle moat, where the willow-trees were; other nights nature made no sound. But at every change of guard on the walls the sentinels cried out one to another, "She hasn't come tonight! Last night she did!" Came the reply, "She will tomorrow. Stay on the alert!" What was the meaning of these strange messages? His curiosity aroused, Bishop Bascapè had inquired of members of his staff, and had received vague replies and embarrassed innuendos; until finally a young priest, Don Delfino, had reported the gossip going all round Novara, but whether it was true or not God alone knew! A Novarese gentlewoman, belonging to one of the noblest and most ancient lineages in the entire district, her yearnings exasperated by her age and by the heat, had two elderly servitors furnished with lanterns escort her to the foot of the city walls, whence she would visit the sentinels in their sentry-boxes, passing from one to the other until the break of day. And this was a lady whom Bascapè saw in the Cathedral at midday Mass every Sunday, seated with veiled face in the front-row family pew marked with a brass plate. A haughty woman famed for her domestic penny-pinching and her public largesse; a devout woman, patroness to many works of piety, both in the city and on her estates. A whore!

Where should he flee to? Under what pretext? And to accomplish what? For many a night these questions thundered in Bascapè's head like the strokes of a passing bell. All is vanity, said the bell: here or somewhere else, what difference could it make? All the world's a sham – all is nothing . . .

Until one evening (the evening before the night of which we speak) the bishop received a message from Milan informing him of the death of Don Pedro Enriques de Azevedo, Count de Fuentes etc., etc., Governor of the State, and of Cardinal Federigo's wish – so pressing as to read like a command – to be attended by all the bishops of Lombardy for the solemn exequies of the deceased. That unexpected and disconcerting message had suppurated a further rebellion in Bishop Bascapè – the resolve to be gone, to flee. At once, at once! To get free of politics. He had every right to, but even if he hadn't, thought Bascapè, as far as he was concerned that changed nothing. Even on the orders of the Pope himself he would not have celebrated the funeral exequies of de Fuentes. Not at any price! For years and years, everywhere and with every means, he had been forced to combat the arrogance and intrusiveness of that iniquitous man, who had tried to deprive him of the Riviera d'Orta and strip him of every one of his prerogatives, even the title of bishop! That man who for more than a decade, there in the Po valley, had represented the very essence of those accursèd politics. Treachery, slander, abuse of power and breach of oath hadbeen his habitual practices, and if now he was dead, thought Bascapè, the verdict on him and his works could not change. If he made a Christian death there was no need for the Cardinal and all the bishops to bury him: the parish priest was perfectly adequate. If not, God rest his soul, for a prayer is not to be denied to anyone. But his works remained: they were there, for all to see, crying for vengeance in the sight of God.

There on the bastions the sentries heralded the second changing of the guard: two hours after midnight, or a little later. Abruptly, as if struck with sudden frenzy, Bascapè crossed to the wall where hung the velvet bell-rope which served to summon his assistant, tugged at it vigorously time and time again, and a bell rang in the upper part of the palace, in an attic where the poor fellow was having goodness knows what dreams, and in those dreams that bell sounded . . . When he had rung long and loud the bishop set to pacing up and down the room, talking to himself out loud about the baggage to be ready before sunrise, the horses to be fetched from the stables, properly curry-combed and prepared for departure, the carriage to be given a thorough overhaul so as not to break down *en route*, as had happened more than once in the past . . .

"We leave at once for Re," he told the luckless Don Delfino who, wearing nightshirt and bearing lamp, had appeared in the doorway of the bishop's chamber and there stood, a bewildered look in his eyes, wondering what was afoot. "We start at dawn, to travel in the cool of the morning. See to giving orders down-stairs and getting the baggage ready. Just a few things . . . the necessaries for two weeks, no more! Fetch my nephew . . . Where are you going?" Don Delfino, who had already turned to leave the room, retraced his steps. "Don Delfino," said Bascapè; and his words were maybe meant to be paternal, but harsh was the tone in which they were pronounced. "Go into my bedroom and wash your face. Use my wash-basin. It's all ready, and I'm not going to use it again today. You're still half asleep, dear boy, and here we need people on their toes! Wake everybody, my nephew, my deputies, the Cathedral canons . . . They shall tell me themselves who will come into the mountains with me and who will stay behind in Novara." He clapped his hands together. "Get a move on!"

He went out into the passage and through his own ante-chamber. As he passed a mirror it threw back the image of a man, indeed of a bishop, that might have come straight from a painting by Cerano, or Tanzio da Varallo: a grey visage, with deeply hollowed cheeks and every bump in the skull already visible beneath the taut skin; a sparse beard; the hand holding the lantern a sheaf of bones; an ample white vestment furrowed with shadows: a ghost traversing the darkness of this world just as if passing through an ante-chamber . . . The ante-chamber of God and of life in God after death, which is the only true life. He who believes in God, say the Scriptures, shall not die, but will share in His joy for ever and for ever; a joy so radiant, so surpassing, that our earthly bodies could not suffer it even for the twinkling of an eye, but would burn up like the gnats drawn to the flame of the bishop's lantern, before that mirror and at that very moment. A tiny flash, an imperceptible sizzle, and the gnat was no more.

Bascapè shook himself out of it, crossed the threshold of his study and went to sit at his work-table. That very evening, or at the latest the evening after – and his fingers, almost without his knowledge, brushed the mask of the Blessèd Carlo in a silent, habitual caress – he would see once more the mountains of "his" Val Vigezzo, the forests of fir-trees, and the tall pines towering against the deep blue of the Alpine sky; once more he would hear the torrents roaring down from the glaciers, once more scent the odours of the earth, and hearken to its silences . . . and deep in those silences the Word of God. He, Bascapè, was convinced of this: the Spirit of God, up there, dwelt in perpetuity, and would never forsake that temple of rocks, of darkest firs and eternal snows, of which He Himself was the Artificer and where He had even seen fit to reveal His presence with a miracle. For at Re, a tiny village deep in the woods of Val Vigezzo, in the spring of the year 1494 a shrine-painting of the Madonna, struck by some sacrilegious hand, had wept tears of blood for twenty days on end; an event which had caused a revival of faith among the locals. Dumbfounded by such a prodigy, the valley-folk had removed the miraculous shrine from its site and transported it to a church, which over the years had grown larger and larger in order to accommodate the pilgrims, and become a great sanctuary: the sanctuary, indeed, of the Madonna of the Blood. A mystic place, thought Bascapè. There God would certainly speak to him once more; and the Blessèd Carlo Borromeo – whose absence, during his time in Rome, he had suffered as palpably as a missing limb or the sudden loss of a belovèd person – would come to meet him along a path, with that shambling gait that was his and his alone –his *own* Blessèd Carlo!

278

By now the courtyard and ground floor of the palace were echoing with footsteps, with voices, with groans; lights were moving in the windows, even in the upper storeys; the somnolent monsignors forgathered, raised their lanterns to identify each other, exchanged commiserations: "You too! There's no consideration for anybody!" "At my age! And me with my pains, my articular fluxions!" "A little more charity towards his neighbours wouldn't do any harm!" "I'd just dropped off," they said, "when they came pounding on my door." Information was exchanged: "He wants to leave! He wants to go to Re! And he's got us all out of bed in the middle of the night because he says we must either see him off or go with him. At once, all in a rush – that's the way he is. Who knows what's going on in his head, that . . . saintly man!"

And they protested. "I'm not going anywhere," declared a short, fat monsignor with gown unbuttoned down the front and nightshirt open to display a whole span of hairy chest. "Next week my nephews expect me at home in Ghemme, and not even artillery could budge me from here now, bishop or no bishop! We're not lansquenets, to be hauled out of bed before dawn to charge into battle! We're priests, of a certain age and a certain standing too, and we deserve a little more respect. Yes sir: respect!"

But they also expressed compassion for the bishop. "He's a sick man," affirmed a priest with a completely red face and prematurely white hair, who prided himself on his medical knowledge. "The sultry heat of recent days is raising the temperature of the fluids, which then plummets in the course of the night and irrepressibly alters the equilibrium of the humours, so that the choleric overflows into the melancholic, the sanguine penetrates the phlegmatic, producing this instability, this constant restlessness, this disorder of thought and action which is a characteristic feature of his illness." But not everybody in courtyard or vestibule was prepared to be indulgent. Many grumbled: "If he's ill, let him get treatment. Off with him!" And, "We can't go on like this. It takes a well-balanced man to manage a diocese. This one's off his head!" They asked, "Where is he now? What's he doing? Why has he had us woken up in the middle of the night? Surely he won't expect us to go with him?"

"No, no!" Don Delfino hastened to assure them. "He only wishes to give you your instructions. He's in his study talking to the deputies. He'll be down in a moment. A little patience, I beg of you."

Above the palace courtyard, still in pitch darkness, the horizon gradually began to glimmer in the east. Dawn was breaking. In the deep deep blue of the cloudless sky was one brilliant star, sole of the thousands which until an hour before had set the summer night athrob. It was Lucifer, son of the morning. In the courtyard palely illumined by the lanterns of the servants and priests the bustle was at its peak. From the upper parts of the palace arrived the bishop's trunks; among the yelling and cursing of the grooms arrived the two carriages, the smaller one in which the bishop would travel and the larger one for his entourage – always assuming, whispered some malicious tongues, that any volunteers would actually be found willing to follow Bascapè at that hour, and in those circumstances, and moreover to such places, beyond the world's end! There also arrived – zigzagging along on horses dreaming they were still in the stable – the "bishop's soldiers". These were two, fetched post-haste from their lodgings on the ground floor of the Chancellery; and from what could be gathered from their sombre expressions and the sour way they cast their looks about them, they were none too keen on setting off like that, at that hour, without a word of warning.

"The bishop!" cried a voice. "The bishop comes!" At which the monsignors still in the courtyard made haste to enter, while those already in the vestibule turned towards the stairway, on which had appeared an ill-matched couple. A young man and an old one – though perhaps we should say one living and one dead – were descending slowly, the old man leaning his weight on the young one. Behind them a servant bore a lighted candelabra, and then came a number of prelates who had gone up to take leave of the bishop before his departure and to receive his instructions for the administration of the diocese. Among them was that "Count Abbot of San Nazario di Biandrate" whom we will meet again as one of Antonia's judges, and who availed himself of this chance to ask the bishop what attitude he should adopt towards the trial of the "witch of Zardino" put in train by the Holy Office. "Let the inquisitor discharge his functions," the bishop replied, "and accomplish what he has undertaken according to the Providence and Justice of God. But the punishment for this offence, if it comes to pass, must be carried out in those parts where the heresy manifested itself, and not in the city of Novara, which is ultimately extraneous to these country rites, with women attending the sabbaths." And that was all.

The young man on whose arm Bascapè leant as he came down the stairs was his thirty-year-old nephew, one Michelangelo Marchesi, a priest himself, who made the bishop's cadaverous appearance even more evident by contrast with his own. This Marchesi had dark eyes and raven hair, a rosy complexion, a robust physique and a general look of glowing health. None of those then present could foretell it, but destiny – fatuous and cynical as it always was and always will be – had already decreed that of those two men in three years' time the young and the live one should die, and that the corpse his uncle should officiate at his funeral in that same place and assisted by more or less the same priests who were there that morning. And this, properly speaking, would have nothing to do with our story, did it not give us that extra incentive to reflect upon the extraordinary vitality of certain corpses, especially when compared with the fragility of the living . . .

As regards the fact that Bascapè was a corpse, no one doubted it, nor had they done so for many years! His carriage and countenance were there for all to see, and in any case he would from time to time speak of himself as a corpse: imperfect and unburied, but none the less a corpse. The wonder of it was, that he continued to breathe, to walk about, to be a trial to those living beings who, when they actually saw him, would often end by forgiving him, thinking: "Poor thing! In the sorry state *he's* in he'll last another few days, a few weeks at the outside!" And this is what happened that morning. The murmuring that arose amongst the monsignors, when the bishop at last appeared before them, was a murmuring of compassion and sympathy. A few even shook their heads: "What's he think he's doing, gadding about the world? He'd do better to stay in his bed and wait for the Lord to remember to come and fetch him!"

"He must weigh about a hundred and sixty Milanese pounds," said the red-faced priest who knew about medicine. "A hundred and seventy fully dressed." (For us today, from fifty-two to fifty-five kilos). "If they let his blood they'll let his soul along with it!"

TWENTY-EIGHT

The Sentence

"*In civitate Novariae die mensis Aprilis 1610. Processus haeresis contra quendam Antoniam de Giardino. Expeditus die 20 mensis Augustus ejusdem anni. In nomine Patris, et Filii, et Spiritus Sancti amen.*

Coram Rev.^{ssimum} D.^{um} frater Gregorius Manini de Gozano diocesis Novariensis Inquisitor haereticae pravitatis . . . " The last phase of the religious proceedings against the "witch of Zardino" began on August 20th at four in the afternoon, on the first floor of the palace of the Inquisition in Novara, in the same audience-chamber where the Inquisitor had interrogated Antonia the very first time. Here, to bestow an air of solemnity on the setting, he had had hung a number of pictures destined for the church of San Pietro Martire; to wit, a *Flagellation of Christ*, a *Deposition* and a *St Jerome in the Desert*. Special decorations had also been arranged on the ground floor: flanking every entrance were holly-trees and other evergreens in terracotta pots bearing reliefs of vine-shoots and leaves and grotesque masks, while a long narrow red carpet had been unrolled in the entrance, up the stairs, and through the ante- room right to the door of the audience-chamber, as if to guide and to muffle the footsteps of the illustrious personages called upon to legitimize the trial by their presence and to decide the fate of the witch.

But without condemning her themselves, you understand! The Church does not condemn or absolve except in purely ritual form; and above all it never kills anyone! The question on which, in trials of this type, the judges of the Inquisition had from time to time to express their opinion was, so to speak, a technical one: i.e. whether the witch was still capable of repentance, and therefore could be permitted the public confession of her guilt that would enable her to save her soul (and life), or whether on the other hand she was utterly irrecoverable, and once and for all at the mercy of the Devil. In the latter case she was handed over to the "secular arm", that is, the authorities of the State, who condemned her to death and also saw to carrying out the sentence. Concerning the bench of judges assembled around Inquisitor Manini and Registrar Prinetti to pronounce sentence on Antonia, we know from the trial records that it was a mixed body, formed not only of ecclesiastical judges but also laymen. A glance at the names and titles of these judges tells us that these assemblies were composed in such a way as to represent all those who counted for something in the society of the time, excluding only the military and the bankers. One wonders if the Holy Office in all times and places acted in this way . . .

That August 20th of the year of Our Lord 1610 many of the bigwigs of Novara were there on the first floor of the Inquisition palace in Piazza San Quirico, all a bustle of starched ruffs, finely chased silver swords, large tonsures and beards of theological cut, friars' cords, priests' girdles, and somewhat crumpled silks all soaked with sweat. It was only the heat that (alas!) impaired the overall spectacle of that assembly of notables, which in any other season of the year would certainly have been more stately, but now, in that oppressive sultriness, appeared a mite fatigued and languid. Though, for all that, distinguished. Among them was the *"magnificus iuris utriusque doctor dominus Petrus Quintanus"*, in other words Dr Pietro Quintano, Mayor of Novara, who by some coincidence was that same "secular arm" to which Antonia must be consigned if adjudged to be incapable of repentance. Present also were the representatives of the magistrature and the nobility: one Giovanni Andrea Castellano, one Giovan Battista Avogadro, one Giovan Francesco Caccia, and one Marco Antonio Gozadini, all of them doctors *utriusque iuris*, that is, of both civil and ecclesiastical law. Representing not the bishop, but the bishop's deputy (*"locumtenens eximii Domini Vicarii generalis curiae episcopalis Novariae"* – for Bascapè wanted nothing to do with this affair, and neither did his deputy Gerolamo Settala), was that highly illustrious "Count Abbot of San Nazario di Biandrate", whose personal name is for some reason omitted. There were the representatives of the ecclesiastical hierarchies, and of the

Chapters: canon Pierangelo Brusati, dean of the Cathedral, one Alessandro Mazzola, canon of San Gaudenzio, one Francesco Alciato, also a canon of somewhere or other (perhaps, and indeed more likely than not, the same Alciato who was once tutor to il Caccetta), and one Gregorio Tornielli, a Cathedral canon. Finally there were the delegates of the most important religious orders represented in the city: an otherwise unidentified Friar Ottavio, theologian and prior of the Carmelite monastery (*"reverendus sachrae theologiae professor frater Octavius, prior in monasterio fratrum carmelitanorum"*) and another friar, Giovan Battista de Casale, a theologian of the Order of St Francis. In all they were fourteen in number, including the Inquisitor and the Registrar; and it would have gladdened the heart of the late lamented Buelli had he seen such a bench of judges brought together in his name and in his Tribunal. Could he but have witnessed his posthumous victory, as a corpse, over a still-living corpse in the person of the bishop!

It was hot, fearfully hot, as we have said and is attested to by one curious particular: that Inquisitor Manini, as a unique exception, treated the judges (and himself) to a glass of iced sherbet ordered from the *Canton Balín* (literally, "Hannibal's Corner"), in 1610 the best-known hostelry in Novara and so called after the proprietor, Annibale Rostiano. It was also the only one with a deep underground ice-house, stocked even in the summer months with snow from Monte Rosa. It goes without saying that the morello-flavoured sherbet is not written into the records themselves, but on a loose sheet on one side of which, marked with the letter A, are registered all the expenses sustained by the Dominicans, and on the verso, marked with the letter B, those sustained by the city of Novara for the trial and execution of the "witch of Zardino", all diligently noted down to the last farthing: so much for the prison maintenance of the thrice-accursèd witch, so much for the sherbet offered to the judges by His Lordship the Inquisitor, so much for bringing master Bernardo Sasso (the executioner) from Milan, so much for his assistants Master Bartolone and Master Jacopo, so much for the "labouring men" who felled and cut up the great chestnut to build the pyre, and so on. After the sentence had been carried out the total bill for expenses was delivered by an official tax collector of the city of

285

Novara to the Nidasios, with a demand for payment within thirty days, delivery date included. So that we may reasonably suppose that the Nidasios ended up destitute, having sold all they had, and spent the rest of their lives share-cropping on other people's land, to the notable satisfaction of those who wished them ill, starting with the Borghesini sisters with their barnyard-feud, the Cucchi with their water-feud, and (why not?) Don Teresio the parish priest: for even priests, like all other human beings, can harbour ill-feelings against their neighbours. Especially priests who fly.

The total bill was in fact enormous: seven hundred Milanese lire, and perhaps more. To make an exact calculation nowadays is no easy matter, for in the days of Devils and witches the decimal system had not yet been introduced, and this complicates things not a little in trying to convert one currency to another and the various appurtenant operations. As regards the sherbets, if this is still of interest to anybody, they cost ten lire, eight soldi, service included. Anyone able to make the correct conversion need only divide that sum by fourteen in order to learn the price of a single morello-flavoured sherbet, chilled with snow from Monte Rosa, in Novara in August 1610.

Yes, it was hot, unbearably hot, hot enough to addle the wits of men and beasts and give rise to collective terrors of portents such as were occurring here, there and everywhere, in the villages of the Flatlands and even in the city of Novara: of monsters or Devils or Fearsome Beasts appearing to scare the wayfarer by night and even in the daytime; of pestilences which began, as in the past, to all appearances quite by chance, but were in fact the plague, the Black Death for which there was no cure. In particular this terror of the plague was widespread at all levels of society and spared no one, rich or poor, learned or illiterate, noble or plebean. It re-emerged each year at the beginning of summer, intensified with the drought, turned to anxiety, to anguish, to agonized expectation of an event which common rumour unfailingly took it on itself to register; so that even when no epidemic arrived the scare of one did. There was always someone who suddenly fell ill with mysterious symptoms, swelling of the limbs, delirium, bubo-shaped protuberances or large purple blotches all over the body . . . Word spread from one quarter of the city to another, from village to village, to this effect: Tom fell all of a heap while walking down the street, Dick saw a gypsy making signs at him and shortly afterwards had terrible pains in his back and chest. We need hardly say that these were news-items which at any other time of year would have aroused very paltry reactions: who on earth gave a damn about the health of Tom, Dick or Harry? At this time of year, though, faces paled in consternation: "Poor thing! My heart bleeds for him! And still so young!" In reality no one spared a thought for the unfortunate to whom the mishap was attributed; they were thinking of themselves. "This is it!" they thought. "The plague is back. St Rock and St Gaudentius, help me not to catch it! St Christopher, you who preserve against all ills, preserve me from this one! Our Lady of Succour, succour me!" The city the Inquisitor found on his return from the Riviera d'Orta was a vile-smelling maze of alleyways full of rats, refuse and excrement, but it was also more than that: a miscellany of fears that took on form and substance in statues of the Madonna, St Christopher and St Rock displayed on little improvised altars at the street-corners, with candles alight all round them and rough garlands of garlic and religious pictures hanging everywhere, from balconies, on walls, above the doorways . . . In the herbalists' quarter, in Monte Ariolo and other parts of the old town, on sale for one *soldo* apiece were bunches of fragrant herbs which people carried around with them in the street, raising them to their noses every so often to sniff the aromas, pungent but considered effective against contagion.

In the churches they prayed for rain, with special prayers repeated during services several times each day, while in the forecourts they spoke of the arrival of rain as depending on the appearance of certain premonitory signs, or the occurrence of certain events. For example, the visit to Novara (announced but never effected) of the new Governor of Milan, Don Fernando Velasquez, High Constable of Castile etc., etc.; or else the death of the bishop (another non-event), concerning which those in the know guaranteed that he had gone to Re, in Val Vigezzo, to die there. (They heaved sighs, they made wide despairing gestures, they said, "His hour is come!") Above all, in the streets and market places people began to talk about the "witch of Zardino" who,

287

being a witch, brought nothing but harm, and began to connect the return of the rain with the death of the witch. "As long as the witch is alive it can't rain!" declared with great emphasis and conviction all those who had experience of the world, and were experts on witches, and knew all there was to know. (That century was chockfull of such men.) They would cite famous cases in Turin, Alessandria and elsewhere, of witches who had managed to prevent rain for six months or, on the contrary, of rains so interminable as to cause the rivers to flood and the hills to landslip; which then had suddenly ceased on the death of the witch. "The sooner she's burnt the better," they decreed; and even those with fewer pretences to wisdom generally agreed. "What sense is there in putting the business off?" they asked. "If she's a witch and has to be burnt, then burnt she should be. That way it'll rain!"

The conviction and sentencing of the witch, i.e. the verdict on the grounds of which she was delivered over to the "secular arm" which would duly rid the world of her presence, was performed according to a text in which each judge recited his part and each part had already been written and allotted, most likely for centuries. It is truly a pity that nothing remains of the archives of the Inquisition of Novara, which with only a few brief intervals was for more than half a millennium in the hands of the Dominicans. Not so much as one other trial to compare with Antonia's, the sole survivor. It might well turn out that all these hearings were identical, or nearly identical, century after century and prisoner after prisoner. In Antonia's case the text first of all included the Inquisitor's harangue, which was ample, detailed and aimed at demonstrating the guilt of the witch, who having admitted her heresies most palpably and indeed brazenly (*"proterv-ius"* is the word Manini used in his summing-up to the judges) must be considered as proved guilty and consigned to the secular arm. After the Inquisitor's harangue came the debate, and here we quote from Registrar Prinetti's report: "The which things having all been examined and considered there followed a long debate, in which the principal speakers were the distinguished Count Abbot of San Nazario, acting for the bishop's deputy, and by their magnificences doctors *utriusque iuris* Giovan Francesco Caccia and

Marco Antonio Gozadini, who maintained that the prisoner must at all costs be consigned to the secular arm as a heretic and apostate (*absolute dicebant ipsam detentam debere traddi brachio saeculari tamque haereticam et apostatam*). Then spake his magnificence the praetor, the learned doctor Pietro Quintano Mayor of Novara, asserting that the matter was not completely beyond dispute, and that it was beholden on the reverend Inquisitor, who had seen and examined the accused and been able to observe when she admitted guilt and when denied it, to say whether or not she seemed capable of a true acknowledgement of her guilt, and was therefore worthy to be allowed to pronounce the abjuration. If not, she must be consigned to the secular arm. Then, the other magnificent doctors and professors of sacred theology taking the floor, all declared that in the course of interrogation the prisoner had never asked for pardon and that even if she had confessed her guilt she had done so without repentance, according to what had already been stated by the reverend Inquisitor, that the accused in her words and deeds had never given the least sign of true contrition (*in dictis eius examinibus ipsam nunquam demonstrasse aliquod signum verae penitentis*), and that she must therefore be consigned to the secular arm; trusting however for every decision in the reverend Inquisitor. And thus in this sentence all concurred."

It reads like the minutes of a meeting of a tenants' association, or of the members of a co-operative. The sentence in which "all concurred", and which in the records of the ecclesiastical proceedings is not even formulated, but merely allluded to in the terms quoted above, was of course to hand Antonia over to the "secular arm" – as was ready written in the text. As regards the other sentence, pronounced later, by which the magnificent praetor Pietro Quintano laid down the when and the how of the witch's death, the words of this are unfortunately unknown to us, but we may imagine them from the results they produced. Antonia was sentenced by the "secular arm" to be burnt alive on the Tree Knoll overlooking the village of Zardino that had been the arena of her sabbaths, on a day to be agreed on with the executioner, but in any case a Saturday, so that all were free to throng there and be present at her execution; and moreover at some hour after sunset so that the flames would be visible from

289

afar, from every corner of the Flatlands. The logs and brushwood for the pyre were to be obtained from the tree which gave the Knoll its name, and orders were therefore given for the tree to be felled and cut up, and for the wood to be carefully laid out in the sun to dry, so that it would burn without giving off smoke. Finally, instructions were given for salt to be sprinkled on the ashes of the pyre, as was the custom, and for a cross to be raised there as a perpetual reminder – in the name of the Father, the Son, and of the Holy Ghost, Amen.

Antonia knew nothing of the meeting of the Tribunal that 20th of August, but even in the early hours of the day on which she was sentenced certain events took place in her underground prison which gave her a presentiment that something big was in the air. Down came her two gaolers, father and son, each armed with bucket and mop. They removed the carrion of the rats and other garbage polluting the air down there, swept away the cobwebs and tidied the place up enough to make it, if not actually pleasing, a little less horrible than before. Taddeo did not of course let slip the opportunity to regale Antonia with the usual, about her and Devils and what she did, or was presumed to do, with the Devils; but the girl was already inured to these scurrilities and didn't even hear them. "I wonder why they are doing all this cleaning-up," she thought in her innocence. "Perhaps someone really grand is coming to see me . . . If *anyone's* allowed down here to see the plight I'm in! I wonder what's happening up there in the world!"

From certain words and truncated phrases of her gaolers she got an inkling that she would soon be out of there, and for a moment a spark of hope kindled in her heart. "You'll see, you'll see," said Taddeo, along with a lot of other balderdash. "You'll soon begin to feel homesick for this place, what with the heat there is above-stairs! You'll miss us too, eh, Bernardo? Say something, you fool!"

"It's true," confirmed Bernardo. "It's so hot up there you really feel you're burning!" He winked his squint-eye at his father. "You feel on fire, you do!"

In the afternoon the two scoundrels reappeared. Over his shoulder each had a straw mattress which he dumped in the cell next to Antonia's – empty like the whole Inquisition prison in

Novara. Since the departure of the "sodomitical cleric" the only sound heard all day and all night was that of the rats, scurrying, squeaking, brawling or coupling amongst themselves. Those beasts were an appalling torment to Antonia; but the darkness and the solitude of that buried place were also terrible. Seeing her gaolers coming back, at that strange hour and with those strange burdens, Antonia began to be afraid. What was afoot? But the coming and going was not yet over. After the mattresses came other stuff: lanterns, flasks of wine, a panier probably full of food, which Bernardo hung on a hook in the ceiling, out of the way of the rats. Every time they passed Antonia's cell Taddeo had something to say: "Perk up, Antonia! Tomorrow it's back to the world for you. You're leaving us!"

"We're giving you a celebration. Aren't you happy?"

"If you want to invite your friends the Devils, by all means do! We're not scared of anyone, not even Devils."

"Just hang on there. We'll be back in a jiffy."

Darkness fell, then night. An hour after nightfall the two returned. They said nothing. They lit the lanterns, opened up Antonia's cell, started undressing. Taddeo passed the tip of his tongue over his upper lip in a gesture so lewd, so obscene, that Antonia shrieked. Bernardo pinioned her arms while his father, as she opened her mouth to shriek again, forced in a torture device he had taken from the cupboard upstairs, a kind of iron and leather bit which he swiftly made fast behind her head. With this between her teeth the most Antonia could do was moan. Then, randy by now, they tore off her clothes, they ripped them off, they struck her with all their might to break down her last resistance. They hauled her onto one of the mattresses and possessed her there in turn, over and over, in a raging crescendo as arousal gave way to frenzy until the two men, gasping and pouring sweat, came to blows over a release by now beyond the powers of either. At last they lay, drained, in a tangle of bodies on which the lantern-flames, flickering in the darkness, threw wavering contrasts of light and shadow, Antonia in the midst as if dead, broken apart, as the last assault of those brutes had left her, a trickle of blood at the corner of her mouth where the torturing bit had rent her flesh.

Only then did her persecutors address her; or rather, Taddeo, croaking with exhaustion, spoke as usual for them both: "So you thought you'd get away with it, eh? you whore you! You thought you'd just go off and leave us flat, after keeping us itching for over a month, damn you! Us up there in our poky little attics thinking about your cunt and you down here in the cool having it off with the Devils! Well tonight you'll have it off with us, believe you me! From now till dawn and then some . . . "

TWENTY-NINE

The Guild Tower

AUGUST ENDED, came September and the heat showed no sign
of diminishing; nor did the rain arrive. Day after day an ever more
pallid, lustreless sun re-emerged at dawn from a sea of vapours:
one could stare at it for a long time without being dazzled. In
town, people moved around as at the bottom of an aquarium, in a
transparent fluid heat that made every movement fatiguing and
magnified all perceptions, so that a sound, an odour, a colour or a
sensation out of the norm produced a state of agitation and distress
wholly out of proportion to the actual discomfort suffered;
thoughts and ideas became unstable, as happens between sleep and
waking. It was difficult to find logical connections with the real
world and between individuals. These albino dawns followed on
sweltering, airless nights plagued by insects and insomnia; and
these in turn came after torrid sunsets, when the sun seemed to
plunge into the vapours like a forge-hot iron plunged into water: it
was almost surprising not to hear it sizzle and hiss.

Out in the countryside parched by the heat and rendered
insufferable by mosquitos, preparations were being made to reap
the autumn crops almost a month earlier than usual. A number of
visions were reported. For example, on August 23rd 1610, on a
farm near Sillavengo, a certain Assunta, the widow Brusati, saw a
smiling Madonna at the well where she had gone to draw water,
and from her received a promise that she would be cured of her
recurrent and troublesome aches and pains – which in fact she was.
At Morghengo on the 3rd of September a girl on her way to cut
brambles to fence the crops and kitchen garden met a young man
on horseback with a nimbus round his head. He conversed kindly
with her and revealed to her that he was St Martin returned to
earth to alleviate the afflictions of the human race. Rain-invoking

processions pullulated, along with novenas to the Madonna and saints to whom popular belief attributed a specific function in this sector, that of combatting drought and furthering the harvests. But above all, throughout the Flatlands, it was ever more insistently claimed that rain would never come to villages menaced by fires and a landscape parched by months of drought until the witch had been executed, and as long as the most infinitesimal vestige of her remained on the face of the earth. At Zardino a gang of woodsmen chosen from among the strongest in the village besieged the great chestnut which had witnessed the sabbaths and now, by Court orders, was to be transformed into logs and brushwood for the witch's pyre. That chestnut was the hugest and most ancient tree in all the Sesia valley, and it held out stubbornly. When at long last it toppled, said the Gossips, the Devil emerged from its trunk in the form of a crested serpent which vanished among the brambles.

Then it was the turn of the shrine frescoed by Bertolino d'Oltrepò. Diotallevi Barozzi in vain attempted to save it from the fury of his fellow-villagers by saying he would whitewash it over that very day and have it repainted. For answer he was told that the very wall was already impregnated by the curse of the witch, and the village must be rid of it. Led by Agostino Cucchi, several times mentioned in this narrative, four farmers arrived, each with his own pair of oxen. They grappled the shrine with chains and stout ropes, uprooted it bodily and hauled it to the banks of the Sesia where they abandoned it, to await the rush of waters that following the death of the witch would carry it who knows whither. Uncouth rites were also enacted in the Nidasios' yard and in the house where the witch had lived. They burnt a scarecrow made with Antonia's cast-off clothes, the furniture in her room and everything they found of hers. There were those who even wanted to set fire to the Nidasios' house and force them to sleep rough on the other side of the yard or wherever they could; but because of the heat, the proximity of other houses and the straw roofs it was feared that once the fire got going it would never have abated until the whole village was burnt to the ground. So "the witch's house" stayed where it was, for many winters to come the subject of cowshed complaint that it ought to be burnt at all costs, that it brought bad luck. Until one day of date unknown – a day like any other in the infinite history of the world – Zardino itself vanished, and its prattle ceased . . .

Taken into custody by the "secular arm", Antonia was transferred on August 21st to the Guild Tower, the ancient tower of the "Broletto", i.e. the municipal palace of Novara before this was reduced to what it is today, bereft of tower and submerged by buildings that in the course of the centuries have come to dwarf it. But at the time of our story the "Broletto" stood aloof, ringed by roads. The Guild Tower rose on the south side of the building, the upper storeys constituting an aerial prison of two chambers one above the other, accessible by way of a hazardous outside staircase. In these two chambers religious frescos were assigned the task of redeeming the prisoners. In the upper room, reserved for women, was a depiction of the Dead Christ in the arms of the Madonna; below, in the men's quarters, St Leonard, patron saint of prisoners. Both these frescos were however scrawled over with signatures, dates and obscene graffiti, and neither was easy to see because there were no windows, only narrow slits which in winter were stuffed with straw and there you were – in the dark. In summer the loopholes were reopened and you could see again, but for anyone entering the Guild Tower at any time of year it was a while before their eyes grew accustomed to the obscurity. And so it was with Antonia: when the iron door closed behind her she groped her way forward, fumbling along the wall, then she sat down. It was only now that she realized she was not alone, and turned her face to the wall, that her fellow-prisoner might understand she didn't want to speak to anyone, and would leave her alone. But when the other told her her name, "Rosalina", she could not but swivel round. Rosalina!

She got up to peer at her more closely: could it really be Rosalina? Her hair was cropped short after the manner of prostitutes (or rather, of streetwalkers), and she looked prematurely wrinkled: her nose, squashed and crooked, evidently broken by a punch, her cheeks disfigured by who knows what disease with hundreds of small scars, on her neck the slash of a wound, probably from a razor: a narrow slit of a scar, but so long it disappeared beneath her dress. She was already hideous, our Rosalina; not downright horrendous, for she was still only twenty-six or -seven, but it was plain that she would very soon become so. The fact that Antonia remembered her and her past left her indifferent, while to Rosalina the face of this new companion was completely unknown and so was the name: "Antonia" meant nothing to her.

She was there in the coop, she said, thanks to a bastard of a Spanish officer who for a short time had taken her under his protection and been her sweetheart and her pimp, until one fine day he announced out of the blue that he had got himself another sweetheart, a younger one, and that she, Rosalina, could pack her bags. "The younger the flesh the better the money." There were already too many tarts around the Castle –this is more or less how that officer and gentleman had the finesse to put it – and every so often a turn-over was needed, as with soldiers. The garrison grows rusty, and it's the same with strumpets: instead of being our sweethearts in moments off duty they become our mothers and our grandmothers. But Rosalina hadn't felt she was anyone's grand-mother, and as for packing her bags, where could she go? Ergo, she said, she went on plying her trade, but without protection, and those cursèd Spaniards started arresting her, saying she was infringing the "proclamation", i.e. the law governing prostitutes. At every arrest they recited this proclamation forbidding prostitutes to circulate without the yellow cape that was their trademark, to approach places of civic consociation, such as the municipality, the churches and the military barracks, to show themselves at windows overlooking thoroughfares or to loiter in the streets going "psst! psst!" to entice men. And they would read her the whole text right down to the "pecuniary and corporal punishments", the latter including the stocks, the lash, imprison-ment and the gallows. Then they would lock her up in the Guild Tower, like this time, all because she was caught without the yellow cape, or near the castle, or going "psst, psst!" to passing soldiers, and because of their oft-deceived mothers and sisters, not to speak of the horns on their own heads – a whole ruddy forest of them!

But this time, said Rosalina, things were more serious: it was going to end in a public flogging. For Antonia too. Whatever they'd sent her to the Guild Tower for, she'd come at a bad moment. The hangman was expected! When Antonia stared at her non-plussed,

Rosalina explained. Master Bernardo was coming from Milan to burn a witch who had committed all sorts of atrocities, including the murder of many babies, and in Novara, alas, this was the way of it: when the Master of Justice was in town the authorities seized the chance to have him flog whoever was in gaol at the time, regardless of why they were there; because the master didn't come every day of the week and the city council paid him a set price and wanted as much work as possible for their money. On the floor below, said Rosalina, there were four poor devils – thieves and tricksters – also expecting to be flogged, and all the fault of the witch! She eyed Antonia as she asked, "And what have *you* done?"

"Nothing," replied Antonia. "I've done nothing." And then, almost in a whisper, "I'm . . . I'm the witch!"

Rosalina goggled at her. "The witch? You?"

"Yes," said Antonia. "So they say." She looked Rosalina in the face and murmured, "I only hope they hurry up and burn me and get it over with! I wish they'd get a move on!"

The most excruciating torment in the Guild Tower was the insect life, the fleas worst of all, but also the lice and the bedbugs. The mosquitoes were almost tolerable, because they did not swarm up there where there were swallows, but stayed below among the buildings, where there were humans. The straw the prisoners slept on was alive with insects, which when necessary served also as a pastime – once you started scratching the days just flew by . . . Towards evening there came knockings on their floor and hollering from below – the male prisoners trying to contact the women; but the cells were so set up that however hoarse they yelled themselves scarcely a word could be understood, "love" being among the foremost. After a while even the prisoners calmed down. At night the world fell silent: no sounds but the cries of sentries on the distant ramparts, the calling of owls nesting in cracks in the tower.

The days went by, one by one, each identical to the one before, not a single event but – once a day – a cowbell ringing in the yard below: time to pull on the cord and haul up their food-basket. Thus was "life" organized in the Guild Tower, and unless new detainees arrived during the week the iron door giving onto the steps opened only on Sundays, for emptying the latrine. You scratched, you chatted, you peered through the loopholes at the outside world, you day-dreamed, you slept. In the Inquisition dungeons Antonia had slept very little indeed; in the Guild Tower she partly made up for this. She slept so long and so soundly as to lose count of the days and nights and madden Rosalina who would have liked a more sociable companion, and – when the stuff in the basket was uneatable – sometimes went so far as to kick her to her senses: "If Her Highness the witch will deign to get up and eat," she would say, "I would inform her that the prison rations are served." On occasions when the food was acceptable Rosalina resigned herself to gobbling it up on her own . . . ("After all," she thought, "if you're asleep you eat in your dreams.") For Antonia each awakening meant coming back to a harrowing and hostile world. She moaned, she wailed, she was all bewilderment. Sometimes she even stammered out "Where am I?"

"You're in the clink, duckie! Where were you dreaming you were, the king's palace?"

Antonia did dream indeed. Grand dreams she dreamt, as intricate and fruitless as life itself; almost all of them beautiful and sometimes, like life, nonsensical. She dreamt of the sea as an upturned sky, the ships ploughing across it, of the city Gasparo had told her about, where the houses were high as hills and they buy and sell everything on the face of the earth, including people, and of the tree-lined avenue along the shore, where the grand ladies parade in their carriages of an evening and people flock to see them . . . She dreamt she was in one of those carriages, attired in silks and velvets and alongside her a beautiful young man who was Gasparo, or perhaps just looked like him. Sometimes enemies would worm their way in among the figures in her dreams: Don Teresio, the Inquisitor, people in Zardino. But far more often Antonia's dreams in the Guild Tower were as aerial as the prison itself, fantasies held together by a plot as tenuous as gossamer. In those dreams she walked through enchanted palaces full of plasterwork flourishes, golden treasures, pictures, tapestries, things she had never seen except, indeed, in dreams. She found herself dancing with handsome young men, went riding with them along white roads that stretched on for ever and for ever, and before them the sun was rising . . . rising or setting. She dreamt in the knowledge that she was dreaming, afraid of waking. "If I wake up," she knew with terror, "I'll go back to being the girl everyone thinks is a witch, and be burnt alive in a few days' time!"

Bernardo Sasso, Master of Justice (i.e. the public hangman of Milano), arrived in Novara with his assistants Bartolone and Jacopo on the evening of Friday, September 10th, sweltering from the journey and in a black mood because of the type of service required of him. With that heat, he had told his assistants while they were ferrying the Ticino at Boffalora, it would have been better and more sensible to drown the witch, rather than burn her. Perhaps right there in the Ticino: why not? If he could have spared himself that business of the death-pyre, and avoided coming to Novara even if it meant losing money, Master Bernardo would have done so. But he could not, for just a month earlier, on August 8th 1610, he had signed a regular contract – perhaps today we would call it an agreement – by the terms of which he, as Master of Justice in Milan, committed himself to exercising his profession in Novara whenever occasion demanded, flogging condemned prisoners in public, executing them in accordance with their sentence and, if called for, drawing and quartering them according to the canons of his craft. As, among other things, is laid down in the contract: "*And there being a call for quartering, and cutting up executed persons, and also for the quarters to be affixed in the allotted places, it is agreed that in such a case d.m.* (standing for *dominus magister) Bernardo is bound and obliged to quarter and affix the pieces where necessary*" etc. This document has come down to us, so we are able to quote its exact words. But should we take them too much at face value we might get the impression that the main square of Novara habitually witnessed the execution of highly dangerous criminals and bandits and every other kind of sentence. The truth, however, was far less grim, and in practice the hangman was required to come every so often for the public flogging, or at the most the hanging, of some petty malefactor or robber, because the more spectacular executions, the beheadings, normally took place in Milan. But burnings, now . . . burnings were something Master Bernardo Sasso considered a barbarous survival from the past, an utter negation of the art of which he was a master, for him not a mere profession, but a life mission! "If all you need to carry out a capital sentence is to light a couple of faggots," he grumbled to himself as they were approaching Novara, "what need of the Master of Justice? Why don't they call any old cook to light their fire for them? What has the justice of a modern State to do with these antiquated rites? Why call the hangman?"

The hangman . . . the hangman . . . Of the characters – or rather, of the unwritten novels – whose stories interweave with that of Antonia, the most singular and maybe also the hardest for anyone today to fathom, let alone write, is his. Bernardo Sasso, that September of 1610, was a man of more than middle age, head and cheeks meticulously shaved and a face that might be thought entirely average, but for the notable trait of a pair of highly spirited blue eyes that looked straight into those of his interlocutor and seemed to divine there even the deepest of thoughts, the most fugitive ideas, the most unavowable temptations. Born to the trade (his father and grandfather, hangmen both) Bernardo Sasso had never in his life done anything that might be called strange or extraordinary; except, perhaps, being a hangman. But it was precisely his absolute normality, his absolute common sense, his almost superhumanly sound judgement, that made him a character not so much uncommon as unique. Those who had chanced to know him from childhood, and had kept up the acquaintance, swore that in his more than fifty years he had never got drunk, not even slightly or even just to see what it felt like, he had never raised his voice in anger, he had never run after a woman. Even his wife he had met during working hours; in the sense (according to his would-be biographers) that it was she who had first set eyes on him while he was exercising his craft in the main square, and had been so favourably impressed that through the good offices of a priest she asked for his hand in marriage. They met, and they married. She was then an inmate of the so-called "Deposit of San Zeno", where they lodged runaway girls whom their parents didn't want back; he was a master of justice, which is to say a hangman, with whom very few women on the face of the planet would have wished to share a roof . . . The result had been a happy and thoroughly solid union, with but one blemish, sadly irremediable: no male heirs. That was the great distress of Bernardo's life. Five daughters but not one son to carry on the craft and mission of the family Sasso. Thus, with no heir to perpetuate the name, Bernardo at length grew fond of the two assistants now at his side, Bartolone – already of mature years and destined to be his successor – and a younger man and distant relative by the name of Jacopo. Both were the result of a long weeding-out of assistants who had in time proved unequal to living cheek by jowl with a man as perfect as Master Bernardo, and had had to find themselves another hangman or another profession. Each was a fairly successful attempt to imitate the master: they had shaven heads, like him; they were dressed like him from head to foot in grey; like him – or almost – they had no bad habits . . .

The three of them, travelling on horseback, must needs knock at the door of the Capuchin monastery, for no innkeeper would have lodged the hangman on his premises for any money, and no publican would have served him food, either in Novara or anywhere else. After a frugal supper with the monks, and a visit from the Captain of Justice, who explained the whereabouts of the village where the witch was to be executed and informed him of the preparations made in the city and at the place of execution, they made their way to bed. However, before taking leave of his assistants and bidding them goodnight, Master Bernardo assigned them their tasks for the following day. Bartolone, he said, was to go with the escort, travelling in the carriage with the witch to ensure her safety; Jacopo was to be at the crack of dawn in Zardino to ensure that everything was ready when he himself arrived.

"Sir, and you, sir?" inquired Bartolone. (Both the assistants addressed the hangman in terms of the utmost respect). "What will you be doing?"

Master Bernardo glanced around him to see if any of the monks were listening. There was no one. "Tomorrow morning," he said, "I have to administer a public flogging to the unhappy mortals now in the Tower, and after that I must attend to another matter: to get a herbalist to make me up something that only I can obtain, and I alone know about." He crossed himself, lowered his voice. "May God be my judge," he said. "Burning alive is the most atrocious way to die, and I do not think I am detracting from the witch's sentence if I lessen her perceptions a little, and with them her suffering. God forgive me if I am about to commit a wrong, and may the Lord be with us!"

THIRTY

The Revels

WHEN IN THE EARLY AFTERNOON of Saturday September 11th, the day of her death, the "witch of Zardino" appeared high up on the Guild Tower, beneath the "Broletto" windows overlooking the main square was a mob of idlers who, what with the heat and mutual incitement, had already worked themselves up into a fine lather, brandishing fists and sticks: "*We want the witch! We want the witch! We'll do the burning!*" Other loafers, superficially calmer, were trying to persuade the municipal sentries to hand the doomed woman over to them: "What's the use of taking her back to her village? We want to *see* her burn! Here in Novara! Right here in this square! Otherwise we can't be sure . . . "

Her unaccustomed eyes blinded by the daylight, Antonia came down the steps seeing nothing or next to nothing, but in her ears the roaring of the crowd, in which single words could be made out – "rain", "death", "witch" but few others. Part supported by whoever was behind her, part by grasping the iron hand-rail, she made it to the bottom. The "Broletto" courtyard was jam-packed with soldiery, horsemen and infantry, Italian militiamen and Spanish Miquelets, halberdiers and harquebusiers, all drawn up in case of need without any specific function, except for those ranged round the carriage and detailed to escort the witch to her place of execution. There stood the closed carriage, a rather shabby four-wheeler normally used to convey magistrates investigating water-feuds to make on-the-spot inspections. Antonia was hoisted up and thrust inside by the soldiers who had fetched her from her cell, and there being only one free seat she took it, beside a stranger all in grey and with shaven head: the hangman's assistant. Two other men sat opposite: on the left the Captain of Justice, a tall, bony senectudinarian with particoloured hair, white at the roots and crow-feather black for the rest, who constantly and in every gesture assumed the airs of a man of consequence, and spared the witch barely a glance before returning to events outside, holding back the curtain and peering through the glass. On the right sat a bald Franciscan with a wooden cross in his hands, a huge black beard to halfway down his chest and two grey, moonstruck eyes which stared hard at Antonia as if she were the Devil in person. A look that meant "I fear you not!"

An agitated voice was heard giving orders and the carriage lurched into motion, turned, and left the palace. The iron hoops of the wheels now clattered on the cobbles, causing the heads and limbs of the occupants to jounce about to curious and sometimes grotesque effect. Antonia squinnied out to her left, through the same window as the Captain of Justice, because on the friar's side the curtain was tight shut. She could see the cuirasses and profiles of the troopers riding beside the carriage, the crowd lining the route, the raised fists, the contorted faces, the mouths wrenched open to execrate and curse and clamour for a death – her own . . . As they neared Porta San Gaudenzio she discovered that to shut out that howling she had only not to listen. The faces, the bodies out there, were like fish in a fishbowl, detached from her and even freakish. Indeed she was amazed at never having noticed the details which now seemed to her so absurd; never before being flabbergasted by those strange shapes, assuming them – as do we all – to be inevitable, completely reasonable, and being always under the impression that they were normal! Those so-called ears, those noses . . . Why were they made that way? Those gaping mouths with that wagging pink nubble inside . . . How imbecile! How nauseating! And that irrestrainable explosion of loathing in people who until a few days ago did not even know she existed and now demanded her blood, her guts, lusting to put her to death then and there, with their own hands . . . Was there a reason, a meaning in all this? If not, why did it happen? I am here, she thought, and don't know why I am here; they are yelling and don't know why they are yelling. She seemed at last to understand something of what life was: mindless energy, a monstrous disease that convulses the world and the stuff things are made of as the "falling sickness" convulsed poor Biagio when it struck him down in the street. Even our much-vaunted intellect, what was it but seeing and seeing not, or a telling of idle tales frailer than dreams: Justice, Law, God, Hell . . .

"Death to you, damned witch! To the stake! To the stake!"

Just outside Porta San Gaudenzio a face more demented even than the rest loomed at the window and opened its mouth: spittle beslavered the glass and the Captain of Justice dropped the curtain. For a moment the carriage was in darkness, but when he peered out again the occupants' faces sprang back into view.

"Make it rain, you foul sow! To the stake! Croak!"

The bald friar with the moonstruck eyes had never ceased to glare at the witch for an instant, not even in the dark. Now he leant suddenly forward, stretched out his arm, thrust the cross at Antonia's face and spoke. "If you still know how to pray," he said, voice quaking and the eyes nearly out of his head, "then the time is at hand for you to repent, and to pray, and to ask God's pardon for your countless sins, however horrible they may be. For men can no longer forgive you, but God can!"

Drawing close to the Borgo San Gaudenzio market the shouts came thicker and faster and more raucous, a riotous, menacing uproar, an uninterrupted hubbub punctuated with increasing force by the thudding of vegetables on the carriage roof and sides and a new and disquieting sound like the rattle of hail. Bartolone had no time to say "It's stones!" but almost together both windows shattered into fragments on the laps of the four and between their feet. That instant the carriage stopped – the coachman in trouble too. As the troopers bawled "Keep back! Keep back or we'll fire!", for a moment – eternity to its occupants – the vehicle was at the mercy of the mob, buffeted, shoved, rocked every which way, like a bark on a stormy sea. The roof-stones ceased; began the thump and thwack of fists and sticks on the carriage sides, a door was wrenched open from without, frenzied faces filled the space, frantic hands reached in to seize the witch . . . But in the nick of time the troopers fired and it was all over in seconds. People trampled on each other in the struggle to escape, scattering in all directions shrieking with terror as the men recharged their harquebuses and the Captain of Justice, hanging halfway out of a window, urged them to reload quicker, aim lower, fire another volley! An invisible hand slammed shut the door, the Captain of Justice withdrew inside, the carriage moved on. But after fording the Agogna came another enforced halt: a wheel had worked loose in the hurly-burly and they had to repair it on the spot with makeshift tools.

This hitch, occurring repeatedly throughout the remainder of the journey, occasioned a notable delay in the witch's arrival in Zardino. Planned for about four in the afternoon it did not come about until close on sunset – and who knows whether Antonia regretted that! We should add that the first halt near the stream provided an opportunity to wash a wound which the Captain of Justice had discovered on his face after the mob assault, caused in all likelihood by a splinter of glass. Painless yes, but the sight of his own blood made that man of consequence fly into such a passion that he did not scruple to give the escort peremptory and ruthless orders: to shoot without warning at body height at anyone even unarmed who came within three paces of the carriage; if armed with sticks or stones to shoot and bring them down as soon as they came in sight; if they were many, to fire into the ruck. After all, grumbled the Captain, pressing a dampened handkerchief to the injured area, however many peasants you kill there are still too many of them.

Practically every step of the way they overtook parties headed for the Tree Knoll to see the witch burn, whole families on the low-sided carts drawn by colossal horses with knee-joints as big as a man's head which at that time in the European countryside were the universal means of transport, for people as well as goods. When the carriage caught up with them the carts pulled aside, or were ordered out of the way by the troops, while everyone aboard, out of their minds with rapture, yelled "The witch! Here comes the witch!" while the dogs (if they'd brought them along) barked fit to burst, the children put both hands to whirling wooden rattles specially made to create a din, the men jangled strings of cans formerly the instruments of the Devil (that is of Carnival, before Bascapè banned it) and now came in handy to celebrate the victory of God over the Devil, and the women and old folks shook their fists and joined in the general cry of "The witch! Here comes the witch! To the stake with her!"

Nearing the Sesia, at each side-turning and lay-by they passed the first vendors of wine and fruit juice, fried fish and water-melon. On either side of the road, wherever the maize or rye had already been harvested, the fields were packed with carts, horses, children scampering after each other and playing hide-and-seek, grown-ups who had stationed themselves there to eat and drink and wait at a distance to enjoy the grand spectacle of the witch's bonfire, expected to be visible for many miles around – no point in pressing on to the foot of the Knoll, where there was sure to be such a crush that close as you were you would see nothing. Better to be a shade further off and a shade more comfortable. In they flocked from every corner of the Flatlands, and even from the towns (Novara, Vercelli, Gattinara . . .) with their families, their friends, their old folks, their children, and their carts stacked with wine and provisions, to make merry and feast themselves and celebrate the end of summer. They were neither bloodthirsty nor wicked. On the contrary, they were decent people: the same decent, hard-working people who in our twentieth century cram the stadiums, watch television, go to vote at election time; and if need arises to wreak summary justice on anyone they do not burn him, but they none the less wreak it. For this rite is as old as the world, and will endure to the world's end. (As Antonia put it, so long as there are men alive there will be Jesus Christs, women as well as men).

"The witch! She's here! Death to her! The stake, the stake!"

"Light that fire! The witch is come! Let's see her sizzle!"

Master Bernardo, on horseback from Novara, had tagged along behind the carriage, observed all its vicissitudes, and came within sight of the Knolls and the village when it was already evening. That steamy hot September Saturday Zardino was living in the spotlight of history for the first and last time in its existence. On the balconies, in token of rejoicing, the crones had hung every bit of embroidered cloth in the village, and in nearly every window shone rows of little lamps, shining brightly now that the sun had already begun to set over the Sesia, and the shadows were lengthening in the courtyards, deepening in the alleyways. Never had there been in the past and never for any reason would there be again such a multitude in and out of the Lantern Tavern, packing the church and cramming the piazza to hear the voice (now hoarse) of Don Teresio pronouncing hair-raising preachments about the snares of the Devil, how he can waylay the steps of man's weak will on their course towards God and turn them hellward. The church doors and windows were all flung wide and Don Teresio, assisted by two priests from nearby villages, had been officiating and preaching non-stop since the crack of dawn, preparing his faithful, and others there on pilgrimage to view the witch, for the solemn procession timed to set out from the church *en route* for the Tree Knoll as soon as the sun dipped below the horizon. Four altar-boys unceasingly prowled the crowd, in church and out, collecting offerings; and so well did they perform this office that the following day, as he counted his heap of coins, it dawned on Don Teresio that the long hankered-after parish was no longer so remote. That maybe even before the end of the current year . . .

"We're here to burn you, stinking witch! It's ready and waiting! Just needs you!"

By now the sun was setting behind the Knolls, and for anyone familiar with those parts the absence of the great Tree was an enormous void, an irreparable blank. On arrival they were stupefied to realize something unnoticed by all while the Chestnut was there at the crest of the Knoll: that the tree, for centuries, had been not only a tranquil presence presiding over the silences surrounding it, but also an essential feature of the landscape of the Sesia valley, which without it would never, never be the same. In its place, as if to cover some nakedness or painful wound, were tidy stacks of brushwood on either side of the witch's stake, and things for the hangman's use, a wooden step-ladder to the top, planks forming a platform . . .

On the other Knoll, unguarded by the military, an irrupting, unstoppable mob had put paid to all legends of supernatural beings there, destroying the vegetation into the bargain . . . Crowds everywhere, wherever the eye could reach – down to the Sesia, on the village roofs, in the trees, up the church tower, hundreds and thousands of people rushing madly, gesticulating wildly, despite the heat and sweat-drenched clothes, scurrying here, scurrying there, ogling the opposite sex, chewing pumpkin seeds, gorging great wedges of water-melon – and all of them dinning it with tin cans or rattles. All of them rejoicing in that day of days when the Flatlands would be rid of a witch who caused children to die, the rain not to fall, and the heat and the summer to refuse to end.

"Filthy witch! Roast her, roast her! To the stake, to the stake!"

It was late already. The red sun, haze-cradled over the Sesia, fired the horizon with the specific trick of refraction which gave rise to the local jingle, "*Quand al sul al varda indré, acqua a secc al dí adré,*" (When the setting sun looks back again/ The next day you'll have buckets of rain). A theatrical, a melodramatic sunset such as only in Italy are September sunsets, lavish with trumpeting colours, resplendent back-drops, chasms of light, of melancholy, of poetry.

Master Bernardo, however, did not number among his perfections that of being a contemplator of sunsets; or even if he did, he would not have been able to indulge it that evening, for sheer lack of time. From his saddle he unstrapped a leather blood-letter's bag where he kept a few instruments and other objects pertaining to his craft; he grasped the witch by one arm and part forced, part guided her to the summit of the Knoll, where the Knights of St John the Beheaded, in black breeches and white mantellettas marked with crosses, stood guarding the scaffold. Beneath this he halted. At his side, chalk-white, wide-eyed, Antonia roved her gaze about her, sightlessly; benumbed but for her heart thudding in her breast, pulsing the blood in her temples, booming in her ears.

"Before I perform this task, assigned to me by divine will and human justice," said the hangman, bowing his head to the girl, "I humbly ask for your pardon." Antonia's lips moved, but nothing came out. Heard instead was the voice of Don Teresio, just leaving church at the head of the procession, singing (or rather, bawling) the litanies of the Madonna. The horde of faithful could be heard, then seen, flooding out of Zardino and making across the field, and finally also the procession wending its way from the village along the track to the Knoll. Don Teresio, his strength almost spent by all the exertions of that age-long day, advanced as we have said, vociferating, tottering and toting the great Crucifix: a prodigious feat, considering

how heavy was the cross and how apparently frail was the man.
Every few steps he cried:

> "*Stella matutina!*" (Star of the morning!)
> "*Rosa mystica!*" (Mystic rose!)
> "*Turris davidica!*" (Tower of David!)

Behind him, holding aloft their respective banners, came the
Christian Brethren of Zardino and the other Flatlands villages, then
the clergy, then the religious congregations, and lastly the pious
with their torches. Their responses came in a great roar, joined by
the multitudes on the Knolls and the river-banks and all the Sesia
valley:

> "*Ora pro nobis*" (Pray for us).

Over Antonia's head Master Bernardo slipped a red habit with two
large white crosses, one on the breast and one on the back. He ought
by rights to have cut off her hair and put a blind cowl on her, but
there was no time for such formalities. In any case these were details
which could be overlooked, at least in Italy, where the preparation
of a witch for the stake did not follow hard and fast rules, as it did in
Spain, but varied according to circumstances, place, and the
discretion of the executioner. Then from his bag he took a glass
phial, poured the contents into a beaker, whispered to Antonia
"Quick! Drink this! It will dull your senses" and steadied her hand as
she drank. Now the friar who had travelled with the witch stepped
forward brandishing his crucifix, and the mob on the Knolls and
around them accorded him a thunderous ovation and many cries of
encouragement: "Out with the Devil! Let's see the Devil come out
of her!" and other crassitudes of like kind which we need not report.
And still the procession wound out of the village, Don Teresio
marched on crying out in the dusk, and the crowds roared back with
the force of a thunder-clap: "*Ora pro nobis*".

> "*Turris eburnea!*" (Tower of ivory!)
> "*Foederis arca!*" (Ark of the Covenant!)
> "*Ianua coeli!*" (Gate of heaven!)

The friar upraised the crucifix against the last embers of the sunset
and, turning to Antonia, "Kneel down!" he shrieked. "Beg God's

pardon!" For some moments she remained quite still, stunned perhaps by the potion; then she made a gesture to embrace the friar, who thrust her away. She was reeling as if drunk. The hangman bound her eyes with a black scarf and led her to the foot of the ladder, where Bartolone was waiting. The whole scene was by now visible from afar, fully illluminated by the torches of the Knights of St John the Beheaded. Bartolone took Antonia under the arms, carried her up as if she were weightless, bound her to the stake by arms and ankles and round the waist too. He lit the brushwood and climbed down at the very moment the procession reached the foot of the Knoll. The responses of the crowd were like the blast of a hurricane: "*Ora pro nobis.*"

"*Speculum justitiae!*" (Mirror of justice!) yelled the priest at the top of his voice. "*Consolatrix afflictorum!*" (Comfortress of the allicted!). "*Causa nostrae letitiae!*" (Source of our joy!).

A dense billow of smoke, then all voices hushed as the smoke began to thin, all eyes strained to see through the smoke to where the witch was. The flames leapt crackling upwards, the night turned bright as day, the tongues of fire converged into a single blast upsurging high into the twilit heavens; even higher – word had it afterwards in and around Zardino – than the tree that had lived a thousand years on that Knoll, and was there no longer. The witch's hair scorched off in the blaze, her mouth opened in a soundless scream. The red dress dissolved, her body blackened, shrivelled, her eyes turned white: Antonia was no more. Out burst the jubilation of the multitude: the drums, the rattles, the trumpets, the tin-can chains were all but drowned in the thunder of voices roaring the incomparable joy of that moment and that blessèd hour. Out burst the fireworks too, from Borgo Vercelli to Biandrate and upstream even further, and at least ten miles of this side of the Sesia dazzled with cascades, rockets, Catherine-wheels, and other devices of colour and light that danced on the waters and dwellings of the Flatlands, admired from all the Monferrato, from Biella, from the Ticino valley . . .

Then, at last, began the revels.

CODA

Nothingness

THE FIRST DROPS OF RAIN, sporadic though weighty as
hailstones, fell at dawn the next day, but soon grew denser,
pelting on the drought-baked earth, entailing a highly disagree-
able awakening for those who, hoarse from much shouting and
stupefied with wine, had at last laid down to sleep in the middle of
a field or by the roadside: and any tardy waker risked death by
drowning. For several minutes the rain was so intense and violent
that nothing could be seen but a wall of water. It doused the last
embers of the witch's pyre, in a trice dispersing the ashes,
mingling them with the soil of the Knoll or sweeping them away
in hundreds upon hundreds of rivulets that, seething and riotous
as rivers in spate, poured one into the other and then into the Sesia.

After that first downpour the rain slackened, and finally ceased
altogether. Huge grey clouds from the southward passed over-
head to mass against the distant mountains, screening them from
sight. The sky turned uniformly grey, lightning darted here, there
and everywhere and the thunder was a blurred, incessant rolling,
as if a thousand carts with iron-hooped wheels were trundling
horizon to horizon above the clouds. Then came the hail, the real
hail, and covered the Flatlands with a snow-like layer of ice,
ankle-deep in places. It did little damage though, because it had
been such an early year that almost all the fruits of the earth had
already been gathered in and garnered away. Then the wind got
up, so violent that it smashed trees and sent roof-tiles flying.
Night fell again at the very hour when the sun should have risen,
and in Zardino and the other Flatlands villages the lamps were
perforce relit for the milking and bread-making. But all this
disturbance, we must admit at once so as not to mislead the reader,
although it happened the day after Antonia's death, was not as

exceptional or unexpected as might appear to one who has never lived in those parts and does not know the climate of the Flatlands. It was not, in short, a token of supernatural wrath, either of God or of Devil; nor even then, in the early seventeenth century, did it cross anyone's mind that it might be. It was more or less normal. Nearly every year in the Flatlands, then as now, autumn forewarns in this way, with half a hurricane; and the more torrid and protracted the summer preceding it the more violent it is, and the more persistent the bad weather in its wake. In far-off 1610 the drought had set in even before Easter, and the summer brought a scorching heat unknown for many years, so that everyone was pretty much expecting what happened that day: hail, rain, scattered whirlwinds, more rain in the afternoon, and then, at sunset, it looked as if the clouds would open and the sky would clear. An illusion though: the night brought another storm, the next morning still another, after which, with short bright intervals of an hour or at most a day, it was rain until nearly the end of September. The streams and ditches overbrimmed and the Sesia, bursting its banks in a reach where the dyke was low or still unfinished, invaded the lanes of Zardino and even the farmyards and the houses themselves, while the inhabitants, fearing the worst, took refuge on the Knolls. But sunshine at last returned, the waters withdrew into their habitual channels, and the whole of the Flatlands shimmered in a sea of mud. Autumn began . . .

Now from the window I look out on nothingness. There is Zardino, its position uncertain but central to the rest, visible or otherwise. In the immediate vicinity, perhaps on the very site, of the present Voltri-Gravellona motorway. There, there was the Knoll, and there died Antonia . . .

What became of the other characters in this story I cannot say because I do not know. I know only a little about a few of them. Bishop Bascapè and Inquisitor Manini, for instance. Bascapè died five years after Antonia, on October 6th 1615, having endured unspeakable physical and above all spiritual sufferings; and it is a great pity that his life – his unwritten novel – was later reduced by his biographers to an edifying fable for persons of piety. During those last five years Bascapè was submitted to the most soul-searing humiliations. Conspicuous among these was that Rome imposed on him as deputy a nephew of Cardinal Bellarmino who without the least concern for the reactions of his superior, considered a madman, began to turn the diocese topsy-turvy and to act as if he were himself the bishop. Against his own deputy, against Rome, against the entire world, Bascapè fought his last, tragi-comic battles. He resigned as bishop. Paul V accepted his resignation and only on second thoughts, when it was brought to his attention that the madman was genuinely about to give up the ghost, and that it would be wiser, as well as more charitable, to avoid the scandal of dismissing him, asked him to remain in office.

Manini, for his part, lived on for many years, and was Inquisitor at Novara until 1623. We know of him only what I have recounted and that he reached the peak of his career immediately after the trial and execution of Antonia. In 1611 we find him in Paris at the "general chapter" of the Dominicans, where he doubtless gave shining proof of his gifts of eloquence and prudence; and who knows if someone didn't even appreciate them! Concerning Master Bernardo Sasso, anyone with a will to hunt for information in the archives of Lombardy would certainly turn something up: a hangman is an historical figure.

As regards all the other characters, who have no place in history and are therefore "earth, dust, smoke, shadow, nothing," to quote one of the leading poets of that age, we can only surmise what became of them after Antonia went to the stake: the Stroller continued to stroll and to traffic in *risaroli*, the whore continued to whore as long as she found clients willing to pay her, and then survived by some means or other, as a bawd or a beggarwoman. And so, each in his own way, did Maffiolo the field-guard, the turnkeys of the Inquisition Tribunal, the priest Don Teresio (who most certainly obtained a parish in Novara), the Gossips of Zardino, the Christian Brethren, Bertolino d'Oltrepò, Caroelli the poet, the peasants, canon Cavagna and all the other monsignors of Novara . . . the idiot Biagio . . . They all went on living in the vast welter and hubbub of their present, that seems to us so silent and so dead, but which with respect to ours was only a whit less well-armed to father forth cacophony, and a whit more downright in its cruelties . . .

Is that the end?

It is, dear reader. Or perhaps not. Perhaps it remains for us to take account of a character in this story in whose name many things were said and many others done, and who in that nothingness outside my window is absent just as he is absent everywhere. Or perhaps he himself *is* nothingness, who can say! He is the echo of all our vacant clamour, the vague reflection of a likeness of ourselves which many, even in our own times, feel the need to project where all is darkness, to mitigate the fear they have of darkness. He who knows Alpha and Omega, the first and the last, the why and wherefore of everything, but alas cannot tell us for the sole reason, paltry as it is, that he does not exist. In the words of another poet, of the present century:

> "He came into men's minds
> And, because he was not, was.
> His non-existence suffices thus:
> That, in that he came not, he came
> And created us."